The SUPERVILLAIN and Me

The SUPERVILLAIN and Me

DANIELLE BANAS

SWOON READS | NEW YORK

A SWOON READS BOOK
An imprint of Feiwel and Friends and Macmillan Publishing Group, LLC
175 Fifth Avenue, New York, NY 10010
swoonreads.com

Our books may be purchased in bulk for promotional, educational, or business use. Please contact your local bookseller or the Macmillan Corporate and Premium Sales Department at (800) 221-7945 ext. 5442 or by e-mail at MacmillanSpecialMarkets@macmillan.com.

Library of Congress Cataloging-in-Publication Data is available.

ISBN 978-1-250-15435-4 (hardcover)
ISBN 978-1-250-15434-7 (ebook)

Book design by Rebecca Syracuse

First edition, 2018

10 9 8 7 6 5 4 3 2 1

Mom & Dad—

Thank you doesn't scratch the surface.

CHAPTER ONE

They never stood a chance.

Tires screamed as the van sped around the corner. It hopped the curb, and the vehicle jolted, the back door swinging open, spilling a sack of priceless artifacts—paintings, sculptures, anything and everything the thieves could snatch from the Morriston History Museum. Not that it mattered. They would be apprehended quickly. They always were.

A golden platter slid from the back of the van, spinning like a top in the middle of Fifth Avenue's busy intersection before falling still. Rotor blades flapped as a helicopter hovered overhead, a cameraman dangling out the door, filming the scene for the world to see.

But the real show was just beginning.

It started with a shadow—long and narrow, stretching over the river where the wharf met the city. The shape grew, widening as it torpedoed to the ground. Blink and you'd miss it. A red blur shot through the air into the back of the van, stopping it from traveling down the ramp to the riverbank, where a boat waited at the docks. Brakes screeched. The van spun in a tight circle, coming to a crunching halt against a guardrail. Dozens more relics fell through the doors, landing in a heap at the side of the road. The camera feed from the helicopter shook as the man inside struggled to get closer.

Smoke curled into the air.

The passenger door opened slowly.

The hero who emerged wore a bright red suit, paired with a mask that covered the cheeky grin likely unfolding across his face. As he forced the thieves—a young man and woman—toward the onslaught of police officers, the crowd on the sidewalks erupted, cheering his name.

"Red Comet! Red Comet! Red Comet!"

I wanted to barf.

"Abby, wasn't that the coolest thing ever?" My best friend, Sarah, put away her cell phone, silencing the video clip of Red Comet's latest rescue as we took our seats in the school auditorium for a Friday-afternoon assembly.

"Anyway," she continued, "do you want to go out somewhere tonight? I just bought a new Taser." She unzipped her purse to show me. "You can't go wrong with glitter and pink."

"Well, at least it's better than the can of pepper spray you accidentally shot in your eye last month."

"Hey now. My screams of agony kept that guy from stealing my car out of the mall parking lot. I call that a win."

I wished I could laugh, but in reality the crime rate in Morriston had grown to such a height that we would be stupid to step outside without some form of protection. Gangs and muggers ran rampant, and then there was that one guy who robbed the mini-mart on Bay Street every Thursday evening like clockwork. After a while, people started making light of the situation just to spare themselves the pain. *The pickpocket stole my homework* was a common joke among students. The police and the supers were stretched thin, and my father, Morriston's longest-tenured mayor, was running himself into the ground to contain it.

Taser or not, I couldn't give Sarah a definitive answer. I was too busy dreading the upcoming assembly. According to Principal Davis, Morriston High had managed to wrangle a famous surprise guest. Surprises had a tendency to make my stomach sour and my palms sweat.

What a shame that Morriston was full of surprises.

It started and ended with the supers. All things did. The nationwide obsession with the heroes had existed far longer than the seventeen years I'd been alive, and would no doubt live on for decades after. Some called them celebrities, others called them gods, but it couldn't be denied that their inhuman abilities had led them to become somewhat of a saving grace throughout the country. Literally. They worked in conjunction with the police forces, but everyone knew the supers stopped crime faster, more efficiently, and . . . they did it while wearing tights.

Only two were currently active in Morriston. The ever-charismatic Red Comet held the top spot in the superhero hierarchy, followed by Fish Boy—an aquatic hero with shiny blue flippers and a gas-guzzling motorbike. Fish Boy showed up late to every crime scene that took place on land, appearing only marginally sooner to those taking place on water. Understandably, he didn't garner much press coverage.

No one could explain how their powers came to be. There were theories, of course. Overexposure to radioactivity, genetic manipulation, popping out of the womb with the ability to use more brainpower than the average human, but none were ever proven true. How did Chicago's favorite hero, the Force, control the weather to strike down criminals with lightning bolts? How did Seattle's Chameleon shape-shift into any animal she desired? Why could Red Comet fly faster than the speed of sound while I was stuck sitting on the bus for thirty minutes on my way to school?

The answer: The supers were exceptional. The rest of us had to work our butts off all day, every day, to get the slightest bit ahead.

"Attention! Attention, students!" Principal Davis tapped the microphone onstage with two pudgy fingers. A loud squeal echoed through the auditorium, ceasing conversations, raucous laughter from a group of sophomores sitting behind Sarah and me, and at least five make-out sessions.

"Who's this assembly for again?" Sarah whispered in my ear.

"Not sure." But I had an inkling.

"I know you're probably curious why we pulled you out of last period," Principal Davis continued. "The faculty has a very special treat for you today. It was hard to track him down, but we succeeded in the end. He's here to say hello and speak a bit about public safety in our fine city of Morriston. . . ."

Oh God, I thought, wiping my palms on my jeans. *Please no.*

"Put your hands together and give a warm Morriston High School welcome to . . ."

No. No way. He's not the only one in the city. It doesn't mean that it's—

"Red Comet!"

I was fairly certain I was the only student who slumped in their seat and groaned instead of immediately jumping up and screaming. The junior and senior boys had decided to stomp and chant, "Com-et! Com-et! Com-et!" and nothing the teachers did could make them stop. Red Comet was the superhero every teenage guy wanted to be and every teenage girl (and a few boys) wanted to be with.

He was also my nineteen-year-old brother, Connor.

If Connor Hamilton was a hurricane, then I was a drizzle. He was popular and athletic, while I didn't care much for either. Where I was book-smart, Connor was street-smart—he never cracked under pressure and always knew what to do. While I clumsily stumbled my way through high school—just ask my PE teacher—Connor flew gracefully above the streets of Morriston, spending his days and nights saving the world.

"Oh my God, Abby! OH MY GOD!" Sarah began smacking my shoulder. "It's him! It's really him! Oh my God, I—I can't! I just can't!"

"Can't what?" I muttered. Connor wet the bed until he was eight, and no amount of muscles or spandex could make me forget the nights he barged into my room, his pajama pants still soaked with urine.

Sarah was too busy losing her mind to notice the scowl on my lips. She was Red Comet's biggest fan. She owned T-shirts and posters and wrote hideously sexual Red Comet fan fiction that I refused to read because thinking about my brother in that sense didn't do much for my appetite.

If Sarah ever discovered that the so-called "sexy superhero" in the red-and-gold suit was the same blond-haired dork who belched nacho cheese in her face at the summer festival, I knew she would immediately burn her Red Comet shrine and repent. But instead she, like so many other rabid fans, was busy snapping away photos of the famous Red Comet to sell or Instagram or masturbate to—whatever people did with his picture nowadays.

Despite the head-to-toe super suit covering every inch of skin, including his eyes and mouth, I could immediately tell when Connor caught my eye and smirked at my agony. He probably also threw a wink in my direction, just for good measure.

Go ahead, Connor. Soak it up, why don't you?

"Quiet! Everybody, quiet!" Principal Davis returned to the

microphone, placing a hand on Connor's shoulder, unaware he was fondling the same kid who only two years prior spray-painted his Jaguar hot pink for a senior prank.

The students continued cheering until Connor calmly raised a hand in silence. One by one they resumed their seats, some kids in awe, some shaking, and others, like Sarah, with tears streaming down their cheeks.

"I can't believe he's here," Sarah whispered, sniffling into her sweatshirt. "I can't believe it."

"I am honored to be here today," Connor began, his voice deepening as part of his disguise. "A hero's job is never easy, and I would like to thank each of you for your support. Protecting a city is not a one-man job, and on behalf of all the superpowered men and women in Morriston and beyond, we are grateful for your vigilance and your devotion to keeping our streets and neighborhoods safe. A few things we can do to improve . . ."

I ignored the rest of Connor's speech, which was probably written by our father, the great politician, and ran through song lyrics to the school's fall musical, *Hall of Horrors*, in my head.

Don't eat the flesh—

"Thank you, have a safe evening." Connor graciously bowed away from the microphone as Principal Davis shook his gloved hand.

"Abby, let's go meet him! I need his autograph! Do you think he'd let me interview him for the school paper? Or for my blog? Oh God, I'm so nervous! His voice is so sexy, I could listen to him talk all day!"

"I don't think he's doing a meet and greet. Come on, I really need to rehearse for my audition next week." *Hall of Horrors* had completely consumed my thoughts for the past month. The show was a rock comedy about a cannibalistic royal family and their servant, who falls passionately in love with the crown prince, and as a senior, I wanted a good part. Theater was my passion; it was *my thing*. Sure,

Connor could surpass the speed of sound, but I could do a kick-ass pas de bourrée.

"What? No! You'll have tons of time to rehearse." Sarah latched onto my wrist and pulled me through the crowd forming at the edge of the stage to get Red Comet's autograph. "Does my hair look okay?" She desperately fluffed up her auburn curls while I contemplated five different means of escape, one of which involved projectile vomiting all over Connor's red suit.

"Hi, Red Comet!" Sarah squealed over the head of a short freshman girl. The girl moved away, tears clouding her eyes, and Sarah pulled us to the front of the line.

"Ladies, how are we?" Connor reached for Sarah's phone, scrawling *RC* on the case with a permanent marker. Sarah looked like she was about to pass out, and judging by the amount of hypothetical if-I-ever-met-Red-Comet conversations I'd endured over the past three years, I knew she was either going to hit the deck or jump his bones.

"Want me to sign anything?" Connor turned toward me. Even though gold lenses covered his eyes, I could imagine his cocked eyebrow and lips smirking at me through his mask.

"No thanks, I'm good."

"Is it, um, is it hard to f-fly?" Sarah stuttered.

Connor shrugged, patting her shoulder. "Easier than breathing, sweetheart."

Lie. Connor put at least ten holes in our walls while learning to control the powers he discovered after his sixteenth birthday. Flying wasn't easy.

"Red Comet, could I—do you think maybe I could get a—a hug? Maybe?"

"Of course, come on up." He gestured for the teachers to let us onstage. A few students yelled in protest, but Connor didn't care. He led us toward the curtain and pulled Sarah into a hug that lasted far longer than he intended. Too bad Connor didn't possess super strength, because it took him three tries to politely extricate himself from Sarah's death grip around his neck.

"Ohmigosh, ohmigosh, ohmigosh!" Sarah was crying again, the ends of her shirtsleeves covered in tears and snot.

"I think I just ruined her life," Connor muttered in my ear as he pulled me to his chest, his voice no longer as husky as when he made his speech. "I was only trying to be nice."

"You definitely made her life, not ruined it. She'll be incorporating this moment into her fan fiction for years to come."

"Awesome," he chuckled, but his voice betrayed him. Connor was as terrified of Sarah's Red Comet fan fiction as I was. "Hey, what's for dinner tonight?"

"Depends. What are you making?"

"Nothing. I think Dad mentioned steaks as long as his press conference doesn't run over."

"You're actually going to be home for dinner?"

"Of course, as long as I don't . . ." Connor trailed off, tilting his head toward the ceiling. I knew that look—his superhuman sixth sense for trouble was tingling. "Shit. See you later, Abby." His hands fell from my shoulders, and he took off, hovering above the stage to many *oohs* and *aahs* from the student body before he flew to save the day—leaving the door dangling off its hinges in his wake.

CHAPTER TWO

"Dad? Connor? Anyone home?" I called out when I entered my house later that afternoon. My voice bounced off the vaulted ceilings and didn't receive a response. Our house was far too large for three people who barely set foot in it, but it was secluded at the end of a quarter-mile-long private drive in the woods, which was exactly what we needed.

My parents purchased the five acres of land and the mansion that came with it three years ago, after Connor discovered his powers and needed a place to practice. I couldn't forget that day even if I tried. We had just returned home from Connor's sixteenth-birthday dinner. At first, he thought he was only coming down with the flu. His head ached from loud noises, and he felt like he would throw up every time he smelled food. Connor went to bed early that night without opening any of his presents, and when he awoke the next morning, his vision had heightened to the point where he no longer needed glasses and he flipped out because he was hovering four feet in the air above his mattress. My family moved to our new house the following morning.

But now Mom was long gone, which was the reason Connor decided to suit up and save the world and hardly eat a meal in our house, and my dad had been reelected mayor and was working around the clock to make Morriston the safest city in America. The large mansion with its tall windows and expensive electronics was only regularly home to me, but because of the secrets my family kept, I couldn't invite any friends over to enjoy it.

"Abby? You okay?" Connor found me in the kitchen an hour later, staring helplessly at some science homework. I was surprised he was home this early after his abrupt departure at school, but even more surprised that his super suit was dirty and ripped and he looked like he was about to cry.

"I'm fine. Are you okay? What happened to you?"

Connor shrugged, throwing his mask on the kitchen table. I was used to Connor wearing his Red Comet getup around the house, but sometimes it still startled me. For as much as I teased him about his nerdy powers or screaming fans, I often forgot that my charismatic, pretentious brother was capable of feeling normal human emotions like exhaustion or sadness.

"Bank robbery downtown," he finally said. "Hostage situation."

I gulped. Of all the terrible things that happened in Morriston, I always was filled with dread at the mention of a bank robbery. Too many bad memories.

"Is everyone all right? I mean, did anyone—"

"No, it's fine." Connor's blue eyes hardened, and he reached to pull me into our second hug of the day. The tang of sweat and smoke clung to his suit, but I didn't protest when he ran a hand over my hair. "You know I'd never let that happen again."

I knew he wouldn't dare lie about that. Connor lied about a lot of things—his secret identity, his grades in his online college courses, whether or not he spent the night fighting crime or in some girl's bed. But he would never lie about saving hostages. Not when our mother was shot and killed in a similar robbery three years ago. Her death was the catalyst for Connor's transformation into Red Comet. Mom had always been too afraid for Connor's safety to let him become a hero, but Connor had pleaded with our dad, suggesting that using his powers to save others and prevent another death like our mother's would be a good use of his time.

Dad never disagreed.

Finally, Connor pulled away and reached for his mask, stuffing it into a pocket in his suit. His eyes were red-rimmed and I knew mine looked the same. Connor and I were two years apart, but we looked more like twins with identical dirty blond hair and bright blue eyes. I knew we looked even more alike when we were crying over our mom. We had done quite a bit of it over the past three years.

I only blamed one person for Mom's death: the man who pulled the trigger. But I would be lying if I said I never wondered why Connor hadn't done something to help her. He wasn't Red Comet at the time, but he still had powers. He could have been *right there*. Yet every time I got close to asking why, Connor would go off on a tangent on some homework problem he needed my help to solve or a new burger joint he wanted to visit with me, and I chickened out, preferring my relationship with my brother over reopening old wounds. Maybe the truth was best left hidden, just like Red Comet's identity.

"Cheer up, kid." Connor flashed me a toothy grin, and just like that, his sadness disappeared from view. If Connor wasn't a superhero, his acting skills, straight white teeth, and sharp jawline could make him a viable candidate for a movie star. "You still need to help me with my calc homework."

Connor may have been a crime-fighting superhero, but I was the straight-A student in the family.

My dad arrived home just as Connor hopped out of the shower. The sound of their conversation drifted from the front hall to the kitchen, words like *assault rifles* and *disaster* reaching my ears. I could picture my father, all salt-and-pepper hair and glasses, running a hand over his jaw before jotting down notes from Connor's afternoon escapade on the cell phone that never left his person. Once he even dropped it in the toilet because he refused to put it down.

"I'll take care of it," I heard Dad say. "We'll wipe all the crime from this city yet, you mark my words."

The stairs creaked as Connor disappeared upstairs to his room.

"Abby, I have something for you." Dad kicked his shoes off on the mat by the back door and pulled a beer from the fridge. A hostage situation so similar to the one that killed his wife undeniably shook him, but he didn't show it. Benjamin Hamilton wouldn't be Morriston's favorite mayor if he did.

"What is it?" I asked, a little skeptical.

My phone buzzed on the table, and Dad grinned, gesturing at the screen. "I sent you a new self-defense video. This one is about escaping choke holds."

"Oh. That's . . . great." This was self-defense video number ten in the past three days alone, otherwise known as my dad's attempt to teach me how to defend myself without superpowers. I'd insisted years ago that I was too athletically challenged to attend karate lessons, and so this was the agreed-upon alternative. Gouging eyes, throwing elbows, escaping zip ties—you name it, Dad found a video tutorial and sent it to me. I understood his reasoning for wanting to protect me from dangerous Morriston criminals; I probably understood better than anyone. And so I watched the videos to appease him, nothing more. Fighting crime was Connor's hobby, not mine.

Dad took a long swig of his drink, then sat across from me. "So how was school?"

I was about to answer when Connor returned to the kitchen. He had changed out of his costume and was now wearing faded jeans and an old Morriston High PE shirt, making him look less like a supernerd and more like the average college student.

Smirking, he dropped a packet of calculus homework on the table in front of me. He'd only completed one problem, and it took me two seconds to realize the answer was wrong.

"I got an eighty-one percent on my history paper," he announced proudly. Rolling my eyes, I fixed the math problem he'd butchered with a stroke of my pen, then threw the packet at his chest. Connor had received his 81 percent solely because of the three closing paragraphs I wrote for him after he'd lost interest in typing and decided to rush downtown to help the victims of a car accident on the Morriston Bridge instead. But I didn't tell Dad that.

"I got a hundred on mine," I said instead, pulling the paper on British literature out of my bag and sliding it underneath my dad's elbow.

He glanced up, smiling. "Really?"

"Really, really. The English department is going to feature it on the school's website and everything."

"That's great!" He actually put his phone down. I beamed. Winning his attention with my brother in the room was never an easy feat.

"And Principal Davis told me that—"

"Oh, Connor, before I forget, I'm thinking of setting up another press conference for you," said Dad. He shifted forward, and my paper slipped off the table and fluttered to the floor. When I picked it up, it was covered in last night's pizza crumbs. *Awesome.* I shouldn't have been surprised. I loved him to death, but everything with

Connor felt like a competition, a giant game that I never agreed to play.

I'd grown used to it. Connor was Connor, and I was just happy he hadn't gotten hurt in his life of fighting crime. After Mom died and Connor became a hero, I worried constantly, but I'd eased up in the years since. Connor was a superhero powerhouse, and I needed to worry less about how many criminals he was punching and more about how often I was rehearsing my lines and lip trills if I wanted to be successful too.

But . . . I still waited up for him to come home more nights than I cared to admit.

Connor reached for my English paper and brushed away a few of the lingering crumbs. He presented it to our dad with a flourish and wrapped an arm around my shoulders.

"I got you," he whispered to me. Then he grabbed a bag of chips from the pantry and floated—yes, *floated* (it's like flying but with a bit more hover)—through the air, landing in the chair next to our dad.

Connor grinned cheekily and shoved a handful of salt-and-vinegar chips past his lips.

Once a supernerd, always a supernerd.

The following week brought record amounts of rain to Morriston, slightly less crime for Connor to fight, and an abundance of nerves as I prepared to nail my musical auditions.

"Abby! Abby, Abby, Abby! Wait up!" Sarah sprinted down the hall to catch me as I entered the auditorium, bumping into anxious freshmen, the night janitor with a bucket of someone's regurgitated lunch, and a group of stage-crew kids having a makeshift sword fight with a pile of two-by-fours.

"Where's the fire?" I reviewed song lyrics in my head while scoping out a prime auditorium seat in the first row, which would provide the most opportunities to brownnose Mrs. Miller, our director.

Foes and rivals, knock 'em to the ground . . .

"There's no fire, I just . . ." Sarah placed her hands on her knees and leaned against the corner of the sound booth, catching her breath.

Feast and bury, never to be found . . .

"I wanted to tell you that . . ."

When we're through, they're merely skin and bone . . .

"That I'm . . ."

We don't care 'cause we're sitting on the . . .

"That I'm auditioning for the musical."

The last lyric flew out of my head faster than Red Comet high on caffeine. I didn't think Sarah could sing. Actually, I was sure she couldn't. She once composed a song about Red Comet and sang it to me and Connor, and we thought our ears were going to bleed. It was so horrible that Connor wanted to make it his theme song just for shits and giggles.

I looked at Sarah. Her big brown eyes lit up with excitement as she bounced on the toes of her sneakers. "You're auditioning for the musical?"

"I'm auditioning for the musical."

Uh-oh. "You can sing?"

"Well . . . no. *But* I really wanted to do this with you because I know all I talk about is Red Comet this and Red Comet that, and I know you don't really like that, and so I thought we could do something that you're interested in—*Hall of Whores.*"

I snickered at her mispronunciation of the show title, but felt a surge of affection for my best friend for wanting to do something with me other than talk about my brother and his bright red tights.

"It's *Hall of HORRORS*, not 'whores.'" I fought to maintain a straight face, but all I really wanted to do was smile. "Are you sure about this?"

"Absolutely. Trust me, Abby," Sarah said. "This is going to be so . . . *so* . . ."

I never found out exactly what it would be because Sarah emphatically spread out her arms at the exact moment that the door to the sound booth opened behind us, punching the poor boy who emerged square in the nose, knocking him to the floor.

"Oh no!" Sarah clapped her hands over her mouth. She gave him a muffled "Sorry!" as her face blushed.

"S'okay," he mumbled. He began gathering the stack of papers he had dropped, so meticulously that I wondered if he was only doing it to stall until he was forced to look up at us.

Sarah and I crouched beside him to help. "I think your nose is bleeding," I said, noticing a few red specks on the paper nearest him.

The boy's shoulders slumped. "Happens to the best of us." He rubbed his nose on his sleeve.

"Do you need a tissue? Or the nurse's office?"

"They have really big Band-Aids in there," Sarah chimed in. "Like almost as big as your head."

"As appealing as that sounds, no thanks." When we stood, the boy finally unglued his eyes from his shoes. He was a good several inches taller than me, which wasn't exactly difficult to accomplish. Dark brown hair fell into darker brown eyes and curled around his ears, which stuck out just a tad too much. The boy rolled a chapped lower lip between his teeth while trying to clean the blood from his face.

"The Band-Aids in the nurse's office really aren't that big."

I laughed, trying to lighten the mood. "You have a very average-looking head, so they should fit you fine."

The frown on his face melted into something slightly softer. "Is . . . that a compliment?"

"Well, it was really just an observation. Your head doesn't look like a cantaloupe, so I thought 'average' might be the correct description. But if I was wrong . . ."

"No. Um . . . no. That's . . . funny," he murmured the last word. But he didn't look like it was funny. He looked anxious and repeatedly scuffed the toe of a sneaker along the floor, his fingers twitching against his thigh.

Don't get me wrong, I wasn't winning the award for World's Most Talkative Human anytime soon—Connor was already a frequent nominee in that category—but I'd never met a guy so painfully shy. A cute guy at that. If Mr. Tall, Dark, and Handsome would crack a smile now and again, then he might actually appear approachable. I knew I recognized him from last year's musical, and I had a vague memory of taking a class with him during our freshman year—or was it our sophomore?—but I couldn't remember his name for the life of me.

"Sorry about all of . . . *this.*" I gestured to his nose, then prodded Sarah when she didn't speak.

"Right. Yep. Sorry." Her cheeks were still pink with blush.

The boy's brown eyes flicked up again before returning to the floor. In that brief moment, an emotion other than anxiety washed over his face. His eyes widened and his shoulders relaxed. He looked shocked that we had bothered to apologize. "Don't worry about it." His voice was the equivalent of speaking near a sleeping baby—so quiet he barely said anything at all.

"I know I'm about to sound like a total jerk," I said, "but what's your name?"

The boy blinked at me, saying nothing.

"I mean, we've gone to school together for a while, but I don't think we've been introduced." I looked at Sarah. "Have we been introduced?"

"Don't think so," she replied.

"Right. So . . ." I offered him my hand. "I'm Abby. This is Sarah."

Another blink. No words escaped his lips. My hand dangled in the air.

I cleared my throat. "And you are . . . ?"

"Oh." He seemed to steel himself, and then he was gripping my hand with calloused fingers and a clammy palm, squeezing perhaps a bit too tightly as he said, "I'm Rylan."

"Ryan?" He was so *quiet*.

"No. Rylan. There's an *l* in the middle." He drew a large *L* in the air with his finger. "Rylan Sloan."

I grinned. "Well, Rylan, it's nice to meet you." He finally let go of my hand. I tried really hard not to make it obvious when I wiped his sweat residue off on my shirt.

"Likewise, Abby." I caught a hint of a smile cross his lips, but a second later it was gone.

"Oooh! Oooh, Abby, it's starting!" Sarah pointed out two empty seats near the front of the auditorium as Mrs. Miller took the stage.

"We're really sorry about your nose," I called back to Rylan. He nodded, never speaking, then returned to the sound booth.

Sarah and I sat in silence while Mrs. Miller passed out sheet music to all the students. The audition song—"The Prince and I"—was one I had practiced forward and backward in hopes of getting the lead role. It was sung during the second act while the main characters, Prince Arthur Delafontaine VII and his starving servant, Angeline, professed their love for each other, and even though it was a bit beyond my vocal range, I'd rehearsed enough that I knew I could pull it off.

"Ladies and gentlemen, do we have any volunteers to sing first?" Mrs. Miller fluffed her bright red bob and tugged on her cardigan. She always wore cardigans, even if it was eighty degrees outside. Today's was pink with too many frilly bows and a cat that looked more like a groundhog.

"I'll go." A guy sitting two rows in front of us raised his hand and sauntered onstage, his lean legs clad in a pair of dark jeans. When he turned around, Sarah pinched my arm so hard that she almost broke skin. Between his glittering green eyes and cheekbones that may as well have been carved from marble, this guy had the potential to put Sarah off Red Comet for life.

The only imperfection on his otherwise flawless face was a tiny bump on the bridge of his nose, like it had been broken once before. Thinking back to Rylan's bloody nose, I wondered if someone clocked his guy by accident or on purpose.

"Hubba hubba." Sarah sighed. "That guy *definitely* did not go here before."

New Guy leaned against the microphone stand at the center of the stage. He started to speak, but the screech of feedback had him pulling away sheepishly.

"Try again," Mrs. Miller encouraged. She was perched on the edge of her seat, eying up her prey, eerily similar to the kitten on her sweater.

New Guy tapped the microphone with his index finger. "Uh. Hi. I'm Isaac. I've never done this before, so . . . yeah. Here we go."

"Very loquacious," I muttered.

Sarah stomped on my foot.

"Ouch."

"Shhh!" she hissed.

Verbose Isaac was not. But *holy hot sauce* could he sing. He belted out the audition piece, his rich baritone voice sliding through the speakers like silk. His voice was every good and every pure thing in the universe. A shooting star. A mug of hot chocolate in front of a roaring fireplace. A deep swimming pool on a hot summer day.

And I was drowning.

"I'll fight you for him," I whispered to Sarah when Isaac stepped offstage to polite, somewhat nervous applause. He would be a tough one to beat.

"I feel like I'd be cheating on Red Comet." She smirked. "But you're on."

"Who's next?" Mrs. Miller asked, clapping her hands together.

Crickets. Everyone looked around the room anxiously, trying not to meet Mrs. Miller's gaze lest she call them onstage to perform. If I didn't do it, then no one would, and if I wanted the lead—and a chance to work alongside *that voice*—it would be best to start showing some initiative.

My hand shot into the air. "Mrs. Miller, I'd like to volunteer."

The audition went better than expected. Meaning it went pretty darn awesome. I sang perfectly on pitch, Sarah sounded *somewhat* halfway decent, and Isaac and his voice of Orpheus offered me brief but still genuine congratulations before rushing out the door. I tried to push the thought of the impending cast list from my mind as I exited the school. There were four days before the results would be posted, but that was more than enough time for me to agonize over Mrs. Miller's choices.

"Want to go eat?" Sarah asked. The invigorating chill of late September cut through me as we stood in the parking lot. "I think I developed acid reflux from that wing place in the mall, but we can get burgers or something."

I hiked my backpack over my shoulder. "Actually, my dad wanted me home tonight. Rain check?"

"Sure thing." She headed toward her tiny red car parked under a row of pine trees. More than once I wished I had one of my own, but after three failed attempts before finally passing my driver's test, Dad didn't exactly trust me. "Do you need a ride?"

"No, it's fine. My dad's coming. Apparently Connor is attempting to make us dinner."

Sarah wrinkled her nose. "Good luck with that. And tell your brother to stop posting pictures of his toenail clippings on social media. I almost barfed up my breakfast today. Toodles!"

As soon as she sped out of the parking lot, nearly sideswiping another car in the process, my phone pinged with a text from my dad.

Did the auditions go well? I'm working late, so I can't pick you up. Sorry.

Seriously? He'd told me last night he was planning on taking the afternoon off. Maybe it was stupid to admit, but I had kind of been looking forward to seeing him.

Don't worry about it, I replied. *I'll call Connor.*

He's working. Big burglary east of Market Street. You shouldn't bother him.

Oh. Of course. My thumbs tapped against the edge of my phone as I thought up a response, but another text came through before I had the chance.

Can Sarah drop you off?

Because he couldn't have asked me two minutes ago when she was actually here? I thought about calling her; I doubted she would mind doubling back, but I knew she would ask questions and suddenly the absolute *last* thing I felt like doing was talking to someone.

Sure, I told Dad. *No problem.*

Dad didn't reply with another message. Instead he sent me a link to a video demonstrating how to execute the perfect roundhouse kick.

Like that would ever happen.

Shoving my phone in my bag, I set off on foot. The buses were long gone by the time auditions finished, but I could walk. I dug my nails into the straps of my backpack as I crossed the street. I'd been waiting all day to tell Dad and Connor about the auditions, to share my excitement over the thing that made me happy—the thing that I was good at. And now . . . nothing. I didn't even know if I would see them the rest of the night. This always happened. They always had another press briefing or another damsel to rescue. And I knew I shouldn't care; I knew what they were doing was more important than a school musical.

But it still stung.

My shoes squeaked through puddles of water on the sidewalks. This was a chance to show my dad and brother that I didn't need them. A forty-minute walk from school to home. No problem. I was fine and dandy on my own.

I hummed a few show tunes to pass the time, occasionally breaking into a little hop, skip, and jump for dramatic effect. Nothing and *no one* would bring me down after my audition.

Sneakers crunched on the sidewalk behind me.

For a minute, I didn't think anything of it. But when the footsteps continued, never veering off onto another street, my heart began to race. I breathed deeply, mimicking the exercises I usually did before singing. *It's fine,* I reassured myself. *You're just paranoid.*

The footsteps quickened.

I knew what to do in these situations. Connor and my dad drilled it into my head years ago. Keep walking. Don't panic. Find an open storefront and hide inside and everything will be fine.

Scanning the street, I cursed under my breath. There were no open storefronts. Most places in Morriston—especially in the suburbs—shut down in the evenings. For good reason.

Feet pounded against the pavement.

Okay. Officially time to panic.

I took off, stumbling in my haste and trying to ignore the angry grunt of my pursuer as his thunderous footsteps gave chase. Fire burned in my throat while I struggled to fill my lungs.

I chanced a glance over my shoulder. The man was about ten yards away, closing in quickly. He was skeletal in appearance, wearing ripped jeans and a football jersey that hung beneath his worn coat. I reached for my backpack, groping through the outside pocket for the can of pepper spray that my dad had forced on me at the start of the school year. I didn't even know if it worked. Suddenly I realized how stupid I was for never testing it out.

Five yards away.

I rounded a corner at the end of the block, failing to dodge a puddle in the middle of the sidewalk. A splash of water filled my shoes, weighing down my socks. I looked back again. Three yards and . . .

The air left my lungs as the man collided with my back. I spun on my heel, firing off the pepper spray. A thin stream made contact with the side of the man's scruffy face, but most of it just dribbled down my hand.

The man grabbed the straps of my backpack, slamming me against the doorway of a closed consignment shop. My head ached, my ears were ringing, but when his hand reached for my throat, some type of primal instinct took over. I slammed both hands down on his forearm. His elbow buckled, and he toppled toward me, mouth agape like I'd actually managed to frighten him. Then, winding up, I punched him right in his lousy face.

The punch wasn't really part of my dad's attempt at Self-Defense 101, but I couldn't help myself.

"Take that, you jerk!" I should have stopped there. I definitely should have run. But I felt rather smug seeing the big dummy crippled by my fist, and so I couldn't help but drive my point home. Raising my knee, I aimed at his groin. But halfway through my attack, I realized my punch hadn't harmed him as much as I thought. The man's hand shot out, yanking hard on my leg, sweeping my feet out from under me.

I hit the ground hard, my forehead smacking the sidewalk. *And this is why Sarah carries a Taser.*

The man recovered quickly. He crouched over me, knees braced on my forearms. My breath came out in quick pants when I noticed the gleam of a knife in his fist.

"Money. Now," he growled.

Fear makes a person do some crazy things. For example, instead of bursting into tears, it made me think that this guy seriously needed a breath mint.

"Now," he repeated, voice sharper this time.

"Oh. Um . . ." I ticked off the contents of my backpack. Student ID. Half a pack of gum. Fifty cents (three dimes, four nickels). Pretty dismal options if I hoped to make it out with my limbs still intact.

"I don't have anything." My voice came out far less firm than I intended.

He sneered. "Nice try." His eyes looked crazed, and I noticed his fingers wouldn't stop twitching. Drug addict maybe? I started to feel sorry for him, but those feelings disappeared immediately as he brought the knife to my throat.

Oh no. Oh God. Oh no. I tried bucking him off, but for a skinny guy, he was absurdly heavy.

"Please," I whimpered. "Please just . . ." I didn't know what. If there was any time for Connor to come to the rescue, it was now. But he was busy being someone else's hero. He couldn't possibly know I was in danger too.

I was utterly and horrifically alone.

I should have asked Sarah to drive me home. I shouldn't have cared that Dad and Connor weren't around to share in my excitement. A great audition wouldn't matter if I was dead.

The knife felt like a bolt of lightning as the man tapped it against my neck. One sharp pain straight through me as I imagined all the hideous things he could do with it. He leaned close, his nose nearly touching mine.

Run on the count of three.

A voice echoed in my head. I knew it wasn't my imagination. My conscience sounded distinctly female and this voice certainly wasn't.

One.

Two.

The man's arm moved. I felt the knife twitch.

Three.

The man was ripped violently away and a rush of air hit my face. I didn't think twice. I scrambled to my feet and bolted, ignoring the thuds and groans that signaled that my attacker finally got what he deserved. I knew only one thing.

My hero had arrived.

CHAPTER THREE

I stopped running halfway down the next block and leaned against a streetlamp, waiting patiently until the moans of the man turned to silence. Connor had finally gotten his butt here. According to protocol, he would still need to call the police station for someone to retrieve the man, but then he could fly me home.

"Comet"—I never called my brother by his real name in public when he was in costume—"do you need my . . ." I trailed off, staring at the guy standing over the unconscious attacker. "Who are you?"

The stranger's green eyes snapped to my own. He wore a black suit, his mask revealing only his eyes, his lips, and a portion of his jawline. Unlike Connor, this guy didn't have a symbol plastered to his chest. My brother's suit sported a shiny gold swoosh that looked mysteriously like a Nike symbol (but he insisted it was a comet). This guy didn't have anything.

"I thought I told you to run," he said, crossing his arms. He was about as tall as my brother, easily clearing six feet, and possessed just as many, if not more, muscles bulging under the dark material of his costume.

"How did you—wait. That was your voice in my head?" I had to admit he had a nice voice—deep and smoky. I wondered if it was real or a disguise.

The super winked at me and tapped the side of his head with his index finger. I didn't know mind-to-mind communication was a legitimate superpower. Connor frequently gushed at other supers' powers and would have told me if someone had such a unique ability.

"Okay, well . . ." I didn't know what else to say. I wished Connor were there to fly me home. I couldn't ask this guy to escort me. I had no clue who he was. "I'll just be going now."

"Don't I get a thank-you?"

"Huh?"

"I mean, a guy puts on a tight rubber suit that crushes his manhood to teleport down here and save a beautiful girl from getting mugged by a creep and he doesn't even get a thank-you? It makes me not want to continue this line of work, to be completely honest."

"Oh, uh . . ." I looked up at the masked stranger. He winked again when he caught my eye, and my stomach somersaulted. "Thanks, I guess."

Turning my back on him, I set off in the direction of my house. If I was lucky, maybe I wouldn't encounter anyone else. I only managed to take a few steps before the stranger began following me, black boots crunching on loose pieces of gravel.

"All right, so either you're extremely prone to confrontational situations and frequently need a super to come save you, thus, you're so used to saying thank you that it's become too repetitive, so you decided to stop being polite, *or* this has never happened to you before, you're rendered completely stupefied by my appearance, and you're so impressed by my lifesaving abilities that you simply forgot to say thank you. Which one is it?"

"Who *are* you?" This guy must have been new in town. Not even Connor was this annoying to civilians after he saved them.

The man—or boy, rather (I'd determined by his voice he was somewhere around my age)—scoffed. "I can't tell you that. Rule numero uno and all."

"I wasn't asking for your real name. What's your superhero name?"

"Oh, right. I can't tell you that either."

"Is it because you haven't picked one yet?" This guy was definitely a newbie.

"Hey, maybe I'm still weighing my options. You know, determining what the public will best respond to."

I glanced up at him. Superdork's green eyes were still trained on me. Was I imagining it, or did he look a little hurt at my jabs to his legitimacy as a hero? It wasn't my fault I was unimpressed by the supers. Living with Connor removed any coolness factor associated with fighting crime in spandex—not that there was any to begin with.

"That was a nice punch back there," he continued. "But you want to keep your thumb on the outside of your fingers next time. You can break it if you clench it inside your fist."

"Wow. Thanks for the critique. I didn't know you were watching. How nice of you to wait to step in until *after* I had a knife pressed to my throat." I sped up my pace, but he matched me step for step. "I had it all under control."

The hair on the back of my neck bristled when he laughed. "Clearly," he said. "That's why you're bleeding, am I right?"

"I am not." I clutched at my neck, remembering only the feel of the knife, so cold that it almost burned. I sighed in relief to find the skin unmarred.

The super shook his head. "Not there." He pointed to my forehead. "There."

I lightly touched the skin, hissing in pain as I examined the slick blood coating my fingertips.

Superdork pulled me to a stop next to the entrance of a small playground around the corner from my house. "Here, let me," he said, crouching to my level to get a closer look. He had long dark eyelashes, leading me to believe the hair hidden beneath his cowl was dark as well. His gloved hand brushed along my hairline, and I twitched away, not wanting another strange man to be anywhere near me again. "Just hold still a second."

I held my breath as a strange heat emitted from his hand, seeping into my skin, making it feel warm and pliable like gelatin. He squeezed his eyes shut for a moment before gently rubbing his thumb over the cut.

"All better," he finally said. "Feel free to say thanks for that too."

"What did you . . . ?" I dabbed the place where the cut was moments before to find smooth, painless skin and only a few dry crusts of blood. "You healed it?"

He shrugged. Now I felt kind of bad. I had been a jerk to this guy when all he'd wanted to do was save me, walk me home, and heal my head. I blamed too many nights making fun of Connor in his super suit.

"Thank you. That was nice of you." I ran my fingers over my healed skin again. "You can't read minds by any chance, can you?"

"No, I can only project thoughts into others' minds. Why?"

"No reason." At least he wouldn't know how embarrassed I felt. "So . . . you don't need to walk me home. It's only another few minutes."

He surveyed the deserted streets. "Are you sure? It's dark—"

"No, really, it's fine. I can make it."

"Okay, if you say so. Stay safe, then."

He tapped the tip of my nose and stepped back, his silhouette blurring slightly and vanishing before my eyes.

The streets were finally silent, but as I hurried home, I got the sense that I was never truly alone.

"Connor, you don't happen to know anyone with a black suit, do you?" I pressed my phone closer to my ear while navigating the pre-homeroom chaos of the hallway the next morning.

I hadn't told my dad or brother about my near mugging or the mysterious super who saved me. I'd thrown my dirty clothes in the hamper, made sure to wash the remaining blood from my forehead, then hid in my room the rest of the night. Though I was still curious if Connor knew of a hero with a similar description. Odds were he would have crossed paths with the guy at a crime scene at some point—or at least heard about him through the rumor mill. There was nothing—well, nothing except my brush with danger—that happened in Morriston that Connor didn't know about.

"What, like a super suit?" he asked.

"Yeah."

"Where are you?"

"School. Homeroom hasn't started yet. Where are you?"

Faint honks of car horns carried through the speaker, mixing with a loud screech of what sounded like a very large bird. "I'm downtown on top of the Steel Building." Of course he was. Because where else would he go at 7:30 in the morning? The bird screeched again, and Connor muttered a string of profanities.

"The guy didn't have a symbol on his chest if that helps," I said, trying to stay quiet so I wasn't overheard.

"Damn bird! Go pick on someone your own size. Just 'cause I know how to fly—" He cleared his throat. "Sorry. I really haven't heard of anyone who wears a suit without a symbol. Why are you asking?"

"Well, I saw that video this morning. . . ." The video in question had been circulating around school like wildfire. Security camera footage time-stamped early this morning showed a guy who looked suspiciously like the super from last night, crouching in front of a homeless man on a sidewalk downtown. There was no audio, but the super could be seen gesturing animatedly to the man before disappearing and reappearing a minute later with two large bags of takeout and a few mugs of coffee. The wide grin on the elderly man's face as he tore into his meal was enough to warm even the coldest of hearts.

It looked like Morriston had a new hero in town. If he kept it up, he could have his own fan club by lunchtime.

"Oh, *him*," Connor said. "I saw that too. My competition." He gagged loudly.

"Be nice," I scolded. "I saw him yesterday after school. It looked like he was helping . . . someone." Twisting the truth never hurt anyone, right?

"We'll see," Connor grumbled. Then he swore so loudly I flinched. "Oh my God! *Get off my roof, you ugly little*—sorry, Sis, I'm having a crow crisis, a herd of them."

"It's fine." I walked farther down the hall and stopped in the doorway of my homeroom, squinting at the news coverage playing on the TV in the corner. "And, Connor, it's a murder of crows, not a herd."

"Who got murdered? Sorry, there's another one attacking me. It nearly shit on my suit."

"I said it's a—"

I was interrupted from telling him the difference between a murder and a herd by the "breaking news" chime on the television.

The screen flashed to a shot of city hall downtown. A helicopter filmed overhead, and massive orange flames engulfed the building's left side. Thick black smoke swirled into the air. As I watched, the flames transferred to the building next door, sprouting along the awning over the doorway, and the fire grew, spreading its germs like a disease.

"Connor—"

"Yeah, yeah, I see it. I have to go." The line clicked and was dead.

I felt a pair of hands brush my shoulders. "Morning, Abby." Sarah smiled, but her grin slipped away when she saw the morning news. "Is that city hall?"

I nodded mutely. Half the students in the room were watching diligently to see if city hall would really burn to the ground before the supers could save it, but the other half were staring at me, waiting to see how I would handle the news that my father's workplace was crumbling to ash.

I looked at the clock hanging crooked above the whiteboard. It wasn't even eight, so logically I knew my dad wasn't in the building. But then I started second-guessing myself. What if he had to go in early today and I didn't know? What if he died before Connor could save him? What if someone else in there died before Connor could save them? What if *Connor* died?

My stomach twisted violently. My heart weighed a million pounds.

I couldn't lose another family member. I wouldn't.

I was halfway through dialing my dad's number, fingers shaking, when a reporter on the television began to speak.

"We have a new development in the act of arson at city hall," the female reporter explained to the camera. She stood downtown, about a block from the building. I caught a glimpse of red flash through the air, and the knot in my stomach lessened knowing my brother was still okay.

The television screen changed to a shaky cell phone video taken from an apartment across the street. "We have obtained video evidence of the criminal traipsing through Mayor Hamilton's office before lighting the building on fire. Thankfully, the mayor and his staff were not in the building at the time—"

I slipped my phone into my backpack, relief flooding through me. I leaned against Sarah, and she wrapped her arms tightly around my shoulders.

The reporter continued. "The man committing the act of arson was dressed head to toe in some type of black suit, and authorities believe that a super is, in fact, the one to blame for the destruction."

The video zoomed in, and even though the footage was grainy, I could still make out the familiar plain black suit and mask. It was clear he was the one standing in front of my father's desk with his hands clasped tightly behind his back. The bright orange fire reflected off his dark clothes. He didn't try to quell the flames; he didn't do a thing. The super spent a few seconds admiring his work before disappearing, just as he had last night.

"The criminal is being called Iron Phantom due to the armored sheen of his suit and his ability to materialize and vanish at will, much like a ghost," the reporter continued. "We are urging citizens to stay alert for any other suspicious activity possibly connected to Iron Phantom, and not to approach this dangerous man if encountered. Developments in this story will be brought to you as soon as they are available, until our supers are able to apprehend this threatening fugitive. Now, back to Robert in the studio."

I didn't need the reporter to spell it out for me. The man who saved me last night was no hero.

He was a villain.

Morriston had never seen a supervillain before. Our supers used their powers for good; the only criminals were ordinary citizens. Thieves, gangs, drug dealers. Never a super. No one knew how to handle a criminal with both evil intentions *and* superpowers. I supposed there must have been supervillains in other parts of the country, but no one heard much about them. They were apprehended quickly, before the problem brought on by their presence could escalate.

The problem in Morriston had already escalated. Iron Phantom had done so much damage during his first official act of evil that the city was terrified to see what he would do next. Thankfully, no one was harmed in the city hall fire. Very few people were in the building, and those inside got out quickly with Connor's help. City hall, however, would be closed until further notice.

Classes continued as scheduled, but no one got much learning done. We were all glued to the televisions as footage of the fire played on a never-ending loop, the video of Iron Phantom's kindness toward the homeless man forgotten. Most students were addicted to the drama, eating up the chance to either gush about or condemn Morriston's first supervillain. For them, he was an excuse to skip out on class for a day. His actions were very real, but he was still a fantasy. For me . . . I didn't understand. Iron Phantom had proven himself to be worse than the criminal he rescued me from. Honestly, I couldn't figure out why he bothered to rescue me at all.

I headed to the library during my study hall, hoping for a quiet reprieve from the news. No such luck. By midafternoon, I'd seen the same clip of the same flames two dozen times, and each one made a golf-ball-sized lump form in the back of my throat.

Even in the library, it was everywhere. A group of girls from my gym class huddled around someone's cell phone, watching a replay at a study table. Gary Gunkle, Morriston's most flatulent member of the senior class, was hunched in front of a computer in the corner, bulky headphones covering his ears as he listened. Upstairs, a group of sophomores from the drama club traded their fears of Iron Phantom as they lounged near the newspaper racks. And in the back corner, near the bay window and the most comfortable squashy armchairs in the library, several stage crew kids hurled an imaginary torch at the wall, shouting Iron Phantom's name.

Ridiculous. Childish, I thought as I headed for an empty table near the stacks of spare history textbooks for rent. Only one other table was occupied. The boy that Sarah had knocked into before auditions—Rylan—sat with a laptop, watching the flames flicker on his screen.

I pulled my chair across the wooden floor with a loud screech that had Ms. Jacobson, the librarian, poking her head out of her office to shoot me the stink eye. I slumped down at the table, trying to ignore the plume of smoke covering Rylan's screen. My fingers rubbed circles into my temples as a stress headache started to form.

"That video is the same now as it was five hours ago," I snapped at Rylan's back. He jumped a little, causing his chair to creak, and pulled out one of his earbuds.

He turned around slowly, raising his eyebrows. His brown eyes blinked, but he didn't speak. When I first met him, his silence unnerved me a little, but after putting up with nonstop chatter all day long, I welcomed the quiet.

The news clip still played on his screen, and I couldn't help but stare, feeling queasy for the millionth time that day.

"Somehow those flames look taller every time I watch that," I said.

Rylan glanced at his laptop for just a moment. "Yeah," he said quietly. We stared at the clip as it played out and the screen went black. With nothing to look at, I started to feel a little awkward, so I watched as a freshman girl pushed through the library doors with tears in her eyes. I wondered if she knew someone who worked in one of the buildings downtown.

I thought back to last night, picturing the boy's bright eyes and the playful lilt to his voice. *Iron Phantom, what did you do?*

"Are you scared?" I asked Rylan. He blinked at me. Such a stupidly personal question, especially after just meeting a person. I tried to backtrack. "I mean, I guess no one likes admitting they're scared. . . ."

"I am," he said, using the half whisper that Sarah and I dubbed the "library voice." But for Rylan it just seemed to be his normal voice. "A little. Maybe even more than a little." He packed up his laptop, gently zipping it into a case before slipping it into his backpack. His shy eyes flicked to me before drifting to the window. The city was too far away to see the buildings, but smoke hung in the sky like a deadly storm cloud.

"Are you scared?" he asked.

"No." That was a big fat lie. "I mean . . . yeah."

Rylan nodded. Gripping the straps of his backpack, he slung the heavy-looking bag over one shoulder. The corners of his lips lifted in an encouraging smile, and he left the library without another word.

"What do you think Dad's plan is?" I asked Connor while we watched our father's press conference from the comfort of our living room couch. Dad was fielding questions from a roomful of reporters who were demanding details on the precautions being put in place to increase our safety from Iron Phantom. He wouldn't go into detail, but said more would be revealed soon. I wasn't even sure if *he* knew what to do. Because of his superpowers, Iron Phantom was quickly labeled as one of the nation's most dangerous criminals. How could my father possibly keep him at bay?

Connor shrugged. He had returned home briefly to make sure I was okay—he was still dressed as Red Comet.

"I don't know. I haven't talked to him yet. He'll probably try to bring in more supers to find this guy. What else can he do? I just don't get it." Connor sighed and started pacing in front of the TV. "We're given these powers for a reason. They're a gift. They help the less fortunate, like you." He pointed a finger at my face.

"Gee, thanks, Connor."

"You know what I mean. We help people. We don't destroy things. We . . ." He sat down again and stared at me. With his blue eyes narrowed and his face covered in sweat and ash, he looked much older than nineteen. "You saw him."

I gulped. "I what?"

Connor's eyes continued to narrow. "You said you saw some dude dressed all in black yesterday and then this happens? That's not a coincidence, Abby. You saw him—"

"Yeah, but he was different then. He was helping. And there was that video this morning—"

"A guy isn't suddenly a saint just because he decided on a whim to feed the homeless. He burned down a building, Abby!"

"Thanks. I wasn't aware." I leaned back into the couch, raking my fingers through the knots in my hair.

I couldn't find a good reason to defend Iron Phantom. He might have saved my life, but he ruined any gratitude I had when he burned down city hall. And yet, for some reason, I couldn't bring myself to tell my own brother the truth about what really happened last night.

"So what do we do now?" I asked.

"We? Nothing. You stay here. I have to get back out there in case something else happens." Connor sighed and pulled his mask over his head, trudging toward the door. "Promise me something, Abby. If you do see him again, you have to let someone know. Me or Dad—let us know and we'll take care of it."

I felt my cheeks start to burn. "Connor, I'm not completely helpless—"

"Abby," he stressed. *"Please."* His voice cracked. Although I couldn't see his eyes, I knew they had that watery sheen to them, the same look he got whenever we talked about our mom or any other victim for slightly too long. He was just trying to do the right thing. Even through his mask, I knew Connor was staring me down, silently begging me to agree. Because that's what Connor did. You couldn't help but listen to him and be on his side. It was the reason he was such a great superhero.

"Promise me," he said again.

I knew the right thing to do. I had no obligation to Iron Phantom. He was nobody. I would always be on Connor's side. He was one of the only family members I had left.

"I promise, Connor. I'll let you know."

When he flew back downtown, I took the steps two at a time to my bedroom. But it wasn't until I pushed my door open and dropped my bag (and all the homework I didn't want to think about) on my desk chair that I realized something was different. I hadn't left my lights on this morning. I knew I hadn't. All my belongings were undisturbed, but I couldn't shake the unmistakable feeling that something was here that shouldn't be.

If I hadn't known that Connor was out of the house all day,

then I would have thought he was playing a stupid prank on me. But as I cautiously padded across the room, my toes sinking into the carpet, I knew that not even my doofus brother was to blame.

Goose bumps crawled up my arms. Placed on my mattress, directly in front of the pillows arranged meticulously against my headboard, was a chocolate bar sealed in a red wrapper and a note written in a messy scrawl:

> *I've heard chocolate helps with head scrapes. I hope you're feeling better.*
>
> *—IP*
>
> *P.S. I'm going to need your help with something.*

CHAPTER FOUR

There was a knife under my pillow. I could say with absolute confidence that I had never slept with a knife under my pillow before.

Sure, it was only a butter knife, but I still felt like I needed some form of protection. He knew where I lived. He had been *in my room*. My promise to Connor played in my head like a scratchy broken record. *I'll let you know.* A load of good that promise did. Connor's cell phone was dead, and once he didn't return home after midnight, I assumed he took up his usual post on a skyscraper downtown, watching for trouble. I just had to hope that if something happened, if Iron Phantom showed up again, Connor would come.

Telling Dad should have been my next move, but after returning home from fifteen hours of dealing with a charred office and a frightened city, he passed out on top of his blankets with his shoes and tie still on. I wasn't about to bother him. I changed my clothes, got my knife, and went to bed. It was just one night. I could take care of myself.

But I had overlooked the fact that it was impossible to sleep when your mind was somewhere else. I rolled onto my side, my back facing the window, while I plumped my pillows and attempted to count sheep in desperation. I had just reached twenty, and was no closer to falling asleep, when I heard a dull thump on my carpet followed by a gravelly voice.

"You should really lock your window. Dangerous criminals are running rampant around this city, you know."

Right, like the window mattered. The guy could teleport. The fingers of my right hand inched under my pillow. I took the knife in my fist, the steel handle freezing against my sweaty skin. Maybe if I didn't move, he would leave. Like an animal playing dead as a defense mechanism. I watched an entire special on opossums doing that on Animal Planet once. If I held my breath and started drooling a little, he would grow bored and walk away.

"Psst. I know you're not sleeping."

The floor creaked as the thumps moved closer. *Be the opossum, Abby. Just be the opossum.*

"Hey." A gloved hand touched my bare shoulder, and I whipped my head around, coming face-to-mask with the guy who'd haunted my thoughts for the past twenty-four hours.

"Get away from me!" I hissed, rolling out of bed. My mattress was the only thing between us. I couldn't work up the courage to throw the butter knife, so I dove for a thick anatomy textbook on the floor instead, hurling it through the room, aiming straight for his dumb, evil face. With a shake of his head, Iron Phantom disappeared, winking back into existence a few feet over. The textbook spun through the empty air, smacked the wall, and hit the carpet. Iron Phantom stepped on it with his boot, and my weapon was rendered useless.

"Easy there, Bazooka." He sounded like he was trying to hold back a laugh, and I hated him for it. In the darkness of my room, I could hardly see him in his black suit, just barely make out the occasional glint of his eyes as they caught the glow from my alarm clock. "I'm not allowed to pay a visit to the damsel in distress I rescued?"

"No. Why don't you pay a visit to one of the people who almost burned alive today in the fire that *you* set instead?" I snatched his note off my bedside table, waving it through the air. "And how do you know where I live?"

"Oh, good. You got it." He noticed the unopened chocolate bar. "You didn't eat it? It's not poisoned."

I blinked. I didn't eat it because I wasn't hungry; I hadn't even thought that it might be poisoned, but now I was starting to reconsider.

"It's *not* poisoned," he repeated. "And maybe I know where you live because maybe I followed you here last night to make sure you got back safe."

I knew I hadn't been alone. I clutched my knife tighter. He knew where I lived. Where I slept. What else did he know?

Connor's plea echoed through my head. *Let me know.* He had to be aware that something was up, right? He had to realize I was in danger.

Iron Phantom leaned against the wall, crossing his feet at the ankles. He looked almost . . . bored.

No. He was messing with me. Trying to get me to let my guard down.

I'd vowed not to wake my dad up, but that was before Morriston's new supervillain made an appearance in my room. Dad was on the other side of the house, but maybe if I screamed loud enough. . . .

"Da—"

Iron Phantom's eyes widened. He snatched one of the pillows from my bed, chucking it at me. It smacked my stomach, then fell to the floor.

"Shh! What are you doing?"

"Getting help. What are *you* doing?"

"Getting you to shut up. If you were really in danger, wouldn't a super have come to rescue you already?"

"I . . ." He had me there. But Connor could just be busy. Wouldn't be the first time.

"Wave that butter knife around all you want," he said, "but if you were really scared, you would have thrown that at me, not the book. Actually, if you were really scared, you would have grabbed a larger knife."

I didn't lower my arm.

"Fine." He hung his head. "You don't like me. I get it. But I wasn't trying to hurt anyone today. You don't understand why I did it." His voice softened as he toyed with the edge of his mask around his jaw. His green eyes were fixed on the collection of photos scattered across my desk, not on me. I could have run out of the room and gotten my dad. Maybe I should have. What if this was some kind of trap?

But looking at Iron Phantom tentatively examining a picture of me and Sarah at the beach last year, a small smile on his face, it didn't seem very urgent that I let someone know of his presence.

"Make me understand," I said.

He dropped the picture frame, pressing his palms against his eyes. "Look, I didn't want to hurt anyone. I was trying to send a message."

"To who?" I glanced at my door. I could still make a run for it. Iron Phantom noticed, but he didn't try to stop me. Instead of stepping closer to the door, or to me, he took a step back, toward my window.

He didn't answer my question, but he did hold out his palm. There was something small and shiny resting on his glove, but with my bed filling the space between us, I couldn't figure out exactly what I was looking at.

Iron Phantom took one small step forward. My muscles tensed, but I didn't move. Then he took another, and another, until his knees were resting against the edge of my bed and his body was leaning over the mattress toward me.

He held up the object between his thumb and index finger. A silver rectangle half the size of my thumbnail.

"What do you know about microchips?" he asked.

"Pretty much nothing. Why?"

Iron Phantom hummed, watching me. What I could see of his face under his mask looked completely blank, emotionless.

"Here's the issue," he said. "I've seen microchips like this before. This looks like a tracking device, the kind that can be implanted under a person's skin, and believe me, there are plenty more where this one came from. But whether they're for people like you or for people like me, I can't say."

"People like you? Supers?"

My heart skipped a beat. *Connor?*

"Someone wants to follow the supers . . . to find out who they are?" I asked, hardly daring to believe it.

"Maybe more," he said. "To capture them, to control them, to test them. Use your imagination, Bazooka. Or *maybe* they're to spy on the rest of Morriston for some inane reason. I don't know. I'm really just spitballing here. You see, this particular microchip is actually empty on the inside." He popped the tiny box open, showing me smooth metal walls and not much else. "From my experience, that's not normal. I want to know what should be there and why it's not. That's where you come in. Think of it as your . . . supersecret mission." He wiggled his fingers, like the whole thing was supposed to be really grand—an honor or something.

"I don't want a supersecret mission," I said.

"Too bad. I need you to find out what's up. But don't ask your dad outright. Be sneaky about it, because if someone catches on, I'm not sure it would be a good thing."

"Wait, wait, wait. Hold up. My father?"

"Yeah, your father. I may be new to the whole superhero gig, but I'm not stupid. I knew last night you were the mayor's daughter." He slipped the chip back into his suit, patting his pocket for good measure. "And I also stole this little guy from his office this morning."

I almost threw the butter knife at him. The only thing stopping me was the knowledge that if I let it out of my grasp, I would officially be weaponless. The memory of the flames flitted through my mind. The fluorescent orange that turned city hall completely black. The smoke. The tears dripping from the freshman girl's eyes as she entered the library this afternoon. Forget the knife. Maybe I would try punching him instead.

"You are no hero," I spit out, my voice wavering in anger.

Iron Phantom looked down at his suit, full lips curling into a smirk. "Is that so? The costume begs to differ."

I clenched my fists as a surge of annoyance bubbled through me. Heroes didn't destroy things—they helped. Connor was a hero. Not this guy. "A hero wouldn't have burned down city hall. You're a villain."

He rolled his eyes and quickly disappeared into the breeze of the air conditioner. I slumped against the wall in relief. He was gone; he'd had enough of me.

"Listen to me." Before I could blink, he was back, one hand holding my shoulder against the wall while the other clamped over my mouth. So this was how it would end. I would die in my bedroom at the hands of the world's most annoying supervillain.

"Abigail," he whispered, his voice so low it nearly got lost amid the hum of the AC unit. "I'm not the bad guy. I'm not a villain. If I wanted to hurt you, I would have done it already."

I didn't register much after his use of my full name. No one called me Abigail. Not because I didn't like my name, but because everyone thought my fair hair and soft bone structure made me look younger—more like an Abby. I guess I wasn't beautiful or sophisticated enough to be an *Abigail*.

Eventually, he realized I wasn't going to fight him and removed his hand from my mouth, resting it on my shoulder.

"Someone in city hall is clearly up to something." He paused, sighing. "I need you to help me."

"Absolutely not." I couldn't believe that after he set my father's workplace ablaze he still had the audacity to ask for my help.

"Please." His fingers dug into my shoulders but lessened their grip when I flinched. "Please, I need you to see if you can find out anything about the microchips. I'll be back again in a few days."

"Why should I help you? You could have killed somebody today."

"You should help me," he said, "because as much as you hate to admit it, you already trust me."

I seethed. "I do not—"

"You do." His words were tentative and quiet, even in the deafening silence of my bedroom, not cocky like he often came across. "You haven't stabbed me with that knife yet." He chuckled. "You didn't run for help or try to force me to leave. Instead, you listened to what I had to say. You trust me." He nodded toward my nightstand. "You should try the chocolate. I've had, like, three bars today. It's really good."

With those final parting words, he vanished before my eyes for a third time, leaving me with a knot of rage in my chest and more questions than answers.

Despite the media frenzy surrounding the city hall fire, I managed to block Iron Phantom from my thoughts almost all weekend. However, in the brief, though irritating, moments he crossed my mind, I couldn't help wondering if he told me the truth when he snuck into my room. Was someone really causing problems inside city hall? Did they put the microchip on my dad's desk and Iron Phantom just happened to find it first, or did my dad know about it? Was it really a tracking device? I wanted to ask, but my tongue felt useless in my mouth. Dad was already so stressed, and for all I knew, Iron Phantom—whoever he was—was just plain crazy and that microchip wasn't even real.

Even though I walked into school on Monday ignoring all traces of Iron Phantom's existence, my nerves were still raging. Sure, I had both a test in statistics and an essay due in English, but my biggest concern was for the sheet of paper tacked up on the theater arts bulletin board.

"I made the chorus!" Sarah elbowed her way past the crowd of students reading the *Hall of Horrors* cast list to reach me when I came through the door. She threw her arms around me, a curl of her hair momentarily getting stuck in my mouth while she squeezed my shoulders. "If my singing managed to get me in the chorus, you definitely got the lead."

"You didn't look to see my name?" Now free from Sarah's iron grip, I eyed the crowd swarming the cast list with trepidation. If Sarah didn't see my name, did that mean I didn't make it? I didn't want to be doomed to spend the next few weeks working in the costume closet.

My best friend shook her head and began towing me toward the list. No. Now I didn't want to see. I tried to dig my heels into the floor, which only resulted in a loud *screeeech* alerting my (possible) castmates of my presence as my shoes skidded along the tile.

"It's not that I didn't see your name," Sarah said. "I was just too busy looking for my own. Here you go!"

Sarah and I came to a halt before the bulletin board. It was decorated with yellow and pink paper and music notes, as if happy colors would somehow make the list showing which part would claim my soul for the next six weeks any less daunting.

"I can read it to you if you want." Sarah laughed and I groaned. Might as well just get it over with. Except . . . Courtney McGuire's audition was just as good as mine. Not to mention her feet fit the extra pair of character shoes backstage whereas mine were much too small. Surely she got the female lead.

All because of her damn huge feet.

But Courtney didn't get it. Her name jumped out to me instantly, and she was in the chorus with Sarah. Which meant . . .

Abby Hamilton. . . . . Angeline

I couldn't believe it. I actually got a lead role in the musical.

Sarah screamed, because that's what Sarah does best, while I stared dumbstruck at the piece of paper fluttering on the board. Suddenly, it didn't seem so frightening. I actually did it. For once I was actually good enough to shine.

Take that, Connor.

"I'm so happy for you!" Sarah twirled me around the hall. "I'm so happy! Wait, why aren't you happy, Abby?"

"What? I am happy." And I was. The news just hadn't hit me yet. I felt like I was walking through a fog.

"You are?" she asked. I nodded. Sarah sighed and began reading more names on the cast list. "Well, then we need to work on your acting skills. You look like I did that time I realized I would never see Red Comet without his mask."

"Hey, that's hardly fair." Sarah moped for days when she reached that not-so-true conclusion. She even whined to Connor. He laughed in her face, then walked away.

The great Red Comet, everyone.

"Fine, maybe you don't look *that* sad, but you look sad. Cheer up, buttercup. Who's your sexy leading man going to be?"

I squinted at the fine print under the fluorescent lights and glanced at the name directly above mine. *Isaac Jackson*. The voice of God's most heavenly angel.

"Ooooh! New kid!" Sarah squealed. "He might just become my new fan fiction project. I mean, that voice and that hair and *those eyes*." She tilted her head to the ceiling. "Is it just me, or is it getting a little toasty in here?"

I scanned the remainder of the list, but my eyes were drawn to the top of the page again and again, landing always on the same name. *Isaac Jackson*. Thinking about how incredible his performance was at auditions was making my palms sweat and my toes curl and . . . I just wouldn't think about him. That was the key. I wouldn't think about him until rehearsals started. I had enough on my mind anyway.

My plan was foiled almost immediately.

As much as I tried to ignore Isaac Jackson until our first rehearsal, he managed to track me down during study hall later that afternoon. He approached me and Sarah at our usual table in the cafeteria—the one closest to the window and civilization—his hands stuffed in the pockets of his jeans, looking wary.

"Abby Hamilton, right?"

"Yeah?"

"Isaac Jackson." *Good Lord.* His voice could melt butter. Isaac held out a hand, and I shook it, his fingers cool against my skin. "Nice to officially meet you. I guess I'll be playing the Arthur to your Angeline this fall."

Sarah's classic Fangirl Squeal of Excitement escaped her lips, and she immediately ran toward the bathrooms, a few girls in our study hall snickering at her unbridled enthusiasm. Sarah was a hopeless romantic. In her mind, because Isaac and I were now starring in a musical, we would obviously end up married with tons of babies and she needed to give us some privacy.

"She's more excited about cannibalistic royals than I am," Isaac said. He took a seat in the chair Sarah had vacated, glancing at her "homework" spread out on the table.

Sarah wasn't doing homework. She was in the process of making a new Red Comet collage for her locker shrine because she claimed the old one was "dated." "Dated" in Sarah's mind meant the pictures of Connor in her locker were from July, and it was now the end of September. Not that anything changed when the public couldn't see Connor's face under his mask. Red Comet could look old and gray as far as anyone knew.

"Are you into superheroes?" I asked, noticing Isaac shuffle through Sarah's Red Comet pictures.

Isaac shrugged. "I don't know much about them. We don't have them where I come from."

I eyed him incredulously. "Where are you from?" I found it difficult to believe there were places in the United States without supers.

"Small town," Isaac said. "Idaho."

"That's far. Why come to Pennsylvania?"

"Oh, uh." He suddenly looked nervous. Isaac played with the corner of a picture of Connor flying over the city. I noticed his fingernails were bitten down to the quick. "I came to live with my uncle," was all he said.

"Oh. Sorry. I didn't mean to pry." The last thing I wanted was to make him uncomfortable if we were going to spend hours together in rehearsals.

Isaac ran a hand through his dark hair, causing it to stick straight up from his forehead. "No, don't worry about it. It's no problem." He didn't elaborate on his living situation or hometown any further. "So . . . do you like superheroes?" He gestured to Sarah's Red Comet photos.

The award for World's Most Unladylike Sound in a Cafeteria went to me as a snort erupted from my nose. Isaac raised an eyebrow while my face turned red. "Sure, I guess you could say that. They have their moments." All I could think about was the five bucks Connor gave me to get a mustard stain out of his super suit last night.

"You must meet a lot of them with your dad being the mayor and all." Isaac leaned closer in his chair. None of my classmates ever bothered to ask about my connection with Morriston's supers. Rightly so because I had never met any of them besides Red Comet.

"I haven't, actually," I said. "Only Red Comet the other week during the school assembly."

"Huh. Interesting." Isaac stared at me intently, his bright green eyes barely blinking. Almost as if he was egging me on to express more about my super encounters and was disappointed by my lack of information.

Realizing I had nothing interesting to contribute to our conversation, Isaac stood. "Well, I guess I'll see you in rehearsals, Abigail."

No one called me Abigail except . . .

I squeezed my eyes shut tight as Isaac walked away, strengthening my resolve not to think about his dark brown hair or bright green eyes if I could help it. Because if I thought too much, I would start to wonder if it was more than a coincidence that Morriston got a new student right before the first appearance of Iron Phantom. But many guys had brown hair and green eyes, and I reminded myself I had never even seen Iron Phantom's hair—only his eyelashes.

His dark lashes meant nothing.

"How did it go, Abby?" Sarah bounded back to her seat after Isaac left, a fresh glue stick in hand for her collage. She applied a generous amount to the back of Connor's head and smoothed it down with her thumb.

How did it go? was a loaded question. Isaac was more inquisitive than most Morriston citizens, who had grown up around supers. He seemed harmless, but I wasn't sure. I had known most of my classmates since we were five. I knew who dated who, who had food allergies, who was afraid of butterflies. I knew virtually nothing about Isaac Jackson, and considering everything that happened over the past few days, that made me incredibly uneasy.

"I'm not sure," I said as I watched Sarah glue cutouts of her and Red Comet atop a skyscraper beneath the sunset. The answer to her question depended on how much I believed in coincidence.

CHAPTER FIVE

The subway was packed to capacity as Sarah and I hopped on the express line from the suburbs into the city center. A new chick-flick was opening at the theater, and Sarah had managed to score us the last two tickets for the evening showtime. There was also an indie rock band playing at the newest venue on Morriston's north shore and a celebrity chef opening a new restaurant in the cultural district. Despite Iron Phantom's recent appearance, it felt like the entire city was out tonight.

The train lurched as it took off from the platform. Sarah nudged me in the back, pointing to a few empty seats in the rear corner of the car. We squeezed through the crowd, collapsing on the plastic bench.

"Is it just me," Sarah asked, "or does this thing smell like BO more and more every time we ride it?"

A group of tourists armed with brochures and thick foreign accents stopped speaking to stare down their noses at us.

"Sorry," said Sarah. "I didn't mean you."

They grunted something unintelligible and moved to the opposite end of the car.

"Whoopsies." Sarah shrugged. She pointed to the spot where the tourists had disappeared. "Ooooh! Abby, hottie alert nine o'clock!"

I couldn't tell if it was his presence that made my stomach lurch or if it was just the ancient subway tracks. I sat quietly as Sarah bounced in her seat and Isaac Jackson edged his way through the crowd, a small group of senior boys laughing and following behind him.

Isaac spun his baseball cap around backward as he turned to clap one of the other guys on the shoulder. His straight white teeth gleamed as he laughed. Sarah sighed.

"I knew joining the musical was a good idea."

"Maybe you should stick to Red Comet," I muttered, but I didn't think she heard me. I still couldn't decide if Isaac was someone I wanted to trust or not.

I hadn't spoken to him since he tracked me down in study hall, and I was trying to forget the resemblance he held to Iron Phantom. They each had green eyes and a similar build, and called me Abigail at least once. Those were the only similarities I had to go by—not a lot. I wouldn't unmask Iron Phantom with those bland observations.

I was irritated at myself for even thinking I might know the supervillain's true identity. He could be anyone in Morriston. It was far-fetched that I personally knew one super in the city, let alone two.

I pushed all thoughts of Iron Phantom from my mind as Isaac approached us, his friends trailing behind him. The subway lurched, and he stumbled into a map of Morriston that was hanging on the wall behind a sheet of glass.

"Dammit. I'm not used to these things at all." He tried to steady himself as the subway jolted quickly in the opposite direction. "Hi, Abigail. Hi, Abigail's friend."

"It's Sarah." She grinned. "Sarah with an *h*."

Isaac nodded. The group of boys he was with passed by us. They unlatched the door that separated our car from the next and ran across the narrow platform. A big no-no in subway safety, but it was also the easiest way to win a game of Morriston truth or dare. Not that I'd ever tried it.

Isaac wobbled as he clutched the handrails above his head. He didn't know what he was getting himself into by jumping cars. Unless, of course, he really could teleport.

Stupid, Abby. I shook myself back into reality as I watched Sarah talk Isaac's ear off. She was trying to get his help with learning lyrics for the musical. Sarah could hardly sing melodies of songs; she was having a disastrous time learning the harmonies.

"Okay, so," Sarah said, sitting up straight and taking a deep breath, "it's *little servant girrrrrrl.*" She pushed her voice as deep as it would go, but the result was less show-tuney-melodic and far more pregnant-moose-about-to-give-birth.

Isaac hacked up a cough. "Ummm . . ." His eyes searched the subway car, landing on the door leading to the outside platform. I could make out his friends on the other side of the glass, waving him forward. His face paled. "I have to go. Nice talking to you, ladies."

He shimmied across the platform, arms spread out wide to brace himself; then he disappeared into the next car.

Sarah huffed. "Was it really that bad? I didn't think it was really that bad."

I couldn't bring myself to shatter her musical dreams. "It was . . . really, really close."

"See? That's what I thought." Sarah looked smugly around the train car, practically daring a young couple reading newspapers beside us to try and outsing her.

"You know, Abby . . . ," she said. "I think I get why you like this whole musical thing. It's fun, and we get to wear costumes—almost like we're superheroes!"

I nearly choked. Superheroes. Right. I didn't enjoy musicals because of the thunderous applause, the sense of accomplishment when nailing a high note or difficult dance step, or the sensation of genuinely feeling alive.

No. Clearly I only did it for the costumes.

I didn't bother to correct her. Instead, I glanced at my phone when it buzzed in my lap. Another self-defense video from my dad. Not surprising considering Sarah and I were venturing out at night, but he could have at least sent a text along with it. A nice *How's your day?* would have been fantastic. Rolling my eyes, I dropped my phone in my purse out of sight and stared out the window.

The train tracks flashed by at a dizzying speed, running parallel to the freeway before beginning their descent into Morriston's famous floating tunnel that traveled under the river and emerged downtown. The pinkish hue of twilight disappeared as the dark hole swallowed us up.

The subway car swayed, screeching over the rails. I tried not to think about how many tons of water rested above us. Too bad parking in the city was so scarce because I would have much rather had Sarah drive into town. Honestly, I would have rather walked into town.

I closed my eyes, trying to think of song lyrics, but nothing would come to mind. Nothing except Angeline's death hymn at the end of act 2, and singing that seemed like a bad omen.

The subway screeched again, slowing its momentum. My eyes snapped open, and I craned my neck to look out the window and down the tunnel. There was no glow of an approaching platform. There was nothing.

The entire car screamed as the lights flickered, winking out in a dull buzz of electricity.

There was only darkness.

I felt Sarah's fingers dig into my wrist. "What just happened?"

"Power," I mumbled, riffling through my purse for my phone. The dark always had a terrifying ability to make my body constrict, growing smaller with each second. Like anything could be lurking inside the black.

The light of fifty cell phones flooded the car, and we all watched as the subway came to a stop in the middle of the tunnel.

"Well. That's not good," Sarah said. Her face was covered in a blue glow from her phone screen. "Do you think we'll miss the movie?"

"I don't know. Maybe someone will . . ." The flashlight on my phone bounced around the car, stopping on the wall of the tunnel. I pressed my face against the glass, watching a thin stream of water trickle from the ceiling. *Drip, drip, drip.* I jerked my flashlight to the left. Another hole. And another. And another. And another. At least a dozen, covering the walls and ceiling, dribbling down onto the tracks.

Nudging Sarah, I pointed outside. One of the cracks on the ceiling was growing wider, gushing water like a fire hydrant.

Around us, other passengers were doing the same, watching the leaks with confusion plaguing every face. For a moment, there was only silence. Then, just like in the tunnel, the dam of calm inside the subway car split wide open.

Sarah and I jumped onto our seats to avoid the stampede as the passengers rushed the doors, not caring if they trampled anyone's bags or bodies to get there. They crashed into the glass, but the seals stayed firmly in place. I leaned around Sarah, tugging at the door leading to the platform of the next car where Isaac had disappeared. It wouldn't budge. The power outage kept it locked up tight.

Like a tomb, I thought briefly. I pushed the horrific image from my mind.

"Abby." Sarah clung to my arm, panic lacing her voice. She pointed outside. "More water."

No longer just dripping, the cracks in the ceiling and walls were all gushing, filling the tunnel with at least a foot of water by now.

I could barely think. There was too much screaming. Too much moving around without going anywhere. The cars in front of and behind ours were doing the same, passengers banging at the doors and trying to break the glass themselves.

Two feet of water in the tunnel. Then three.

I looked at my phone. I didn't even have service to call for help.

A red blur flashed past my eyes.

The subway car behind us rocked on its track, and a deafening cheer went up inside the tunnel.

"Abby!" Sarah pulled at my arm again. "He's here!"

A window in our car shattered, and Red Comet flew inside. He collided with a metal pole, crashing to a halt.

Smooth, Connor.

Red Comet stood rather ungracefully, brushing dirt and whatever other grime that lurked in the subway off his suit.

He made quick work of prying open the exit doors with his bare hands. "Citizens of Morriston!" he boomed. "I have come to save—"

No one bothered listening. Connor was a forgotten superhero as the passengers rushed into the tunnel, climbing the steep slope of the tracks toward the pinprick of light and the outside air. When the car emptied out, Connor's shoulders drooped. "Way to make a guy feel good."

Beside me, Sarah squeaked.

Connor's head snapped up. He ran the length of the car, skidding to a stop in front of us.

"What are you still doing here? Go!"

I gripped the front of Connor's suit so he couldn't shove me away. "You'll get everyone out, right?" I thought of Isaac and his friends in the next car over. I even thought of the snooty tourists and anyone else we might know but couldn't see down here in the tunnel's dark depths. He had to save them. We couldn't leave anyone behind.

Connor pulled at my wrists. "I will once you let go of me. This isn't amateur hour, you know. Now run!" He gave me one final shove before flying off. He crashed through the next car and the next, the tunnel filling with wave after wave of desperate passengers.

Sarah and I waded with the crowd, our clothes waterlogged as we slipped up the tracks. A suffocating mass of passengers pressed in from all sides. An elderly man tripped, and a woman hoisted him to his feet. In front of us, a father carried two sobbing children on his shoulders. The mob edged forward as one. We reached the mouth of the tunnel, where Sarah and I helped haul the last straggling passengers onto shore just as the water bubbled up behind us. As far as I could tell everyone made it out safely, but the tunnel was officially flooded.

Panting, I whirled around, searching the sky for Red Comet.

The air was empty.

"No," a tiny breath of air escaped my lips. "No, no, no." He wasn't with the passengers onshore, he wasn't in the sky. The river gurgled, churning into a fierce undertow as the tunnel began to crack apart, collapsing.

One person was left inside.

"No!" Sarah held me back when I made a break for the tunnel. The water continued bubbling as I watched, helpless to stop it. He would make it out. He always made it out.

My thundering heartbeat was muffled by the roar of the crowd when two dark shapes burst from the middle of the river. The first, Morriston's favorite B-list superhero, Fish Boy, with his bright blue flippers. And the second was Connor, looking like a drenched rat as he coughed and wrung water from his gloves. He hovered above us for a moment before flying toward our house. He moved slowly, much slower than normal, and I knew instantly that Connor didn't escape without injuries.

"Don't worry about him. He'll be fine." A shadow fell over my shoulder, and I turned, finding my nose nearly pressed up against a chest covered in spandex. White letters—an *F* and a *B*—glowed against the navy-blue super suit.

"Facebook?" I said dumbly, still distracted by Connor's well-being.

"Uhh, no," he laughed. "Fish Boy. But I'll forgive your slight faux pas on account of your near-death experience."

I leaned back from Fish Boy's chest to get a good look at his face. I'd seen him in photos but never in person. If I could describe him in one word, it would be *blue*. A navy-blue mask covered the top half of his face, and ocean-blue eyes peeked out beneath a mop of curly brown hair. His blue super suit was much more revealing than most supers' costumes. The sleeves cut off like a vest around his muscular shoulders, and the material of the legs stopped just above his knees. The fabric was thicker, more like a wet suit, which made sense because Fish Boy's favorite activity was obviously swimming. Shiny, neon blue scales covered his arms from wrist to elbow. My eyes traveled farther south, moving past his webbed fingers and finally coming to rest on the infamous flippers replacing his human feet. Briefly I wondered whether Fish Boy would grow a mermaid tail if submerged in water long enough.

"Did you ladies lose anything in the water?" he asked. "I'm trying to recover everyone's stuff." He pointed to a small black circle clipped onto his suit near his shoulder. "And I just got this new video camera. It kind of sucks about the subway, but I filmed *everything*. It's going up on my website. Do you want the link?"

Sarah blinked at him. She glanced at the sky.

Fish Boy followed her gaze, looking a little crestfallen. "Like I said, don't worry about Red Comet. He's tough. So . . . do you need anything? No? Yes? Your blatant staring is *filleting* me alive." He pushed his wet hair out of his eyes. "Ha. *Fillet.* I love a good pun."

"We're fine over here," I told him. "Thank you."

"Suit yourself. If you need me to *fish* anything out, let me know." He patted Sarah on the shoulder. "Take it easy, sweetheart." He moved farther down the line as the crowd jostled for his attention.

Sarah was still staring at the sky. I wondered if I needed to slap her.

"Sarah, a super just touched you and you're still breathing." I chuckled nervously.

She slowly turned around. She looked from me, to the sky, then back to me. Her brows furrowed before her eyes snapped open, wide and unblinking as she made the connection.

"Abby," Sarah whispered, "when Red Comet was inside the subway, why did he sound exactly like your brother?"

I knew I made a mistake screaming when Connor didn't show up right away. I was so afraid for his life that I panicked and didn't care about being reckless. I could have completely blown his cover, and it looked like I did—for one person at least. Red Comet's biggest fan.

Connor would understand. I thought he was dead, and he knew as well as I the heartbreaking punch in the gut that accompanied the loss of a family member.

"Because . . ." Sarah could keep the secret. She didn't have a choice. "He is my brother."

CHAPTER SIX

"I can't believe you told her," Connor moaned from the living room couch while I finished tending to his wounds. A hospital visit was out of the question because his abnormal DNA was a dead giveaway he was a super. Just a single blood test would be enough to condemn him. My mom had been a nurse once upon a time and I knew a little about sterilizing injuries, but I had to admit that I was clueless when it came to removing the broken glass lodged in my brother's side. The amount of blood staining his skin was enough to make me woozy. But I tried my best. For Connor's sake.

"It's your own fault you weren't disguising your voice," I muttered, gathering the shards in one hand while I used the other to dab antibiotic ointment on his cuts. I tried to keep my eyes averted from the blood.

"Maybe it's your fault for freaking out with a crowd of people around."

I pressed harder than necessary on a particularly deep wound, making Connor hiss in pain. "Oh, sorry. I didn't really think twice about your secret identity when I thought you drowned."

"Come on, I'm fine. Aren't I fine, Sarah?"

Sarah hadn't said a word since I told her the truth. The only reaction she gave when I told her she couldn't tell anyone was a slight shake of the head. We took a bus from the city to Sarah's house, then drove to mine. All in painful, gut-twisting silence. When we arrived home, Sarah nearly fainted seeing Connor struggle to remove his super suit without aggravating his injuries, his mask lying on the ground. She had taken up refuge on an armchair by the television and barely blinked since.

"We ruined her life, didn't we?" Connor asked, throwing an arm over his face to shield his eyes from the light. Now that I removed the glass and cleaned the cuts, he looked much better, though his bare torso was marred with four long gashes on the right side of his chest. They extended around to his back, but it took more than a few injuries to keep Red Comet down. In a few days, he'd be back to normal.

"Is she going to speak at all?" Connor snapped his fingers in Sarah's direction, and she jolted in her seat. "Sarah, you aren't going mute or anything, are you? Because that would suck. I'm dying for you to read me some more Red Comet fan fiction."

Ah, my kind, compassionate, sensitive brother.

Sarah looked at Connor's super suit as if it would suddenly grow legs and try to attack. "You're—you're really him, aren't you? I mean, he's—he's really you. You . . . him . . ."

"Yeah." Connor tousled his dirty blond hair that appeared more dirty than blond after his dip in the river. "You can't tell anyone. It's really not as cool as it seems. I mean . . ." He gestured to the needle I was using to slowly stitch his midsection. "This is pretty painful right now."

"But for the last three years all I did was . . . was talk about you!" Sarah cradled her head in her palms. "That's so embarrassing. All the things I said . . ." Her eyes locked with mine. "Abby, how could you never tell me?"

"Hey, I was sworn to secrecy." I tied off the thread and held my hands up in surrender.

"It's true," Connor said. "I make everyone take an oath. I blindfold you and light candles and then we chant."

"Seriously?"

"No." He slumped down on the couch cushions and fluffed his pillow. "Not seriously. Just don't tell anyone. I'm not creative enough to invent another secret identity if you screw this one up."

The doorbell rang as I was cleaning up the first-aid kit ten minutes later. Connor's eyes were closed, but he pointed at the front door, wiggling his fingers in an obnoxious shooing motion that only he would be obtuse enough to try. If he weren't injured, I would have hit him.

"Abby, get the door please," I imitated my brother's deep voice under my breath.

Connor's lips lifted in a weak grin. "Thank you."

Shaking my head, I kicked Connor's suit behind a potted plant, stepped over Sarah's feet, and headed down the hall as the bell chimed a second time. "I'm coming, I'm coming," I grumbled.

A young man was sitting on the porch swing. He jumped up when he saw me, turning his Morriston High School baseball cap around backward. The tail of his flannel shirt fluttered in the breeze.

"Hi, Abby!" He grinned like we were old friends. Which was kind of a problem because I had no clue where I'd met him before. "I came to see how Connor's doing. Is he here?"

"Ummm . . ." I looked back into the living room. "He's . . . uh, who . . . who exactly are you?"

He removed his hat, revealing a messy poof of brown hair. He sighed, though still smiling. "How soon they forget. It's been what, two hours? I know you said you didn't need my help, but I'd still think you'd remember. Maybe I should have given you the link to my website after all."

"Wait . . . *Fish Boy*?" But that couldn't be right. My brother told me he never gave his identity out to anyone, not even other supers. I rolled my eyes. Connor seriously whined after I told Sarah his giant red secret? What a hypocrite.

I crossed my arms over my chest. "So you know my name, but I don't know yours?"

Fish Boy laughed. "I guess that's a little weird for you, huh? I'm Hunter." He held out his hand. I didn't take it. I was feeling oddly protective over my brother at the moment, collapsed on the couch while the city was falling to pieces around us. Could I trust Hunter? I didn't know.

"Abby, let him in," Connor called from inside, his voice groggy. "We got drunk together a few months back. Our names just slipped out. He's cool."

"Oh, of course." I nudged open the heavy oak door with my foot to let Hunter pass into the foyer. "Staying out all night, getting drunk. What next? Impregnating fans?"

"There are perks to the job," Hunter said with a wink. Then he cleared his throat heavily. "Not that that is necessarily one of them."

"Sure." I rolled my eyes a second time. I immediately understood why Hunter and Connor were friends. Their vulgarity knew no bounds.

I followed Hunter down the hallway and into the living room. He seemed to know just where to go, and it made me feel a bit like a stranger in my own home, wondering how many times he had a little playdate with Connor when I wasn't around to witness it.

"You look a lot different without your scales and flippers," I observed. Hunter's arms lacked shiny scales, and the toes showing at the tips of his brown flip-flops were distinctly human.

"Don't worry, I get that all the time. The ladies love the flippers." I wasn't sure if he was serious. I hoped he wasn't. "Check this out."

Hunter stretched out his forearm, flexing his fingers. Blue scales popped up one by one along his skin. He flexed his fingers again and they disappeared. "All my fishy parts come and go as I please." Hunter shot me another wink while I stared wide-eyed at the place where the scales sank into his flesh. "Cool, right?"

A loud squeak punctured the otherwise silent living room. Connor covered his head with his pillow as Sarah bounced in her seat, her mouth hanging open. She was completely lost for words . . . and thoughts . . . and as I looked closer, I realized that she was probably just plain lost. Too much new information in one day had zapped her dry.

"Hi there!" Hunter waved. "It's you again. How are you?"

Her mouth moved like a fish out of water. Oddly ironic.

Hunter leaned close to me. "Does she ever talk?"

"Usually, yes," I said. "Today? Not a chance."

"Okeydoke." He clapped Connor on the shoulder, making him groan, then ventured through the swinging door that led to the kitchen. "Do you guys have food? Saving people makes me hungry."

Sarah wouldn't leave our house until Connor and I reassured her that I didn't have a superpowered bone in my body, and Hunter wouldn't leave our house until he consumed all the food on the top shelf of the fridge.

When they finally headed home, I flipped through the television channels, ignoring any news related to the flooded subway, while Connor napped on the couch. The grandfather clock in the hall just struck eight when the door opened and my dad hurried in. He dropped his briefcase and phone to the ground while he examined Connor. My brother tried to push him away and continue sleeping, but Dad relentlessly made certain he was stitched up and bandaged correctly and wasn't bleeding anywhere I might have missed.

As I watched my father's meaty fingers poke and prod at his son, I remembered my mom's funeral. Her skin looked so fake in the coffin, like someone carved her from wax and put her on display. There was no trace of the grin she wore while teasing Dad or Connor or me. No evidence of the tan she earned from spending hours lounging by the pool during our summer vacation. She looked pale and plastic in death, and I understood why my dad checked and rechecked Connor's injuries. He had to do what he was unable to manage for our mother. My dad had to keep us safe.

"I'm going to fix this," Dad said, reaching for his phone. Suddenly my father the politician was back. The tender way he eyed Connor disappeared and was replaced with a stony frown while he tapped away at his touch screen. My dad was granite. No one could stop him now.

"What caused the flood?" I asked.

Dad lifted his eyes from his phone for a brief moment. "Not *what*, Abby. *Who.*"

"Iron Phantom," Connor quickly supplied, then groaned and reached for a bottle of painkillers.

My father nodded, looking back to his screen. I didn't understand. Iron Phantom saved me, set city hall on fire, asked for my help, then flooded the subway? He was the king of mixed signals.

"Iron Phantom is a menace." Dad began pacing in front of the couch. "He can't be trusted. The public knows he's evil, and they'll support city hall's plan to have him dealt with."

"What's the plan, Dad?" Connor was already rubbing his hands together, eager to get back to work.

My father straightened his tie. It was red and gold striped, matching Red Comet's suit. Dad insisted red and gold had always been his "power colors." I just thought he liked to match his son. "Don't worry, Connor. I'll take care of everything. The demise of Iron Phantom will be the first step in the reduction of crime in Morriston."

"What did you have in mind?" Connor pressed on.

My eyes flitted back and forth from my dad to my brother. Connor sat up as much as his bandages allowed, ready to exercise justice, but my father's eyes were narrowed, deciding how much he wanted to reveal.

"I'll let you know soon," he said hesitantly. "I'm still waiting on a few things to fall into place." I knew he didn't want to speak because I was in the room, which annoyed me to no end. Whether his silence suggested he didn't want to scare me or he thought I was incapable of helping, the joke was on him. I was the only one in this house who had any contact with Iron Phantom, and if he stayed true to his word, the villain's late-night return to my room was well overdue.

I wasn't sure if the butterflies in my stomach were from fear or excitement.

When I was a kid, my dad decided it would be a good idea to sign me up for a summer soccer camp. Sports, he said, would help me get stronger. They would enhance my fragile human body and protect me from danger. As the crime rates in Morriston skyrocketed, so did my dad's determination. Soccer was followed by boxing, which was followed by fencing. (I put my foot down pretty firmly on that one.) I failed to see how sweating all day would help me fight evil, so I quit athletics and allowed my interests to gravitate toward performing instead. This switch was not beneficial to my safety, as I discovered later that evening. Because I hated sports, I had zero muscles to protect myself against the supervillain who came knocking just after midnight.

But I did have a steak knife.

"Holy shit!" Iron Phantom ducked as the knife whizzed over his right shoulder, the tip embedding in the wall. "And *again* with the throwing."

"I have more than one tonight." I pulled the second knife out of my pocket as I stood my ground on the opposite side of my bed. I didn't plan on throwing knife number two, but if he tried anything funny, then it just might slip. . . .

Iron Phantom yanked the blade out of the wall, a bit of plaster breaking away with it. Dammit. Now we were even.

I expected him to keep it for himself, to taunt me with it. What I didn't anticipate was for him to toss the knife onto my bed and turn his back to me.

"This is an interesting change, Abigail." His laugh sounded like honey—sweet and sticky and something I didn't trust myself to be around without encountering a huge mess. He shut my window with a soft thump and held a hand to his eyes, shielding them from the lights in my room.

Because Connor was temporarily out of commission and I knew I didn't have a shot in hell of fighting off Iron Phantom should he try to attack, I decided to use my intellect for protection. My bedroom was flooded with light—the overhead light, the lamp on my bedside table, my bathroom light, even my night-light. I wouldn't give the supervillain the advantage of the dark again. Tonight I hoped the bright lights would give me the opportunity to discover his true identity. Though I didn't want to admit it, talking to a super whose name I didn't know unnerved me.

I made a grab for the second knife. One in each hand. "Don't come any closer." I was proud that my voice held steady. Iron Phantom's eyes raked over my body, which was braced against the wall beside my closet door, and the corner of his lip curled upward.

"What's with all the lights? If I knew I was being interrogated tonight, I might have worn a different outfit." He looked down at his black super suit and shrugged.

"I didn't want to give you the advantage of being in the dark." I decided to tell him the truth. If I told him lies and he figured me out, then he wouldn't trust me. And if he didn't trust me, I would never know who truly was under the mask.

"Ah, I see." He continued to smirk at me. "But between you and me, Abigail, dark or light, I still have the advantage."

I winced when I realized he was right. Of course he had the advantage. His powers didn't diminish if it was light out. He was a supervillain, not a vampire.

But the lights did allow me to get a closer look at him. The portion of his jaw that was visible was sprinkled with light stubble, and a single bead of sweat dripped down his chin from under his mask. His bright green eyes appeared more vivid now, filled with suppressed laughter and sparkling in the glow from my lamp. I could give credit where credit was due, and even for a supervillain, he had really pretty eyes. Gorgeous, luminescent . . .

Iron Phantom cleared his throat, and my jaw quickly snapped shut. God, I felt like Sarah, drooling over a super's presence. The supers never affected me before. But this guy did. This guy made my heart pound in my chest, and I didn't know why.

"Mind if we sit?" he finally asked. "I want to talk to you about something."

"No." My voice cracked. Crap.

He laughed. "No, I can't sit with you? Or no, you don't mind?"

I didn't know exactly what I wanted, so I didn't respond.

"Okay. Well, don't stab me. I'm coming over." He limped to the bed, cradling his left arm against his stomach. The handles of my knives dug into my palms, leaving deep impressions in my skin, but I couldn't help my feet from carrying me closer. Was he injured?

"Do you think we can kill a few of these lights?" he asked. "They're giving me a migraine."

Once again I didn't answer, so after checking to make sure my knives were (somewhat) lowered, he took it upon himself to pull the chain on the ceiling fan to turn off the overhead light.

"Yeah, that's better." We sat on the bed, him on the left side of the mattress and me on the right. His knee brushed mine while he settled himself, and I flinched, eyes wide. "Relax, Abigail. I just came for a friendly chat about what happened today. I won't hurt you." Judging by the way he still clutched his arm, he looked temporarily incapable of hurting anyone. Though his presence wasn't enough to make me forget about all the people he could have killed today.

"You flooded the subway, you asshole!" I punched his shoulder and he groaned, leaning away from me. "Why did you do that? People could have died!" *Connor could have died.*

"I didn't do anything," he snapped. "If you could see what I have going on under this suit, you would realize it wasn't me. I just came to talk to you about it."

"What do you mean? What's under your suit?"

More beads of sweat dripped down his jaw as he shut his eyes. One gloved hand tugged hard at his suit near his shoulder blade; he was too preoccupied to answer.

"Hey!" I slapped his arm again. His muscles of steel probably hurt me more than my punch hurt him, but that didn't stop him from shooting me an angry look. "What happened to you?"

"I was in the tunnel trying to . . . I don't know, help I guess. But when the water swept through, it knocked me against the tracks. A piece of concrete broke off from the wall and . . ." He shook his head, like he was trying to dislodge the memory. "Let's just say that it's not easy to stitch a wound one-handed."

I thought of Isaac hopping the subway cars with his friends. The water came through so fast, and the subway had been so packed. Would he have had time to help anyone?

But it was possible I wasn't even talking to Isaac right now.

Iron Phantom mistook my silence for disbelief. "I'm not lying to you. If I wanted to cause a flood, I would have made sure I wasn't in its path. I'm a lot of things, Abigail, but I'm not an idiot."

The key to spotting the difference between the truth and a lie is to look for a tell. Most people don't make steady eye contact when crafting a lie. But Iron Phantom did. He scooted closer until I could smell the sweat on his skin and the peppermint gum hiding somewhere in the back of his mouth. The hand not gripping his shoulder reached toward me, his rough glove holding my chin in place.

"I'm. Not. Lying. I know everyone thinks I did it, but someone set me up. I had nothing to do with it. I'm not who you think I am."

I'm not who you think I am.

He wasn't a villain, or he wasn't Isaac? Or both? Whoever he was, I wasn't about to let him bleed out in my bedroom. His eyes were turning glassy, and more drops of sweat stuck to the sides of his mask. He flashed me a hopeful smile, then dropped his hand from my chin, our bodies still so close. I wanted to know who he was, and only his mask hid his face from view.

"Just sit here for a second, okay?" I scooted to the edge of the bed and walked to the bathroom, pulling the first-aid kit out from under the sink and studying myself in the mirror. My blond hair was in a knot on top of my head. I was short and skinny and had an annoyingly persistent row of acne near my hairline, which required a gallon of makeup to cover on a good day. I severely lacked superpowers. But for some reason, Iron Phantom thought I could help him.

"I thought you could heal people," I said, dumping my supplies on the bed. Scissors, tweezers, bandages, and a lot of antibiotic ointment. I'd left my knives in the bathroom sink. The super was now leaning against my pillows, but his hand still clutched the fabric over his wound like a lifeline.

"I can't heal myself. That's probably my only hamartia."

"Hamartia," I repeated.

"It's a tragic flaw. Better known as an Achilles' heel." He eyed the scissors I held warily, but allowed me to turn him on his side so his back faced me. "Another hamartia might be allowing you near me with sharp objects, for example."

"I know what a hamartia is." Frankly, I was shocked that *he* knew. "And I'm not going to stab you . . . with *these*."

"That would be a plot twist," he muttered. "For future reference, I'd much prefer poison. It's quick. Usually painless."

"Where's the fun in that?" I knelt on the bed and hovered over him to get a better angle.

"And you call *me* a villain." He tried to turn and look at me, but I held my hand firmly on top of his head. It suddenly struck me how simple it would be to unmask him. With a flick of my fingers, just one little tug on his cowl . . .

The fingers of Iron Phantom's uninjured arm grasped my hand, jerking it away. "Less thinking," his deep voice growled. "More fixing."

I blew a loose strand of hair away from my face. "Fine. Is it okay if I ruin your suit though?" I positioned the tip of the scissors over the black fabric just above his left shoulder blade. "Last chance to take it off."

"Hardy-har-har," he deadpanned. "Just cut it open. I'll find a way to fix it."

The first thing I noticed when I sliced through his suit was a thick smear of blood that made my fingers tremble. Ragged, torn skin surrounded the wound that stretched from his shoulder to the top of his ribs, and dirt and debris covered his sweat-drenched skin. The second thing I noticed was that he was in ridiculously good shape. Not like body-builder-ripped or anything, but the kind of intimidatingly toned that makes it obvious when someone seriously takes care of themselves. I told myself that it was likely just his super DNA . . . because that made me feel a bit better about the two frozen waffles I ate for dinner.

"It's really bad, isn't it?" he asked.

"What?" I stared at the definition in his triceps while I wiped the blood away.

"I couldn't clean it properly. It's going to get infected."

"Not if I fix it." I reached for tweezers to remove a piece of rubble jutting through the blood. He flinched before I even touched him. "I won't make it any worse. I've done this before."

"To who?" he asked, aghast.

"It doesn't matter." I thought of Connor, snoozing down the hall. "My mom used to be a nurse. She taught me a bit. You can trust me."

"You and your knives?" he scoffed. "I don't think so."

"Well, I'm not the one with superpowers, you know. I'm just human." My mom's best approach to patching people up had been to talk to them until they forgot there was anything that needed fixing. So far it seemed to work with Iron Phantom. He watched me suspiciously over his shoulder, but he didn't flinch when I came at him with the tweezers a second time.

"You're right about that, Abigail. Powers are intimidating. I kind of miss being 'just human,' to tell you the truth."

"How old were you when you got them? Your powers?" A jagged piece of metal wedged near his armpit pulled free and fell on my mattress with a soft thump. Half a dozen fragments of crumbled bedrock and concrete followed next.

If the amount of debris alarmed Iron Phantom, he didn't say, and he barely noticed when I unscrewed the cap on the antibiotic ointment and started dabbing it on the laceration.

"My powers? I was nine," he said.

"Nine?" I shrieked, and immediately covered my mouth. The last thing I wanted was for Dad or Connor to find me tending to a wounded supervillain on my bed. I waited for the sound of heavy footsteps or the pounding of fists against my door, but it never came. "You were so young," I whispered in awe. According to Connor, most supers received powers between ages fourteen and sixteen. Any time under thirteen was unheard of.

"I can't believe you were teleporting and reading minds when you were nine years old." As wary as I was about Iron Phantom, I was also incredibly impressed. Pulling out a needle to stitch his wound, I felt him tighten his muscles, but he didn't protest.

He sighed. "I told you, I can't read minds. If I could, I would have you figured out already. Ouch!"

"Oh, sorry!" I had stabbed him with the needle by accident. But in my defense, what he said had shocked me. I bit my lip as my face flushed red. "You would have me figured out?"

"Yeah . . ." He picked at the edges of his mask, fixing his eyes on my hands as they carefully resumed stitching. That was his tell. The almighty Iron Phantom was nervous.

"You, like . . . ," he continued, sounding more like the teenage guy I suspected he was and less like a supervillain. "You're so confusing, like, you seem to think I'm an okay guy, but then you hate me and think I'm evil. Then you try to stab me, but now you're helping me out even though it's obvious how much you want to rip the mask off my face."

"No, I—"

"Don't lie, Abigail."

All right, so maybe I did want to tear off his mask and see if I knew the owner of the mysterious green eyes and husky voice. But I had some self-restraint. For a little while.

I finished stitching, his back now covered in a crooked row of sutures, and began packing up the first-aid kit. "Okay, maybe I am curious." He chuckled at that and licked his lips. "But, I don't know, I mean, I guess you're all right. You've never tried to hurt me, but you just seem to hurt everyone else. . . ." His eyes narrowed into slits. "Wait, no, that didn't come out right."

"How many times do I have to tell you? I had nothing to do with the accident in the subway. Maybe some mind-reading powers would have done *you* some good." He swung his legs off my bed, his boots almost kicking me in the process. "Someone set me up, and I thought you might have an idea of who it could be. Or I thought *maybe* you did your homework and found out something about that microchip I showed you, but I'm going to guess you didn't do that either. Those were the only reasons I came here tonight. I just wanted to talk about that. Not my powers, not you and me. Just that."

I was briefly hung up on the phrase *you and me*. Was there a *you and me* when it came to me and Iron Phantom? I felt like I always spent half our time together bickering with him and the other half checking him out.

"You have no proof that there was ever anything inside the

microchip," I pointed out, immediately feeling small when his anger appeared to double. If steam shot from his ears, I wouldn't have been shocked. "No tracking device. No nothing. How do I even know it's real?"

"How do you know it's *real*? How . . . ? Why would I lie to you?" He slapped a hand over his eyes. "Thanks for the vote of confidence, Abigail. It's not like I saved your life or anything."

"And it's not like I saved yours. We're square."

Iron Phantom examined his wound, now only a red line between the split black material of his super suit. When he spoke again, his voice was rougher than usual. I clearly pissed him off. "Tell your mother thanks for giving you the first-aid lesson."

My body ached at the mention of my mom. I could handle talking about her myself, but when others did it, it still caused my heart to feel like a block of cement in my chest. "My mother's dead."

I wished I could have filled my voice with the same level of venom and seething disgust his held, but I couldn't reach anything except a monotone.

It was a fact of life.

The sky is blue. The grass is green.

My mother is dead.

Iron Phantom's eyes widened a fraction, but he managed to contain himself. "My condolences," he muttered. "I know how it feels."

And then he vanished.

CHAPTER SEVEN

"I'm contemplating writing anti–Red Comet fan fiction. Thoughts?" Sarah asked as we headed toward the auditorium for our first *Hall of Horrors* rehearsal. I couldn't form any cohesive thoughts about stories featuring my brother. My mind was occupied with the nervous anticipation of building a quality show from the ground up, as well as the not-so-villainous super who paid me a visit the other night.

"I guess it's an okay idea." I shrugged, pulling open the auditorium door. The drone of twenty chattering cast members met my ears, and a few goose bumps rose on my forearms. "Any story about my brother is bound to suck, though. No offense."

"None taken. I can't believe he's really—*you know.* It just seems so insane. Like, it makes you wonder who the rest of the supers are."

"Yeah, it really does." I snorted, thinking about Iron Phantom lying on my bedspread. I may have told Sarah all about Connor's abilities, but I hadn't breathed a word of my connection with Iron Phantom to anybody.

I walked backward down the narrow aisles, continuing our conversation while we made our way to our seats. "So what would anti–Red Comet fan fiction feature exactly?"

"Mostly jabs at his emasculating spandex. I haven't thought that far."

"Sarah, you are a girl after my own—"

I meant to say *girl after my own heart*, but my shoe caught the carpet at the exact moment I was about to end my sentence. As a result, I crossed *heart* with everyone's favorite curse word, *fuck*. And so, on the first day of rehearsal, in front of the entire cast, I screeched *"FART"* while I plunged to my doom.

I was about to drown in an abyss of embarrassment when two hands appeared out of nowhere and wrapped around my waist. My equilibrium was in the middle of that not-so-pleasant experience where your stomach feels like it just dropped out your butt, when I noticed my rescuer. His dark hair flopped across his forehead while he stared at me, a little slack-jawed. I tried, unsuccessfully, to ignore the snickers of my castmates while he pulled me to my feet.

"Hey, Isaac." My breath came out as one long pant while the remaining adrenaline worked through my body.

"Are you okay, Abigail?" This close, I could finally get a good look at him. The hard lines of his jaw and his pale milky skin resembled someone else I'd encountered recently. But would a supervillain wear a pair of ripped jeans and a Pac-Man T-shirt? I had no clue.

"I'm fine, thanks." I grinned what I hoped was an award-winning smile and not a grimace of I-Think-You-Might-Be-a-Dangerous-Supervillain.

"Good." Isaac nodded and glanced at his watch. "Let's get this show on the road, then."

My near-death experience before rehearsal was an omen. The first run-through of *Hall of Horrors* was a disaster.

I spent at least an hour tripping over Isaac's ginormous feet—not to mention the props and the slick wooden floor of the stage—but my suckage wasn't the worst of it. A junior girl in the chorus started a conga line (for what reason I was unsure) and sprained her ankle, Rylan blew a fuse while operating the stage lights, leaving us stranded in the dark for ten minutes while we called the janitor to fix it, and Isaac spent half the rehearsal alternating between texting and playing games on his cell phone. Then he shouted at Mrs. Miller when she shook her Director's Stick in his face. The stick was a long, gnarled tree branch Mrs. Miller doused in holy water, then shoved in our faces. It was only used when our cast performed so horribly we needed extra help from "the big man upstairs"—and she didn't mean Principal Davis. When Mrs. Miller used the stick on Isaac, he told her he had an emergency and sprinted from the auditorium.

Sarah offered to sing Isaac's parts in his absence, which made rehearsal that much worse. She was my best friend, but she sang herself hoarse in five minutes, sneezed when she came too close to the prop flowers covering the stage, and stepped on my toes while we learned choreography. By the time Sarah accidentally hip-checked me across the stage and headfirst into both Courtney McGuire and the giant papier-mâché crocodile in a moat around the castle, Mrs. Miller decided to call it a day. At least, I think that's what she said. She was sobbing rather loudly, so it was difficult to tell.

"That is *so* not what happens on *Glee,*" Sarah groaned as we walked outside toward the parking lot. I was busy obsessively checking my arms and legs for bruises. Already a rather large green one had manifested around my elbow. It held a striking resemblance to the Statue of Liberty.

"Hollywood is misleading. It's the reason why people think musical rehearsals are magical places where everyone gets along and superheroes are charming and always get the girl in the end."

"Speaking of superheroes . . ." Sarah led me to her car parked near the curb. "I just hung up some new Fish Boy posters. Want to see?"

"Not particularly, but you're driving me home, so I guess I don't really have a choice."

"That's the spirit!" She opened the passenger door for me and I slumped inside. Like most other things Sarah owned, the interior of her car was plastered with posters of my brother. She taped them to the doors, dashboard, even the ceiling. Most were Photoshopped to include Sarah hanging from Connor's back as he flew through Morriston, but I noticed that a few had been replaced by Fish Boy doing the backstroke in the river.

"This one took me *five hours.*" Sarah pointed to a drawing of Fish Boy kicking his flippers. "It was so hard to get the shading right on his scales."

"Mmm-hmm . . ." But another photo hanging from her rearview mirror had caught my attention. Sarah, Connor, and me at the summer festival last August. He had his long arms wrapped around our shoulders, and we grinned manically while Sarah reached out to snap the photo. I'd forgotten all about that day. Right after we took that picture, Connor had to rush off to save someone from a burning semitruck.

Sarah was still admiring her posters as she started the car, a small smile on her face. Her red hair covered her eyes, so she couldn't see me watching. We had been best friends for years, ever since she repeatedly pulled my ponytail in the lunch line in fifth grade, but I'd always assumed she would hate me if she ever found out about Connor's superpowers. Sarah and I shared everything, but I had lied to her about her celebrity crush's true identity for three years. If I were in her position, I would hate me. But Sarah always had been more forgiving than me.

"Hey, Sarah?"

"Yeah?"

I gulped. Ever since my mom died, feelings and honesty were hard for me to admit to anyone other than Connor. But I owed them to her. "I'm really glad you know the truth."

She smiled. The top row of her teeth was perfectly straight and the bottom slightly crooked.

"Me too."

I could always tell when Connor was home by the way the house smelled like salsa. When Sarah and I stepped in the kitchen, my brother was pacing in front of the microwave, wearing his super suit and stuffing his face with tortilla chips.

"Wow, okay." Sarah nudged me with her elbow. "I know I said I was writing anti–Red Comet fan fiction, but this is still really cool."

Connor crunched the chip bag in his fist as soon as the microwave beeped. "Abby, you will not believe what just happened," he snapped, pulling a burrito from the microwave and taking a massive bite. Pieces of ground meat rained down on the counter.

"You forgot to buy sour cream?" I asked.

"You realized tacos are better than burritos?" Sarah chimed in.

Rolling his eyes, Connor took another bite. "Oh, please. Everyone knows the burrito is the thicker, manlier, *sexier* cousin to the taco. No one wants the skimpy, crusty hard-shell taco when you can have the juicy, succulent burrito. It's the obvious choice."

"So then what's the problem?" I pulled out a pitcher of lemonade and filled glasses for me and Sarah.

"What's the problem?" Connor shouted through another bite of his burrito. "The problem is that lousy Iron Phantom keeps trying to kill people!"

I froze. I didn't even realize I was overflowing my glass until Sarah grabbed a handful of napkins and started mopping up the lemonade I'd spilled all over the counter.

"What do you mean? What happened now?"

Connor finished his burrito in two more bites, licking the salsa off his gloves. "Well, it started off as a great day. I was floating under a cumulus cloud, throwing birdseed at pigeons and listening to 'I'll Make a Man Out of You' from *Mulan*—"

"You're a Disney fan?" Sarah asked.

"Who isn't?" Connor shot back. He pulled out another burrito from a fast-food bag on the kitchen table and popped it in the microwave. "Anyway, I was listening to music when I felt my good old sixth sense for danger, and I just barely made it over to Adventure Land in time to save two ten-year-olds from meeting their doom on the Loop-da-Loo."

Ah, the Loop-da-Loo. The roller coaster perfectly mimicked what it was like to soar around Morriston with Connor after he chugged an energy drink—you strap yourself in, regret almost every life decision you've ever made as you're launched out of the gate to an altitude higher than most birds dare to fly, then swear like a sailor as you plummet toward the ground through a slew of corkscrews, zero-gravity rolls, and something that Connor lovingly referred to as "the pretzel knot," positive you're about to die a gruesome, bloody death, before screeching into the station, massively shaken but also kind of contemplating doing it again. Zero to one-fifty and then back again all in under a minute.

"Their car disconnected from the train as soon as it launched and then made a ninety-degree drop back into the station," Connor continued. "The hydraulics malfunctioned and everything. It was pretty awful."

"And you think Iron Phantom did it?" I asked. Part of me didn't want to believe it was true. I trusted my brother . . . but did anyone even see Iron Phantom near the roller coaster?

"Abby, I don't *think*," Connor said, slamming his fist on the counter. "I *know*. The guy is a master villain; I'm pretty certain he can figure out how to break an amusement park ride. We should just be glad no one died." Grabbing his snack, Connor left the room.

"What do you think?" I asked Sarah once we were alone.

She eyed Connor's fast-food bag, abandoned on the table. "I think . . . that there's one burrito left and I'm going to eat it before your brother does."

Shaking my head, I ushered her toward the microwave. "Give me half and I promise I won't tell him."

The next day at school was filled with speculations over whether or not Iron Phantom was responsible for the Loop-da-Loo mishap. According to the media, he was a thief, an arsonist, even skilled at attempted homicide. His one publicized moment of good with the homeless man had been officially eclipsed. Everyone in the city was convinced he did it—the news anchors, my father, my brother, the lady who served the mystery meat in the school cafeteria, even Sarah. *Clearly* no one other than a supervillain could be the cause of a broken amusement park ride.

Everyone believed Iron Phantom was to blame. Everyone, it seemed, except me and one other student.

"I'm calling bullshit on the whole Loop-da-Loo thing," Isaac grunted from behind me in the lunch line. He elbowed his way between two freshmen to stand next to me, and we peered through the grease-stained glass separating the students from the lunch ladies and their heaps of mushy food. Isaac's lip curled upward at today's special: Potato Salad Surprise. The "surprise" was likely last week's fish tacos . . . or the hopes and dreams of former Morriston High School students.

"What about the Loop-da-Loo?" I narrowed my eyes at Isaac, trying to figure out if he was who I thought he might be. He certainly was tall enough, broad enough.

Isaac and I gagged as a cafeteria worker unceremoniously plopped a spoonful of potato salad on my plate. Isaac reached for an apple instead, groaning when he noticed it was bruised. He kept it anyway, polishing it on his shirt before moving forward in line and pushing my hand away when I tried to give my money to the cashier. He tossed five dollars at the woman, covering us both, and tugged me by the elbow to a nearby table. Sarah was already seated there, pulling a container of pasta salad from her bag. She glanced at Isaac when we sat down, one of her eyebrows raised in a silent question. I shrugged. I had no clue why Isaac decided to sit with us. Usually he ate alone and only spoke to us during rehearsal.

"I know I never lived in a city with supers before," Isaac began, taking a large bite from his apple, "but it seems kind of dumb to blame everything bad that happens around here on just one dude. I mean, do you really think that Iron Phantom guy managed to sneak into the park and break a *roller coaster* without anyone noticing? That's impossible."

"Well, he *can* teleport," I said.

Isaac laughed, scooting closer. He bumped his shoulder against mine, and a prickle of heat rolled down my arm. "That's not what I asked," he said. "I don't care if he can teleport to Australia and back, there's no way he set a building on fire, flooded the subway, and almost killed two kids at an amusement park. I mean, how would a guy find time to take a piss if he's planning that much destruction? I'm just saying, Abigail."

I glanced over to Sarah. A forkful of noodles was suspended in midair on the way to her mouth. So far, eating with Isaac proved to be much more eventful than our usually silent lunches.

I speared a chunk of potato salad. A piece of gray fuzz protruded from my fork. I dropped the fork to my plate with a clatter.

"I don't think Iron Phantom did anything yesterday," I said.

One of Sarah's noodles fell from her mouth, landing on her sweater. "Abby, seriously?"

"And what about that Red Comet guy?" Isaac continued. "Why does he get to save the day all the time? Let someone else get a turn, you know?"

"Oh, puh-lease!" Sarah enunciated her syllables like a prepubescent girl whenever she got angry. "Red Comet saves people because he's an amazing superhero, right, Abby?" My best friend was in complete Red Comet Protection Mode, the sassy attitude she adopted every time one of our classmates jokingly told her that her favorite super might really be a wrinkly old man under that suit.

"Abby?" Sarah nudged me and I jerked in my chair. I was busy thinking about Isaac's voice and if it could be disguised to sound like Iron Phantom's. I was also curious as to why Isaac suddenly seemed to be pro–Iron Phantom and anti–Red Comet.

"Oh! R-right, yeah," I stuttered, looking at Isaac. His eyes were really green, but were they the right shade of green? A bright, electric green that looked more like spring grass and less like pine needles? "Red Comet *is* a great superhero," I finally muttered.

"Whatever." Isaac sighed and pushed away from the table, throwing his apple core over his shoulder. It landed in the trash without him even looking. "At least *you* don't believe only one guy is responsible for all the crime that goes on around here. It's like the rest of the city is brainwashed or something. See you guys in rehearsal," Isaac called over his shoulder, practically plowing through half the student body in his haste to leave the cafeteria.

I sat in the library later that afternoon, memories of Iron Phantom's irritation slicing through me as I recalled our last conversation. There was no way he had been faking. No one was that good of an actor. Not even me.

He swore he wasn't to blame for the subway flood. I didn't want to admit it, but I believed him. There was no proof otherwise—for the subway or for the roller coaster. Yes, Iron Phantom was annoying, I'd give him that. And aloof. But after he came to me, broken and bleeding, and asked for nothing except for me to help him, something changed. For a moment, right before he got angry with me, Morriston's big bad villain seemed just like anyone else. Nervous and a little unsure of himself. He was a super, but if you took away his powers, he was every bit as human as I was.

Whether he knew it or not, Iron Phantom had guilted me into researching Morriston's mysterious microchips. Not an easy thing to do with the amount of information he'd given me. The chips had *nothing* in them. He'd literally given me *nothing* to work with. How considerate.

Iron Phantom had overestimated my abilities. This wasn't the kind of thing I could just look up online, and he'd deliberately told me not to ask my dad. Not like that would have made a difference. Every time I asked about Dad's job, he'd just say, "Politics, Abby," in a gruff voice that reminded me of a pissed off bear. Vague to the tenth power.

"How am I supposed to research nothing? It's like walking into a black hole." I slapped my hand on the desk, rattling the keyboard. "He's so *stupid*."

"Trust me, hurting the computer doesn't make it work any faster."

The voice came from the row of monitors in front of me. I stood up to look over the partition and found Rylan typing frantically at a homework assignment.

"What are you working on?" I asked.

"Schoolwork," he muttered. His fingers dashed across the keys. *Clack-clack-clack-clack*. "That's what people usually do in the library."

"You don't say. What an astute observation." I rubbed my forehead, slouching in my chair. All I'd gained from this library trip was a headache from looking at the glow of the screen for far too long.

Clack-clack-clack-clack.

I poked at the keyboard with my middle finger. The screen flickered, but it didn't do anything particularly exciting—like give me all the answers I was looking for. It wasn't a genie, unfortunately.

I poked the keyboard one more time, just to make sure.

Nothing.

"Ugh!"

Clack-clack . . . clack. Silence. Rylan's head popped over the partition. He'd cut his hair since the last time I saw him. It made his ears look a little bigger, but it also drew more attention to the various shades of brown in his eyes. Like a cinnamon stick dipped in caramel.

"Sorry," I said. "I'm not disturbing you, am I?"

He paused for a moment. "Well . . . yeah. Kind of."

"Sorry."

"It's okay. Do you need help . . . or something?"

I leaned back in my chair. "Or something."

He stood so he could look at my computer screen. I wanted to close the window so he couldn't see, but I wasn't fast enough. Rylan brought a hand to his mouth, failing to cover a wide smirk once he noticed the hand-drawn Wanted poster of Iron Phantom done by a sketch artist at the Morriston police department. Whoever drew it had obviously never gotten a good look at the super. He appeared at least twenty years older on paper, complete with a little goatee and everything. The mark of true evil. I rolled my eyes.

"You're not one of those weird superfans, are you?" Rylan asked.

"No!" I closed the browser and shut the entire computer down. "That's Sarah, not me."

"Oh. Okay." He looked around us. The dull hum of the computers was the only sound puncturing the silence of the library's bottom floor, but a few giggles floated down from upstairs. Rylan rubbed the back of his neck. It seemed like he had a time limit before he would get all awkward and silent in a conversation, and I wondered if that had something to do with him being alone every time I saw him. I honestly wasn't sure if he had any friends at Morriston. It made me kind of sad.

"So . . . what do you think about the supers?" I asked, determined to continue the conversation. "Like Iron Phantom. What do you think about him?"

Rylan laughed. The sudden noise coming out of his usually silent mouth startled me. "I think he's an idiot."

"You do?"

"Yeah. Honestly, he just got here and I'm already sick of hearing about him."

"Go ahead, tell me how you really feel. It'll be cathartic for you." I leaned forward, resting my elbows on the wooden partition that separated his row of computers from mine. "Maybe he's not as bad as everyone thinks."

"Abby." Rylan looked at me like I just told him I had a third foot growing out of my ass. "He burned. Down. A building."

"Yeah, I saw it on TV fifty times over."

"So . . . ?"

"So there's no proof he did anything after that. It's just people making up stories."

He shook his head and started gathering his books spread across the computer desk. "True, but . . ."

"But what?"

He turned back around, staring at me curiously. "But he's a criminal. He's obviously got issues." He grimaced. "I guess I'd just hate for this to end badly. The crime rate's high enough as it is."

The bell signaling the end of study hall chimed. Outside the library, doors creaked open and the rapid beat of footsteps filled the halls.

Picking up my backpack, I trudged past the computers. "Great. Back to hell."

Rylan followed behind me. "That's an insult. Hell is far more pleasant." He held the door open so I could pass through first. "At least in hell there's no gym class."

We parted ways at the stairwell, him going upstairs and me going down. My heart swelled with a silly sense of pride as I recalled our conversation. Maybe he hadn't agreed with me, but getting Rylan to talk felt a lot like coaxing a tiny butterfly to land in your hand or teaching Connor not to crash into the ceiling after taking flight. It wasn't that big of a deal, but it meant a lot to me.

CHAPTER EIGHT

"Isaac Jackson pisses me off," Sarah said over the phone that evening. My feet dangled from a swing in the park near my house while I listened to her find fault in everything Isaac had said, done, or worn since his arrival in Morriston. I'd ventured to the park earlier in the evening to rehearse choreography on the empty basketball court (it was roughly the same size as our stage and posed minimal risk of Connor walking in on me and making fun of me), but my dad hadn't let me outside without first presenting me with a brand-spanking-new Taser, which was currently shoved in the pocket of my jeans. I wished he'd instead presented me with a brand-spanking-new coat as I rubbed my arms to keep warm. It was only the beginning of October, but the oncoming chill of winter was already evident.

"Like, what the hell, Abby?" I could picture Sarah pacing back and forth in her bedroom, her walls completely plastered with superhero posters. "I know Red Comet's your brother and all, but he's still the best super in the country! How could Isaac say that?"

I dug the toes of my sneakers into the sand beneath the swings, tracing a few letters. I hastily wiped them away once I realized I wrote the initials *IP* on the ground.

"I thought you liked Isaac. Yesterday you said, and I quote, 'His face makes my pants tingle.'"

I heard the springs of Sarah's bed squeak as she flopped down on her mattress. "Yeah, well, that was before he opened his smart-ass mouth."

Isaac had spent our last rehearsal mimicking Mrs. Miller behind her back in an attempt to make me smile and forget how much of a train wreck *Hall of Horrors* was turning out to be. I wouldn't admit it, but part of me was starting to enjoy his smart-ass mouth.

"Sarah, Isaac can say whatever he wants because he doesn't know the truth. And we probably shouldn't be talking about this on the phone. . . ." The small park was deserted except for me, but I didn't want to take any chances on someone walking by and listening in. I'd already blown Connor's identity once.

Sarah's long sigh echoed through the speaker. "Fine. Yeah, you're right, but you have to admit Isaac's the most annoying kid in the senior class."

"Oh, come on, he is not."

"Okay, maybe he's not worse than Gary Gunkle when he eats beans, but he's *totally* worse than Fanboy Kenny and his cousin, even when they try to beat me at Red Comet trivia."

"No way. Kenny and his cousin top Isaac on the aggravation scale." I ignored another one of Sarah's exasperated sighs as I drew a flower on the ground with my shoe.

"What's his name again?" she asked.

I added a stem and leaves to my sunflower in the sand. "Kenny's cousin? The hell if I know—"

Hey, Abigail.

My phone nearly slipped from my hand as the swing set creaked. I turned around to find the source of the noise, but nothing was there. No one was standing beyond the park's fence, and no one seemed to be within the park itself. But I knew it was *his* voice in my head.

The swings were next to a large wooden play structure filled with tunnels and monkey bars, but I didn't see anyone there either. I was still very much alone. I must have imagined his voice because I was thinking about him. But even still, maybe it was time I went home. . . .

"Abby? Are you still there?" I suddenly became aware of my fingers, slippery with sweat as they clung to my phone.

I was halfway between sitting and standing when a *whoosh* and a loud *crunch* sounded from my left, near a rusted blue slide. A shadow moved closer, exposing itself in the crisp fall air.

Nice night for a stroll in the park, wouldn't you say?

"Sarah, I'm going to have to call you back. . . ."

"What? Why? What's going on? Abby, I'm in the middle of a serious rant and—"

I ended our call and slid my phone into my pocket. The mysterious Iron Phantom walked closer, cracked his neck back and forth, then collapsed on the swing next to mine.

So do you think I'm responsible for what happened at Adventure Land?

"Get out of my head!" I jumped up and took a few steps back, nervous knowing Iron Phantom could invade my privacy and there was nothing I could do to stop him. I hoped if I moved away then he couldn't speak into my mind. Of course any attempts to thwart his abilities were futile. Superpowers superseded logic.

Sorry.

My eyes narrowed at the masked man. He chuckled sheepishly. "Oops. Sorry. I didn't know you'd hate it so much."

"I don't hate it, I just . . ." I just what? I just don't like the tickle in my stomach when your husky voice is so close to my brain? I just don't like that I'm turning into a crazy fangirl? I finally settled on, "I just didn't expect to see you here tonight."

Iron Phantom hummed and tapped the swing I had vacated. "I see. Well, I guess I just wanted to tell you that—to tell you . . ." He refused to look at me as I sat back down. Instead, he stared at the empty playground. A car drove down the road behind us, and I feared the glow of the headlights would alert the driver of the super next to me, but thankfully the vehicle continued on. I didn't want anyone else knowing about the masked man. Alone in the park, it felt like he was my own twisted little secret.

"Pretty depressing, isn't it?" He spoke suddenly, still staring straight ahead. "Playgrounds in the dark—that's like some warped metaphor for adults realizing their hopes and dreams died once they grew up."

"Wow, Eeyore. You have to be one of the gloomiest people I've ever met." I tried to laugh to show him I was joking, but the noise came out as more of a pained squeak. Away from musicals, my acting sucked. I couldn't pretend to be funny when my palms dripped sweat and my mouth was as dry as a desert. The last time I saw him, he was furious. I didn't know what to expect tonight.

"I'm sorry for getting angry with you the other night," he muttered quietly. He looked down at his shoes, drawing a circle in the sand with the tip of a slick black boot. Apologies seemed just as hard for him as they were for me. I was filled with dread at the thought of acknowledging I did something wrong, and having superpowers didn't seem to make him any less inept at admitting fault.

"I'm sorry for thinking you flooded the subway," I replied. "And I don't think you tried to hurt those kids at Adventure Land either, just for the record." I drew a square next to his circle. A breeze blew through the trees, and I rubbed my hands along my arms to smooth out the goose bumps.

"Thank you. Apology accepted, glad we're done with that. Are you cold? Do you want a sweatshirt?" He leapt to his feet, towering over me.

"Oh, no. You don't need to—"

"Hang on, I'll be right back."

"Wait, I—"

He was gone. My heart was in my throat.

"I'm nervous to get a sweatshirt from a superhero," I spoke aloud. "I'm such a fangirl."

A warm breeze blew across my cheeks moments before he returned, and a black sweatshirt flew at my face seconds later. "Is black your favorite color or something?" I asked, glancing at his sleek suit and mask.

"My favorite color's green, actually," said Iron Phantom, winking an appropriately colored green eye at me. "What's yours, if I may ask?" he inquired, his tone absurdly serious. I burst out laughing, and Iron Phantom picked at the side of his mask while he waited for me to sober up.

"I like blue," I said once I pulled myself together.

Iron Phantom hummed. "Blue. The color of peace and tranquility. No, that doesn't sound like you at all." He sat back down, intentionally bumping his swing against mine. "You should like red. The color of violence. Considering you throw knives at people."

"That was one time! You burned down a building!"

"That was also *one time.* And if you must know, I only did it to stall. I was hoping the fire and the investigation and the inevitable chaos of it all would be enough of a distraction to give me time to determine what the microchips really are. I'm not sure it worked out like I hoped." A teasing grin took over his face. "We're quite the pair, aren't we?"

"Who says we're a pair?" I tried to play coy, but my pulse *thump-thumped* erratically, blood rushing in my ears.

"I don't know." He winked again. "I didn't hear a thing."

Unfolding his sweatshirt, I ducked my head inside just so I would have an excuse not to look at him for a moment. I wasn't very cold anymore. The rush of heat to my cheeks had taken care of that.

I could still feel his eyes burning into my temple. I balled up my fists inside the sleeves of the sweatshirt and held them to my cheeks. Fresh laundry detergent greeted me, mixing with a touch of warm and spicy soap. Smiling, I pulled the sweatshirt tighter, breathing perhaps a tad too deeply as I said, "You smell . . ."

He looked offended. "I *smell*?"

"You didn't let me finish. You smell good. I mean . . . your sweatshirt . . . um . . ."

Yikes. Sentences were great. I really needed to try using them sometime.

His laugh echoed through the park. He patted my fist with his gloved hand. "Thanks. You smell too."

I quirked an eyebrow at him, my lips tingling as I tried to hold a straight face. "Only like good things, though, right?"

"The best," he assured me. "Flowers and freshly mowed grass and the smell of the ocean when it's stuck to your skin after a long day at the beach. Oh, and cookies."

"And cookies," I repeated, my voice only half the size as before. His fingers still lingered on my hand.

I glanced away to break the spell. It was frightening being this close to him when he kept looking at me like . . . like *that*. I didn't know what else to do, so I pulled away to take another subtle sniff of the sweatshirt, hoping he wouldn't notice.

"What on earth are you doing?" he wondered. *Oh.* So he noticed. "Don't rub your nose all over it. That's my favorite sweatshirt." He reached forward to shove my arms into my lap, looking at me like I was nuts.

I jumped up and thought about running from the park, just to see if he cared enough about his sweatshirt that he would chase me down for it. I never got the chance. Before I could blink, he was standing before me, gently pressing my back against a wooden rope wall.

"You're not trying to steal it, are you?" he asked, taking hold of the dangling sleeves, which were too long for my arms. "Because, you know, stealing is against the law. Being a superhero and all, I'd hate to . . . what do they call it? Exercise justice and all that jazz?"

He stared at me, not blinking, not smiling, completely serious. I don't think I ever gave anyone a more dramatic eye roll in my life. I could just picture it: Superhero 101. First rule: Use Cheesy Clichés in Attempts to Look Badass.

"You did not just use the phrase *'exercise justice.'* "

He shook his head and looked at his feet. "It sounded a lot better in my head," he admitted.

"Why is it that all superheroes are so lame?" I smirked and tried to push him back a step. He didn't budge.

"Me? You think I'm lame?" His hands reached for my ribs. I couldn't move. Honestly, I wasn't sure I wanted to.

His fingers descended on my sides, moving under the hoodie to tickle up and down my shirt. I squirmed, gasping for breath. Iron Phantom didn't let up. He only laughed. "Do you still think I'm lame now? Really, Abigail?"

I fidgeted under his fingers, pulled at his wrists, but he didn't let go. If Iron Phantom's hamartia was the inability to heal himself, then mine certainly was incessant tickling.

"Yes," I gasped in between laughs. "You're—so, *so*—lame! Stop it!"

The tickling continued. "What's the magic word?"

The super's index finger hit a particularly sensitive spot on my ribs, and I squeaked and tried to shy away. "Please! Oh my God, *Isaac*, please stop it!"

His gloved fingers stilled on my sides. Neither of us moved.

My breathing shook as I tried to steady my heartbeat. Iron Phantom stared at me, his head tilted to the side, not blinking. Was he angry because I finally figured out his identity? Or did he think it was funny that I couldn't be further from the truth?

A low chuckle rippled through his chest, shaking my own because he refused to let me step away. His lips broke into a smile, blindingly white teeth a stark contrast against his black mask. I couldn't believe how straight they were—like movie-star teeth. Did Isaac have movie-star teeth? I couldn't remember. That seemed like something I would be unlikely to forget.

The super tilted my head up so I couldn't look away from his eyes. "What did you just call me?" he asked.

"Huh? What?"

Every idiot's best defense against inquisition: *Huh? What?*

"You called me Isaac." He couldn't keep the smirk from spreading across his lips.

I then decided to use every idiot's second-best defense against inquisition: Deny everything. "What? No, I didn't."

Iron Phantom didn't buy it. Damn him. "Yes, you did," he said. "Do you think my name's Isaac?"

Of course I thought he was Isaac. A new guy comes to Morriston and defends the city's newest super at the same time Iron Phantom makes his first appearance. Who else would he be?

But I didn't want to tell him my suspicions. I wanted him to admit it to my face. "Who's Isaac?" I asked.

Isaac/Iron Phantom shrugged, looking annoyingly devil-may-care about his potential unmasking. "I don't know. You tell me."

I stared at him. He stared back. Unblinking. Again. A dog howled on the next street over, and I jumped. Iron Phantom steadied me, and I looked at his hand gripping my elbow. I followed the curve of his muscular arm up to his shoulder, across his wide chest, to his chiseled jaw. He finally blinked at me behind the eye holes of his mask.

"You have the same build as him," I slowly said.

"As who?"

"Isaac Jackson."

"Am I supposed to know who that is?"

"He—" *He's you,* I wanted to say. But I couldn't. I now knew why Sarah never figured out Connor was Red Comet. No matter what you think you know, with a mask involved it's impossible to be certain. "Never mind," I muttered, dropping my gaze to his chest.

Iron Phantom sighed and released me. Slowly, he turned and leaned his forearms on the wooden fence surrounding the park. Now free from his grasp, I hugged his sweatshirt closer as a gust of wind blew through the trees.

"I never said I wasn't him." His back faced me and the wind blew stronger, but I could still hear the tortured croak in his voice. "This Isaac guy."

I joined him at the fence. "You never said you *were* either."

"Touché," Iron Phantom grumbled.

"So who are you, then?" I asked. "Behind the mask?"

My fingers twitched toward his face. I didn't stand a chance. His lightning-fast reflexes caught both of my hands, pressing them tightly between his own.

"Don't you dare, Abigail. Wow, would you look at the time?" He glanced at his wrist, but he wasn't wearing a watch. He probably told time using the position of the moon or something bizarre and had no need for one. "We both need to get out of here." Iron Phantom held on to my hand as he pulled me from the park.

"*We?*" I couldn't imagine he would take me anywhere significant. He was far too secretive.

"Well, I'm not leaving you alone, and I need to get back to my house for *The Big Bang Theory*."

My steps faltered as the super tugged me down the dirt road toward my house. I wasn't sure which part of his sentence surprised me more—that he lived in a house or that he actually had time to watch television.

"You live in a house?" I bumped his shoulder jokingly with my own. "Not in some secret supervillain lair?"

Iron Phantom bumped me back, though he misjudged his strength and unfortunately sent me tripping toward the ground. He steadied me with an arm around my waist, and we continued toward my house. Tall maple trees on both sides of the road blocked out the glow from the moon, and when he spoke again, it appeared his voice came from the depths of the shadows themselves.

"Ha. Ha. Ha. Not amusing. Tonight's the episode where they go to a superhero costume contest. I don't know why, but something about it really strikes a chord with me."

I snorted in a very unladylike fashion and carefully stepped over a ditch in the road. "You don't say. You know, I tried to partake in your 'secret mission' today." I held up little air quotes around the words. "I couldn't find anything about city hall's mysterious microchips. Sorry."

He sighed. "That's okay. I don't have much to go on either." He kicked a rock, and it soared off the road, landing in the underbrush. "I guess we'll just have to try harder."

I shook my head in amusement. I was about as useful to him as a parka in the Caribbean, and I was still waiting for him to figure that out. "So if they aren't tracking devices, then what do you think is wrong with them?" I asked. "You must have suspicions, right?"

"I do," he said. "But I never said they weren't trackers."

"Seriously? Can't you give a straight answer to anything?"

"I can, but . . ." He paused, scratching his chin. "I'd rather not right now. I . . . I just have my reasons. That's all."

I tried not to let it show how much that saddened me. I didn't like secrets, but lately I'd found myself entangled in more and more of them. Dealing with Iron Phantom was exactly like dealing with my dad and Connor. Either I needed to keep the information I knew to myself, or I wasn't trusted enough to keep the information at all.

"Hey." He reached out an index finger to poke me on the nose. "Don't look so sulky, Abigail. It's just for now." I wondered if he was serious or just being kind.

We walked the next few minutes in silence. I could feel Iron Phantom glance at the side of my face every so often, but I never looked back to him. Other than *"Are you Isaac Jackson?"* I didn't know what else to say. Except his favorite color (green), his favorite television show (*The Big Bang Theory*), and his special skills in teleportation, healing, and telepathy, I didn't know much about him. Though, I couldn't blame him for keeping quiet. Supers were never very forthcoming.

I wished he would tell me who he was. I could keep a secret. I'd kept Connor's for years. But I could never tell Iron Phantom that. Apparently the relatives of supers aren't very forthcoming either.

So where did that leave us?

"Okay, question." He broke the silence, plucking a fallen leaf from his shoulder and tossing it to the ground. "If you were a super, which one would you be?"

I pretended to ponder his inquiry, hand on my chin, eyes scrunched up in mock thought. "Well, definitely not the Burning Babe," I said, thinking of one of Philadelphia's finest. "Could you imagine dealing with all that fire power? She destroys her clothes at least twice a week. That would suck."

He snickered. "All right, fair enough, fair enough. Red Comet?"

I pushed him away, catching him off guard and causing him to stumble. *One point for Abby!* "No. No. No. No way. That would suck even worse!" Thinking of stepping into my brother's bright red spandex for a day made my gag reflex twitch.

He held his palms up in surrender. "Sorry! I really thought all the girls were into him, my mistake. Okay, what about . . . Iron Phantom?"

We had reached the edge of my driveway. Towering pine trees blocked my house from the road, but I leaned against the mailbox, casually crossing my arms over my chest while I eyed the super before me.

"That would suck worst of all," I said.

Iron Phantom threw a hand over his chest, tilting his head to the sky. "You wound me." He leaned toward me, his voice sly. "Maybe I should have masqueraded as a jock instead of a super. I might have been better liked."

I hummed in thought and edged closer, wondering if he had terrible hat hair under that cowl. "I'm not really into jocks either. Try a member of the drama club maybe."

"I'll see what I can do." Iron Phantom tugged on the sleeve of his sweatshirt, which I was still wearing. "Keep it." He grinned. "It looks better on you anyway."

He disappeared into the breeze, and I slumped against the post of the mailbox.

CHAPTER NINE

I crouched behind the table, my knobby knees unsteady against the hard linoleum. My chest shook. Everywhere screaming. Sobbing. Pleading. A gunshot into the ceiling. Silence.

I couldn't move. If I moved, I would die. The men reached for my mother, pulled her to her feet, dragged her to the front of the bank, spoke in a loud guttural growl. If they didn't get the money, she would be the first they would kill.

A siren echoed through the city. They wouldn't get here in time.

"No!" I ducked out from under the safety of my table. "Please! Let her go! Please!"

The man holding the gun to my mother's head grinned. His teeth were yellow and crooked. He pulled the black mask from his head.

"Abigail."

The killer's green eyes narrowed. He aimed the gun at my heart.

My mother screamed for me to run, but no words came from her mouth.

The lobby of the bank slowly melted away. The three of us stood in an empty room with white walls. My mother, the killer, and me. I wouldn't run.

"Abigail."

He pushed the barrel of the gun into the back of my mother's head. I felt the pain against my own. A cold, hard circle at the top of my spine. I couldn't think. I couldn't breathe.

"Abigail."

His finger tightened on the trigger.

"Say good-bye."

My mother's blond hair hung limp around her face. Tears dripped down her cheeks. His finger moved, quick like lightning.

Red.

Pain.

Screams.

"Good-bye."

Black.

"Abigail!"

I jolted, thrashing in my covers, my breathing ragged. I could still feel the pain at the base of my skull, still hear the screaming, the echo of the gunshot.

I jumped again when I noticed the figure next to my bed. The moonlight streaming in from the window silhouetted his body as he leaned over me. His eyes peeked through the holes of his black mask, so similar to the killer in the dream. I lunged for his face.

The man shushed me, pinning my arms to my sides. I thrashed a few seconds more, my legs intertwining with my sheets and trapping my body. I tried to head-butt the stranger away, and he cursed, his voice eerily familiar.

"Jesus, Abigail, it's okay. You're okay. I'm here. It's okay. Everything's okay."

The shock of the nightmare receded, and the masked man

hesitantly released my arms. I reached past him, flipping on my lamp with trembling fingers. Bright light flooded the bedroom. We both groaned and shut our eyes against the glare.

"Why are you here?"

Iron Phantom ignored me. "What were you dreaming about?"

I cracked my eyelids open, then immediately shut them. Beside me, the light clicked off, and the room was dark once more.

"Nothing," I said.

"Didn't look like nothing. You can tell me, you know."

I didn't know exactly when I decided to tell him—if it was before or after he knelt beside my bed, resting his chin on the edge of my mattress. I didn't know *why* I decided to tell him either. Maybe because behind his black mask he could be anyone I wanted him to be. A friend, a partner, a confidant. I took comfort in that.

"Fine. It was my mom. The day she was murdered."

I expected him to pause, to dish out some profound advice I didn't ask for or to change the subject as quickly as possible. Because that's what most people did when faced with murder—they either faked sincerity or they refused to talk at all.

What I didn't expect was for him to ask without missing a beat, "You were there?"

I shook my head. I couldn't imagine how bad the dreams would be if I actually witnessed my mom's death. "But that doesn't keep me from having night terrors about it."

"Night terrors." His distaste for the term indicated he was all too familiar with the disorder. "Yeah, I used to have those. And I was an insomniac for a year after . . ."

"After what?"

He gulped and whispered, "After my parents died."

I wanted to reach for his hand lying so close to mine on the mattress and tell him it was okay. But I would never be dumb enough to tell him that. Dead parents weren't okay. So I said something slightly less stupid than *it's okay*. I said, "I'm sorry."

I knew from personal experience that *I'm sorry* didn't cut it either. It's just another thing to say. Another thing to fill the awkward void of silence that death creates.

"Do you still have insomnia?" I asked.

"No. But I still get nightmares from time to time. I don't think they'll ever go away."

"Yeah," I muttered. I had wanted to find out something personal about Iron Phantom, but dead parents and insomnia weren't what I had in mind. Sure we had stuff in common, but I wanted him to tell me something pleasant about himself, something to take me away from the sudden bouts of depression that arrived after dark.

"Hey," he said suddenly. "It'll get better. I promise." The smile he wore mirrored Connor or my dad when they tried to look calm in the midst of catastrophe. His lips quirked upward, but the light didn't quite reach his eyes. I had seen that smile enough over the years to know it was likely a lie.

I scooted up in bed, away from him. "Don't make promises you can't keep, Iron Phantom." That was the first time I called him Iron Phantom to his face. Although the name sounded weird hanging in the air instead of tucked safely in the corners of my mind, the last thing I expected was for him to laugh.

"What?" I felt more self-conscious than usual around him.

"It's just funny to hear you call me that, Abigail."

"Well, I don't know your real name. . . ."

"Don't you?"

"Oh, cut the crap," I scoffed. "I'm not really in the mood to play your mind games."

Iron Phantom was silent, watching me. I tried to go back to sleep but felt his gaze burning a hole in my head. When I opened my eyes, he was still kneeling next to me, green irises staring through his mask.

"C'mon." He patted my shoulder, which for the record is probably the least sensual place you can pat somebody. Not that I wanted him to be sensual . . . at night . . . in my bedroom . . . but just saying. "Let's go somewhere. It'll make you feel better."

If I had known our nighttime excursion would involve teleporting to the Great Unknown, I wouldn't have agreed. But by the time he dropped the bomb, after I got dressed in the hoodie he lent me yesterday and a pair of jeans, I couldn't back out.

"Just trust me." He held out a hand and I skeptically placed my palm on top of his. This was stupid. So, so stupid. And reckless. Very reckless of me to trust a guy whose name I didn't even know. But I had stitched him up, and he gave me his sweatshirt and woke me from a night terror. We had bonded . . . right?

"So where are we going?"

"You'll see." That seemed to be every superhero's favorite phrase.

"Will this hurt?" Shockingly enough, I had never teleported before. My ears still popped every time I went up in an airplane, let alone disappeared into a cloud of mist. I wanted to be certain Iron Phantom would get me to wherever and back in one piece.

The super shook his head. "It tickles a bit in your stomach, and it might make you dizzy the first time, but it's harmless."

"Is teleporting difficult? I mean, you're good at it, right?"

"It's hard to learn at first. One time I overshot my destination and ended up on the Great Wall of China—"

My fingernails dug into his forearm. "Wait, you did *what*?"

"Yeah, no, I'm good at it *now.*" He rolled his eyes. "Relax. I was only eleven at the time, cut a guy a bit of slack. You ready?"

Oh, crap. It was happening this soon? "No, wait, I don't think I—"

"Yeah, I think you're ready."

And then the ground dropped out from under me.

My stomach followed suit.

Akin to pulling a plug free from a drain, we raced like water into the abyss. I couldn't see a thing. The silence filling the void around us was deafening, like being trapped inside an invisible bubble. Teleporting was different than flying with my brother. With Connor, I always feared for my life as he raced through the air. The g-forces stretched my lips, and the wind flapped my cheeks. But right now, I just felt woozy—like my insides turned to jelly and were squeezed through a narrow straw. My skull felt tight against my brain. I resisted the urge to throw up, knowing if I did it would likely get sucked right back inside me.

But as quickly as it began, it stopped.

"How was that?" he asked once my world stopped spinning.

Even with my feet planted firmly on the earth, I still felt like we were moving through the air. "Ugh. I think I need a moment."

"Don't take too long." His hand brushed over the small of my back, and I felt an entirely new type of jitters unrelated to teleportation. "You don't want to miss out."

When my stomach finally settled, I glanced up to see where he had brought me. We stood in a large field. Tufts of green poked around the tips of my sneakers, and the faint trace of white paint lined the grass. A large red barn with rusted doors reflected in a pond at the bottom of the hill. Somewhere nearby, a goose honked. Though it was dark, I could still pick out the shapes of gargantuan trees lining the road that curled around the edge of the property.

"Is this a soccer field or something?" I noticed the goalposts looming out of the shadows. I kicked some of the flaky paint off a patch of dead grass on the sideline.

"Sometimes it's a soccer field," he corrected me. "Other times it's just where I come to think."

Warning me to be careful of potential goose droppings and holes in the field, Iron Phantom led me past the barn to a tree at the pond's edge. It was old and gnarled, chunks taken out where people carved their initials or professed love for one another. Things like *Jamie hearts Chris* or *RJ+MB. 2gether 4ever!* I wondered if they really were "2gether 4ever," or if their lack of grammatical skills ruined their relationship.

"So this is it." He smiled, patting the bark happily. "My thinking tree."

"Do you bring all the girls out here?"

He rolled his eyes, and we both plopped down at the base of the trunk. I tried to adjust my position so I wasn't sitting directly on top of a root, but that caused me to topple sideways, my head coming to rest dangerously close to his—right in the crook between his neck and shoulder. I jerked away immediately.

Iron Phantom pretended not to notice. He tossed a small pebble into the pond, where it landed with a *plink* before sinking, ripples spreading across the surface.

"No, Abigail, you're the privileged one." He searched the ground, collecting more stones. "I mean, you did a pretty impressive job of cleaning up my shoulder for me. I think that alone deserves special access to the thinking tree."

He handed me a pebble, and we tried to see who could throw the farthest. His just barely reached the center of the pond. Mine made it about three feet farther.

"Did you let me win? It's lame to let someone win."

"I can assure you, Bazooka, letting people win isn't something that's ever on my radar." He wound up and threw another pebble. It soared across the water, landing on the opposite shoreline. I took another one from his outstretched hand, but it only reached three-fourths of the way across the pond before dropping with a tiny splash.

"See?" Iron Phantom grinned.

I pushed a piece of hair out of my eyes. "How do you know I didn't let you win to spare your feelings?"

"Did you?"

"I'll never tell," I said with a shrug. I hadn't, of course, but if he could keep all his secrets locked up tight, then so could I.

"You're something else." Iron Phantom leaned his head back against the tree, watching the leaves rustle in the breeze. "So . . . I think you should tell me a story."

"A story?" I wasn't very good with those. I could act them out, sure, as long as someone else wrote the lines. Making one up from scratch was something I could never quite figure out.

"Yeah, a story. Something other than you like the color blue and have horrible nightmares. Tell me something fun."

"Fun?"

He laughed. "Stop repeating everything I say." He grazed his fingers over the grass, searching for more stones to throw. "C'mon, you must have hobbies, right? Everyone has hobbies."

I raised an eyebrow. "What are yours?"

Iron Phantom lunged for my sides with his fingers. "I asked you first. Just start talking, Abigail."

I wasn't about to be subjected to another tickle fight, so I gave in. Reluctantly. There wasn't really anything interesting about me, and I didn't want him to find that out. He had superpowers for crying out loud. He was the emperor of the Land of Interesting and could probably find someone more worthy of his time if I turned out to be a dud.

"Um, I like musicals. And I like traveling, like going on vacation and stuff?" It came out more like a question, like I *sometimes* enjoyed leaving Morriston, but only on Tuesdays. Basically I sounded like a confused fool, but his small smile and encouraging nod helped me continue. "When I was little, my dad took us on a trip to Australia. I got to pet a kangaroo." I smiled remembering that moment—the baby kangaroo all brown fluffy fur and tiny T. rex arms.

"Your turn." I'd had enough sharing for the moment.

He tapped his chin, thinking. "Well, before I learned about my powers, I always wanted to be a doctor. Honestly, I kind of still want to be a doctor." The surprise must have shown on my face because he looked away, as if embarrassed. "An oncologist, actually," he clarified.

"Did you know someone with cancer?"

Iron Phantom scratched the back of his head, tugging on his mask. "Sort of."

And on went the rest of the night—him teasing me, me getting twice as many hits back, and a round of Twenty Questions in between. I wanted to ask how he learned about his powers when he was a kid, but I didn't want to ruin the moment. Even though he wore a super suit, talking about favorite foods (his—pizza, mine—triple chocolate fudge cookies), favorite movies (horror and comedy), and favorite animals (we both agreed wolves were kick-ass) made me forget he was a little abnormal. Regardless of who he was with or without his mask, I knew, no matter what my dad or brother said, I wanted to spend more time with him.

"Thanks for this," I said after we teleported back to my room. It was after two in the morning, but I wasn't tired. I could have listened to him talk about the new mystery novel he read or his trip to Italy all night if I wasn't scared someone would try to check on me at home and find my room empty. Connor had that weird sixth sense thing going for him after all.

"My pleasure. Thanks for coming." He leaned against my windowsill, squeezing my fingers in his gloved hands.

"You're welcome. . . ." I shook my head in disbelief.

"What?"

"I just realized that I still don't know your name."

He shrugged. "So? You know *me*. Does my name really matter?"

"I just feel weird calling you Iron Phantom."

He reached into a pocket in his suit and pulled out a folded piece of paper. He held it behind his back, out of reach. "Yeah, that makes two of us. I never asked for a fancy superhero name; it just sort of happened because I kept pulling that disappearing act." He shrugged again. He shrugged a lot when he talked to me, I noticed. Like all our conversations were one big leisurely stroll through the park. Maybe they were for him. For me, they were more like a stumble down a dark alley. "Call me whatever you want."

"Even . . . Steve?" Steve was the first name that came to mind. I reached for the paper behind his back, but he switched it to his other hand.

"That sounds nothing like my real name, so go for it."

I made another grab for the paper, laughing. "Then I shall call you Steve."

"All right," he said.

"All right," I replied.

"You're still doing it—repeating me."

"Sorry, Steve."

The corners of his mouth crinkled when he grinned. He tapped me lightly on the head with the paper, then pressed it into my palms. "Good night, Abigail. I'll see you sooner than you think."

As I stared at the spot where he disappeared, a single question formed in my mind:

Was this a date?

I thought back to how he appeared in my room, seemingly for no real reason at all. How he kept finding excuses to brush his fingers against me. How he sat next to me under his tree, far too close to be friendly . . .

A date. Holy crap. That was totally a date.

With shaking fingers, I slowly opened the paper he'd given me. A *Hall of Horrors* poster. I'd heard they'd been printed, but I hadn't seen one yet. It featured a cartoon drawing of the Delafontaine royal family, blood dripping from their sharp teeth.

Beneath the picture, in highlighted letters, were the words *Starring Seniors Abby Hamilton & Isaac Jackson.*

Oh. My. God.

CHAPTER TEN

It didn't matter that I got only three hours of sleep. It didn't matter that I had a test during third-period world literature that I was totally unprepared for. What mattered was that I had rehearsal after school today.

I would get to see my superhero again.

Despite what he told me about his name, he wouldn't have given me a *Hall of Horrors* poster unless he was in the show—unless he was Isaac.

"What's up with you this morning?" Connor grumbled through a mouthful of cereal. I skipped into the kitchen wearing a bright green dress and rushed around, throwing open cabinet doors in my haste to make breakfast. Dad raised an eyebrow over his phone, then continued to tap at the screen.

"Nothing. Nothing's up," I said far too quickly to be considered innocent. I smoothed down the eyelet fabric of my dress. "Does this look okay?"

Connor snorted and reached for the backpack containing his Red Comet suit. My heart skipped a beat when I thought of my late-night date with another Morriston super. "You trying to impress someone?"

"No!"

"Weirdo," he countered.

My brother was right. I was acting like a weirdo, but I couldn't wait for rehearsal. Isaac, Iron Phantom, Steve—whoever he was, I knew I would get to see him today. He couldn't leave me hanging; he had to make some reference to last night's thinking tree by the pond.

Connor took a whiff of the air near my face. "You smell strange."

Self-consciously, I made sure my hair was covering my neck. "It's perfume." Dad and Connor stared at me. I never wore perfume. "All right, I have rehearsal after school. Seeyalaterbye," I yelled quickly, and ran toward the door.

"Girls," I heard Connor say. "Can't live with them."

"Can't live without them," Dad finished.

"Nope," Connor corrected. "Just can't live with them."

It amazed me how hard it was to track someone down in Morriston High when you actually *wanted* to see them. If you didn't want to find someone, then they were everywhere. That ex-boyfriend who broke your heart, the lab partner you couldn't stand, the teacher whose class you skipped—they would pop up everywhere all day long. A superhero who took you on a date last night—nowhere to be found.

"You're acting like a complete weirdo," Sarah said as we walked down the third-floor hallway to my statistics class. Isaac didn't take statistics, but that didn't keep me from craning my neck every few steps, trying to find his dark head of hair over the basketball players, cheerleaders, tiny freshmen, and a group of Goth kids in trench coats lurking in a corner near the elevator.

"Why does everyone keep saying that?" I stood on my tiptoes in the doorway of my classroom, still surveying the passing students.

"Um, because you're acting like a weirdo? What's up, Abby?"

"Nothing. Just excited for rehearsal today—was that Isaac?" I thought I saw a tall boy with brown hair leave the bathroom, but he disappeared.

Sarah followed my finger pointing down the hall. "No, that's Fanboy Kenny."

"Oh." My shoulders slumped.

The bell rang, and the hallway cleared. Sarah took a step across the hall to her French class. "We're talking about this later. You're acting really weird."

But I couldn't talk to her. I couldn't talk about Iron Phantom to anybody *except* Iron Phantom. And just like so many times before, he had disappeared.

I'd never cared so much about seeing a guy before. I would have been embarrassed for myself if I wasn't so certain that the mysterious Iron Phantom and I had connected last night. He was kind to me and he made me laugh. Being with him, reclined against the bark of his thinking tree, had felt incredible, like neither of us wanted to look away for fear the other might melt into thin air. Like snow in the springtime. Ice cream on a hot day.

I was crushing on him hard, and I couldn't help it.

"Spill." Sarah appeared in the auditorium and dragged me behind the curtain. Mrs. Miller was starting rehearsal any minute, and if I wasn't out there and ready, she was bound to shake the Director's Stick in my face.

A few stage crew kids moved around behind the curtain, pushing set pieces across the floor and flicking lights on and off to run tests. Rylan gave us a small nod as he rushed by with a wrench in his hand and scaled a ladder to the castle balcony. Sarah pulled me to a dark corner primarily used for quick changes between scenes. Her shrill voice hurt my eardrums. "You haven't listened to a word I've said all day, you keep looking for Isaac, and you're wearing . . ." A pause. "You're wearing a *dress*. What did I miss?"

"What? I wear dresses."

"On Easter you do. Never to school." Sarah swept her auburn hair into a ponytail, something she only did when frustrated.

"Look, Sarah . . ." I didn't want to keep lying to her. I'd lied enough about Connor and Red Comet. We had just figured everything out. But I couldn't risk her telling Connor that I knew who the dangerous "villain" was. Though, maybe I could clue her in a little bit. Not so much that she would figure anything out, but enough that she would leave me alone.

"There's this guy," I began.

"Isaac the Red Comet hater?" Sarah looked like she was trying to brush the taste of his name off her tongue.

"Yes. Maybe. I'm not sure yet—"

"Where's Abby?" Mrs. Miller yelled from the auditorium.

I ran to center stage and poked my head through the curtain. "Right here!" The rest of the cast laughed. My breath caught when Isaac winked at me from the front row.

"I'll admit that he's hot, but his taste in superheroes sucks," Sarah muttered before taking her seat.

Today's rehearsal turned out only slightly better than our previous one. Only slightly—meaning not very much. Isaac flubbed his lines, one of the lights came loose from the ceiling and nearly fell on a sophomore girl in the chorus, and I tripped every time Isaac wasn't there to catch me when we ran choreography. Jimmy Stubbs, a junior boy who played Felix Frye, the sadistic town executioner, nearly sliced off his thumb as soon as he was presented with a sword and had to be rushed to the hospital. So much for sadistic. How he managed to injure himself with a blunt prop sword was anybody's guess.

"I'm going to kill all these idiots," Isaac whispered in my ear while Mrs. Miller directed the chorus girls to "stand in the windows so people can see you." He pulled his phone from his back pocket, looked at the time, then roughly shoved it back in. "I really don't have time for this."

"Do you have somewhere to be?" I tried to inconspicuously straighten my green dress. Green. His favorite color. Isaac raised an eyebrow at me, then shrugged.

"Here. There. Everywhere," he said. "My uncle wanted to take me out to dinner. He's trying to start some family tradition since my parents are . . ."

"Are?" Dead. I knew they were dead. He told me last night.

"Not around." He pulled out his phone again.

"I'm sorry," I offered. I hated saying sorry, but I wanted to get back to the place we were at last night, where we both understood how much death sucked but tried to make each other feel better.

He didn't look at me, still engrossed in his phone. Last night, in the darkness of my room, he sounded tormented when talking about his mom and dad. Today, he didn't seem to care at all, and it made me want to rip out my hair. He had been there for me, and I would be there for him too. Didn't he get that?

"Isaac! Abby! We're running the finale again. Get in position, please." Mrs. Miller pressed a button on the CD player at the foot of the stage.

I tried my best to remember the dance steps while pondering my partner. I knew he was trying to keep his identity a secret, but radio silence wasn't exactly what I'd been expecting.

The upbeat show tune played through the speakers. The choreography called for me to do two pas de bourrée—a kind of crisscrossy dance step with my feet—then spin counterclockwise directly into Isaac's chest. But of course, right as my body was about to make contact with Isaac's, his phone beeped with a text. He answered right in the middle of our dance and didn't catch me like he was supposed to, and as a result, I overspun, tripped on his shoe, and landed on the stage with a crash.

The shock of the impact rattled my spine. A collective *ooooh* sounded through the auditorium, and the dance screeched to a grinding halt. Lying sprawled out on my back, I looked up to see Isaac grinning.

"Don't worry," he said. "I tend to make all my dance partners weak at the knees."

"Isaac, *you* tripped *me*!"

"Right. Sorry." He ran a frazzled hand through his hair. "Let me get you, uh, ice. You definitely need ice. Sorry."

His phone beeped again as he hurried from the auditorium. He typed out a reply, fingers flying across the screen. Somehow I doubted he would remember the ice.

"I knew we should have done *The Sound of Music*!" Another rehearsal ended with Mrs. Miller's tears. She wiped the sleeve of a bright orange cardigan across her eyelids, clutching her Director's Stick so fiercely I thought it would snap. *"Hall of HORRORS,"* she wailed. "This show is horrid! I should have known it would be *horrible*!"

I picked my head up a few inches, then let it drop back down with a dull *thump*. If I did that enough, maybe I would get a concussion or amnesia and forget ever being excited to have a lead role in this show. So far the only thing I learned in rehearsals was that Mrs. Miller sounded like an injured sea lion when she sobbed, and Isaac could use proper instructions in the art of phone etiquette. The thing was practically glued to his person. He was worse than my dad.

My head thumped against the stage again.

"Need a hand?" A voice from above startled me, and my eyes snapped open. *God? Is that you? Forgive me, Father, for I never should have auditioned for this show.*

The voice didn't belong to God but to Rylan, staring down at me with his hands on his hips. He wore the traditional stage crew uniform: dark jeans, a black T-shirt, and a weary scowl stemming from heaving around set pieces between scenes. He held out a hand in a silent gesture of assistance.

"Oh, uh, thanks." I gripped his hand, and he easily pulled me upright. "But you should have just left me down there to die. The captain always goes down with the ship."

He smiled. "Not if you're a pirate. Pirates are notoriously selfish. Not that I'm saying you're selfish . . . or anything," he added. He crossed his arms over his chest, then uncrossed them and shoved his hands in his pockets, like he didn't know what to do with them.

"Right, but even pirates abide by some kind of code, don't they?" I asked, straightening a fold in my dress.

"Perhaps," Rylan said. "Which is a lot more than most people here can say for themselves." His brown eyes flickered to the door where Isaac had vanished. "He likes to disappear a lot, doesn't he?" Rylan observed.

"Isaac?" I snorted. "You have no idea."

"Hmm . . ." Rylan leaned against the pulley behind the curtain. I examined my elbows and knees, checking to see if I accrued any more bruises after today's fall. Rylan pointed out a long snag at the bottom of my dress. I groaned. Bruises were easier to deal with.

"That looks bad," he said. "Sorry. Was that rude?" he asked when I stared at him.

"Not necessarily . . ." I watched as he gathered a handful of fake flowers that someone had knocked to the floor. He wrapped a rubber band around the stems, then dropped them in a vase on top of a checkered tablecloth that was part of Angeline's kitchen scene. "I'm just a little surprised you're so chatty today. Usually you clam up."

Rylan's shoulders tensed. "Oh." He moved around the stage, avoiding eye contact, while he straightened the sets and collected stray props. "Well, I guess I warm up to everyone eventually. I'm not a robot." He bent over to pick up two more fake yellow roses, dropping them in another vase. "I thought we were kind of, like, friends . . . maybe. Or maybe not—"

"Abby!" Sarah called out from the door. "Are we still getting pizza?"

"Yeah, I'm coming." I turned back to Rylan. He had moved on from the props and was counting out a handful of screws in a toolbox. A friend. I wasn't very good at dealing with secrecy and superheroes, but friendship—that was something I felt like I had somewhat of a grasp on.

"Rylan," I asked, "what are your thoughts on pizza?"

"Sarah, your car frightens me."

That was the third time Rylan made that statement in the past ten minutes. Sarah and I hadn't exactly prepared him for what he would find inside her superheromobile.

"You get used to it," Sarah said, crunching an empty coffee cup in her fist and tossing it behind her. The cup bounced off a poster of Fish Boy kissing a baby that was taped to the window and landed in Rylan's lap, where he brushed it to the floor with a frown.

I turned around in the passenger seat to look at him. "That's a lie. No one ever gets used to it." To prove my point I kicked my feet up on Sarah's dashboard, effectively covering a picture of Connor flexing his biceps with a glob of mud from my shoe. Rylan laughed to himself.

"Okay, enough about the car," Sarah said. She swung into the parking lot of the pizza parlor, stalling with a *clunk, clunk, clunk* before cutting the engine altogether. "He has feelings too."

"She knows it's just a car, right?" Rylan whispered to me as we pushed through the doors of the restaurant. It was one of the only eating establishments nearby that didn't shut down once the sun set. Todo, the large bearded owner, once told me and Sarah that he wasn't afraid of any criminals. No wonder—the guy was built like a sumo wrestler.

We took a seat in a booth near a row of televisions mounted on the wall. Sarah ordered our usual—a pepperoni pizza and a large breadstick bucket with extra cheese sauce—while Rylan ducked into the bathroom.

I fiddled with the straw in my cup of water, absentmindedly staring at the TV above our booth. The evening news had just started, and Kip Snyder, the weatherman, was in the midst of predicting how much snow Morriston was likely to get over the winter. Sarah loudly cleared her throat from across the table.

"Do you need a throat lozenge?" I asked politely. I'd watched her sneak looks at Rylan the whole ride here; I knew where she was about to go with this.

Sarah rested her elbows on the table. "He's a cutie." She wiggled her eyebrows.

"He's afraid of you," I countered.

She scoffed. "Not for me. For *you*."

"Hmm . . ."

"Oh, come on, Abby! Yes, Isaac is gorgeous, and my God, the boy can sing, but he looks like someone is eternally shoving a stick up his ass."

"I never said I liked Isaac." I liked someone who I thought was Isaac, which may or may not have been the same thing.

Sarah pulled the straw out of my drink and flicked a drop of water at my face. "Just think about it."

"I . . ." I trailed off as Rylan returned from the bathroom, scooting into the booth beside me. He ripped the paper off his straw and stuck it in his water glass.

"What did I miss?" he asked.

"Nothing at all." I shot Sarah a look when she winked dramatically, then allowed my attention to drift back to the television. The weather report had finally ended, but a bright red stripe across the bottom of the screen declared a report of breaking news. The entire restaurant stopped eating to stare. Todo dropped a glass in the kitchen, and it shattered to the floor. Rylan braced his hands on the table, his eyebrows furrowed.

"What's he doing now?" Rylan asked. His voice was sharper and louder than I'd ever heard it. He was afraid.

My shoulders twitched in a semblance of a shrug, but I didn't answer. The restaurant watched silently as live footage showed Iron Phantom firing a round of bullets into the front window of a fancy uptown jewelry store. The super ran inside before exiting with a bag strapped to his back. He started down the street, but Red Comet intercepted him, knocking him to the ground. Iron Phantom rolled onto his back. He fired off another shot, and Connor ducked as the bullet whizzed by. That moment of hesitation was all Iron Phantom needed. He bolted for a boarded-up building at the end of the block, dodging Fish Boy, who sped down the street on his motorcycle. Iron Phantom knocked in the door with one firm kick before slamming it behind him. Red Comet raced after him, police and media not far behind. When Connor finally opened the door, with the officers' weapons trained on the building, there was nothing to see except a brick wall. Iron Phantom was gone.

"We should get out of here." Rylan grabbed my arm and pulled me from the booth. "He was only a few blocks away. We're too close for comfort." The pizza parlor was emptying out, most diners begging Todo for take-out boxes. Sarah swiped a handful of lollipops from a bowl beside the cash registers, and we rushed to her car in silence.

Predictably, my house was empty when Sarah dropped me off. I headed up to my room, my mind racing. I didn't care how much my brother would rage when he finally got home—something about that scene wasn't right. The Iron Phantom I knew wouldn't do that. After spending so much time convincing me he was innocent, he wouldn't—

I halted, noticing a piece of paper taped to my window, fluttering against the glass as if it were begging to be let in.

Crossing the room, I unlatched the window and pushed it up. I half expected him to be standing on a tree branch outside, his lips quirked up in the constant state of amusement that I'd come to associate with the super who visited me after dark. But he wasn't there. All I had were five words scribbled in green ink:

That wasn't me. I swear.

CHAPTER ELEVEN

The auditorium was abuzz with theories when I stepped inside the door. *Iron Phantom is a murderer. Iron Phantom is going to take over Morriston and force us all to wear black. Iron Phantom is the most entertaining bit of reality television since that matchmaking show got canceled last spring.*

I leaned against the doorway, apprehensive to walk through the sea of chatter to find a seat. If I had to hear one more person spewing fallacious gossip, then Iron Phantom wouldn't be the only villain in town.

"Hey, Abby." Rylan entered the auditorium and climbed the three steps into the sound booth. "You made it home okay last night, then?"

"Yeah. I'm guessing you did too?" The last I saw of Rylan, Sarah was dropping him off in the school parking lot, where he'd taken his own car home.

"Safe and sound." He pulled out a chair, taking a seat amid a tangle of colored wires scattered across the table. I watched as he chewed on his thumbnail and flicked a switch on one of the boards on the desk. The lights hanging above the stage turned purple, and Rylan quickly programmed something into the computer on his right. He hit another switch, and the lights glowed gold.

"That looks complicated." Standing on my toes, I peered into the sound booth and watched the numbers scroll across Rylan's computer screen. "Is it complicated?"

"Not really. Mrs. Miller wrote out all the lighting cues. I just have to enter them into the computer, and it remembers them from there." We looked to the stage, where Rylan made a few lights swivel in circles and flash red and white, turning the room into an afternoon disco party.

"See?" He glanced over at me before returning to the screen. "Not too difficult."

I snorted. It didn't sound difficult, but the pile of wires and hundreds of buttons on the board sure made it look impossible.

"Want to try?" Rylan asked. He pushed open the door of the sound booth.

"No thanks. This show's already off to a rocky start. If I break something, Mrs. Miller might have a heart attack."

"Nah, she'll just shove her Director's Stick down your throat. Come on." He cleared his backpack off the folding chair beside him. "It's a piece of cake, I promise."

Apprehensively I sat on the edge of the seat, my fingertips digging into my knees as I awaited further instructions.

Rylan showed me a piece of notebook paper covered in Mrs. Miller's swoopy cursive. "Okay, so I already did the first couple lines . . . um . . . let me see if I can find you something really difficult—"

"Rylan."

"Kidding. I'm just kidding. Oh! Here, try this one." He pointed to a string of numbers halfway down the page. "Literally all you're going to do is make a blue light swivel across the stage and then hit this blackout button right here." He jabbed his finger at a large square button on the upper right corner of the lighting board. "Annnd . . . go."

"Right now?"

"Yes, now. It's recording, so if you don't go, you'll mess everything up."

"What?"

"Go!" Rylan shook the paper at me. "Type a five-one-seven into the computer. Quick!"

"Oh my God, I can't stand you." I laughed as I punched in the numbers. At the front of the auditorium, to my surprise, a blue light began its journey across the stage.

"Eight-eighteen!" Rylan instructed. I did as he said, and a second light panned in the opposite direction.

"Four-one-two!" Four white lights began to shimmer like rainwater and I turned to Rylan with a scowl.

"That's not what you said was going to happen."

"I omitted a bit." He shrugged. "Oh, Abby! Blackout button!"

I slammed my hand down on the board, and the lights shut off all at once. A few screams filled the auditorium, followed by nervous laughter. Rylan flicked on a lamp at the corner of the desk, bathing us in a bright yellow glow. He slowly brought the houselights back up while keying a few more numbers into the monitor. I sat back in my chair. Between Rylan's frantic directions and the fact that his voice was louder than I'd ever heard it, I was left dazed.

"See, Abby? You're a pro." We sat still for a moment, staring at the stage. The lights flickered, casting shadows on two girls goofing off while doing cartwheels. Sarah joined them, and they collapsed on the floor, giggling. Rylan pulled his keyboard toward him, bringing up a pair of soft pink lights that twinkled on the castle and the small-town backdrop.

I'd never thought about it before, but I kind of liked the view from the back of the auditorium. When I was onstage, everything was all action and adrenaline. *Go, go, go.* Back here it was quiet. Peaceful.

"Hey, Abigail?"

The rhythmic tapping of Rylan's keyboard was interrupted when Isaac leaned over the wall of the sound booth.

"Yeah?"

"Uh . . ." He swallowed hard. "I just wanted to say that I'm . . . I'm sorry about tripping you yesterday. It really was an accident and—"

"She smacked her head on the floor," Rylan grumbled, barely audible. Isaac didn't appear to hear exactly what Rylan said, but he shot Rylan a look all the same.

"Anyway, I'm sorry," Isaac said. "Here." He rummaged through his bag. "Do you like chocolate? I got you a bar of chocolate."

I reached out, my fingers brushing his as I took the candy bar. A jolt shot through my chest. My eyes widened as the red wrapper crinkled in my fist, identical to the wrapper that was once left in my room by a certain super—

"Abby! Isaac! Has anyone seen my leads?" Mrs. Miller's cardigan covered with sparkly pumpkins fell from her shoulders as she shuffled up the aisle to locate us.

Isaac waved a hand in the air. "Back here, Mrs. Miller!"

I couldn't move. The candy bar weighed my hand down like a brick.

"Oh!" A bony hand fell over Mrs. Miller's heart. "I swear you two disappear faster than that superhero. What's his name? Iron something . . ."

"Iron Phantom!" a freshman boy in the second row yelled.

"He's evil, you know!" another girl shouted, though her high-pitched giggles said otherwise.

Isaac took a step away from the booth, adjusting his backpack, frown lines creasing his mouth.

"Isaac," I started.

"Abigail, I need to run lines at the top of act one. Can you help me?" He took off down the aisle before I could answer.

I glanced at Rylan. His fingers *tap-tap-tapped* across the keys, but he smiled when he caught me watching. "Break a leg, Abby." Offering me a hand, he helped me down from the sound booth.

"What's up with you and Rylan Sloan?" Isaac demanded when I took the stage beside him.

"What do you mean?"

He sat on the steps leading up to the castle, flipping a page in his script with much more force than necessary. "Never mind. Scene two. Let's start there."

Iron Phantom's name wasn't mentioned the rest of rehearsal. I tried to grill Isaac for information to see if I could glean more similarities between the two of them, but he dodged all my questions like a pro, pressing my script harder into my hands and forcing me to recite entire scenes with my eyes closed. As soon as Mrs. Miller called it a day (she wasn't crying this time; it was pretty impressive), Isaac darted out the door.

His silent treatment was right on par with Iron Phantom's. I'd expected the super to contact me again, but he was disappointingly silent. Not another note, not a word, not even a breath. Maybe he was afraid that I would blame him for yet another crime, but that was the furthest thing from my mind. I knew he was innocent. The real Iron Phantom would have disappeared right in the middle of the street—he wouldn't have run from the police, and he certainly wouldn't have shoved his foot through a door, hiding in a building before teleporting.

Which made me wonder if the Iron Phantom from the surveillance video had teleported at all.

Someone was framing him, and I wanted to know why. And if the man who dressed up in an imitation of Iron Phantom's super suit had any connection to the microchip that the real Iron Phantom had stolen from city hall, then I knew there was only one logical place to start my search: my father's office.

I hadn't wanted it to come to this. The mayor and his entire cabinet had switched offices to a skyscraper farther uptown after the fire, and the last thing I wanted was to go poking around. I never enjoyed visiting my dad at work. Everyone there was so serious, rushing around with harried looks in their eyes—but not rushing so fast that they made it obvious that they *were* harried—griping about the best spots to place new traffic signals and the rise of potholes in suburbia and who might challenge my father when it was time for a reelection. There was a lot of arguing without any action—except for drinking coffee. Walking into city hall always had a way of making me feel impossibly small, and as I stepped out of the elevator in my dad's new building, I knew today would be no exception.

"Abby, sweetie!" A middle-aged woman dashed out from behind the reception desk, her heels clicking on the clinically white tile floor.

She smiled down her pointed nose at me. "I'll call your daddy to come get you."

I grimaced. This woman was probably nice, but she, like all the secretaries before her (whose names always seemed to start with a *B*—like Bertha and Betty and Beatrice), had a tendency to treat me like I was five.

"No, that's okay," I told her. "I'm, er, actually here to . . ." My voice wavered. What would Iron Phantom do in this situation? He wouldn't stutter, that was for sure. He would straighten his shoulders, clench his jaw, and charm the pants right off her.

"I'm actually here to surprise him." I plastered a smile on my face. "There's this little game we play. He leaves a gift for me; I leave one for him." I shrugged bashfully. "I know it's dorky—"

"Not at all! Oh, aren't you the sweetest little thing!" Her voice got all high-pitched like she was praising a puppy for finally learning not to pee on the carpet.

"The absolute sweetest," I agreed. I took a step to the side of her desk, looking down the narrow hallway. "My dad isn't in his office, right? That would sort of ruin the surprise."

The receptionist tapped her keyboard. "No, I believe he's in a meeting for the next half hour." She shooed me toward the hall. "You go make his day, sweet pea."

The bitter taste of guilt coated my tongue as I hurried away, but I ignored it.

Supervillain Mission Impossible: officially under way.

Dad's office was easier to locate in this building than it was in city hall. Instead of hiding in the back corner of no-man's-land behind oak double doors and a tapestry of the American flag, it was only just around the corner, next to a fake potted fern and a black-and-white photograph of the Morriston Bridge. Much homier, but not exactly my dad's style.

I checked for the patter of approaching footsteps before ducking inside. The room was clean, just the way he liked it. His computer hummed on the glass desktop. I didn't know the password, but I could settle for snooping through his drawers.

The top one was full of manila folders and a package of thumbtacks. I pulled each item out, careful not to disturb the papers, and placed them on the corner of the desk—right beside two school photos of me and Connor in our awkward braces phase.

Contracts, housing permits, notes for speeches written in chicken scratch—nothing helpful. The second drawer was full of last year's Halloween candy. That was interesting in a rather bizarre way. I couldn't save candy for a month, let alone a year.

The bottom drawer yielded something that might have been halfway helpful—an empty brown envelope wedged behind a three-ring binder. Three letters were written on the front, underlined in bright red ink: *E.D.D.*

Kneeling on the floor behind the desk, I struggled to come up with a meaning for the envelope. It had to be significant; Dad's pristine office made it obvious he didn't like trash lying around. Initials, perhaps? But I didn't think I knew an E.D.D.

Soft whistling filled the hall outside the door.

Dropping the envelope back where it belonged, I crouched farther under the desk. *Don't come in here. Please don't come in here.* I'd reached my lying quota for the day, and I didn't know if I'd be able to make up another excuse on the spot. Maybe I could say I dropped an earring? Or I fainted. Or—

"Shake your flippers. Shake, shake your flippers, yeah!"

Thank God. I stood, pushing my hair from my eyes as Fish Boy opened the door and stepped inside the office.

He froze when he saw me. "What are you doing here?"

"What are *you* doing here? This is my dad's office."

"I'm aware." Hunter shut the door behind him. He pulled his mask up a few inches to scratch his cheek. "Your dad left his tie clip in here." He reached for a small silver bar sitting on a coaster. "Your brother and I are doing a superhero photo shoot with him on the roof. It's for the *Morriston Gazette* or something. Do you want in?"

"I'm not a super."

Hunter slapped a webbed hand to his forehead. "Duh. Sorry, I forget sometimes. I'm filming the whole thing for social media if you want to check it out later." He leaned back against the wall, flippers crossed at the ankles. "So . . . what *are* you doing here?"

"I'm looking for . . . uh . . . you know, just . . ." Somehow I knew Hunter wouldn't believe a fib about a lost earring. The scales and the gills did a good job of making him look like the ultimate supernerd, but there was a sharpness to his eyes as he scanned the room, sucking in every detail before his ocean-blue gaze eventually settled on me. He was more intuitive than he let on.

"I'm looking for . . ." I crossed my fingers behind my back. "Tampons."

Hunter paled. "I beg your pardon?"

"Tampons," I repeated. "My mom died shortly after I got my . . . *you know* . . . so Dad started buying me tampons and sometimes he . . . keeps them around . . . for me?"

Did that even make sense? I wasn't sure, but Hunter's face grew steadily redder beneath his mask each time I said the t-word, so I kept at it, hoping if I said it once more he'd forget seeing me at all. "He keeps them in his desk," I said. "The tampons."

"O-kay, then." Hunter tripped over a flipper as he struggled to turn around. "Uh, okay. Right. You seem like you have this under control. I'm going back to the photo shoot."

"Cool." I tried not to grin as he shuddered. "Oh, and Fish Boy?"

"Yeah?" he croaked.

"Can you not tell my dad or Connor about this? They get a little squeamish whenever I say *tam*—"

"Okay! Yep! Gotcha! I'll do that—or I won't rather. Don't worry, they won't hear a thing from me." With another flipper-flapping shudder, he stumbled from the room.

"Boys," I muttered.

I shielded my eyes against the setting sun as I hurried back to the bus stop. My mind was whirling. *E.D.D.* Who was E.D.D.? Were the letters even significant, or had I spent too many evenings listening to Iron Phantom's vague conspiracy theories?

I tilted my head to see the top of the nearest skyscraper, wondering if the photo shoot had ended. Connor wasn't visible up there, but then again he never was unless it was necessary. Superheroes were champions at Lurking Creepily Out of Sight.

The crossing signal turned green, and I jogged to the other side of the street. It was nearing that time of day when Morriston's creepy, crime-ridden streets turned even creepier and more crime-ridden and most people called it a day and drove home. I pulled my Taser from my bag—just in case. I wasn't crazy about walking to my bus stop in the growing twilight, but I found myself pausing on the street corner anyway, my heart thudding painfully. The quickest way to the bus was to pass the City Bank where my mom was murdered.

I weighed the pros and cons. I could take a longer route, but if I did then I might miss the bus. I'd have to call Sarah to get me—or admit to my dad that I ventured downtown without his knowledge. No. I would have to risk it. If I held my breath and walked really fast, then the bank would be out of sight before I knew it.

I took off at a brisk pace, trying to think of song lyrics. *Feast and bury* . . . and something else. The hulking marble building with its golden doors and tinted windows was at the forefront of my mind. Admittedly, I was far too distracted by memories of my mom to really pay attention to where I was going.

And of course that was when I felt the hand on my arm that pulled me into the alley.

I shrieked, driving my Taser toward the attacker's ribs. They dodged me once, then dodged me twice when I thrust my elbow at their jaw. I aimed another attack with the Taser, but they caught me easily, clamping a palm over my lips. I opened my mouth, determined to bite their fingers in half, only stopping once they snickered and stepped back.

As my eyes adjusted, his tall figure emerged from the shadows. The black super suit made him practically invisible, but no one else had bright green eyes like his.

"You have got to stop trying to hurt me," he said.

"*You* have got to stop showing up out of nowhere! What the hell, Steve?"

The super chuckled. "Steve. That sounds almost as strange as *Iron Phantom*." He peeked out of the alley, looking right then left before tugging me toward a darkened alcove between a run-down movie theater and an apartment complex. "And showing up out of nowhere is kind of what I do—teleportation and all. A big, bad supervillain has an image to keep up, do I not?"

"You're not a villain."

He flashed me a toothy grin. "I have a feeling that means you got my latest note."

"Possibly." I grinned back at him. "If that wasn't you yesterday, then where were you?"

"Would you believe me if I said I was at home, thinking up really cheesy superhero one-liners that I can use the next time I stop a mugger from attacking a pretty girl?"

"Oh?" I felt myself blushing. "And what have you come up with so far?"

He cleared his throat. "Well, this one is my big opener. I think it's important to knock their socks off right away. So here it is." He cleared his throat again. "Hey, you. *Stop.*"

"Wow. I'm shaking. You've put me on the straight and narrow with that one. Never will I have dreams of thievery again."

"Hey, you're the one who said supers were lame."

I shrugged, sheepish. "Maybe I changed my mind."

"I'm really glad to hear that."

"Me too." I scanned the seemingly deserted streets. "Someone could see you around here, you know."

"Then what a lucky day it would be for them." We ducked into another alley, but if someone crossed our path, a six-foot-something guy wearing a mask would be hard to miss. "Maybe *they* won't try to kill me when they see me."

"You're so full of crap."

He nodded. "I'm just emotionally constipated. It'll pass."

I laughed, causing his fingers to tighten around mine. Everywhere he touched tingled, like I'd shot myself with my Taser by accident. The skin on my palms, the back of my hand as he grazed his thumb over my knuckles, my hip bone when he brushed against me while moving farther into the shadows. Each point of contact. I was on fire because of him.

"I . . . I . . ." And I stuttered. Fantastic. "I was in city hall's makeshift offices today," I told him after I regained some composure. "Snooping. I might have found something."

"You did?" His voice leapt in excitement.

"Possibly. Do the letters E.D.D. mean anything to you?"

"Ed?"

"No, E.D.—"

"I know. I'm just saying it sounds like Ed. Not that I know an Ed. Or an E.D.D. Is that a person, do you think? Or . . . ?"

I shrugged. "I don't know. I was thinking the same thing. I'm not even sure if it's relevant. No one at my dad's office was acting weird—well, no weirder than usual."

"Hmm . . ."

"But I am wondering if there's a connection between whoever ordered the microchips and the person who's framing you."

Iron Phantom pointed a finger in my face, less than an inch from the tip of my nose. "See, Abigail? That's how I knew this arrangement would work. You're smart."

"Are you saying you're not?"

He rolled his green eyes. "Not at all—"

"Thank you for your modesty."

"—but it's nice to have someone on the inside, you know? So . . . has your dad said anything, uh, *off-color* recently?"

"Not that I've noticed. We barely talk. He's working all the time. He's freaking out, thinking you're to blame. He has no clue what's going on."

I peered out of the alley. We were only a few doors away from the dreaded City Bank, and I didn't feel like having another freak-out about my mom in Iron Phantom's presence. He pulled me back into the shadows, out of sight of a mother and daughter standing in front of the bank's ATM machine, frowning while he watched me.

I gulped. "Things have been different . . . since my mom died. He tries to act otherwise, but I can tell he's still hurting."

"You all are, I'm sure," Iron Phantom said. He crouched against the brick wall behind us, watching the bank. The mom was still pressing buttons at the ATM while her little girl tossed a teddy bear in the air, then spun around to catch it.

I nodded. "I guess he's under a lot of stress."

"I suppose. But . . ." I watched as he wrung out his hands. "Maybe—and don't get mad at me for saying this—but maybe your dad is just . . ."

He fell silent. Blinked.

"Just . . . ?"

"Abigail, maybe he's just—"

The rest of his sentence was left hanging in the air when a silver van screeched around the corner and opened fire on the City Bank.

Bullets shattered the glass front door. They left deep grooves in the marble face of the building, making pinging sounds as the shells bounced along the ground. I felt hands press my body into the sidewalk, Iron Phantom's heavy weight on top of me before he disappeared and materialized in front of the bank. He'd wasted time protecting me, I realized with a sharp twist in my gut. But I wasn't the one who needed saving.

Iron Phantom bent over the woman as the dented van screeched around the corner and raced out of town. A shredded teddy bear rolled into the center of the street.

Murder.

As the sticky puddle of blood spread along the sidewalk, I doubted the victims would make it. A child and a . . . a mother. Dead in front of the City Bank. Two innocent people murdered in cold blood. And for what? The criminals hadn't taken any money. They fled like cowards instead.

I suddenly couldn't breathe. I was frozen.

The woman's limbs were sprawled at awkward angles, her blond hair fanned out like a halo. Was this how my mother looked when she died?

Iron Phantom's lips moved, but I couldn't hear his voice. My eyes had shifted from the mother to the little girl's fingers as they twitched on the concrete toward her teddy bear.

She was still alive. We could save her.

Seeing her move broke my trance, and I raced down the sidewalk. Connor would be here soon. And the police and the media were never far behind.

"You can help her, right?" I knelt next to the girl and examined her fragile body. So much blood. Far too much to tell the extent of her injuries. But judging by the way her chest barely moved, I knew she was moments from death.

Iron Phantom turned away from the woman on the ground by the front door. She wasn't moving. We both knew she was already gone. "What?" he asked, his voice cracking.

"You can heal people! You can heal her! You have to do something!"

The girl's eyelashes fluttered open for a second, and her tiny fingers splayed across the sidewalk. "Mommy?" Her voice was a whisper, barely there.

I squeezed the girl's bloody palm and looked up at my superhero. Another life couldn't be taken outside this bank. He had a chance to save somebody—that's what he was supposed to do. He was one of the good guys. I knew he was.

Blood oozed over the girl's white sweater, staining the knees of my jeans. I opened my eyes wide, pleading.

"Abigail," Iron Phantom said. "I can't fix this. It's . . ." He gestured at the dark puddle of blood circling the girl's body. "It's too much. It won't work. I—"

"Can't you try?"

Iron Phantom bit down hard on his bottom lip, turning it bright white where teeth met skin. Before I could beg again, he dropped to his knees, his hand hovering over the girl's chest. Clenching his fingers into a fist, he slowly lowered his hand into the blood.

When he had used his healing powers on me, it seemed easy. Over in a few seconds. But now coming in contact with such deep wounds caused his entire body to seize up. His hand shook violently, smearing his glove with blood. He held in his pain for only a moment before it burst forth. His screams bounced off the buildings, howling as if he was being subjected to torture. His skin was paper white. Tears trickled down his mask, falling onto my fingers.

The little girl sat up slightly, sucking in a deep breath of air. Her big brown eyes opened wide, but she just as soon collapsed in my arms. I felt for a pulse, dizzy with terror. A faint *thump-thump* greeted me. She was still alive. But only just.

Iron Phantom cradled his hand to his chest, leaning down to rest his head on his knees. Hesitantly, I placed a hand between his shoulder blades, where the stickiness of sweat seeped through his suit. A distant cry of sirens grew closer. Connor and Hunter would be here any second. They couldn't find Morriston's supervillain crouching over a crime scene on the sidewalk.

"Red Comet is bound to show up soon," I said.

"I know."

"You need to get out of here."

"*I know.* It's a bit . . . difficult . . . at the . . . moment." I couldn't see his face, but a soft weeping met my ears. I settled the unconscious girl on the sidewalk, using my jacket as a pillow under her head before standing over the super.

"Come on, you need to get up!" I pulled at his arm.

"Abigail, I—" He couldn't catch his breath. "I don't think I can." His right hand—the hand he placed over the girl's chest—still shook uncontrollably, like he had been electrocuted. He took another deep breath and managed to flex his fingers.

"Please help me. Please," he said. I started to pull him up by his underarms, but stopped when a soft whimper escaped his lips.

It sounded like *Mom*.

I pulled him a little straighter. "Stay with me, okay?"

He continued to mumble as I dragged him, his boots scraping across the sidewalk, to the side of the bank. Two words, over and over and over again. "I'm sorry. I'm sorry. I'm sorry."

"I know," I tried to console him. "It's okay. I promise it'll be okay. Please, just move. It's not safe."

"My fault," he mumbled, half conscious.

"No. Not your fault. You did great, all right? Just . . . keep . . . moving." With a final tug, I dragged him around the corner and propped him against the building. I swiped my fingers under my eyes, shocked to see tears glistening on my fingertips. I hadn't even noticed I'd started crying. I just witnessed the murder of a woman—one who looked extraordinarily like my mother—and all I felt was numb.

"You need to leave," I told him.

It looked like he was regaining some strength. His head wasn't drooping to his chest at least.

Clenching his fists, he breathed deep. "I don't have the strength to teleport you with me."

"That's fine. I'll stay here." A loud thump from the front of the bank indicated that Connor had finally shown up. Iron Phantom didn't know it, but Red Comet was capable of taking me home too. He opened his mouth to argue, but the squeal of sirens had him backing into the shadows. "Go!" I pushed his shoulders. "Please go."

He gritted his teeth in pain, and soon I was left staring at the side of the building.

When I returned, the front of the City Bank was a mess of caution tape, television cameras, and superhero spandex.

An ambulance screamed as it fled down the street, and I said a silent prayer for the little girl inside, trying to push away the thought that she would be yet another girl who would have to grow up without a mother.

Red Comet stood motionless on the edge of the sidewalk. I knew what he was thinking. Three years ago, it was our mom lying torn and broken at this very spot.

My brother looked at the police and reporters gathered at the scene. Nearly twenty people surrounded the bank, but the air was frighteningly still.

"What are you waiting for?" Connor roared. "Someone fucking do something!"

Our eyes met across the sidewalk. I wanted to run to him, I needed to run to him, but with the crowd pressing in, I knew that was impossible. Too suspicious.

Digging my fingernails into my palms, I desperately tried to push away the images. But the crescent moons of blood that beaded through my skin had the opposite effect. They brought it all rushing back. Blood, pain, death. Blood, pain, death.

Mom.

I wanted to shove the crowd aside; I wanted to wrap my arms around my brother's waist and lose control. But I couldn't. And that made the pain hurt a million times worse.

CHAPTER TWELVE

Dad sat on the couch nursing a glass of scotch when Connor and I came home. His tie dangled loosely around his neck, and the television remote was clutched in his fist. I was shocked to see him home, sitting on the couch like everything was normal after today's tragedy. Normally he would work late into the night and barely get an ounce of sleep. He never relaxed in the living room and watched . . . home videos of Connor and me?

We hadn't seen these videos in years, mainly because they featured my mom just as much as they featured me and my brother. We couldn't bear to see her moving or breathing on-screen when she was incapable of singing in the kitchen or even walking through our front door in real life.

Connor looked from my dad to the television. The video currently playing featured a five-year-old Connor and a three-year-old me making mud pies on the back porch of our old brick house. As we watched, the tiny version of Connor smeared mud on both our cheeks like war paint. Or like a mask. A blue blanket was tied around his neck like a cape. Eleven years before Connor received his powers, he was still a superhero.

"Connor, sweetie, smile for the camera!" our mother's voice called from offscreen. Tiny Connor grinned, his mouth full of baby teeth and sticky peanut butter, and waved at the lens. Tiny Abby was busy drumming a plastic shovel on a bucket.

In our living room, I noticed my brother's shoulders tense under his super suit. After the scene at the bank, the last thing we needed was to hear our mother cooing like everything was okay.

Everything was not okay.

"Turn it off," Connor growled. Most humans would show fear if a super angrily advanced on them, but not my dad. He crossed his legs and patted the cushion next to him. The video paused on a shot of Connor pulling his pants down and mooning the screen.

"I'm proud of you," Dad said. Ice cubes clinked as he twirled them in his glass. "I'm so proud of you. You are both so strong. We all miss your mom, and sometimes I wish . . . I wish I could be a better father. But I'm trying." His lips quirked up in a weak smile. I wondered if he was only being heartfelt because of the scotch.

My dad stood before me and placed his hand on my cheek. It was cold and damp from holding the glass. I wasn't used to him touching me. When I was a kid, he always gave me hugs, was always really affectionate with both me and Connor. But as the years went on, the hugs and kisses grew few and far between. He became mayor, and it was like he suddenly forgot all about the bear hugs or piggyback rides he used to give me. We both grew up, I guess. But tonight I didn't know whether to welcome his tender touch or be angry it took my dad this long to remember what we used to have. I wanted my daddy back, but I didn't know if he was still there.

"It's going to get better, Abby," he said. "You'll see." His hand slid from my cheek, and he walked from the room. His bedroom door slid closed with a soft click seconds later.

Normally after returning home from his superhero life, Connor was in a great mood. He never stopped talking, and he ate everything in sight while laughing loudly at reality television. But today, he fell on the couch and threw the remote at the ground. The TV clicked off. The room darkened.

"I failed, didn't I? I never failed before."

Here it was. The perfect opening for the question I was dying to ask. *If you never failed, then why didn't you save Mom?* But it wouldn't be right to bring it up. Not now. Not when I was hiding so many secrets from him in return.

"Connor, that woman never stood a chance. Everything happened too fast."

"But if I got there sooner—"

"It wouldn't have mattered. It was over even before it began." I remembered Iron Phantom's hand shaking over the girl's chest. *He* could barely save her. Red Comet couldn't have done a thing.

"There's a reason why I work so hard, Abby," Connor said. "So nobody dies. And I can't even do that right."

I knelt next to him on the floor. Blood still soaked the knees of my jeans, cold against my skin. I waited for him to ask why I was downtown today, but the question never came as Connor met my eyes through the dark. I needed to squint to see his face, but he didn't have a problem seeing me with his heightened vision. He told me once how clear everything looked through his eyes, like the entire world sparkled in a sea of diamonds and every detail was magnified to the nth degree. Only Connor Hamilton would think of his world as being covered in diamonds.

I ruffled his hair with my fingers. It fell limp in my hands. "You don't always have to be Red Comet, you know. Sometimes you can just be Connor."

"No, I can't." He gestured to his suit. "Connor Hamilton is a nobody. You take away my powers and I have nothing. I'm a C-average student with zero plans for my future. Without my powers, I'm nobody."

I shook my head. He couldn't be further from the truth. "You're not nobody. You're my brother."

"Since when is that enough?"

I pried his mask out of his grasp and threw it across the room. It hit the wall and slid behind a cabinet. "It's always enough."

When I entered my bedroom later that night, Iron Phantom was sitting on my floor against the wall. He must have washed his suit—it was no longer bloody. He didn't speak, but I knew he noticed my bloodshot eyes and sweaty hair. He might have cleaned up, but I still looked like a mess.

"I'm fine," I said.

"No, you aren't." He nervously pulled at the fingers of his gloves, but his eyes never left mine. "My parents were in a car crash. Drunk driver ran a light just as they were making a left and smashed into the car. I was there, right in the back seat, and I tried to heal them . . . but I couldn't. So they died. It wasn't nearly as gruesome as what happened to your mom, and I wasn't *'fine.'* You don't ever need to say you're fine when it's so obvious you're hurting. Not everyone gets it, but I do. Please don't pretend around me."

His words touched me, and I tried to hold back sniffles. I was so used to keeping secrets and pretending things were different than the truth. Maybe that's why I joined the drama club. Faking things had become my forte. "It's ironic you tell *me* not to pretend when you're the one wearing a super suit and won't even tell me your name."

His lips twitched. He motioned at me with his index finger. "Just come here, Abigail."

He held me on the floor of my bedroom, and I tried my hardest not to cry. But eventually, I stopped pretending.

"How's your brother doing?" Sarah asked as the stage crew wheeled our eight-foot-long papier-mâché crocodile onto the stage during rehearsal.

I shrugged while I glanced over my script. "He's had better days."

That may have been an understatement. Connor was throwing himself into his Red Comet duties harder than ever, spending almost every waking minute up in the sky, but no one was taking notice. All anyone cared about was his failure and what it meant for the safety of the rest of the city. Connor had been a complete stranger to bad publicity, but now he couldn't escape it. *Has Red Comet Finally Burnt Out?* was the latest headline in a string of less than positive articles about Morriston's favorite super, accompanied by a photograph of Connor angrily throwing his hands into the air outside the City Bank. I'd caught him reading it obsessively this morning, and then he immediately threw the newspaper in the trash. And of course it didn't help that Fish Boy was actually managing to pull off rescues by himself for once. Yesterday he saved a kitten from drowning in a swimming pool. It made the five o'clock news, and the city cooed over the cuteness. Connor's ego had completely crumbled.

Sarah started onstage when Rylan pushed a wooden wall of the Delafontaine castle dangerously close to her foot. "Poor guy." She lowered her voice. "Tell him if he needs a sidekick to help him out, I probably have more Red Comet memorabilia than he does."

I snorted. "I don't doubt that. By the way, how's your Fish Boy memorabilia coming along?"

Sarah winked. "Swimmingly." She jumped offstage, leaving me alone.

I pressed my palms over my eyes, silently counting the minutes until I could go home. I hadn't been sleeping well the past few days, ever since Iron Phantom and I witnessed the murder. It came as no surprise that all of Morriston blamed him for the death—someone needed to be accused after all. But if they could have seen him that night, immobile and shaking, they wouldn't be so quick to judge.

I hadn't seen Iron Phantom since that evening. We didn't talk much in my room, and he disappeared in the middle of the night after I fell asleep on his shoulder. I missed him. I wanted to know if the horror we witnessed affected him as much as it affected me.

"Stressed out?" a soft voice spoke from backstage. I looked behind the curtain and found Rylan sipping from a water bottle, his lanky body hunched over the wooden podium that Principal Davis used during assemblies. "You look exhausted."

"Awesome." I stifled a yawn. "Do you think I could pass off the rings under my eyes as bruises and tell everyone I got into a fistfight?"

"Doubtful."

"Bummer." Another yawn worked its way out of my mouth. "I haven't been sleeping well." My nightmares had been steadily growing worse. I jolted awake almost every night screaming and crying, cold sweat soaking my sheets. "I'm just really tired."

"Speaking of tired . . ." Isaac sauntered out of the wings and took

Rylan's water from him, gulping it down. "I'm so exhausted I can't even stand up straight. Thanks for the drink, man." He tossed the bottle back, and Rylan caught it, a scowl on his face.

Mrs. Miller motioned for us to get into positions to run the final scene of the show. Spoiler alert: Angeline gets bitten by the Delafontaine's ferocious pet crocodile and dies, and then Prince Arthur feeds her to the reptile before his family eats her first. He then commits suicide by jumping into the crocodile's mouth. It's a funny musical . . . I swear it is.

Anyway, Isaac was supposed to pick me up bridal style and roll me down the ramp inside the crocodile's jaw, but because he was so "tired" he could barely lift me.

"What's up with you?" I asked him, though I had a potential idea of what might have been the cause.

He yawned, then cracked his neck. "I've just been, you know, here, there, and everywhere."

Like the scene of a murder, perhaps?

"You're a very vague person, Isaac Jackson."

He shrugged. "Not really. But if you want the truth, I'm so tired because, funny enough, I've been having nightmares."

I stiffened. "Why is that funny?"

Isaac winked. "I have dark humor."

"Is that so? What are they about?" I took a step closer to him, trying to appear approachable. I was sick of playing a constant guessing game. Sick of the fact that he could spill his heart out one minute, then barely look at me the next.

Isaac studied his fingernails. "They're about death mostly. Well, sometimes they're about failing English, but mostly they're about death. Not hard in a city like this. Oh! Sorry. I heard you were at the bank the other day when those people . . ." He trailed off, staring at me, his green eyes never blinking. His fingers twitched like he wanted to reach out to me, but he seemed to think better of it and stuffed his hands in his pockets. "How was that?" he asked softly.

Like he doesn't know. "Not good, Isaac. Not good."

He yawned again, and the sincerity in his voice vanished as quickly as it appeared. "I can imagine. I'm sorry you had to see it. Must have sucked."

Isaac's eyes shifted away from me, and he fiddled with his watch. "Look, I'm too tired to be here today. I need to go home."

"What? You can't just ditch rehearsal. Mrs. Miller will kill you."

He rolled his eyes and made a dash for the door when our director wasn't looking. Unfortunately for the rest of us, Mrs. Miller immediately realized his absence when she turned back around. Her red hair resembled fire, the flames licking up and down the sides of her face. We now had no one to play Prince Arthur, and Mrs. Miller was convinced *somebody* had to practice rolling me into the crocodile, lest I do it wrong during the show and accidentally puncture its papier-mâché mouth with my foot.

"You!" Mrs. Miller pointed behind me and snapped her fingers. "Stage crew boy, can you lift her?"

I turned and caught Rylan looking frantically around himself, hoping Mrs. Miller was talking to anyone but him.

"Well, *can you*? You look strong."

"I—I mean, yeah. Yeah, I guess. But I don't . . ."

Mrs. Miller either didn't hear him or didn't care. She snapped her fingers again. "Pick her up."

"N-now?"

"Of course right now! This is the theater, boy. Time is of the essence. The show must go on!"

"The show must go on," Rylan mocked under his breath. He approached me warily, like he expected me to backhand him for touching me. I didn't really care. Participating in drama club had

forced me not to mind who touched me or saw me half-naked as I changed my clothes. It wasn't like Rylan looping his long arms around my waist and cradling me against his chest meant anything. Strictly professional.

I leaned my head against his shoulder and tried to relax. His soft cotton shirt brushed against my cheek, and his hands wouldn't stop shaking. *Poor Rylan.* It was obvious from the moment I met him that he was the kind of person who got stage fright. Parading a "lifeless" girl around the stage in front of thirty people certainly wasn't helping.

"I'm not cuddling with you or anything," I whispered, trying to keep my lips still so Mrs. Miller wouldn't notice. "I'm supposed to be dead, you know."

"Yeah." His breathing sounded labored. "Yeah, I know."

"Am I too heavy or something?"

"Nope." More hard breathing. "You're fine."

"You're supposed to drop me now."

"Yeah. Okay, right. Yeah."

Fortunately for Rylan, his fifteen seconds of fame was coming to an end. But unfortunately for me, he was so nervous that he confused *drop* with *throw*, and he chucked me into the crocodile's mouth so forcefully that I landed in a heap on the reptile's squishy red tongue (which was actually a bathmat). The top set of its teeth crashed down on my head. Mrs. Miller screamed. The rest of the cast burst out laughing. But at least my foot didn't break through its mouth.

Oh. No, wait. It did.

CHAPTER THIRTEEN

"Go away. I'm mad at you." I fluffed my pillow and forcefully flipped a page in the book I was reading when Iron Phantom appeared in my room later that night.

"Me?" He threw a hand over his heart. "What did I possibly do?"

"You mean other than being all sweet and consoling when we're alone together and then basically acting like a jerk at school? It's not really fair." I turned another page without even reading it.

Iron Phantom sat on the edge of my bed, drumming his fingers on his leg. "I think you're overreacting."

A short laugh ripped through my chest. "Okay, Isaac. Whatever."

"Abigail, last time I checked my name's Steve. I don't even know an Isaac."

I gripped the edge of my book. He was trying to be cute, and I wouldn't smile. I wouldn't give him the satisfaction—

"Hey, are you ignoring me?" Iron Phantom lay on his stomach

beside me, his black combat boots waving through the air as he kicked his feet. I held my book a bit higher.

"I'm trying to," I said.

"And how's that working out for you?" His gloved fingers crawled across my mattress and started poking me in the arm.

I would not smile, I would not smile, I would not . . .

"Why is Abigail Hamilton's face frozen into a look of constant constipation?" Iron Phantom began in a low, dramatic voice. "A shitty story that. She was once a fair maiden, but she frowned so much her lips got stuck that way forevermore."

"You don't say."

"Oh, I do. And no one would kiss her. And then she died. It was tragic."

My book fell to my lap.

Kiss her.

The words echoed in my head as they fell off his lips.

Kiss her.

I totally caved. I smiled. "This Abigail died just because some guy wouldn't kiss her? Sounds like a pansy to me."

"Definitely. Thank goodness that, although that Abigail shares your name, she isn't you." Iron Phantom placed my book on my nightstand and tugged me off the bed. "And now that I've distracted you—"

"I wouldn't go that far."

Iron Phantom riffled through a pocket in his suit. "Okay. Fine. I apologize. I know I'm not always as charming in the real world as I am when I'm here." He pushed something at my chest. "Now, come on. We have work to do."

"Huh?" I examined the object he shoved at me. A black mask covered in delicate lace flowers. "What's this?"

"Abigail, I know you're smarter than that question." He took the mask from me and got to work tying it behind my ears. "I tried to look up that E.D.D. you mentioned, but I didn't find anything. *However*, I do know that there's a shipment of microchips arriving at a warehouse by the river, so we're off to do a bit of reconnaissance. Do you still have that sweatshirt I gave you?"

My mind was working overtime as he dug through my closet, eventually tossing me his black sweatshirt and a pair of black cotton gloves. He thought he'd distracted me, but I was still drawn to his identity, puzzled why he wouldn't just give up and confess already. He was infuriating. If I hadn't already let myself be dragged into the mystery—of him and of the microchips—then I would have ignored him completely and told him to get lost. But I was already in so deep that I couldn't crawl out of the hole I'd dug for myself even if I tried.

"How do you know about the new chips coming in?" I asked as I pulled on the sweatshirt and the gloves. Dressed all in black, we totally matched. We just needed a dorky team name to go along with it.

He reached for my hand. "I know things, Abigail. You know, you'd make a pretty cute superhero," he added, flicking the side of my mask. "Time to go."

When I blinked, my room dissolved before my eyes. We were huddled behind two thorny bushes, dirt and tiny stones pressing into my knees. The warehouse at the bottom of the hill was alive with a flurry of activity. It was an old building, rusty, with holes in the roof and graffiti on the walls. Pretty inconspicuous as far as shady warehouses went.

Under the cover of darkness, an assembly line of men and women passed wooden crates from the hull of a vessel on the river. Flashlights reflected off the water and the steel beams in the building. None of the workers spoke, their movements perfectly choreographed for maximum productivity. Pick up crate. Turn.

Hand it off. Pick up another crate. Rinse and repeat. They looked like robots. And that made my heart pound all the more.

"They're very efficient." I felt the overwhelming need to make small talk, anything to reassure me I wasn't kneeling on the dusty ground alone.

Iron Phantom chuckled darkly. "Got that right. Do you recognize anyone? Anyone your dad works with?"

We were far enough away that our whispering couldn't be heard. But we were also far enough away that I couldn't see anyone clearly without super vision.

"We can get closer," Iron Phantom suggested. He squeezed my hand, and suddenly we stood by a cluster of trees halfway down the hill. I peeked between the branches, aware of the super's shallow breaths on the back of my neck. From this angle, we could see through an open garage door on the side of the warehouse. Inside, men wearing gloves and surgical masks took objects from the crates, injected them with something in a syringe, then gently replaced them one by one.

Nothing about this looked right. Why bring a group of people out in the dead of night to unpack boxes and use needles if what you were doing was ethical? You wouldn't. You wouldn't do that unless you were up to something, unless you were trying to keep a secret from someone.

A man in a suit and tie approached one of the workers. His bald head caught the light from one of the flashlights. He was built a little like a boulder—short, but as hard as a rock. The buttons of his shirt stretched over his muscular chest. He cupped his hand over the man's ear, muttered something, then carried on his way with his hands behind his back. He reached the end of the assembly line and turned around. Seeing the familiar handlebar mustache, I gasped.

"I know him, I know him," I whispered. "That's my dad's security advisor. His name's Wallace."

"You're sure?"

I nodded. "Positive." I'd recognize that furry caterpillar on his face anywhere.

"Security," Iron Phantom mused. "Let's see how secure he's keeping those microchips." He stepped away from our hideout. "I'm going in. Stay here."

"What? No way." I wouldn't let him drag me out here just to leave me standing in the woods. Absolutely not.

"Unless you learned how to teleport this afternoon and didn't tell me, you're staying here. You're not risking your safety," he hissed, eyes flashing dangerously.

"Steve—"

"No. I'll be right back, I'm stealing one of those chips."

I bit back a retort, but it didn't matter. I blinked and he was gone. If I squinted enough, I could just pick out the curve of his shoulder hiding behind a dark sedan. Teleportation or not, I didn't see how he would get close enough to swipe a chip. There were too many people around, and if memory served me right, Wallace had eyes like a hawk.

"You have five minutes to get those crates into the truck!" Wallace announced. He walked over to a semitruck parked next to the warehouse and greeted the driver. Iron Phantom took the opportunity to sneak into the building.

"This is ridiculous," I muttered. Leaving the safety of the trees, I crept down the hill. Immediately I stepped on a particularly crunchy leaf. I froze in my tracks. I counted slowly from ten, waiting for a shout or the glow of a flashlight to signal my cover was blown.

Three . . . two . . . one . . .

Nothing.

I reached the riverbank with no further complications. Iron Phantom hadn't come out yet. I scanned the inside of the warehouse, looking into the shadows—anywhere a super could find a good hiding spot.

I jumped back when the men and women filed out, carrying crates toward the truck. Should I try to steal a chip? I didn't see Iron Phantom, and this could be our only chance to find out what these things really were. My arm flinched, fingers begging me to reach out, trip the woman with the perfect bun on the crown of her head, and take the crate. I could do it. I wasn't a super, but I could be one just this once. I could save the day if I just reached a little farther. . . .

The woman stepped away from my hiding spot on the side of the building. Slumping against the wall, my fingers fell to my side. This superhero thing was a lot harder than I thought.

Slowly, I edged around the doorframe. Only one person remained inside. A skinny man wearing an oversized lab coat fumbled with the final crate, and a few of the chips rattled on a metal tray.

"Drat," the man grunted, wiping his brow. I could see his hands shaking in the moonlight filtering through cracks in the roof.

How did I approach this? Did I announce myself? Smack him on the head with something? My dad and brother always taught me how to avoid people, never how to confront them.

Finally, placing a lid on the crate, he turned to leave. His breath caught when he spotted me standing just inside the door, still deciding whether to run in fear or punch him in the face.

"A super," he whispered, clutching the crate to his chest.

I tilted my head, confused. *What?* Then I remembered. *The mask.*

"You—you're a super," he said again.

"Uh . . ."

"Actually, you're mistaken," Iron Phantom called from atop a ceiling beam. He teleported in front of the man and cracked his knuckles. "She's not a super." He flashed the guy a wide grin. "But I am."

When the man's face paled and he let out a nervous squeak, I almost felt bad. Almost.

"Whatcha got there?" Iron Phantom moved toward the crate.

"Wallace," the man tried to yell out, but his voice reached only a whisper.

"Nope, not Wallace. I just want to see. Give me one of those chips, and I won't throw my elbow into your temple."

Way to be persuasive.

I took a few steps across the floor. "Is that really necessary?" Iron Phantom had never displayed any type of violent tendencies before—at least not ones that I was privy to. Seeing him this way, shoulders stiff, ready to strike, shocked me.

"W-Wallace!" the guy screeched. "Wallace! It's him!"

"Goddamn," Iron Phantom groaned. A flash of a fist. The man crumpled to the ground.

"What did you do?" My voice shook. I thought he would just steal a chip and get out, not hurt anyone in the process.

"I didn't kill him. He'll live." Likely not without a concussion was what he failed to mention. A punch from a super must have hurt like hell.

Iron Phantom was busy collecting the chips that had scattered across the ground when three gunshots echoed outside the warehouse. A scream tore through my throat. Wallace, along with two other men, ran into the building. Ducking into the shadows under a ladder, I found a long plank of wood. Light enough to lift, but heavy enough to hopefully do some damage. I didn't want to do this—injure someone. But the crate of microchips lay abandoned at the center of the floor, Iron Phantom hidden in another patch of shadows kitty-corner to me. We hadn't come this far to leave empty-handed.

A warm breath crested over my ears as Iron Phantom appeared behind me. "So I'm thinking I'll be the distraction while you snatch the chips," he whispered.

We watched Wallace prowl toward the unconscious man. He picked up a stray chip, rubbing it between the fingers of his left hand while he held his gun steady in his right.

Iron Phantom patted my shoulder before vanishing, and then his voice was in my head. *Give it all you got, Bazooka.*

He reappeared on one of the ceiling beams, whistling. Wallace and his two comrades looked up, distracted, leaving my path to the microchips clear.

"This isn't the venue I would have chosen for my criminal activities," Iron Phantom said, looking around. "But I suppose there's a certain charm to it."

Wallace responded by firing off two shots, but they pinged against the rusty walls, passing through air that hadn't been empty two seconds ago.

"Down here." Iron Phantom stood in the farthest corner from the door, drawing Wallace a few steps closer to him and away from me. I crept out of my hiding spot, carrying my two-by-four. I was twenty feet away. Then ten.

"So what are these things?" Iron Phantom asked, pacing along the wall. Wallace followed the super's movements with his gun, but he didn't shoot. "Because if it was something that could be bought in a grocery store, then I have a feeling you wouldn't be pointing a gun at me."

"I'm pointing a gun at you because you're a danger to society, you imbecile," Wallace snapped.

"Imbecile. Never been called that before. I'll take it."

I was five feet away.

Iron Phantom continued. "Those microchips of yours seem to be very valuable. Why is that?"

Two feet away. I bent over, scooping up a handful of fallen chips and shoving them in my pocket.

Take a few more, Iron Phantom said. *I want to make sure we have enough.*

I did as he said, then straightened up.

Three tiny microchips tumbled free of my pocket and scattered across the ground.

"Crap," I heard Iron Phantom say.

Wallace's men turned, weapons raised. I knew I didn't have another option. Hurt or be hurt. Survival of the fittest. Hiking up my two-by-four, I spun in a half circle, smacking the man closest to me in the back. He fell to the ground, chin cracking loudly when it met the concrete. Blood dribbled from his mouth.

Wallace whirled at the commotion. "There are two of you?" he yelled. "Who are *you*?"

I pretended my plank of wood was a lightsaber as I swung it near his face. "I'm your worst nightmare." I'd always wanted to say that to someone. Unfortunately my voice wavered just enough for it to sound unconvincing.

"I don't think so." Wallace chuckled and pointed his gun between my eyes.

My two-by-four fell to the ground with a clatter.

The world faded away. The barrel of the gun was all I could see. A black hole growing larger and larger, consuming my vision. The very thing I dreamt, the end of the nightmare that kept me awake for hours screaming. Here it was in stunning Technicolor. Like in my nightmares, I couldn't find the strength to move. Wallace's finger tightened on the trigger.

Iron Phantom took out the third man with a swift kick to the head before materializing right behind Wallace. He wrapped one arm around Wallace's neck, the other smashing his gun to the floor. Wallace squeezed his eyes shut and wailed at the sound of his wrist snapping.

"Give me a reason," Iron Phantom snarled. "Give me a reason why I shouldn't snap your neck right now."

"I—p-please," Wallace wheezed. He tried to throw a punch, but the bones of his wrist stuck out unnaturally, and the large man slumped against Iron Phantom's chest in pain.

"Not good enough." Iron Phantom's grip tightened. Wallace's face turned purple.

If I was a good person, I would have told him to stop. But tonight I didn't feel like being a good person, not when Wallace had just come *this close* to putting a bullet in my brain.

"What are those things?" Iron Phantom nodded to the half-empty crate at our feet. Wallace opened his mouth but couldn't speak through Iron Phantom's chokehold. "Tell me! Tell—"

The three of us froze at a loud *flap, flap, flap, flap* coming from the sky. Lights shone down through a hole in the roof, illuminating the floor, putting us in full view of the helicopter in the air. A voice yelled from a speaker above, but it was impossible to hear over the drumming of the rotor blades. Or the sound of my heart pounding out of my chest.

"You lucked out," Iron Phantom said to Wallace. His fist reared back, ready to strike again. But before he could move, my plank of wood came crashing down on Wallace's head. The board snapped in two, and Wallace hit the deck like a sack of potatoes.

A good person would have felt sorry.

I didn't.

"Did you really just knock him out with a chunk of wood?" Iron

Phantom asked. Above us, a door on the side of the helicopter slid open and bodies began rappelling toward the ground. Iron Phantom held out his hand expectantly and wiggled his fingers.

He didn't look anxious to escape our new pursuers. A grin split across his face, excited and powerful and full of adrenaline. A nervous chuckle escaped my mouth. Then, suddenly, it was like a dam split open, and I couldn't stop laughing.

I took Iron Phantom's hand. "I couldn't let you have all the fun, now could I?"

CHAPTER FOURTEEN

I expected him to teleport me home, but home wasn't where we ended up.

A mad-scientist laboratory was.

We appeared in the room a little after midnight, surrounded by humming machines and winking, colored lights. Iron Phantom swiped a stack of papers from a computer desk nearby, shoving them in one of the drawers and locking it before taking the microchips I'd collected off my hands. My heart beat a heavy rhythm in the back of my throat. We actually did it. I couldn't believe we *actually* managed to steal the chips without getting caught . . . or killed. Forget landing the lead in the musical, tonight had to be my proudest accomplishment. A damn shame I couldn't write *villainous activities and superhero stealth* on my résumé.

I tugged the knot out of the ribbon at the back of my head and peeled my mask from my sweaty cheeks as I followed Iron Phantom across the floor. As fluorescent lights flickered to life, more machines emerged from the shadows. The back wall was covered in screens revealing security cameras in various sectors throughout the city. A large monitor showed the deserted entrance of the City Bank downtown. Another, on the far end, displayed the red tile floor of the Morriston High School lobby.

"What is this place?" I asked, watching Iron Phantom carefully place a chip under a large microscope. If the countertops weren't covered in computers or microscopes, they were obstructed by beeping metallic boxes with antennas and glass observation windows. Rows of red lasers scanned back and forth along an empty tray in some type of futuristic microwave. In the back corner sat a cylindrical MRI scanner, blue and yellow wires trailing onto the floor from its disabled body. If he told me he was building a flux capacitor in a DeLorean to take us back in time to 1985, I would have believed him.

"All good supers have a secret lab," Iron Phantom grunted. He turned a dial on the side of his microscope, his eye still pressed into the lens.

Not Connor, I thought. My brother was lucky he could do long division; science wasn't his thing. Of course, he wasn't alone. I could comprehend what they taught us in school. But here, with Iron Phantom's pinging computers and pulsing lasers, I was so out of my league.

I spun in a slow circle, taking it all in. A small glass ball covered in clear spikes sat on top of a map of Morriston's bus system. It looked like something belonging to a punk rock band, not a superhero. But it seemed innocuous enough . . . until the glass glowed bright blue as my hand moved closer. I quickly pulled back—you know, in case it electrocuted me or whatever.

"That's just a paperweight." Iron Phantom laughed. "It changes color when it senses body heat. It doesn't bite."

The glass turned yellow this time as my hand closed in. I backed up. It faded to clear.

"And you can sit down if you want," he continued, rolling a stool next to his workbench. I started to move forward but paused as soon as I noticed a wrought iron staircase curling upward on the other side of the room. Fancy flowered designs were twisted into the railings, far too decorative for just an ordinary laboratory.

"Are we in a house? Is this—is this *your* house?" I took a step toward the stairs and the wooden door gleaming at the top. This was where Iron Phantom lived, it had to be. Upstairs there were surely more rooms and maybe photographs and possessions and—

"Don't go up there." In a blink, he was blocking my view, his eyes wild but also a bit cautious. "Please don't go up there."

"Why? Is that where you store all the dead bodies?"

He wrapped a hand around my elbow and led me to the stool beside his workbench. He sat beside me, absentmindedly fiddling with a knob on his microscope.

"Believe it or not, we're not the only ones home," he said. "So try to be quiet. I don't want someone coming down here and seeing me dressed like . . ." He gestured to his suit.

"Your family doesn't know that you're . . . ?"

"No. Not the family that's upstairs anyway."

As he preoccupied himself with the microchips again, I couldn't help but wonder who was upstairs. Isaac had mentioned once that he moved in with his uncle after his parents died, but was there anyone else? I kept waiting for him to tell me the truth—after what we'd just gone through it only seemed logical—but the words never came.

"How do you know what you're doing?" I asked, watching Iron Phantom pry one of the chips open with tweezers. His tongue poked between his lips.

He patted the table with his palm, and a glass beaker shook in its holder. "A lot of this stuff used to belong to my parents. They were in love with science. They did experiments on everything, even on the perfect plant food to make my mom's rosebushes grow." He laughed, but the hint of moisture gathering near the corners of his eyes betrayed him.

I decided to steer the conversation to something that didn't involve parents—his or mine. "Why didn't you kill Wallace?" The morbid question made me flinch a little. "You could have, right? You looked like you knew what you were doing."

Iron Phantom hummed in agreement. "Yeah," he said carefully. His tongue swiped over his teeth, tasting his words before deciding which to use. "But heroes don't destroy things. They help. I want to help people."

I smiled, remembering Connor saying something similar after Iron Phantom set city hall on fire. My brother and I thought he was dangerous back then—we were afraid. Now I didn't know how I could have been so wrong.

"Did you want me to kill him?" he asked.

For a moment, I did. That endless moment between Iron Phantom knocking the gun from Wallace's hand and his frantic gasps for air. He tried to kill me. I wanted him to get what he deserved. But I knew how it felt to lose a family member. Surely Wallace had someone out there who cared about him. No matter what he almost did to me, it would have been a horrible crime to steal him away from them.

"No." I sighed. "No, I didn't."

"Good. I didn't want to either." He reached for my hands, tracing his fingers along the lines in my palms. His lips were puckered and red and raw as he dragged them over his teeth. I scooted forward in my seat, my heart pattering against my ribs.

As I glanced down at our fingers intertwined in his lap, I found myself unable to stop thinking of a different evening. His hands, covered in blood as he pushed his power into the young girl's chest. What happened after wasn't something I could have anticipated, but I still felt a sense of responsibility, the guilt weighing like a stone on my chest.

"The other night . . . ," I began tentatively. "When I asked you to heal the girl outside the bank, I didn't realize it would . . ."

"Hurt me?" he finished, offering me a sad little smile. "Pretty ironic, isn't it?"

"Pretty sad is what I was thinking. I'm almost sorry I asked."

Iron Phantom's eyes widened. "Don't apologize. I knew what I was getting into." Pinching the bridge of his nose, he looked past me to the staircase at the opposite side of the room. "Powers don't come without consequences. I can mend broken bones or close up cuts. I can take away pain. But when I take it away from someone, it has to go *somewhere*. So, as you noticed, it gets absorbed into me. For a period of time, I feel whatever they were feeling, no matter how painful."

"So with that girl—"

"She was dying and bleeding out, and I felt that. I'm good at healing smaller things, but fatal wounds I can't handle. Believe me, I've tried more times than I can count."

Like with his parents. He hadn't just seen them die; he'd felt it too.

I was sick to my stomach.

"That girl wasn't the only one who took a bullet to the chest that night," I said.

Iron Phantom looked at his shoes. "Not really."

I had hoped I'd been wrong. God, I had never wanted to be wrong more than in that moment, staring at the boy with too much blood on his hands to bear. When he first healed the girl, a part of me thought he only trembled and screamed from the amount of energy he needed to exert to heal a gunshot wound. I hadn't wanted to believe he was experiencing one himself. But really I just hadn't been able to admit what was happening until now. If Iron Phantom was in any more pain, he wouldn't have been able to teleport to safety when the police arrived. Someone could have caught him. Someone could have exposed him as a dangerous criminal before the entire city, and he would only have me to blame.

"I'm sor—"

He held up a hand. "I told you not to apologize. It's not that big of a deal."

"Yes, it is. You healed me once too."

Leaning close to me, he tucked a strand of hair behind my ear. "I'd do it again. And again, and again." His hands skimmed up my arms, resting on my shoulders. "Thanks for all your help tonight," Iron Phantom said. A shy smile lingered on his lips. "We make a pretty great team, huh?"

His face was getting closer, less than a foot away. I leaned forward, bracing my hands on his knees. The green in his eyes looked impossibly bright and his smile impossibly happy.

"I guess you're okay," I told him.

"You guess?"

I shrugged. "I make really educated guesses. Ask anyone."

"That's okay. *I guess* I'll take your word for it." He was closer now, closer still. His head tilted to the side, the warmth of him flowing across the small space between us, settling into me.

I leaned farther, my chair creaking slightly beneath me.

Then he pressed his lips to mine.

Kissing him was like teleporting, but without ever leaving the ground. I couldn't tell where my stomach ended and the rest of my body began. My heart beat against my ribs so quickly that it felt like my chest had been set on fire. Everything tingled. It was slow and smooth and sweet. It was perfect.

I scooted to the edge of my seat, nearly falling into him. One of his hands wound around my waist, while the other tangled in my hair. He pulled a bit too hard, and I released a muffled squeak.

"Sorry," he chuckled awkwardly, pulling away. Shaking my head, I drew him back again.

I couldn't take it anymore. I needed to know his name, if not solely for my sanity than at least for my sense of logic. There was no way this relationship could grow into anything more than flirty jabs and nighttime confessions if I didn't know who he really was.

Without breaking our kiss, I found the edge of his mask a few inches beneath his jawline. My fingers touched sticky, warm skin as I pushed it up, up, over his chin toward his lips. I was so close to discovering his identity. If I could just keep going . . .

A timer beeped on one of his machines.

I jerked back, gasping for air, but Iron Phantom held me in place with a hand on my wrist. "If we ignore it, it might go away," he said, his breathing equally as labored.

I raised my eyebrows.

"It was just a suggestion." He moved away to tap at a keypad attached to the machine.

As I raked my fingers through my hair, I noticed they were shaking. *Did that seriously just happen?*

"Uh . . . Abigail? Come here a second." Iron Phantom was comparing some type of data from the beeping machine with a slide under his microscope. I didn't know what he could need me for, but his voice had dropped all the humor it held before he kissed me, so I did as he asked.

"What is it?" I leaned over his shoulder, watching while he pressed his eye against the microscope. Underneath the lens, one of the chips lay open, a tiny silver tube inside the metal cover. Iron Phantom hummed to himself, sounding a lot like my anatomy teacher when he got excited about dissecting fetal pigs. Picking up tweezers, Iron Phantom poked at the silver tube and refocused the lens with a twist of a dial.

He hummed again. "Look at this." He pushed the microscope in front of me.

"What are *those*?" At first, I nearly cringed away, repulsed. The objects under the lens looked like little silver bugs. They had round bodies and pointy pincers for legs. Spiders maybe. I shivered. Creepy crawlies and I didn't exactly have a healthy relationship.

"What am I looking at?" Whatever those things were, they weren't moving. Completely still, they gathered in clusters along the inside of the tube. Maybe they were sleeping. Or dead. I hoped they were dead.

Curling his lip in disgust, Iron Phantom plucked the tube of metal spiders off the tray. "Nanobots," he said.

"Oh, come on. What kind of cheesy science fiction film did you fall out of?"

Iron Phantom walked past the beeping machine and dropped the tube inside one of the metal boxes with pulsing red lasers instead. He spent almost a full minute programming codes into a keypad on the glass door before shutting it and letting the box whirl to life.

"It's not science fiction," he said. "I have superpowers. Don't tell me you don't believe in nanobots."

I watched the lasers sweep back and forth inside the box. To me, superpowers weren't that weird. Some people had green eyes, some people had blue eyes. Some people had superpowers, some didn't. But something a scientist engineered in a lab freaked me out.

"So what do they do?"

"Whatever you want them to." Iron Phantom sighed. "That's

kind of the problem. Usually, they're used for medicinal things, but you can program them to do just about anything."

"Anything?" Suddenly, Iron Phantom's mad-scientist laboratory seemed a million times smaller. Someone in city hall ordered an entire boatload of those things, and they could do *anything*? "Why do I have a sneaking suspicion that these aren't tracking devices?"

I watched his Adam's apple bob as he swallowed. "Because, Abigail, I honestly don't think they are. I think they're something far more complex."

"But . . . but you can figure out what they do, can't you?"

"I hope so," Iron Phantom said, though he sounded uncertain. "It might take a while. I don't know how many tests I'll need to run. They're safe as long as someone doesn't activate them."

"That's going to be a bit of an issue eventually, don't you think?"

Squeezing his eyes tight, Iron Phantom tugged at the back of his mask. His classic nervous tell. My confidence in the fate of Morriston began to wane.

"We'll figure it out," he promised. "I swear we'll figure it out."

We watched the red lasers. They blinked quickly, multiple times a second. But every now and then, they slowed down, and the interior of the machine shined blood red.

"So . . ." I leaned against Iron Phantom's shoulder. "Now what?"

"Now," he said, "we wait."

CHAPTER FIFTEEN

Waiting was taking longer than I anticipated.

Iron Phantom hadn't contacted me in over a week. Connor was working nonstop after failing to save the woman outside the City Bank, and my dad was partaking in nightly televised press conferences, during which he assured the city he would put Iron Phantom and his evil ways to rest—though he refused to give details.

All the details I needed were locked in a laboratory in Iron Phantom's basement. The mystery rolled around in my head at all hours of the day. Whose orders had Wallace been working on? My dad's? Every time the thought crossed my mind, I shook it violently away, my nerves plummeting.

And yet . . .

The worst part was that Wallace had opened his big mouth and spilled the details of the new "supervillain" aiding Iron Phantom. He didn't reveal much, just that it was a girl and she had a wicked arm with a two-by-four. I would have laughed if I hadn't almost choked on my breakfast when I read the article in the *Morriston Gazette*. Hands shaking, I proceeded to stuff the mask Iron Phantom had given me safely in the back of my bra drawer, where Dad and Connor would never dare to go.

The only thing that remotely distracted me from agonizing about the nanobots was my next musical rehearsal. *Hall of Horrors* wasn't improving, but I was hopeful that would change. Isaac was actually making a commitment not to cut out early for once (he even shut off his cell phone), meaning that the number one item on Mrs. Miller's rehearsal agenda was to block Isaac's and my most pivotal scene.

Because our characters were supposed to be in love and whatever, we had to kiss. Our beautiful, romantic, heart-stopping lip lock occurred at the top of act 2. Honestly, I hadn't thought about it once with everything else that was going on, but today I found I couldn't stop. Last week, in Iron Phantom's lab, I hopelessly struck out when I tried to uncover his identity, but I wouldn't make the same mistake twice. When Isaac kissed me, he would either make my heart lurch and my toes curl . . . or he wouldn't. One way or another, I would finally know the truth.

"You need to give me all the dirty details." Sarah smirked after Mrs. Miller announced the day's rehearsal schedule. Isaac was busy bouncing on his toes and stretching. He looked like he was preparing to run the Morriston Marathon, not peck me on the lips. I tried to remain calm. If Isaac was who I had a hunch he was, then this kiss had the potential to be so much more than just practice.

I climbed the wooden steps on the side of the stage, following Isaac into the glow of the spotlight as we awaited Mrs. Miller's instructions. "I promise I'll go easy on you," he said, grinning. My stomach flopped.

"Put your hands on her waist," Mrs. Miller coached Isaac. His fingers were freezing, like he had shoved them in a bucket of ice. Mine weren't much better. I was so nervous that I couldn't get them to quit trembling.

"Tilt your heads to the right. We don't want anyone smacking noses in front of an audience." The corners of Isaac's mouth quirked into a devilish grin. I tried to smile back, but nothing about a choreographed kiss was particularly romantic.

"Pucker up." We did. Mrs. Miller waved her hand like she was conducting an orchestra. The bracelets on her wrists jingled loudly. "And . . ."

He moved toward me. I couldn't see anything except glittering green eyes and a thin strip of perspiration dotting his hairline. A guy in the audience wolf-whistled. Our lips touched.

Yikes.

Isaac didn't quite grasp the concept of the stage kiss. The whole point of stage kissing is to look like you're passionately kissing the other person *without* actually doing it. Pucker up and *don't kiss*. It's like kissing your grandma. No emotions, entanglements, or tongue. Especially no tongue. Lips only. Isaac didn't get that.

As soon as our lips touched, his tongue thrust into my mouth like troops rushing a battlefield. He did some weird thing where he licked the back of my teeth so I could taste the cafeteria macaroni and cheese he ate for lunch. (Just a note, the macaroni and cheese had a tendency to taste like old socks.) His mouth kept making these weird clicking noises, reminding me of a giant crab waving its pincers on the beach. And as if all that wasn't fantastic enough, then he gripped my ass like he was trying to start a weed-whacker. *Vroom, vroom.* Tug on my butt. *Vroom, vroom.* Lick my teeth.

Yuck.

This had to be a joke, right? This most certainly was *not* what happened in the lab. He was trying to confuse me, throw me off Iron Phantom's trail. People didn't *seriously* kiss like that.

When we broke apart, our castmates cheered, stomping their feet. Sarah held her phone high above her head, snapping pictures. I only had to think of Sarah's massive Red Comet shrine to remember that collecting embarrassing photos was what my friend did best.

Isaac watched me with a smug smile on his lips, looking like he was ready for round two. All I wanted was to take a shower to wash the slimy remains of that assault off my body.

"You're screwing with me, right?" I demanded. "Is this a joke?"

For a split second, he almost looked hurt. "Whatever do you mean, Abigail? I'm not laughing." Then he winked. "See you later."

Isaac walked offstage just as Rylan pushed through the curtain and approached me. A soft purple towel bearing the Morriston mascot—the Fighting Frog—dangled from his fingers.

"You have a bit of spit on your chin," he said. "So . . . if you want to wipe it off or something . . ."

Talk about majorly embarrassing. I hid behind the towel while I wiped the spit—Isaac's spit—from my face. "Rylan Sloan, you are a born romantic."

Rylan scuffed his sneaker across the stage. "I try."

I tried to force myself to do homework that weekend, but as I threw down my pen, leaving a streak of blue ink on my notebook, I knew it wasn't going to happen. The sky was cloudy and gray, and I hadn't received a nanobot report from Iron Phantom in approximately eleven days, eighteen hours, and roughly thirty minutes. (But who was counting?) I honestly couldn't figure out if I wanted to see him or not. After the stage kiss from hell, I knew if I saw him—or Isaac—I might kick them both.

Dropping my unfinished homework on the floor beside my backpack, I retreated to my bed. I had been attempting not to think about him for the past few days . . . and I was failing. Miserably. I hated admitting it, but I often found myself sitting in school wondering what he could be up to. Did he teleport to another country for the afternoon, or was he sitting in the same classroom as me without my knowledge? Did he forget about me? I'd seen Iron Phantom so much lately, but now it was like he disappeared from Morriston.

"Knock, knock."

I jumped, almost shrieking when my window slid up a few inches and a gloved hand poked through.

Look who finally decided to show up. If he expected me to think everything was fine and dandy between us, then he had another thing coming.

I climbed off my bed. He was balanced precariously between my windowsill and a tree branch, grinning.

His smile did horrifically stupid things to my stomach.

"Can I come in?" Iron Phantom pushed the window up several more inches.

I frowned. "You can teleport, can't you? You don't need to wait for an invitation."

"Yeah, but . . . I thought it might be nice if I did, for once."

"Is that why I haven't heard from you in almost two weeks? You were waiting for an invitation there too?" I shoved the window up, and he took it upon himself to clamber through. Connor and my dad weren't home, but I shut my bedroom door out of habit anyway, taking a seat at my desk chair.

Iron Phantom leaned against the wall beside me. "You look pissed about something," he observed.

"Do I? Why could that be?" I tapped a finger against my chin while his eyes narrowed.

"Abigail, I've told you before, I can't read minds. If I did something to upset—"

I couldn't stop the words from spilling out. "You're an idiot, you know that?"

He recoiled. "Why's that?"

"Why's that?" I pushed out of my chair and stood before him, our chests nearly touching. "Should I spell it out for you, or would you prefer a diagram? As a general rule, it's usually frowned upon to kiss someone and then disappear for two weeks, especially if that someone has been testing nanobots with you. I thought we were a team, Steve."

He had the nerve to look relieved, like he thought that's all I was mad about. "I didn't show up because I don't have anything to report. I've been running a lot of tests, but nothing is conclusive." He rolled his bottom lip between his teeth. "Abigail, we are a team. I promise. We'll get matching T-shirts and everything if it makes you happy."

He gave me another one of those wide, charming grins, but I wasn't having it. "You could have just told me what was going on instead of leaving me in the dark."

"You're right, I could have." Iron Phantom winced. "Sorry?" He reached for me, tracing his fingers along my palms, just as he had when we were in his lab. I tried to fight it, but I could feel myself melting, my anger ebbing away. Like we were picking up exactly where we left off.

He was too good at trying to make me feel better. But this time I didn't want to feel better. Not after the way he lied to me and completely humiliated me at rehearsal.

I pulled my hands away.

"It's not right," I said, my voice surprisingly much stronger than

I anticipated. "What you've been doing. I'm not going to keep putting up with it."

"Abigail, we can get matching hats too. It's no big deal."

"No, that's not what I—What are you even doing here? You said you didn't have anything to tell me."

Iron Phantom shrugged. "Do I have to have a reason? I like coming here." He looked around the room, straightening a stack of textbooks on my desk. "You're here."

I snorted. "You say that like you actually missed me or something."

He moved on from the textbooks and started sorting through a coffee mug full of pens, separating them by color. "I think we're both guilty there. Of course . . ." He leveled his gaze at me. "It's not like we haven't seen each other in the *real world*."

The way he said the words had me jumping back like I'd been slapped. *The real world*. The one with musical rehearsals and stage kisses and boys who whispered one thing in your ear in private just to deny the truth in public. He was playing head games with me, just like before, and he needed to throw in the towel and admit it. If we really were a team, like he said, he finally owed me the truth.

"What crap were you trying to pull in rehearsal?" I let all my anger rush off me, flooding the space between us, sending the temperature in the room sky high. "Sucking my face off? We had a great kiss in your lab, a *perfect* kiss even, maybe the best kiss anyone could ever have, and then you thoroughly ruined it! You did a one-eighty like it was no big deal, like you were trying to throw it all back in my face. Like—Hey, why are you smiling?"

"You . . . you thought it was a great kiss?" he asked. *Pompous prick*.

I pushed my hands through my hair, groaning. Nothing was changing. He was as infuriating as usual. "Stop messing with me!

You were *there*. You *know* it was a great kiss. Just like you know that what you did to me in rehearsal wasn't fair. What you've been doing this whole time isn't fair. Now just fess up! Tell me. Tell me, once and for all, what is your name?"

The room grew silent. I didn't even think he was breathing. I knew I wasn't. He leaned against the wall, head tilted to the side like I'd spoken gibberish or something. I crossed my arms over my chest. If he told another lie, after everything we'd been through, I didn't know how I could move on from that.

"You . . ." Iron Phantom cleared his throat. "Abigail, you . . . you don't know?" Before I could answer, he pushed past me, pacing at the foot of my bed. "I can't believe you *really don't know*."

"Not true. You know exactly who I think you are. I know you aren't just some random person."

"Aren't I?"

"Oh my God." More head games. My fingers curled tight against my palms, so hard that my skin stung. What I did know was that the only guy with a big enough ego to pass as a super was Isaac Jackson. Like Connor, most supers were full of themselves, and Isaac was certainly no exception.

Isaac had been a fan of Iron Phantom from the start. It was Isaac who had gotten all anxious at rehearsal when Mrs. Miller mentioned Iron Phantom's name. Isaac who kept looking at me like he was privy to some giant joke that I didn't know the punch line to. *Isaac. Isaac. Isaac.*

Iron Phantom faced me. "You said you know who you *think* I am. *Think*," he spit the word back at me, his eyes blazing. "But you still aren't positive. Not after all the time we've spent together. Not after the first kiss, or hell, not even after the second!"

I could feel my face burning. How did he manage to turn this around so it was suddenly my fault?

"Go ahead!" he goaded. "Toss out a name, any name, and see what happens."

I opened my mouth, then promptly closed it. I couldn't say it. He needed to be the one to do it. That was the only way I would know if he was being honest.

Maybe this was another prank. Just another way for him to confuse me further.

"See?" Iron Phantom said. "You can't do it. You aren't sure."

Right as I was getting ready to lash out at him again, his anger faded completely, replaced by a sadness large enough to consume my entire bedroom. His tall frame seemed to shrink a little, curling in on himself.

"I guess I thought if anyone could figure it out, it would be you." He headed for my window. "I need to go."

"Are you kidding?" I finally regained my voice. "Go where?"

"I'm a superhero, Abigail. Duty calls." Any other super would have sounded suave when saying that. All macho in a let-me-flex-my-biceps-in-your-face-because-I'm-a-man kind of way. But he just sounded exhausted, like he wanted to be anywhere other than standing next to me. He sounded like he made a mistake. Like I was a mistake.

"Who are you off to save? No one in Morriston likes you, you know." *I like you,* I thought. *I really, really like you.* But I was so pissed off at him for being pissed off at me when I didn't even *do* anything that I almost didn't care if I hurt his feelings.

His lips lifted into a weak smile. "You like me." Iron Phantom's eyes no longer burned with an annoyed intensity but softened with compassion, like he forgave my sudden animosity toward him. "And I like you too. That's why I need to do this right. Let me do this the right way, please."

"What does that even mean?"

He shrugged. "Just have a little faith, Abigail."

Headlights flashed across the window, their glow momentarily flooding the room. I tore aside my curtains just in time to see my dad climb out of his car and stroll into the garage, cell phone pressed to his ear.

I glanced over my shoulder to Iron Phantom. "You're lucky he didn't come home five minutes soon—"

My bedroom was empty. He was gone.

CHAPTER SIXTEEN

Dear Abigail,

I will be at the Coffee Cabana on 2nd Avenue today at noon. I'll be there as me—the real me, no spandex necessary. I'd love to see you, if you are willing.

Sincerely,
The guy who can't wait for you to start calling him by his real name—not Steve

P.S. I put in an order for our matching T-shirts.

I found his note when I rolled out of bed the next morning, scribbled in green ink and taped to my window beside another one of his chocolate bars. Stuffing the candy in my mouth, I contemplated what to do next. Obviously, I wanted to know who he was, but I was also nervous that knowing would change everything between us. Right now he was an enigma, but what—or *who*—would he be in a few hours? If the mystery surrounding his identity disappeared, would we have anything left?

It would be almost too easy to call Sarah, confess everything, and ask for advice. I could trust her. She'd kept Connor's secret so far. But part of me didn't want a second opinion on Iron Phantom. Part of me was scared Sarah would convince me that meeting him in real life without his mask would be a bad idea. I was afraid she, like the rest of Morriston, would think he was dangerous and then run and tell my father with the intention of protecting me.

When Connor received superpowers, my mother's biggest fear—besides him being in constant danger—was that his personality would be different. That he wouldn't be Connor anymore. That he would become so consumed by his new abilities he would forget what really mattered and think he was above everyone else. What she failed to notice was that, at sixteen, Connor was already on the fast track to narcissism with or without the power to fly. He may have learned to defy gravity and spot an object the size of a Ping-Pong ball across a football field, but on the inside Connor remained a lovable doofus who sucked at doing math and spent far too much time fixing his hair in front of the bathroom mirror.

And so, by the time I finished debating whether or not I should meet my superhero, it was nearly time to leave my house. No matter what happened after I met him, I vowed not to let the discovery of his name change anything between us. Take away Connor's powers and dorky costume and he was still the same guy. Underneath Iron Phantom's mask, he was the same too. The Iron Phantom that took me to his thinking tree and to his lab—that was the real him. Whatever happened between us at school, for whatever reason, had been an act.

After making up my mind, I rushed into the kitchen, formulating a grand plan that involved snatching Connor's keys off the hook by the back door and driving his truck to the coffee shop without wrecking the darn thing. Riding the bus would take far too long. This plan would be perfect. I would write Connor a note, making sure to mention something about going to buy coffee or doughnuts—any type of food that would distract him enough so he wouldn't freak out. He would read it and smile, scratching his belly in anticipation, and *voilà*! He would completely forget I ever drove his truck in the first place.

The plan was flawless. Or it would have been . . . had Connor not already been waiting for me when I stepped through the kitchen door.

"Abby." He set his cereal bowl on the counter and wiped his mouth with a napkin. Immediately I knew something was off. Connor never used napkins. "Going somewhere?"

"Just to get some doughnuts." I stepped around him, snatching his truck keys. His eyes tracked me as I crossed the kitchen. He was acting like a weirdo, as usual, but I decided to ignore it. Until he cut me off when I tried to exit the room.

"Why don't I believe you?"

"I don't know, Connor. That's on you." My heart started to race. My master plan was falling down the drain, but I could still escape if I hurried.

"You're getting doughnuts, you say?" Connor put a hand on his chin. "But who are you getting doughnuts *with*?"

I answered just a bit too fast. "No one. Why?"

Connor pursed his lips. He took a step back, prowling in front of the cabinets like some kind of jungle cat. "It's interesting, Abby. Very . . . interesting." His teeth bared in a grimace.

"What's interesting, Connor?"

"Oh, I don't know. Just that you conveniently happened to be downtown two weeks ago when that woman was shot at the bank. It's interesting that her daughter didn't die after being injured so severely."

"It sounds like a miracle to me. If you're done playing detective, I'm going to—"

"Hold up." His fingers clenched around my elbow. "At first, I didn't think much of how convenient it all was. So what if you were downtown? Sure Dad would be pissed, but I didn't tell him. So what if the little girl lived? Like you said, miracles happen. But then, last night when I was working, I flew to the children's hospital to visit Kelsea—that's the little girl's name. *Kelsea.* And *interestingly* enough, she mentioned a girl who tried to help her. A girl who looked just like . . . you." Connor's fingers tightened on my arm. "She mentioned someone else too."

"Connor . . ." But I didn't know how to finish. He knew. He knew everything. I tried to pull away from him, but he held firm. As his fingers pierced my skin, I knew this wasn't a bluff.

"Kelsea said there was a man in a black mask who tried to heal her, and then when she looked back he was gone. *Disappeared.* Hmm . . . I wonder who knows how to do that?" Connor cocked his head, pretending to think. "Oh, right. Iron Phantom."

"You don't understand."

His laugh was as sharp as a knife. "I understand that I told you to stay away from him. I understand that he's dangerous."

"Connor, he tried to save that girl. You just said it yourself."

"Abby, he's earning your trust so he can stab you in the back!"

Finally I managed to get out of his grip. I pushed him back, and he stumbled into the refrigerator. Annoying or not, Iron Phantom was good and kind. He'd been there for me, even when my father and brother were not, and Connor was just spewing lies.

"You're wrong," I said.

"No, I'm honest."

"Honest?" I finally snapped. Long overdue. "You want to talk about being *honest*? Okay, let's do that. Iron Phantom is *honestly* trying to save this city, and you're too busy catering to your screaming fans to pay attention. Maybe if you took a minute to listen instead of checking out like you did with Mom, then you could save people too!"

Connor's face went pale. My hateful words hung in the air between us, like smoke after a fire. Our entire house might as well have been in ruins.

"What?" he asked in a whisper.

"Where were you when she died?" The words to the question I'd been too terrified to ask for three years spilled out in a rush, stabbing the air around us, causing Connor to take small steps back with each syllable. "Why didn't you do something? You had your powers. You could have tried—"

"Who says I didn't?" He raised his voice to a hysterical level, loud enough to match mine. I hadn't seen our father all morning, but I knew he had to be at the office or else he surely would have come running.

"You don't know a thing, Abby." A muscle ticked in Connor's jaw. "Maybe I did try. *Maybe* I felt something that day. *Maybe* I clumsily flew downtown because I still wasn't good at using my powers." He advanced on me, backing me up until the knob on the pantry door dug into my spine. "Maybe I looked for Mom and maybe there were too many people running around the bank and maybe . . . maybe when I heard the gunshot . . . maybe *I froze*." He spit out the words through clenched teeth. "Maybe I froze like a scared little child, and maybe if I hadn't done that, she would still be alive."

We stood staring at each other, chest to chest. I could barely breathe.

"Why?" I asked him. My whisper sounded like a scream in the stillness of the kitchen.

"Why didn't I try harder?"

"Why didn't you *tell me*?"

"Because no one wants to hear the story about how the hero failed to save the day." Pushing around me, he headed for the door. "You're blinded by your naivety, Abby. I'm going to protect this city, and if I have to take down your supervillain friend to do it, then I will."

After a minute, I heard the front door slam. A red streak flew past the windows moments later. When he was gone, I slumped to the floor, leaning my head against the wall. It wasn't Connor's fault that our mother was gone, even if he thought otherwise. Even if maybe I thought otherwise too. But we had been kids back then; things were different now. Connor needed to realize who the real enemy was. And if my words had managed to break him instead of forcing him to see sense, then this time, that heroic failure was all on me.

I sat on the kitchen floor replaying my fight with Connor in my head for fifteen minutes before I remembered I was supposed to be meeting Iron Phantom downtown. I rushed to the Coffee Cabana, squealing the tires as I swung Connor's truck into the parking lot at five minutes to twelve.

The café was filled with a dozen fake palm trees—a small one on every cherrywood table and tall ones towering near the cash register. Colorful lanterns hung from the ceiling, and reggae music played through the speakers. The shop was a pile of sand and one dolphin shy of becoming a beach. A fine substitute if a family couldn't afford a vacation.

I ordered an iced coffee from the barista, a tan guy with a head full of dreadlocks, then took a seat near the front window to wait. The café was empty, and I felt uncomfortable being the only one there—especially because dreadlock boy wouldn't stop staring at me over the top of the Harry Potter novel he was reading—but at least there would be no confusion over my superhero. The next guy who walked in would be him.

It only took me a few quick gulps to finish half my drink. My mouth felt parched, and my lips dry no matter how many times I reached in my purse to apply lip balm. I wiped my palms—hopefully wet from my iced coffee and not from sweat—on my jeans and then checked my watch.

12:01.

Only a few people walked past the storefront while I sipped my coffee. A woman with kids, a little boy riding a skateboard, an elderly couple holding hands, a father with a toddler throwing a temper tantrum and spilling his juice box, a young couple arguing. No superheroes, no single guys looking to meet a girl in a coffee shop.

Maybe he was running late. Yes, that was definitely it. He was testing the nanobots or he had to save a kitten stuck in a tree or a lost little kid or something and lost track of time. He would come. He would.

"You need a refill?" the barista asked as he wiped muffin crumbs off the table next to mine. The rag he used was stained brown with dried coffee, which I thought sort of defeated the purpose of cleaning anything.

I anxiously chewed on my lip and looked at the cars driving down the city street. No one approached the door. "Yeah, sure. Thank you."

The barista paused, flinging his rag over his shoulder. A few stray drops of coffee flew through the shop. "No offense, but I dunno why people come in here and order this overpriced crap."

"You guys sell pastries too," I pointed out. "They're less expensive."

"I dunno why people order pastries either. They're always stale. Which is probably why you aren't eating one."

I gestured to the front door. "I'm just waiting for my friend. He'll be here any minute."

The barista shook his head. His hair swung around his face, slapping his cheeks. "That's what they all say, girly." He walked behind the counter, and the hum of the coffee grinder started seconds later.

"He *is* coming!" I yelled over the noise. "He's just stuck in traffic!"

I knew I was lying to myself. The guy could teleport. Trivial human things like traffic jams were beneath him.

By 12:30, I'd finished my second coffee and needed to run to the bathroom to pee. Bursting back into the café with my shirt halfway untucked, I feared he would be sitting at a table thinking he missed me. But the shop was still empty.

"No one came in for you," the barista mumbled from a barstool behind the counter, loudly flipping a page in his book.

By 1:00, I'd read three articles from the Sunday paper, checked my social media accounts four times, and heard the same reggae song play through the speakers twice. I encountered zero superheroes.

When 1:30 rolled around, I'd given up hope. He wasn't coming. Ten people had entered the café in the past half hour, but none of them spoke to me. Iron Phantom said he would be here. What happened?

I should have known he wouldn't show. I should have stayed at home, where it was safe. I should have run to Connor when Iron Phantom first began talking to me, and then maybe my brother wouldn't be so furious. Should have, should have, should have. But I didn't. Maybe Connor was right after all. A supervillain couldn't be trusted.

"Hey, wait!" The barista ran over to me as I opened the café door. He plucked a pink hibiscus flower from a nearby plant and offered it to me. His white apron was dirty with spilled coffee and the heat from the shop caused him to sweat, but he still managed to give me an encouraging smile. "Whoever he is, he's an asshole for standing you up. You deserve better."

Holding back tears, I jumped in Connor's truck and peeled out of the parking lot. I may have waited almost two hours for that jerk, but I wouldn't cry. I wouldn't prove he had some type of hold over me by shedding tears after a missed coffee date. Crying would show I was weak. I wasn't weak. I was Mayor Hamilton's daughter. My brother was a famous superhero. My mother was dead. I knew how to be strong.

I ended up at the mall, operating purely on autopilot as I walked through the food court and stood in line at the froyo stand. Sugar. I needed a ton of it, and then when I was done, I would get some more. And I would completely forget about superheroes and boys with emerald-green eyes and lips that tasted like the chocolate bar he'd left on my pillow and—

Oh my God, I needed to stop. Less thinking, more eating.

I ordered a large chocolate fudge in a waffle cup (because even the most broken of hearts will mend when eating fudge) and grabbed a handful of napkins from the dispenser. As I was looking for an open spot to sit, a hand shot out of nowhere, sending a pile of napkins fluttering to the ground.

"Sorry!" Rylan called to the girl working behind the counter. She rolled her eyes and continued making a milk shake for the next customer.

Rylan dabbed at a spot on his shirt. "Crap. This is going to stain."

"What is it?" I leaned close, noticing a bright blue blotch on his plaid shirt.

Rylan jumped, like he hadn't even noticed me. "Blue raspberry slushie." He gave me a nervous smile, and I noticed the blue staining his teeth. "What's yours?"

"Chocolate fudge."

He nodded, crinkling his napkin in his fist. "Why do all girls like chocolate?"

"Um . . . because it's chocolate."

Rylan laughed. "Fair enough." He spotted an empty booth across the food court, and we headed toward it in an unspoken agreement. Rylan slurped at his drink while I prodded at my ice cream with my spoon.

"You look a little glum," Rylan said.

"Glum?" I looked across the table at him. He swished his drink around in his mouth before swallowing. "Do people still say 'glum'?"

He shrugged. "I do. Now spill."

I thought about it for a second. Telling him wouldn't hurt.

I stabbed my ice cream with my spoon, putting a deep crater right in the middle. "I got stood up."

Rylan's eyebrows shot up. "By who?"

"Just by . . . someone."

"Does he have a name? I hope you know his name."

Rage burned through my cheeks. I almost cut it loose, making Rylan the target of my white-hot frustration, but the only thing holding me back was the fear that I would drive him away. Being alone right now, stuck with only my thoughts for company, would be torture.

I watched him watch me for a moment. Rylan was so sweet. He never would have left me sitting in the coffee shop without an explanation.

I smashed my spoon farther into my melted frozen yogurt. "Isaac." I muttered his name like it was something rotten. "Isaac stood me up."

Or maybe he didn't. Who cared anymore?

Rylan bit the end of his straw. "Oh man, I really don't want to tell you what I'm thinking right now."

I sat up straight. "No, please. Tell me. On second thought, tell me everything you've ever thought. *Ever.*" I leaned toward him.

Rylan grimaced. The blue was gone from his teeth. "Abby, I don't want to be mean, but have you ever noticed that Isaac kind of only cares about Isaac?"

"He's an . . . acquired taste," I countered, thinking more of Iron Phantom than Isaac Jackson.

Rylan took another sip from his drink. "Abby, Isaac is . . . well . . ." He shook his head. "Anyone who would stand you up is an idiot."

"Thanks."

"My pleasure." He pushed back his chair with a screech. "And on that note, I'm going to make you feel better."

"How? Where are you going?"

He jerked a thumb over his shoulder. "Well, first I'm going to the bathroom, but *after* that, I'm going to make you feel better. Promise."

"How?" I asked again, but he was already weaving through the crowd to the restrooms.

"If one more person ever tries to be cryptic with me again, I swear . . . ," I muttered, stirring my spoon in my cup. I wasn't particularly hungry anymore.

After throwing away my ice cream, I glanced at my watch. Rylan was taking such a long time that I wondered if something had happened. Like if he fell in the toilet. Or maybe he got held up. I shivered just thinking about gentle Rylan with a gun to his back. With the amount of crime in Morriston, I wouldn't be shocked.

I'd just stood to check on him when the sound of a gong cut through the air. I glanced around the food court, looking at the ceiling. Around me, other shoppers were doing the same. A loud *tick-*

tock was coming from the speakers instead of the usual oldies music the Morriston Mall favored. The noise reminded me of the large grandfather clock in the entryway at home. When that thing chimed, the whole house heard it.

Goose bumps prickled my forearms. In the same way the supers always knew when danger was beginning to unravel, I had a strange feeling that something wasn't right.

Another strike of a gong. I looked at the nearest television screen hanging on the wall behind a sports bar. Highlights of a baseball game were playing, but the station suddenly changed, now showing a countdown of sixty seconds. With a flicker of lights and a loud *click*, every screen in the food court flipped to the same picture. The digital numbers had now reached fifty-five and were moving quickly. *Ticktock. Ticktock.* The noise grew steadily louder as the numbers grew smaller.

Whether this was caused by the same person who had been framing Iron Phantom for months or by a new criminal, I wasn't sure. I had no idea what the end of the countdown would bring. But it couldn't possibly be good.

There was a fire alarm across the food court. I raced to it, scrambling to lift the cover and slam my hand down on the lever. The shrill ring mixed in with the ticking from the speakers, jolting the mall into action. Chairs screeched, toppling over. Shopping bags were left strewn across the floor as people bolted for the glass doors by the parking lot.

The ticking grew to a near deafening volume. Thirty seconds on the clock. People pushed from all directions, trying to escape the mall.

Ticktock. Ticktock. Ticktock. Ticktock.

I stopped in my tracks. Rylan hadn't come out of the bathroom . . . had he?

I'd never forgive myself if I left without checking. I ran against the flow of the crowd, hopping over fallen chairs as I rushed toward the empty hallway that led to the restrooms.

Something crunched beneath my shoe, and I pulled up short.

I lifted my foot, finding a small cracked key chain. A glass cylinder hung off a metal loop, a few broken pieces scattered across the floor. Not knowing exactly why, I bent down to retrieve it, hiding my fingertips in my sleeve so I wouldn't cut myself.

As my hand neared, the glass started glowing, first purple, then blue, cycling through the entire rainbow in quick succession. I jerked my hand back a few inches. The colored glass became clear.

Iron Phantom's words came back to me, as hard and fast as a thunderclap. *That's just a paperweight,* he said when we visited his lab. *It changes color when it senses body heat. It doesn't bite.*

I held the key chain in my palm again. Through the glow of bright green glass, I could just make out two initials carved on the side.

R.S.

Out in the food court, the ticking stopped.

A rumble rocked the mall, dust falling from the ceiling. I felt the vibration under my shoes, but I barely heard it. I barely heard the screams. I barely heard the breath wheezing through my lungs over the ringing in my ears.

R.S.

A second explosion, this one harsher than the first. The floor shook so violently I feared it would split and swallow the world whole. I was pitched sideways, my head slamming into the cinderblock wall before my body crashed to the ground. Through the stars of color popping before my eyes, I noticed the ceiling beam directly above me, cracking apart, starting to fall. . . .

"Abigail!"

Iron Phantom appeared in front of me, his rough black gloves clinging to my arms as he tugged me upright. My stomach dropped.

I felt the same nauseating, chest-tightening sensation I'd experienced twice before. Momentarily weightless, when I touched solid ground again I pulled away from the arms wrapped around my shoulders. We were outside, at the farthest end of the parking lot. The Morriston Mall quaked in the distance, spitting singeing debris into the air like a fountain.

I rounded on the boy standing beside me, his mouth hanging open as he took in the damage. "Thanks for your help." My gaze was firm, but my insides were shattered. His key chain was still clutched in my hand. I thrust it toward him, and he barely managed to grab it before it fell. *"Rylan."*

His shoulders pulled taut as he blinked behind his mask. His eyes were Iron Phantom green, not brown, but his soft voice was unmistakably Rylan's—he hadn't bothered disguising it.

"Abby, I . . ." A third explosion had us both ducking for cover. By the time I oriented myself and turned back to him, he was already gone.

Goddammit, I was going to murder Rylan Sloan.

Sirens wailed through the air. A red blur shot overhead, but Connor's suit was quickly obscured by the thick smoke unfurling from the depths of the mall. Over the shouts of the terrified crowd, I thought I heard the engine of Fish Boy's motorcycle.

My feet pounded across the parking lot. Connor couldn't go in there. Not now. Not when the mall was so close to reaching its breaking point.

A fourth explosion sent everything over the edge. I squinted in the sunlight as the roof burst into bright orange flames. Metal beams creaked and snapped. The building buckled. A gust of hot air hit my face, scorching my cheeks as the Morriston Mall imploded.

With my brother trapped inside.

"Connor!" The sting of my last words to him haunted me, bitter and biting and so, *so* pointless as the mall came crashing down.

Maybe if you took a minute to listen instead of checking out like you did with Mom, then you could save people too.

Hunter appeared behind me, holding me steady as my screams seared my vocal cords. My throat was on fire. Everything was on fire. Connor was burning alive in that crumbling building. His body would be found amid charred rubble, his bright red suit black from the ash.

He hadn't saved our mother, but this was never what I wanted. I may have teased Connor about his superhero status and grudgingly did his homework, but he was my family. I loved the infectious smirk that proudly graced his lips every time he used his nerdy powers. And his confusion over sugar and salt, which resulted in baking sickeningly gross brownies that we fed to our dad as a prank. I loved the way he recited lame knock-knock jokes to cheer me up after a rough day at school. The way he treated me as his friend and not his powerless little sister.

"Abby." Fish Boy's fingers dug into my shoulders. "Look."

A familiar streak of red finally flew between two metal beams. His suit was burned and ripped, but his mask still remained intact. He cradled an elderly woman in his arms, setting her down gently beside an ambulance as the crowd cheered.

"Thank God," I murmured, falling slack against Hunter's chest. Connor managed to extract himself from his legion of fans and limped toward us, trailing blood from a wound in his leg the whole way over.

"Does anyone have some OxyContin?" he mumbled, then cursed in pain when I threw myself into his arms. Our relationship may have looked suspicious, but I couldn't bring myself to care.

"You're okay. You're not dead." My voice came out muffled against Connor's chest. He rocked me back and forth, refusing to let go. He didn't care what we looked like either. "I'm so sorry."

"Me too. Look, I'm not upset about what you said. You're right. I didn't save her. And if anything, that helped me realize that I need to try harder." He pulled away just a bit so he could look at me. He seemed like he wanted to say something else, but he was prevented from speaking when my phone started beeping with a video chat request from our dad.

I answered quickly, honestly a little shocked that he found the time to call instead of sending another text.

"Abby! I was so worried. I tried the house and you weren't home," Dad said as soon as his haggard face filled the screen. Sunlight streamed in through the office windows behind him. Connor took a step away from me, pretending he wasn't part of our reunion, but I caught him give our father a reassuring nod all the same. "When I saw the explosion, I thought . . . well, I'd never forgive myself if something happened to either one of you."

"Dad, it's okay. We're both—"

"Benjamin." Wallace opened my dad's office door and stepped into the room. His right wrist bore a cast from Iron Phantom's attack at the warehouse. Wallace's piercing gaze looked from my father to his phone and finally to me, but if he recognized me as Iron Phantom's accomplice, he certainly didn't show it. "Is everything all right?"

"Yes, thank you." Dad gave me a quick smile before lowering his phone to his desk. His face disappeared, and only his tie filled the screen. "Wallace, make sure you bring in an adequate amount of security. I'm going forward with the press conference."

"On Tuesday, sir?" I heard Wallace ask.

"Yes. The big one. I just need to draft the speech." His excitement carried him away and he ended the call, without even remembering to say good-bye.

Beside me, Connor gave Hunter one of those complicated man-fives where you slap each other at least four times and fist bump all in the span of about three seconds. He towed me across the parking lot as the crowd started to press in.

"Abby, I know how you feel, but we're still going to find him," Connor said. "We're going to end this."

"Comet—"

"No. Iron Phantom isn't going to hurt anyone else. He isn't going to hurt you again."

But Connor was wrong on two accounts. First, Iron Phantom hadn't bombed the mall. He wouldn't have teleported me out if he did, meaning the real culprit was still at large. And second, Rylan Sloan was every bit capable of hurting me again. In fact, he already had.

CHAPTER SEVENTEEN

Abby,

I never wanted you to find out this way. I know I hurt you, and for that I'm sorry.

—Rylan

Well, at least he wasn't dead. That was a good thing, right? The note was shoved inside my locker the next day, but I couldn't find Rylan anywhere. I looked for him before homeroom, in the halls between classes, and in the cafeteria during lunch. He wasn't in the library, and I even arrived to rehearsal early that afternoon, hoping to catch a glimpse of him testing stage lights in the auditorium. Nothing. If a super didn't want to be found, it was nearly impossible to track them down. Nearly impossible, but not completely. I'd looked up Rylan's address in the school directory and was taking a bus to his affluent Morriston gated community as soon as rehearsal ended to demand answers. Rylan may have saved my life yesterday, but he still owed me.

"Abigail, are you all right?" Isaac's shadow passed over me as I sat on the floor outside the auditorium. The *Hall of Horrors* script clutched in his fist was covered with doodles of cars, geometric boxes, and girls with boobs larger than their heads.

"Yeah. I'm fine."

"Are you sure?" The distress and confusion I felt over Rylan the Idiotic Iron Phantom must have shown on my face if Isaac Jackson was taking the time to question my feelings.

I tried to smile. I hoped it looked convincing because, to me, it just felt fake. "Yeah, Isaac, thanks."

Clearly unsatisfied with my lame attempt to persuade him I was okay, Isaac sighed and sat down beside me. He pulled his knees up to his chest, mirroring my position. "Think about this," he began. "Whoever upset you, are they really worth your time? Life's too short to be moping around about things, you know?"

I raised my eyebrows, scrutinizing him. How did I ever believe he was Iron Phantom? His eyes were a darker green, his shoulders narrower, even his legs looked shorter. Now that I knew the truth, I wondered how I could ever be so blind.

"Why are you giving me advice? You're being nice to me."

Isaacs's head cocked to the side in confusion. "I can be nice."

"Not without turning to stone or melting into a puddle."

"Oh, really?" For once, he looked genuinely apologetic. "Sorry. I have a lot on my mind, I guess. Remember how I told you I moved in with my uncle because my parents are . . . gone? Well, it's been stressful to say the least." A harsh bark of laughter escaped his lips. "He's my dad's brother. He's not the greatest person to be around during the best of times, and he's been even grumpier since my dad died, but . . . Sorry, you probably don't care about that."

I frantically shook my head. I shouldn't have cared—not after all the rehearsals where he acted like an arrogant asshole. But I liked hearing him open up to me, and I understood why he came across as a jerk. It was a front he put up from dealing with so many bigger issues than dumb high school musical rehearsals. I guess, in a way, we were all like the Morriston supers. We all wore our own masks.

"No! I do, I do," I said. "It's just I'm a little confused—"

"Why I told you all that?" He folded a loose page of his script into a paper airplane. "To help, I guess. This is going to sound weird, but I kind of had a little, uh, crush on you when we first started rehearsing. Just a minuscule thing. Insignificant really." His ears grew red around the edges.

"Oh. Um . . ." Briefly I wondered how things would have turned out if Isaac had been wearing Iron Phantom's mask instead of Rylan.

"Like I said," Isaac continued, "it was stupid. You and Rylan seem to have some weird, mushy thing going on and"—he shrugged—"Jimmy Stubbs has been looking interestingly attractive lately."

"Oh? *Oh!*" I gave him a genuine smile this time. "Go for Jimmy. He's nice."

Isaac started sputtering, his ears redder by the second. "Well, erm, maybe. I'm not sure if it'll work out. He's probably a moron. . . ."

"God, Isaac. Just shut up and go talk to him."

Laughing, Isaac stood, throwing his paper airplane into the auditorium. It got caught in Mrs. Miller's frizzy hair and went unnoticed. He linked his elbow with mine—very uncharacteristically Isaac, but I didn't mind. "C'mon, Hamilton," he said. "Let's get to rehearsal. I need to practice throwing you into that damn crocodile half a dozen times."

Rylan's neighborhood only had ten houses because they were so *massive* that's all that could fit. I used to think my house was huge. My home was full of useless space, but looking across the pond—or was it a lake?—in the front yard of Rylan's family's mansion, I knew the Hamilton household just got put to shame.

The estate looked less like a family home and more like Buckingham Palace with its luscious gardens and rows upon rows of red-trimmed windows. Already it was growing dark, and a few of the upstairs lights cast a glow on the front lawn. Through one of the downstairs windows, I noticed a baby grand piano in the middle of a room with white marble floors. An enormous glass chandelier hung from the ceiling. Tall white columns bracketed the porch.

A knocker shaped like an eagle's head glared at me from the middle of the front door, daring me to reach for the handle. I took a deep breath. I shouldn't be nervous. Rylan was the one who withheld his identity from me for so long, then stood me up. He should be scared, not me.

The knocker dropped loudly on the wood three times. I took a step back and waited. Maybe he wouldn't be home. Maybe he put on his stupid super suit and went out to his thinking tree in the middle of nowhere. Maybe . . .

The front door opened with a loud creak. Rylan peered out of the house, looking sickeningly handsome in jeans and a button-down shirt. He nervously licked his lips and opened his mouth to speak, but no sound came out. Rylan looked like a fish without water—a superhero without his mask. He tried twice more, running a hand through his dark hair and glancing back into his house as if hoping someone, *anyone*, would come to his rescue. Finally, he leaned against the doorframe and groaned. "None of this turned out the way it was supposed to."

He was right about that. The tense moment stretched between us, but all I could think to do was stick my nose in the air and snap, "Your lab is much more impressive on the outside."

"Yeah." Rylan sucked in a breath and glanced at the porch, disinterested. He flinched forward, like he wanted to touch me, but thought against it. "Abby, I never meant to hurt you."

"Never meant to hurt me?" My shrill voice could have doubled for bat sonar. "You know, Rylan Sloan, I've had a lot of firsts with you. First time I've crept around a shady warehouse in the middle of the night, first time I've been stood up . . ."

"Abby—"

"Why didn't you tell me? You had a lot of opportunities."

"Abby—"

"Were you afraid? Did you think I wouldn't like you or something? Because news flash! I like you. A lot. Even when you're you. Even when you're shy and quiet. And you liked me too, or was that just another thing you lied about?"

"Abby—"

"What? Aren't you going to call me *Abigail* anymore? Or do you only reserve that for when you're Iron Phantom?"

With a sharp yank on my arm, Rylan dragged me over the threshold, shutting the door firmly behind us before rounding on me. "Would you please be quiet about that kind of stuff?" he snapped. "I don't want my neighbors and Franklin to hear us."

"Franklin? Who's *Franklin?*"

"He's my butler. Well, my grandfather's . . ."

"Oh, a butler! Righto, old sport!" I laughed, mocking an English accent. Nothing about having a butler was that funny. I only laughed because I realized that Rylan had at least three personalities: at school, in costume, and at home in his megamansion with his fancy manservant. And the problem was, I didn't know which was real. I didn't know if I wanted answers to my questions anymore. It felt pretty cathartic just chewing Rylan out in his foyer.

"Can you stop, please?" he asked, looking uncomfortable again.

"Sure, Rylan. Whatever you want. Cheerio." I turned to reach for the door handle.

"No, stop! Abigail, wait." His fingers clenched around my wrist. "Just wait. I like you too, okay? I more than like you, I . . . please stay." Rylan jumped in front of me, blocking my path. "Please. Just give me a chance to explain. I'll answer all your questions, and if after that you still don't want anything to do with me, I'll leave you alone. For good."

I wasn't sure if I wanted to remain in the house—where we kissed in the basement—and yet I didn't have the heart to tell him no. I tried to buy myself some time before I had to answer. "Your eyes are brown now," I said, confused. "Whenever you're . . . *him*, they're green. What color are they really?"

A timid smile came to Rylan's mouth. "Brown. I bought colored contacts a while ago, hoping they would keep people from thinking I was . . . *you know.* I guess my plan worked a little too well." He stared at me pointedly. "Are you really sure you don't want to stay?"

His deep brown eyes pleaded with me—the same unblinking stare I'd seen so many times before. And with his glassy eyes and rumpled hair, he looked so sad. I took a step away from the door. "Okay."

The interior of Rylan's mansion looked so white and sterile it could pass for a hospital. The furniture, the walls, the two spiral staircases leading upstairs were all bright white and free from specks of dirt. *Poor Franklin must keep himself busy.*

Speaking of Franklin, Rylan gestured to a middle-aged man descending the stairs. His white hair blended perfectly with the house, but instead of a suit and tie—the typical butler attire—he had on jeans and a worn leather jacket. Not exactly what I was expecting. Franklin reminded me of Sarah's dad that one time he tried to start a motorcycle gang and barhop along Morriston's South Side.

"Franklin, this is Abigail."

"Hi, Franklin." This was too weird. My family didn't even have a housekeeper and my dad was the mayor. Instead of hiring help, my parents used to punish me and Connor by making us scrub the bathroom floors with a toothbrush.

Franklin nodded in return. "Miss Abigail," he said with a deep southern twang. Not only was Franklin dressed like a biker, he wasn't British. He was just full of surprises.

"Does he know what you are?" I asked Rylan as he guided me through the twisting hallways of the megamansion, out of earshot of the butler.

"No. The last time you were here, I told you I had family upstairs who didn't know. That's who I meant. Unlike you, Franklin is blissfully unaware."

"You could always let him in on the secret. He could be your sidekick. The Super Server! Fighting crime one hors d'oeuvre plate at a time!"

Rylan halted in front of a door at the end of a white-carpeted hallway. An oil painting of an incredibly obese bulldog hung on the wall. He cocked an eyebrow. "You turn to sarcasm to deflect stress in your life."

I shrugged, following him into the room. Unlike the rest of the mansion, this space had blue walls and dark wooden furniture. Newspapers and books were scattered across every surface in the open living area. A box of Chinese takeout sat on a shiny kitchen countertop. Beside me, a door was cracked open just enough to see the edge of a green bedspread. A ball of black fabric sat crumpled on the floor by the hamper. Iron Phantom's super suit.

"This is the guesthouse," Rylan said. "I'm not really a fan of my grandfather's decorating choices, so I stay in here. It's a bit more homey, I guess."

"This is your grandfather's house?"

He nodded, looking around the room. "Yeah. He doesn't live here, though. He lives in Florida, but this house is his backup. More on that later." He ruffled his hair, causing a few pieces to stick straight up. "Anyway, I moved here after my parents . . . well, you know." He glanced at a copper frame on the mantle, where a mini version of Rylan grinned beside a dark-haired man and woman. They all sat on a checkered picnic blanket, and orange Popsicle juice stained Rylan's lips, dribbling onto his T-shirt.

Rylan methodically straightened the newspapers on the coffee table. On the front page was an article condemning Iron Phantom for blowing up the mall. Rylan sneered at the paper and threw it in the garbage before collapsing on the couch. He picked at his fingernails, refusing to look me in the eyes, even as I awkwardly hovered next to him. I couldn't believe how much braver a mask could make a person. Rylan as *Rylan* and Rylan as *Iron Phantom* were complete opposites. Like the sun and the moon. The sweetness of vanilla and the bitter taste of dark chocolate.

"So . . . ," I said. "Tell me everything."

"Everything?" he chuckled, sounding bitter. "Wow. That's a lot of things. Are you sure you have enough time in your schedule?"

"You turn to sarcasm to deflect stress in your life."

Rylan patted the couch cushion beside him. "Take a seat. We're going to be here a while."

I wanted to bombard him with questions, but I refrained, watching his eyebrows scrunch together in thought. It dawned on me that Rylan Sloan and I were about to have our longest conversation to date where he wasn't hiding behind his alter ego.

"Okay," Rylan sighed, fidgeting in his seat. "Okay. So, I guess I should just start at the beginning. Um, when I was eight, I, uh, I started to get a lot of headaches. Really bad ones, like someone was smashing a brick into my skull. I got dizzy a lot. Once, I tripped and almost fell down a flight of stairs. My parents thought I was just suffering from really bad migraines. But when I started to have trouble walking, they obviously realized something was wrong. Really wrong. So I went to the hospital, they did an MRI . . . and they, um, they told my parents that I had a brain tumor."

I felt like someone punched me in the chest. His desire to become an oncologist finally made sense.

Rylan scratched at the back of his head. Turning, he parted his hair a few inches above the top of his spine and showed me a long line of scar tissue. "They call it medulloblastoma. It's cancerous, and it's pretty much the worst kind of brain tumor a kid can get." Dropping his hands, he leaned forward, resting his elbows on his knees.

"Obviously, they did surgery to remove it. I had a round of radiation and chemo after, which was miserable." His head twitched like he was trying to shake the memory from his brain. "And then they pronounced me cancer-free. My doctor said I had about a seventy percent chance of survival, which are good odds, but it still pissed me off that I went through brain surgery and chemo and there was still a chance I could die.

"But I went back to school and tried to forget. A few months later, I started to develop my powers. The telepathy came first, then the healing, then the teleportation. My parents knew about it, but no one else in my family did. They tried to help me cope the best they could. They took me on vacation and to baseball games, camping and to the park, trying to make me feel normal. But then they died a few years later, and I haven't told anyone since. On the bright side, the cancer never came back. Supers have different DNA than the normal population; I've done a few tests on myself. We're immune to pretty much every human disease or illness there is. I don't know if you know that."

"I do." Connor was the same way.

"I figure the tumor must have had something to do with developing powers. Cancer is caused by DNA mutations. I get cancer, and then I learn to teleport? What else could have caused it?"

"The radiation, maybe?"

"Yeah." Rylan nodded. "Or that. I'm sure not every super is a cancer survivor. Either way, if I never had it I would still be normal."

I took a deep breath, trying to absorb everything he just threw at me. Rylan's story made me want to cry for the sad little boy who experienced so much pain all before the age of twelve. And as I looked at the guy next to me, head lowered to the ground and knuckles clasped so tightly they turned white, I noted that the little boy from the Popsicle photograph on the mantle may have grown into a handsome superhero, but that didn't make him any less sad. My brother's powers literally came out of nowhere. I never would have guessed Rylan went through something so terrible to gain his.

"You don't like having superpowers?" A lot of people would kill to be a super. Personally, I could take it or leave it. But Rylan sounded like he wished his powers could just disappear. Ironic, really—he could disappear, but his powers couldn't.

"Remember when I said I was sick of hearing about Iron Phantom? It's because I was—am. I never wanted powers. I never even owned a suit until I learned about the microchips. What was the point, you know? There are other supers around to take care of everything. I . . . I can't help wondering what life would be like if

I didn't have powers," he said. "Would I keep to myself as much? I don't know. It's isolating. It's hard to explain. . . ."

"No, I understand." My brother might be the one with the powers, but I lived with him. I knew what it was like to keep secrets, or divert conversations away from superheroes, or be forbidden from inviting friends over. Connor's superhero life affected me and my dad as much as it affected him. I felt terrible that the same thing that empowered Connor made Rylan feel so utterly alone.

"You're not hiding superpowers from me too, are you?" Rylan asked.

"No, but . . ." Should I tell him? He was finally being honest, and even though I was angry with him earlier, I knew I needed to reciprocate if we were going to get anywhere. Besides, who was Rylan going to tell? Not his butler. Not anyone else either.

I exhaled a long breath. "My brother has superpowers too."

Rylan eyed me like he expected me to shout, "April Fools'!" When I didn't, the amused smirk slipped from his face. "Wait, you're serious? Connor?"

"You know my brother?"

"Abigail, we've gone to school together since sixth grade. No, don't be embarrassed," he said when I started to apologize. "I know we never talked before this year. So . . . Connor, huh? Who is he?"

"Red Comet," I muttered.

Rylan laughed. "That doesn't surprise me at all. He hates me, you know. Want some water?" He stood, pulling two bottles from the fridge.

"He doesn't hate you," I said. "He hates Iron Phantom."

"What's the difference anymore?"

"You're practically two different people!" I laughed when Rylan wrinkled his nose in disgust. "Don't disagree. You're much more outgoing with a super suit."

"I'm not outgoing now?" He brushed a piece of hair from my face, letting his fingers linger on my cheek.

"Don't go there." I took a sip of water, hoping it would eliminate the sudden rush of heat coursing through me. I wanted to tell him that yes, he's becoming quite outgoing in the privacy of his home. But as much as that excited me and caused my nerves to tremble, I wanted to stop him before his knuckles on my cheek turned into hands around my waist or lips crushing lips. I wanted to know why he left a note on my window but didn't bother to follow through on his promise.

"Why didn't you come to the coffee shop the other day? I waited an hour and a half for you."

Rylan's fingers stilled near my earlobe. "Because most people don't realize what they're doing when they do it. They're selfish, and they don't think about who they will hurt." He frowned. "I was going to come. I had this whole speech planned out where I presented you with a giant stuffed crocodile like in *Hall of Horrors*. And then you would laugh because, hey, look, I guess Rylan can be witty—it turns out he's not an awkward mess *all* the time. And then I was going to buy you coffee and take you back to my thinking tree, and we were going to talk." He paused to tip some water down his throat, but then he fell silent.

I searched for a way to keep him talking. "Why did you tell me you thought Iron Phantom was an idiot? That's a little strange to say about yourself."

"Because I wanted to know what you really thought about him, if you'd defend him. And then once you did, all I wanted was to work up the courage to tell you the truth and have you not be mad when you found out that he was really me. This all started with me needing your help with the microchips, but then it turned into so much more between you and me. Or at least I thought it did."

"You're not wrong."

"I didn't know what to do." He clenched his hands in his lap. "I never meant to stand you up, but then I started freaking out. I didn't want to be . . . to be . . ."

"Rejected?"

Rylan stared at a stain on the carpet. "Yeah. So I went to the mall instead, and then once I saw you I thought, 'This is a sign. I'm *really* going to do it this time.' But everything got so crazy and . . . I know I'm not the person you were expecting when you thought of Iron Phantom."

I laughed. "Yeah, you're a lot better." After all the time I spent with him, I thought he was smarter than this.

Rylan slowly lifted his head, his eyes alight with the beginning of a smile that he seemed too apprehensive to share. "Really?"

"Do you even have to ask? You or Isaac? There's no contest."

His smile spread a bit wider. "Yeah, I guess I am a better kisser."

"Among other things."

Rylan grinned. "How many other things? I'm thinking I should make a list."

I lightly pushed his shoulder. "Reel in your ego." I looked out the window, spotting Franklin emptying a trash can at the back of the main house. "What else were you going to tell me about your grandfather?"

Rylan frowned. I got a sense that he wasn't very fond of the man. "Like I said, he lives in Florida, but he owns an electronics manufacturing company here in Morriston—Sloan Manufacturing. I used to call it S&M when I was thirteen and kind of angsty . . . and now I'm rambling. Anyway, they make computer chips and stuff." He paused. "Conveniently, they made the same microchips that we've been testing."

I gaped at him. "That's how you knew about them?"

"Correct. I was snooping through his computer one day right before summer ended, just because I was bored. I never expected to find anything, but then I saw that an order of microchips was getting sent to city hall. Originally, I thought it would be a good way to track which citizens had superpowers. It would be easy—inject people without their knowledge, then see who shows up to save the day whenever someone is in danger. But obviously now we know that's not the case."

"But, Rylan, we still don't know *what* they do."

He scratched at the back of his neck. "I know. I'm working on it. There's nothing in my grandfather's e-mails to indicate that he knows anything about the nanobots. He just signed off on the microchips." Shuffling through a stack of papers on the table, he located one of the many chips we had stolen and held it up to the light. "Maybe they do have something to do with the supers' powers."

"But it wouldn't make sense for my dad to do that. He already knows about Connor. If he wanted more information, he could just ask." I swallowed hard, looking away. Since we took the microchips at the warehouse, I'd thought about my dad's involvement a million times, but actually believing it made my stomach sour. If I was being completely honest with myself, I'd thought it could be possible ever since Iron Phantom first showed me the empty microchip in my bedroom. But he was my dad. The mayor. He just wanted to keep Morriston safe.

Rylan looked at me out of the corner of his eye. He wouldn't say it, but I knew what he was thinking. He thought I was being naive.

Rylan dropped the chip into the pocket of his shirt, right above his heart. "We're getting closer, Abigail. I know it. And I have a feeling we won't like what we find."

CHAPTER EIGHTEEN

Rylan didn't act much differently toward me the next day at school. We met up in the library during study hall, where we sat at two adjoining computer stations and did our homework in comfortable silence. But he did surprise me when he briefly held my hand as we walked back to class, our palms lightly touching. Sarah caught us in the act, and although she didn't pester me about my feelings for Rylan, I could tell she wanted to by the way her lips pursed like she was holding in her last breath of air. I think she knew something was going on when Rylan gave me a timid, one-armed hug and a small smile as he asked if I needed a ride home from school. I knew *ride home* was Rylan's code for teleport, and even though I wasn't crazy about entering the Black Vortex of Terror, I obliged. It was either that or ride in the Red Comet–mobile. The exaggerated wink Sarah gave me as I exited the building behind Rylan told me that she didn't mind riding home alone.

I didn't want to admit it, but I was starting to get used to teleporting. My body felt much more tummy-dropping-on-a-roller-coaster and much less need-to-excessively-hurl when Rylan and I arrived in my bedroom.

Rylan was all smiles as he took me by the hand and sat with me on the squashy armchair by my window. I'd expected him to act serious, still pondering the purpose of the nanobots, but he didn't mention it once. I couldn't say that I minded.

Rylan brought my face close to his, our lips stopping just short of meeting. His brown eyes were alight with something that looked suspiciously like mischief.

The tip of his nose brushed against mine. "I *really* want to kiss you right now," he began, "but I don't know if that will be frowned upon."

My mouth popped open in surprise. We hadn't kissed since before I found out Rylan was Iron Phantom, and I would be a liar if I said I wasn't craving everything about him. "Why don't you try it out and see?"

"You know, I thought of that, but I'd rather not get slapped across the face if something goes wrong."

"Why would I slap you?" I laughed, taking a moment to tangle my fingers in his hair.

"Because you're quiet," he said. "It's always the quiet ones you need to watch out for. You never know what they expect from you or what you should expect from them. They have the power to turn the world right on its head."

I ran my nails along his scalp, and his eyelids fluttered shut. "Yeah, well, you're pretty quiet yourself, you know."

Rylan smirked and tugged my chin down to meet his mouth. "Exactly," he whispered against my lips.

"Knock, knock. Your brother wants you downstairs." Hunter popped his head around my doorframe after Rylan left. We'd been trying to keep quiet the past two hours in case Connor came home, and once we heard my brother and Fish Boy loudly barge into the house, shouting about football and the new taco joint that opened downtown, Rylan thought it would be best to make himself scarce. As much as I didn't want to, I knew I would have to go downstairs and force myself to socialize. My dad was making a "very important speech on the local news this evening, Abby." I was forbidden from missing it.

"Your room is more . . . beige than I imagined." Hunter turned in a circle, studying my walls and curtains.

"Did you expect pink?" I got up from my desk, being sure to stuff a note from Rylan in the top drawer, out of sight. As a joke he'd written, *Do you like me? Check yes or no,* and drew two large boxes underneath. Much to his amusement, I'd drawn a third box and wrote, *Only when you bring me chocolate.*

Hunter trailed his fingers over the photographs on my walls. "I expected there to be, like, a dollhouse in the corner or something."

"Seriously?"

Hunter laughed. "I guess Connor always makes you sound really young whenever he talks about you. Not in a bad way, though."

I huffed. It wasn't like I'd proven I could take care of myself or anything. This was just more of Connor's Iron Phantom bullshit. He thought I was too young to realize what was going on. If he only knew.

"I'm not five," I told Hunter. "I'm perfectly self-sufficient."

Hunter pushed a few scales through the skin on his forearms and started picking at them. "I know you are, Abby."

"Right. Yeah." I nodded, like I needed to convince myself. "Well, tell that to Connor. Tell him I'm not a total idiot. That I'm smart and . . . and mature . . ."

"Abby, he knows that. He trusts you. He's just worried about the Iron Phantom thing. Everyone is." Hunter ruffled his curly hair and gave me a look like he knew there was more going on. More than I was willing to share.

He cleared his throat. "Anyway, the press conference is on soon, so . . ." He jerked his thumb toward the door.

As we headed down the hall, my brother's voice floated up the stairs. "You guys aren't making out, are you? Because I just ate a plate of nachos and they were too tasty to puke back up."

"Actually we're dating now," Hunter called back, joking. We stumbled into the living room to find my brother flipping through television channels, searching for the press conference.

Connor choked on a sip of pop and crumpled on the couch in a coughing fit. "Wait, *what*?"

"Nothing," I said. "He's being stupid. He's too old. You're, like, what? Thirty?" I asked Hunter.

"Ouch. I'm only twenty-three."

"Close enough."

Connor continued coughing, his face looking like a giant beet with blond hair.

"God, Connor, stop choking!" I yelled.

"I'm a certified lifeguard," Hunter chimed in, puffing out his chest. "I'm a pro at the Heimlich."

I rolled my eyes. "Oh, I bet you are."

"I'm fine—I'm good! Don't touch me!" Connor pushed Hunter away as his coughing ceased and our father appeared on the television screen. "It's on! It's on!"

I felt light-headed from my nerves. My dad never demanded that Connor and I watch one of his press conferences. It was suggested but never mandatory. The news he was about to deliver was either very, very good, or horribly, horribly bad. I didn't have to guess to believe it would be the latter.

Dad straightened his red-and-gold tie, stepping up to the glossy wooden podium bearing the Morriston crest—a bald eagle spreading its wings over a skyscraper.

Connor scooted to the edge of the couch. Hunter kicked up his legs on the table, relaxed as could be. I felt like I was about to throw up.

"Ladies and gentlemen of Morriston, good evening," my father began. His voice was clear and strong, never wavering. "I come to you tonight to make an announcement—an announcement that, with your full support, will radically change our fine city for the better. In the past month, the already disturbingly high crime rates in Morriston have skyrocketed. The death toll has risen. Fear has plagued our city. Our heroes can only do so much to protect us from evil, from the villainous acts committed by the criminal known as Iron Phantom." I held my breath. *Poor Rylan*. I knew he was at home, watching.

"Fortunately, after much deliberation, city hall has reached a solution to better equip citizens against any further felonies by Iron Phantom and his associates. Effective immediately, with approval from the governor, all Morriston residents will receive an emotion detection device from their primary health care provider." He held up one of the chips from the warehouse, the silver glinting in the flash of the cameras.

"These devices recognize chemical changes in the brain associated with premeditation, high levels of malice, and the intent to commit a heinous crime. They then transmit a signal to the authorities, who will alert the nearest superpowered citizen, causing them to come to the rescue quicker and more efficiently. With emotion detection devices, we save lives otherwise threatened by Iron Phantom and criminals like him. We protect our beloved city from evil. We win.

"On behalf of city hall and those families affected by violence in Morriston, I truly appreciate your cooperation in this matter."

Benjamin Hamilton stepped away from the microphone to thunderous applause. I clenched my fingers in my lap until I surely thought they would break. Emotion detection devices.

E.D.D.

Cold sweat broke across my hairline. The file I'd found in Dad's desk drawer—this was it. He did know about the microchips. He was behind it all.

As soon as my dad mentioned them, I thought at least one person in his audience would object. I guess my father was right about one thing. People were afraid of criminals, and after the mall explosion, they were *especially* afraid of supervillains—of Iron Phantom. If this magic chip would keep them safe from violence, they would surely be on board.

And yet I could just imagine Rylan pacing in his lab, inspecting the nanobots through his dozens of microscopes, suspicious of everything. Spending so much time with him had made me suspicious too. If the nanobots could do *anything*, then how did we know they were solely limited to stopping crime?

"Those chips aren't going to work," Hunter said. I'd forgotten he was sitting next to me, his arm draped casually over the back of the couch behind my head.

"What do you mean?"

He raised an eyebrow, and it got lost amid the tangle of his tousled hair. "Connor and I—all the supers—we use instinct to save people. By the time the police alert us, we'll already know someone's in trouble and be on our way. And think of the logistics. If someone is contacting us all the time, they run the risk of finding out who we are. And isn't that the point? No one knows who we are. No offense, but your dad's just wasting time and money by making everyone get injected with those things. I'm not even sure he can do that anyway."

"Of course he can," Connor cut in. "The state signed off on it. If people don't like it, they can move out of Morriston. Everyone knows we're all going to turn into cyborgs anyway, haven't you been watching the SyFy channel? Inject me with a microchip, I don't care. Even without Iron Phantom running around, the crime around here is out of control." Connor stood, walking to the kitchen to grab another can of Coke and a bag of chips. "I bet Dad's going to tell us more about it when he gets home. It sounds cool to me."

Hunter leaned close to my ear, whispering, "There's still no way in hell it's going to work."

"So I guess we know what E.D.D. stands for," Rylan said as soon as he appeared in my room.

I looked up from the poem I was reading for English class, propping my head in my hand as I lay on my side in bed. "Rylan, isn't it creepy to keep showing up in a girl's bedroom at night? I could've been naked for all you knew."

He tugged on his mask. Dressed as Iron Phantom, he approached the bed, climbing on top of me and holding himself up with his elbows. My textbook fell to the carpet with a thump.

"But you weren't naked," Rylan stressed. "And it's only creepy if the girl doesn't want me here, but you aren't exactly telling me to go away, Abigail."

He was right, of course. I wasn't telling him to leave. What I *was* doing was tugging the satiny mask over his head and dropping it on the floor. Rylan shook out his hair and smirked at me. Seeing Rylan wear his super suit without his mask was weird. Actually, it was more than weird. It blew my mind—like he was revealing his secret identity all over again while lounging on my purple sheets.

"Your hair is a mess." I patted his head, trying to fix his hair, but static electricity from his mask kept it sticking straight up. He looked like he had an unfortunate run-in with a light socket and lost.

Rylan shrugged. "Occupational hazard. Oh, and FYI, I know for a fact that those"—he made a face—"emotion detection devices don't do what your dad says they do."

I sat up so fast that Rylan rolled off me, nearly falling to the floor. He stood, leaning against my windowsill. "What did you find out?"

"Well," he said, "three things. The nanobots don't paralyze people, they unfortunately don't cure cancer, and most important . . . premeditation my ass." He scoffed. "They can't sense that either."

"So my dad lied? Why?" My heart sped up.

"Maybe he truly doesn't know. Why was Wallace at the warehouse instead of your dad? If I was in charge of something like this, I would want to be there. I wouldn't have sent my security guard."

"Security advisor," I corrected.

"Same thing."

I swallowed hard. I needed to believe my dad was doing the right thing. My daddy, who used to build sand castles on the beach and braid my hair after I took baths when I was six. I knew I had to keep the option open, but right now Wallace was the only person we could truly blame. Considering he almost shot me and everything.

"Rylan . . ." I got out of bed and stood before him, struck with a brilliant idea that I hoped would end better than some of my previous ones. "Indulge me for a second."

"I'm indulging." He scrubbed his hand over the back of his head. "I'm a little nervous, but I'm indulging."

"Have you ever gone on a stakeout?"

"No, but I watch a lot of cop dramas. I'm familiar with the concept. Whose place do you want to stake out? Wallace's?"

I nodded.

Rylan rubbed his chin. "Interesting. I'm assuming you know where it is?"

"I haven't been there since I was little, but I think I could find it."

"Good enough for me." He pulled his mask back on. "Let's go back to my place first. I want to grab snacks."

"Snacks?"

"Abigail." He pulled me close, and I felt my limbs turn to jelly as we disappeared. "All stakeouts have snacks."

I didn't realize that when Rylan said snacks, *holy cow* he meant *snacks*. He had a greater variety of junk food in his house than you could find in a convenience store. I stood in his driveway, leaning against the back bumper of his small black sedan while he changed out of his suit and gathered our food.

"I got you fudgy cookies." Rylan tossed a box at me. "I also have pretzels, extra-crispy potato chips, both regular and diet pop, red licorice, *blue* licorice—which sounds weird but I'm willing to give it a shot—three varieties of bubble gum . . . and carrot sticks."

"Carrot sticks? Who's going to eat carrot sticks?"

"I don't know. We might have to lure a wild animal or something. I was trying to think outside the box."

We climbed in the car, and I lined up our snack options across the back seat while Rylan studied the directions to Wallace's house that I attempted to write from memory. They were pretty vague. One of the lines included the phrase *Turn at the big tree by the mini-mart.*

"Franklin won't wonder where your food went, will he?" I looked back at the expansive front yard of Rylan's house as he drove through his neighborhood.

"Franklin actually isn't home. It's knitting night."

"*Knitting* night?"

Rylan nodded. "Franklin likes to challenge gender norms." He started to laugh. "He also likes to makes scarves, so it's a twofer."

I turned sideways in my seat so I could see him better. "You smile a lot when you talk about him."

Rylan flicked on his blinker and we cruised onto the interstate. "Do I?" And now he was blushing. "I guess he's been like my dad for the past few years. We have a lot of fun together. Oh, like this one time last year, we built one of those papier-mâché volcanoes and I put some diet pop and Mentos inside and the whole thing blew up. It got *everywhere.* All over the walls and the ceiling." He chuckled as he pulled off the highway, turning onto a back road. "My grandfather got so mad. So mad," he repeated, frowning a bit.

"He's not around a lot, is he?"

"My grandfather?" Rylan shook his head. "Not particularly. He likes his privacy. He likes his work too."

The silent echo of my house crossed my mind. "I know the feeling."

Rylan reached for my hand, and we stayed that way, our fingers tangled like vines, our palms warm and touching, all the way to Wallace's house.

When Rylan cut the engine at the corner of a tree-lined street south of the city, I had to squint through the dark to make sure we had the right place. A two-story brick monstrosity stared at us from the end of a cul-de-sac, each of its white shuttered windows blacked out. A large SUV was parked in the driveway, the engine off.

"Do you think anyone's home?" Rylan asked.

"There's a car in the driveway. I don't see anything, though."

"Here, use these." Rylan reached into the glove compartment and pulled out a pair of binoculars. When I looked at him in surprise, he hunched over his steering wheel. "I was a Cub Scout when I was seven. What do you expect?"

While I spun the knob to focus the binoculars on Wallace's front door, I tried to picture Rylan wearing a teeny-tiny uniform with a teeny-tiny tie. I couldn't do it. Too much black spandex had tainted the image.

"I still don't see anything," I said. I panned the binoculars across the front yard. A raccoon hiding under a shrub near the garage was the only movement I detected. Like all my other ideas, maybe this one was a bust too. What had I really expected us to learn about the nanobots while stalking my dad's security advisor?

I made another sweep of the yard with the binoculars, and then back again.

"Oh! Wait!" A light flicked on above a side door next to the garage, spilling across the grass. The raccoon darted down the street.

Rylan's hand made contact with my head. "Get down, get down." We held our breath, peering over the dashboard while two shadows appeared at the door. The first one stayed put, their body invisible in the dark, but the second grabbed a trash can and dragged it to the edge of the road.

"That's *it*?" I muttered, feeling the irritation creep up the back of my neck. Wallace deposited the trash beside his mailbox, dusted his hands on his jeans, and returned to the house. Both shadows disappeared as the door closed, but the light remained on.

"Maybe there's a dead body in it?" Rylan suggested half-heartedly.

"Or maybe he doesn't recycle. Wouldn't that be a scandal." I dropped the binoculars in a cup holder. "This was pointless. Sorry I dragged you out here."

"Okay, that right there is how I know you don't watch nearly enough crime dramas. Abigail, everyone knows that nothing good happens until hour three of the stakeout." Rylan reached blindly into the back seat, retrieving the snacks. "Licorice?"

Stakeout, hour one: Rylan and I ran out of napkins to wipe the potato chip grease off our fingers. We had to resort to using Rylan's floor mats, something he cringed about but eventually got over.

Stakeout, hour two: I impressed Rylan with my ability to recite the alphabet backward. He reciprocated by reciting every element in the periodic table in under forty seconds, giving me a headache for the next ten minutes.

Stakeout, hour three: The raccoon returned to Wallace's shrub . . . followed by a second raccoon that appeared slightly too . . . *excited*, for lack of a better word.

Stakeout, hour three and a half: I'd officially eaten more fudgy cookies than my stomach could hold. Wallace hadn't made another appearance.

"I'm bored." I nudged Rylan in the shoulder. "Entertain me."

He pushed me back—just barely. His eyelids were drooping shut. "You entertain me. You're the thespian. Tell me a story."

"I don't know any stories."

Rylan yawned. "Dirty lies. Tell me the most embarrassing story you have. I promise I won't laugh."

"Now *that* is a dirty lie."

His only response was to recline his chair back, closing his eyes while he waited for me to continue.

"Fine. Jeez," I said. "Okay, how about this? Do you remember in seventh grade when we had Miss Gentilli for gym class?" Rylan nodded. "Do you remember how terrifying she was?"

He chuckled. "Sort of. She was ex-military, wasn't she? I just remember teleporting in and out of the showers that year so none of the guys had to see me naked. Didn't want to blind anyone or anything," he added.

"Yeah, I'm sure twelve-year-old Rylan was positively horrific."

"Horrific wasn't really what I was implying."

"You're as awful as my brother." I slapped the console between us. "And this is my story, not yours."

"Sorry, sorry. Continue, please."

"My pleasure. Anyway, one day in class Gentilli made us play football. And I'm bad at almost all sports, but football was the worst. I couldn't grasp the concept that you don't pass the ball once you get it. You just kind of run until someone hits you, which never seemed very team-oriented to me. And so I kept trying to pass the ball, and of course Gentilli just got really angry really fast. So she took me out of the game and made me stand in the corner all alone. That didn't bother me because I hated gym anyway . . . but then I needed to use the bathroom."

"Oh no."

"Oh yes. I thought Miss Gentilli would yell at me if I asked—she probably would have made me do, like, fifty push-ups or something. And of course I was too young to just say 'screw it' and go anyway. So I stood there. And stood there. And stood there. And eventually, I couldn't hold it anymore, so I just peed all over the gym floor."

Rylan curled up on his seat in a fit of laughter. "No way!" Even in the dark, I caught a tear slide down his cheek. He wiped it away and continued laughing.

By now, I was laughing too. I hadn't thought of this story in years—I'd done a fine job of blocking it from memory. But here it was. And somehow, it was hysterical this time around instead of absolutely mortifying.

We were trying so hard to be quiet as we sat in the car that we just ended up laughing harder. Rylan pounded the seat with his fist, and I started smacking his stomach, and then we were just laughing and hitting each other for no reason at all. I was grateful I didn't drink much pop. My bladder didn't want to go for round two.

"That's classic," Rylan said at last. "Everyone has a urine story."

"Yeah? What's yours?"

"Abigail, that's between me and Mr. Brown from sixth-grade bio. I'll never tell," he said with a wink. "I can't believe you told me yours, though."

I tried to pinch him in the arm, but he dodged me, leaning against the window. "You're so mean."

"I'm a supervillain," Rylan said. "We're supposed to be mean." He moved toward me, reaching for the binoculars and flipping them between his hands. "Hey . . . Abigail?"

"Yeah?"

"You . . . you're . . ." He put the binoculars back down, stalling. "You're really beautiful, you know."

I snorted. "I just told you that I peed on the floor in gym class and that's what you come up with?"

Rylan chuckled. "Well, you also have a cookie crumb on your face. Is that better?"

"Oh, God. Where?" I scrubbed my palm against my left cheek, down my jaw.

"Other side. Let me."

He leaned close enough that I could smell the sugar from the pop on his breath. Fingers brushed down my skin, his hand cupping my jaw as he whispered, "Got it."

"Thanks." For some reason, my heart suddenly felt two sizes too big for my body.

He was still *so close*, looking at me in that unblinking way of his. Then finally, he smiled. A wide, bright smile that could extinguish the sun and knock the moon right out of orbit.

If I was beautiful, then he was radiant.

"You know," I said, "nothing very exciting is going on at Wallace's house. . . ."

Rylan's lips quirked up further. "I've noticed."

"I doubt we would miss much. . . ."

"Highly doubtful," he agreed.

"So if we were to . . ."

I edged forward. His arm found the curve of my waist, and he met me halfway.

His lips brushed over my cheeks, nose, eyelids, the corner of my mouth. My stomach felt tight, hot, like something was crawling around inside and needed release. His kisses made me feel warm, loved, truly powerful for once in my life.

I hesitated.

Loved?

I hadn't acknowledged the extent of my feelings until that moment. They had always been there, I realized, lurking under the surface, but I never thought about how serious this could get. Love. I was inching toward it. That was big, huge. I wasn't in love with Rylan yet—it was too soon—but I would be. Maybe in a day. Maybe in a week. Our relationship was moving full steam ahead, and eventually my heart would catch up. And when it did . . . My God. When it did, there would be no turning back.

Rylan pulled back, cracking a lazy grin, his eyes hooded from being kissed. "See?" he said. "Beautiful."

Crash!

The sound echoed through the neighborhood, destroying any hope I had of crafting a decent response.

We reached for the binoculars simultaneously, which resulted in Rylan looking through the left lens while I peered through the right, focusing on Wallace's house at the end of the street. Glass from two broken headlights glittered on the concrete, and a dark shape was lying on the driveway, its torso beneath what I assumed was Wallace's car.

"What are they doing?" Rylan asked. He jostled the binoculars a bit as we leaned forward.

There were five houses between Rylan's car and Wallace's home, just far enough away that I couldn't make out the identity of the figure. It was wearing dark baggy clothing with a hood pulled over its head. As we watched, the figure picked up a brick and smashed it through the windshield of Wallace's car.

The alarm blared. Wallace's porch light flickered on, and throughout the neighborhood, dogs started yapping uncontrollably. Rylan had just tossed the binoculars in my lap and was about to teleport outside the car when Wallace flung his front door open and barreled into the yard. He fired two shots into the air from a pistol, but the criminal was already running, vaulting over the next-door neighbor's fence and taking off into the woods behind the house.

"Come on." Rylan pulled at my hand, and suddenly we were standing behind a cluster of pine trees, my head spinning. The crack of Wallace's gun cut through the air once more; then his door slammed shut. We jogged into the woods, trying to listen for footsteps to signal that we weren't alone, but the night had fallen silent. Whoever the criminal was, they had gotten away.

"Great." Rylan spun in a circle, but the woods pressed in on all sides, blinding us. "Iron Phantom will probably get blamed for that one too."

"I know. The guy didn't even steal anything from the—wait a second. Rylan . . ." I gripped his arm. "What if that was no regular Morriston criminal? What if that was the man who's been framing you?"

CHAPTER NINETEEN

Time has a way of flying when you're most ill equipped to chase after it.

We were no closer to uncovering the secret of the nanobots or the man who vandalized Wallace's car, but to the rest of Morriston that didn't matter. To my father that didn't matter. When I walked into school, Rylan cornered me and dropped the bomb, effectively turning me into a stuttering, anxious mess. City hall was starting their microchip injections, and they were sending medical representatives to Morriston High School. Today.

"Rylan, we have to tell somebody."

"Who?" He pulled me off to the side of the hall, out of earshot of the students scurrying to class. No one was running, no one was crying, no one realized they were about to get a tube of nanobots shoved inside their body. To them, Iron Phantom was the enemy. If this was the only way to deal with him, then so be it.

"Abigail, I'd take this to the police if I could, but—"

"But then they'll know you stole the nanobots, and they'll know you're *you-know-who*, and then they'll chain you up somewhere so you can't teleport away despite being innocent." Rylan couldn't teleport if he was attached to something heavier than he could carry, a weakness he had told me about two nights ago when I asked him how it worked.

"We could talk to Hunter," I offered.

Rylan's lips puckered. "Who the heck is Hunter?"

Was that a hint of jealousy I detected?

"Relax. He's Connor's friend, uh . . ." I cupped my hand over my mouth as we huddled in the corner by the elevator. "Fish Boy." Maybe I should have felt bad about spilling another super's identity, but I didn't have the time. I couldn't stomach keeping secrets any longer.

I continued. "Hunter's already suspicious that something isn't right. Maybe he could help."

"I don't know. . . . Do you really think we can trust him? Can we trust anyone?"

I wished I could say that we could trust my dad. He'd spent breakfast reciting all the benefits of using the chips to Connor and me, all the lives we would save by detecting premeditation. Dad's goal was to keep Morriston safe—the chips would do that. Connor excitedly bounced at the kitchen table as he listened. I just focused on not throwing up my cereal.

How could my dad lie to us—to the entire city?

Or was he even lying? I was still holding on to that shred of hope, as delicate as a piece of tissue paper, and praying it wouldn't tear completely in two.

"You can't ask him," Rylan stressed. The warning bell chimed a few seconds later, leaving the halls nearly deserted. "I really don't think we should ask anyone. The nanobots need to be activated by an outside source before they can start working. An injection technically won't hurt anyone. But if your dad thinks we're suspicious, he can order them to be activated right away—before we figure out what they really are. And then we're screwed."

"So we're just supposed to let some nurse stick us with a needle?" We headed down the hall.

"I was stuck with so many needles when I was a kid," he said, rubbing over the scar on the back of his head. "It barely fazes me anymore."

"Um, hello? Nonpowered human over here. It kind of fazes me just a little bit."

Rylan pulled me into a hug outside my homeroom. Inside the doorway, Sarah caught my eye and made a kissy face. When I looked back to Rylan, a red tint covered his cheeks.

"Everything's going to be okay." He quickly kissed my cheek. "I promise." He jogged up the stairwell, chased away by Sarah's catcalls.

My legs felt like jelly when Principal Davis called my history class down to the cafeteria in the afternoon to receive our microchips. Most other students lined up in the hall without complaint, busy chattering about their weekend plans and who was hooking up with whom, happy for the ten-minute reprieve from class. I, however, had spent the morning biting my nails down to nubs and struggling to swallow the golf-ball-sized lump in my throat.

"Just relax." Rylan sidled up to me, cutting in front of a giggling group of underclassmen. "Just pretend like nothing is wrong."

The people in front of me took a small step forward. I craned my neck, looking over the long line zigzagging through the hall into the cafeteria. Multiple chairs were set up inside the doors, but I couldn't tell what was happening.

Being almost a head taller than me, Rylan could see no problem. "There's a woman and man in there. It looks like they're injecting people in the forearm."

"Rylan, we need to go home." I clutched at his hand, hoping if I squeezed hard enough I could will him to disappear.

"Maybe you could get away with it, but I can't," Rylan said. "If I leave, they'll just come to my house and inject me there. Principal Davis said city hall isn't letting anyone avoid them. They're treating these chips like seat belts. They're 'for safety.'" He rolled his eyes, leaning against a row of lockers. "If someone refuses an injection, they can get arrested. And besides, I can't just hide at home. That's not very heroic," he muttered.

"We can't get those things shoved inside us either," I protested.

"We'll figure something out. We'll take them out."

"But—"

"Miss Hamilton!" Principal Davis appeared behind Rylan and me, clapping us on the shoulders. I jolted, but Rylan remained completely still, lips turned into a frown. "You're holding up the line. Kindly move forward." Grinning, he gestured to the ten-foot gap in front of me that I'd been too busy freaking out to notice.

I couldn't go through with this. It wasn't safe. We didn't know what the chips would do to us. Before Rylan or Principal Davis could take another step, I shouted, "Rylan has a fear of needles!"

"What?" Davis asked.

Rylan hung his head. When he looked up for a second, I caught a glimmer of amusement in his eyes.

Principal Davis studied Rylan. "You're afraid of needles?"

"Yes!" I interjected. Davis looked from me to Rylan like he was watching a game of Ping-Pong. Rylan—shrugging, hands stuffed in his pockets—and me, waving frantically like a madman.

"He has a *very bad fear,*" I continued. "Horribly, horribly terrified. In fact, he might pass out."

"Really?"

"Yep. Just fall to the ground. Just hit the deck like *that*!" I smacked my hands together. By now, half the student body had turned to watch the spectacle. "*Splat!* Like a—a bug! Just down on the ground like a—like a dead man. Just *dead.*" I clapped my hands again, half-heartedly this time, when I realized my argument was losing steam and didn't seem to be changing the principal's mind. With hands crossed over his chest and lips pursed tightly together, he looked about two seconds away from bursting into laughter.

"Just . . . gone," I said quietly, realizing how stupid I sounded. I had an A-plus in my speech and debate class, but the only time I really needed to craft an excellent argument to save myself and my maybe-boyfriend from potential destruction, I couldn't come up with anything better than an amateur attempt at sketch comedy. Failure, Abby. What a complete joke.

"I should take him home," I mumbled to no one in particular. "Just to make sure he's okay."

Principal Davis shook with silent laughter. Glancing at Rylan, he asked, "Mr. Sloan, do you have a paralyzing fear of needles that may cause injury or death?"

Yes! Yes, you do! I thought. But I seriously lacked Rylan's superpower of mental communication. Of course, my idiot brother got superpowers even though I was the one who obviously needed them.

Rylan knew I was trying (and failing) to perform telepathy. *Don't worry, Abigail. I got this.* Then to Principal Davis, he said, "No. I'm not afraid of needles."

The students still eavesdropping on our conversation laughed. For a moment, I thought of smashing my hand in the door of the nearest open locker to create another distraction.

Davis clapped his hands together and motioned for everyone to turn around. "Okay, okay! Now that we've gotten that settled, Mr. Sloan, please return to your place in line. And, Miss Hamilton . . ." He shook his head, scratching his hair. It looked a lot like a toupee, but no one could prove it.

"I really thought you were different from your brother. I thought surely you weren't disruptive. Don't prove me wrong. Make your way into the cafeteria *quietly*, please," he said, walking in the direction of his office.

You'll be okay, Abigail. Rylan's voice slithered into my head. I used to hate when he did that. It felt invasive. But now I took comfort in knowing he was so close.

I'll come find you after. It'll be fine. But as the nurses came out to take down our names on their clipboards, I noticed that a hint of doubt slipped into his voice. Before I could say anything else in our defense, he was following a man across the cafeteria while a woman led me to a table set up behind a flimsy blue curtain.

She had me take a seat while her cold hands swiped an antiseptic wipe over the inside of my wrist. There was a bright red mark on the inside of her arm. I really hoped it was only a rash, but somehow I doubted it.

"On a scale of one to ouch, how much will this hurt?" I asked.

The nurse gave me a sad smile. "Honey, I'm not sure you want to know."

Rylan and I returned to his guesthouse when it was all over, where I shakily lowered myself into a chair in the corner of his bedroom. There was a bump in my arm and tears in my eyes, and no matter how hard I rubbed I couldn't get either to disappear. Once the nurse had pulled out a six-inch-long needle, I looked away, but I still felt the burn when the microchip entered my wrist, like my skin had been blistered with a blowtorch.

And this was the thing that my dad was convinced would make Morriston safe?

After the nurse was finished with me, I had lingered in the hall for a while, waiting for Rylan and watching groups of students leave the building, rubbing their arms at their injection sites. Most didn't seem to care much, but every now and then, a few would shoot me dirty looks, like Mayor Hamilton's precautions were somehow *my* fault.

Even Sarah had looked a little pissed off as she headed out the doors. And that almost never happened. I'd thought about grabbing her, telling her what we knew, but I didn't have to think twice to know that would be a horrible idea. It was bad enough she thought city hall was treating her and the rest of Morriston like potential criminals. If I let it slip that something was wrong with the metal chip bulging under the skin of her forearm, Sarah would panic. And if Sarah panicked, everyone in the city would know about it. Her screams couldn't be quelled.

As I settled into the armchair in Rylan's bedroom, I asked myself if I had made a mistake keeping another massive secret from my best friend. I didn't have an answer.

If lies were dollar bills, I'd be a millionaire.

A shadow appeared above me, and a handful of peppermints fell into my lap. "Eat some sugar," Rylan said. "It helps."

"Thanks." I popped one into my mouth, studying Rylan as he gingerly poked the lump under his skin, disgusted. "So what's your grand master plan for taking these out?"

Instead of answering, Rylan pulled a thin, shiny object out of his backpack and headed for the bathroom. I followed apprehensively, my heart thudding double-time.

Like most things in the megamansion, the size of his bathroom easily doubled my own. It was spotless, smelled sweet like lavender, and housed both a shower and a massive claw-foot tub. Because why not take off your clothes and mix it up a little?

"So . . . um . . . I should probably practice on myself first. Can you make sure this towel stays in my mouth?" Rylan tossed a white hand towel across the room. He was now in the process of disinfecting something in the sink. Upon closer inspection, I noticed a gleaming silver scalpel.

"Rylan, you're kidding!"

"Hmm?"

"We're cutting the chips out?" I started to feel queasy. I couldn't do this to myself, and I couldn't watch him do it either. I may have stitched him up after the subway flood, but this felt different. I had known Rylan longer now; I was emotionally invested. Seeing Rylan harm himself, in my mind, was infinitely worse than seeing Rylan harmed.

"We shouldn't have even gotten them. You have such a superhero complex! What if we get infected?" I clutched my forehead, pacing in front of his toilet.

"You're in the clear. I can heal you just fine."

"But what about you? Oh God, what if you slice an artery?"

Rylan took the towel from me and bit it between his teeth. "Oooh gun?" he asked.

"What?"

Pulling the towel out, he tried again. "You done? I'd really like to get this over with."

I glanced at the chips under our skin. Looking closer, I could just make out the pulsing of a faint blue light. I knew we had to do this whether I vomited all over his bathroom floor or not. Who knew what those nanobots could do to us. To everyone.

"What do you need me to do?"

Rylan held out his left arm. "Just hold this steady for me. I don't want to flinch."

I gulped when he poised the sharp tip of the scalpel over his skin. It was impossible to tell whether mine or Rylan's hand was sweating more.

The blade glinted under the lights, and before I knew it, a scarlet line dotted his flesh. Rylan moaned, the noise slightly muffled under the towel. He made another cut perpendicular to the first, forming an L. A tear streaked down his cheek.

Rylan's fist squeezed my fingers, and I feared they would break. Sweat flecked his hairline. Another grunt beneath the towel yielded two clinks in the sink. The first, the scalpel, blade stained with blood. The second, a red—formerly silver—microchip.

"Shit!" Rylan spit the towel to the floor. The underside of his forearm was a bloody mess.

Rylan disinfected the scalpel. He reached for my arm, but I swayed, suddenly too dizzy to feel much of the pain.

The steady *drip, drip, drip* of Rylan's blood soaked the marble floor. I dove for another hand towel, clenching it between my teeth as he dug in with the scalpel. My blood and another microchip joined his seconds later.

I spat out the towel. "Oh, God. Oh, God. Oh, God." My stomach quivered with the cafeteria hot dog I ate for lunch. I didn't think I would make it. Oh, no way. The hot dog was getting its revenge.

"Oh shit . . ."

I reached the toilet just in time.

"You have such a superhero complex," I muttered. We moved from the bathroom to his bedroom after I purged my lunch and brushed my teeth. I was surprised to find he slept on a waterbed. How 1980s of him. I sat down, scooting against the headboard to put some space between us. Rylan had been trying, unsuccessfully, to heal my arm for the past five minutes.

"It's not a superhero complex," he insisted. "It's just a decent human being complex. Now let me see your arm."

"It's fine."

It wasn't fine, but I knew what healing did to him. I picked at the towel wrapped around my wrist, wound tight enough to make the cut burn. Rylan had his own pain to worry about. I wouldn't add to it.

"Whatever, Abigail." Rylan sat beside me with a sigh, dropping a roll of gauze bandages into my lap. "At least help me with mine, would you?"

I leaned toward him, unraveling the gauze in a long spiral between us. Just as I was about to tie it around his arm, he jolted forward, ripping away the towel covering my cut to place his palm over my wrist.

"Gotcha." He grinned, but it was strained as he leeched out my pain. After a few seconds he sat back, wincing as he massaged the underside of his right wrist. Predictably, my skin had knitted back together, like the scalpel never even touched it.

"Superhero complex," I repeated, rolling my eyes as I secured a strip of gauze around Rylan's cut.

"You know I had to do it. Your intentions, though noble, wouldn't have worked if your dad saw a huge scab on your arm. He'd know you took the chip out."

"And what's going to happen if someone sees the huge scab on your arm?"

"They won't. I'll wear long sleeves, I guess. I don't think anyone's really looking anyway."

I taped the bandage in place, watching Rylan roll his wrist in a slow, painful circle. I'd never wanted superpowers, but I wouldn't mind having them just this once, if only so I could heal his wound and repay the favor.

"That's going to leave one gnarly scar," I pointed out.

Rylan snorted. "Yeah it can match the one on my head." He tugged his hair. I could hear the rough scraping of nails against his scalp.

"You always scratch at it, you know."

"Do I? Bad habit." As he spoke, he did it again. Nails against skin. Like he was trying to erase something that no longer existed. Or trying to erase the memory of it. "Does it bother you?"

"Not at all." The waterbed formed around the contours of my body as I relaxed into it. I closed my eyes and bounced a little, the bed sloshing loudly beneath me. When I opened my eyes I found Rylan lying on his side, grinning at me.

"Does it ever hurt?" I asked. I brushed my fingers through the hair at the back of his head.

"It feels numb a lot, so no. I used to think it was disgusting when I first got it." He laughed, but there was no humor in it. "Man, did I hate it. But now I don't mind as much. The scar isn't me. I'm me. The scar is just something that's there. It took a while to figure that out." He paused for a second. "Scars say a lot about a person, you know. What you've been through. What you defeated before it defeated you. Your fears. Memories. Strengths. Weaknesses. The things you love, the things you hope will never slip away. They tell a story," Rylan said. "And I'm always a sucker for a great story."

He always had such a unique way of looking at things. It would be easy for him to stay bitter. To shut down instead of opening up about his past. But the right thing and the easy thing are rarely the same. I think Rylan knew that.

"You could always tell people you got it in a fight with a super. You won, obviously."

Rylan smirked. "Clearly."

"Say you fought Iron Phantom. They'll love you forever. They might even throw a parade in your honor."

"True. I've always hated that guy."

"Oh, I don't know. Peel off all that spandex and I bet he's a real sweetheart underneath."

Rylan's eyebrows raised. "I'm not sure how I feel about you ogling other men, Abigail."

He held a straight face exceptionally well. Though, I guess the whole secret-identity thing helped his acting chops. "Okay. I guess I'll have to give Iron Phantom a call and break up, then. . . ."

"Don't do that; I'm pretty sure he'd do something crazy if you broke his heart. Like cry or something emasculating." He scrunched up his nose. "He doesn't seem like a crier."

"Are you sure? I've seen him cry before."

"He must really like you then—to let you see him like that. Vulnerable."

My eyes lowered. "I really like him too."

"He'll be pleased. I'll inform him immediately." Rylan winked. "I bet he'd ship it."

I wasn't sure whether to laugh or be horrified. "I'm pretty sure that's Sarah's favorite phrase."

Rylan shrugged. "I'm sure she'd ship it too. I would. Wouldn't you?"

I grinned so wide my cheeks hurt. "Definitely."

We grew quiet. I brushed my fingers over the healed skin on the underside of my wrist, trying not to think of what had been buried in there less than an hour before. Trying not to think about what would happen next. Somehow Rylan and I would have to find a way to cope with it, whatever it would be. We wouldn't have a choice.

The soft tick of Rylan's alarm clock filled the room.

"Rylan . . . I'm scared."

The smile curving his lips disappeared. His eyebrows furrowed. "Me too."

"I keep expecting the worst."

He reached an arm around my shoulders, pulling me to his chest. He smelled warm and safe, though I knew we were anything but. "So do I."

CHAPTER TWENTY

We didn't get many chances to talk the following week. Opening night of *Hall of Horrors* loomed closer, and if Rylan and I weren't stuck in rehearsals until an ungodly hour, we were slowly digging our way out of piles of homework, papers, tests, and presentations.

In short: Tech week was miserable. Commonly known as "hell week" in the theater community, it consisted of late-night rehearsals, nearly twenty costume fittings, and standing onstage doing absolutely nothing for an hour while Mrs. Miller patronized Rylan over whether yellow or pink lighting best complemented my skin tone. Yellow won out, much to Rylan's dismay.

Wednesday's rehearsal was the least painful. No one (specifically me) fell, the cast actually knew their lines, Jimmy Stubbs didn't slice off any more of his extremities, and Isaac's singing sounded better than ever. He totally nailed one of my favorite moments in the show—"My Hunger," a song where his character Prince Arthur debates whether he should give up the throne and turn in his family for cannibalistic crimes against the kingdom.

Isaac and I didn't even mess up our big dance number during the finale. I spun downstage and gracefully landed in his arms without causing injury to myself or others.

"Hey, that was great," he said during our break. "Good job."

"Thanks, Isaac."

"My pleasure, Hamilton." Isaac patted my shoulder and smiled. He had been on a nice streak lately, which made the hours I spent with him during tech week actually bearable. As I watched him walk backstage to grab a snack, I started to have faith that maybe this show wouldn't crash and burn after all.

Friday rolled around, and along with it came opening-night jitters. Morriston High had an early dismissal due to a faculty luncheon, so I had the entire afternoon to myself until showtime.

Rylan returned home to check on the nanobots. After weeks of testing, he hadn't determined their purpose. So far, no one in Morriston exhibited questionable behaviors or strange illnesses, which put my mind slightly at ease, but many citizens were still taking action. Plenty were accepting of the microchips, but that didn't include the protesters with their handmade signs, the rioters overturning vehicles, the groups staging sit-ins outside city hall. As far as anyone could tell, the crime rate remained unchanged. If anything, it might have gotten worse, although I suspected that was only because the chips hadn't been activated yet. The Morriston City Police Department had been tasked with using census data to ensure everyone received an injection—even those who hid at home hoping to avoid it. Last I heard, my father said everyone was accounted for.

Except Rylan and me.

I'd expected my house to be deserted when I kicked off my shoes at the back door, but my dad apparently had other ideas. He was seated in the living room, grasping the sports page of the newspaper between his fingers, holding it far enough away so no ink would stain his crisp white shirt. I didn't know whether to ignore him or scream in his face. Because of city hall, Rylan had a scar the size of Texas on his arm, and I could barely sleep with the terrible thoughts racing through my head in addition to my usual nightmares.

But when my dad dropped the paper from his face, all thoughts of yelling and temper tantrums vanished. A wide smile formed wrinkles around his eyes. It wasn't his politician grin—that one was sly, like a snake. It could convince anyone of anything. But this was his real smile. It spoke of bedtime stories, campfires, chocolate chip cookies, and kisses with Mom under the mistletoe. It had been ages since I'd seen it.

"Hey there, Abby!" He waved me over to the couch. Dad noticed when I hesitated, and his smile dropped for a fraction of a second before coming back even brighter. "Come on over! I haven't seen you in a while, honey."

I took the comics section when he offered it, skimming them over. My dad used to read the comics to me every Sunday, even before I was old enough to understand most of the jokes. That tradition stopped once he ran for reelection.

"Aw, man, that Charlie Brown gets me every time." Dad laughed and squeezed my shoulder. I tensed up. Chastising myself, I relaxed. This was my dad. This was fine. But why was I so nervous?

"So, what have you been up to, Abby?"

"Oh, nothing . . . nothing much. Been busy with school. Things have been pretty stressful."

Dad furrowed his brow. "Really? Anything I can help with?"

"No. Just—" I'd planned on crafting a stupid lie. Boys, classmate drama, maybe something girly that would have him turning back to the comics without question. But this was my chance. Rylan told me no, but surely I could ask one tiny question about the EDDs without raising suspicion? "Actually, the EDDs seem to be making a lot of people really anxious." I yawned, hoping to convince him my inquiry wasn't cause for concern. "Why do we need them anyway? I get that they're for premeditation, but I'm not a criminal. Connor obviously isn't a criminal either."

Maybe my overactive imagination caused me to think he flinched when I mentioned the chips. Maybe he was just taking his time folding the paper before answering. Maybe I needed to calm the heck down.

"Well . . ." He smiled at me. It was his politician's smile. "I don't want anyone thinking I'm giving you or your brother preferential treatment. And there's really no harm in getting one, even if it's not necessary. It won't hurt you." He glanced down at my wrist. I bunched up my sleeves in my hands, covering my skin even though Rylan had made sure there was nothing to see. I searched my dad's arm to see if I could find the soft blinking of a chip under his skin, but his cuffs covered his wrists.

"Don't worry," he continued. "I know people are angry. Change is an adjustment, but it won't always be this way. Pretty soon this will just be a thing of the past." Somewhere between his rubbing of my shoulder and his encouraging words, his grin morphed back to his real smile—the Dad Smile. "I can't tell you how excited I am about the E.D.D.s, Abby. They'll change the city forever! Finally, we'll be able to put an end to crime. Morriston will be a better place."

He relaxed into the couch, closing his eyes. He looked . . . happy. Really, truly happy for possibly the first time since Mom died. He was either the world's greatest actor, or he honestly believed the microchips would help the supers save people.

Which was worse? For me to tell him he was misled and ruin his happiness, or let him go on thinking everything was okay? Did I owe him the truth? He hadn't been around much; he'd been too busy with work to care. But he was still family. We protected our family.

"Dad . . . ," I began.

"I think we should go on a vacation, Abby," he said suddenly. "Me, you, and Connor. We deserve it, don't you think?"

We hadn't gone on vacation since my mom died. Dad couldn't bear to travel without her. If he truly wanted to go somewhere without my mom, he was finally healing. And I knew as well as anyone how long that took.

I wanted to tell the truth about the E.D.D.s, but I couldn't. Kind of like when you're in school and want to raise your hand, but refrain from fear your answer might be incorrect. Most of the time, you were right anyway. But you still don't raise your hand, even the next time. And the next. And the next. And the next.

I couldn't ruin his happiness with the possibility of being wrong.

"One day, Abby, we're going to live in a world full of peace," he said. "And what a beautiful world that will be."

Dad disappeared to the office, promising to be back in time for my show, and I headed into the kitchen, leaning against the counter while I rolled an apple between my palms, my thoughts raging. It was easy to believe he was innocent when I was sitting next to him, watching him smile and laugh and remember how things used to be before Mom died, but now that I was alone again, I wondered how much of what he told me was a lie. Did he know more about the microchips than he was letting on? I couldn't tell.

I glanced at my phone. Rylan promised he would call after he finished checking on the nanobots so we could meet up. But school let out over an hour ago, and Rylan assured me he only needed to visit his lab for a few minutes. I already felt nauseous over opening night. If something happened to Rylan . . . *No.* My imagination couldn't get the best of me. But still . . . a quick call wouldn't hurt.

My throat tightened while I listened to the phone ring. I felt like a nervous little girl calling a guy for the first time. Sweaty. Out of breath. But I should have heard from him by now. Rylan was nothing if not punctual.

Hey, this is Rylan. Sorry I missed you, but leave a message and I'll call you back as soon as I can. The beep's coming up in about two seconds. Aaaand . . . go.

"Hey, Rylan, it's me . . . uh, Abigail. I just wanted to make sure you're okay because you said you'd call and come over, and it's been over an hour and . . . I totally don't want to sound needy or anything, but . . . yeah. Just checking on you. Call me, or I'll call you or come over or something. Okay, bye."

Behold: World's Most Awkward Voicemail to Maybe-Boyfriend. Ever.

I waited about thirty minutes before totally freaking out. Rylan and I didn't talk on the phone much, but he'd never left one of my messages unanswered before. I didn't want to take any chances. I rushed around my house, searching for my wallet and the abundance of stage makeup I'd need for tonight, then sprinted to the nearest bus stop. I tried to convince myself everything would be okay. I'd go to Rylan's house and confirm he was still alive, and then maybe we could relax for a few hours. Maybe.

My fist pounded relentlessly on the front door of the megamansion. *Come on, come on, he has to be here.* Any second, he would open the door. He would smirk and make fun of my urgency. I would laugh, and he would laugh. And then he would invite me in and offer me some cookies. Except he wasn't opening the door.

I pounded harder.

The door flew open. My hand hovered in the air, midknock.

"Miss Abigail? One knock would have sufficed. I was in the middle of making dinner."

I looked up, staring at Franklin's white collared shirt and equally-as-white hair. Studying his face, I noticed he wasn't really that old—probably not much older than my dad. Franklin gazed at me with a mixture of joy and concern, and I suddenly felt the need to explain myself.

"Rylan? Is he here? Can I—I mean, I need to see him. Now. Could I—um . . ."

I was such an excellent speaker. What a stroke of luck that English happened to be my first language.

"Rylan's in the basement," Franklin said. "He hasn't come up since he arrived home. Can I get you something, Miss Abigail? A glass of water, perhaps?"

I shook my head and ran through the house before Franklin could stop me.

The basement steps were hidden in the corner of the kitchen. They were covered in a layer of dust, like Franklin didn't clean them often. Or at all. I reached the bottom, and the lab unfolded before my eyes. The thuds of equipment, flashing of lasers, and Rylan—hunched over a long table in the back corner.

"Rylan?"

He wheeled around. When I got closer, I noticed sweat soaking the back of his T-shirt. "Abby?" His voice sounded thick, pained.

"What happened? Are you okay? I tried to call, but you didn't answer."

"You did?" He pulled his phone from his pocket and glanced at the screen. "Oh, you did. Sorry. Did Franklin let you in?"

I nodded, and Rylan said, "You didn't tell him why you're here, did you?"

"No." *I* didn't even know why I was here.

"Good." He looked up the stairs to make sure we were alone. "I have to tell you something."

I could always count on Rylan not to sugarcoat things for me.

"One of my tests came back positive today," he said, forcefully rubbing the back of his skull. "God, I'm such an idiot! I should have checked this last week, but I didn't think it would be possible. I only ran it as a last resort, but I should've done it sooner. I'm such a—"

"Rylan!" I pulled his hands to his sides, forcing him to look at me instead of the ceiling. We wouldn't get anywhere if he kept babbling. "Tell me what happened. What did you find?"

Rylan gulped and glared at the microchip open on the table. "The nanobots were never meant to detect premeditation or malice or any other kind of emotion. They were meant to *change* emotions."

"Wait, *what*?"

"You heard me. They target the part of the brain that processes emotional reactions—the amygdala. The nanobots change a person's emotions depending on how they were specifically programmed by the scientists who engineered them."

"English, please?"

Rylan groaned, though I suspected it had little to do with my lack of scientific knowledge, and more to do with his anger at himself. "For example, if the nanobots were programmed to make you feel happy, then you become happy all the time. You could break your leg and still be happy about it. Sad, angry, scared, whatever—that's the only emotion you get. They completely control your brain. You don't get a choice in what you feel."

I didn't want to ask, but I had to. "What were these nanobots programmed for?"

Rylan slumped in the nearest chair and put his head in his hands. "Submission. If the nanobots work, which I'm positive they do, everyone who received an injection will obey anything they're told. If someone told Sarah to jump off the Morriston Bridge, she'd do it. If Franklin was commanded to drown himself, he wouldn't think twice. Anything to keep the peace."

The nanobots sounded anything *but* peaceful.

My stomach curled into knots. This couldn't be happening. I had too many nightmares while sleeping; I didn't think it was possible they could exist while I was awake. Not anymore. Not since Mom died.

Rylan reached for my arm. "Abigail . . . I don't want to say this, but your dad . . . I think he's responsible—"

I swallowed hard. I knew he was right, but I found myself shaking my head anyway.

"Abigail, listen. His whole thing is about bringing peace to the city. If he tells the citizens not to kill or steal or fight, they'll listen. Once the nanobots start working, their brains will be wired that way. They won't argue. And, *ta-da*, Morriston suddenly becomes the most peaceful city in America."

I was crying now. Big fat tears that kept coming and coming down my cheeks without end. Connor and I had been ordered to receive the injections just like everyone else. Did our dad mean to brainwash us too?

Rylan handed me a tissue, and I wiped my eyes and nose, my makeup coming off in big dark splotches. "So the chips are basically turning everyone in the city into robots?"

"Pretty much," he said.

"Is there a way to stop it?"

Rylan picked up the chip sitting on the table and slid it under a microscope. "They have to activate the nanobots from a computer, likely multiple computers considering how many people are involved. They need to be located somewhere in the city so the signal is strong enough to reach all the microchips. *If* we find the server before the nanobots are activated, I could destroy the data."

"And if we find the server after?"

Rylan sighed. "I don't know. I never expected it to be this bad. I don't know if this is something we could reverse."

There was a time, right after my mom died, when I was excellent at choking back tears. I'd hold my breath and pinch my arm until it bruised, and I wouldn't cry. I got so good that there were days when Dad or Connor asked if I was even upset at all. Of course I was. But I was selfish. I hid the pain inside, I kept it to myself. It hurt less that way. I convinced myself that if I didn't cry, her death wouldn't be real.

Eventually, I did cry. And it was real.

But now, I was severely out of practice at holding in my emotions. I sobbed and couldn't breathe, and suddenly found my cheek pressed against Rylan's damp T-shirt while I hiccupped my tears away.

"I need to call my dad," I said at last. "I need to find out where he is. If we find him, we might find the server."

I dialed my dad's number with shaking fingers. The phone rang and rang and rang. And finally . . .

You have reached Mayor Benjamin Hamilton. Please leave your name, phone num—

I hung up and dialed again. And again. And again. I didn't bother leaving a message. If my dad cared at all, he would see my multitude of missed calls and wonder what was the matter.

"Do we have a plan B?" Rylan asked.

I dialed the number of the office building Dad moved to after Rylan set the fire in city hall, but the line was disconnected. It was possible he'd switched offices again without telling anyone, probably out of paranoia that someone would find out what he was up to and try to track him down. But if he moved to another building, I didn't know where it was. It wasn't like my dad ever told me much of anything. But there was one person . . . one person who knew plenty more about my dad's career than I. And I knew exactly where to find him.

"Rylan, every good superhero knows there's *always* a plan B."

"Plan B is the Bookworm?"

The Bookworm was a large independent bookstore down the road from the Morriston Mall . . . or where the Morriston Mall used to be before someone blew it up. Nevertheless, the Bookworm lived on, and today it just so happened to be packed with screaming, swooning fangirls.

"Abigail, I like books as much as the next person, but why are we here?"

I pointed to the long line stretching out the door and down the sidewalk. Teen girls and their moms chattered and squealed in small groups. They came armed with life-sized posters, handmade T-shirts, and Sharpies in every color. Rolling my eyes had never turned into such a workout.

Rylan eyed two girls standing just outside the shop. They both wore matching red bodysuits with a familiar gold swoosh on their chests. "Your brother's here?" he asked.

I hit him with my right elbow while using my left to dig our way through the crowd to get inside. "Don't mention him! Do you want them to attack you? They'll take you prisoner if they think you know him."

"They won't."

"Oh yeah?" I cocked an eyebrow. "Don't be so sure. Super fangirls are completely different than casual fangirls." I pointed out two sleeping bags on the ground and a sign reading, *We waited 52 hours for Red Comet!*

"These fans will *eat you*," I said.

The inside of the Bookworm was more crowded than the outside. The gossiping, crying, obnoxious line wound between bookshelves all the way to the back of the store where Connor sat behind a long table. Two burly security guards stood on either side. I wasn't really sure they could protect Connor in any way his superpowers could not. But they did look intimidating, which I guess cut down on the number of girls willing to leap across the table and offer up their virginity.

"Huh. I've never been to a meet and greet before. Do you think I could get one of these?" Rylan's eyes grew wide as he took it all in. The posters and the cleavage, the chanting and the short skirts. And the cleavage. Did I mention the cleavage? I flicked the side of his head, snapping him out of it.

"Rylan, keep staring and you won't get much of anything from anybody. Get your head in the game."

"Yes, ma'am," he grumbled.

Girls whined and threw tantrums as we brushed past to the front of the line. One mother tried pulling Rylan's hair to hold us up. And all over Connor, my dorky brother who could burp the alphabet—one of the least classy celebrities in the country.

"Still want a meet and greet?" I asked Rylan.

He rubbed his head where the woman's long nails scratched him. He pouted. "No."

Rylan suggested we approach the shortest security guard. Unfortunately, the shortest guard was also the widest, and looked like he could run me over like a tank. He stopped us twenty feet away from Connor, holding his arms out so we couldn't slip by. My brother was too busy signing posters for fans to notice.

"Hello," I greeted the guard. Kill 'em with kindness. "We need to speak with Red Comet. It's really important."

The guard snorted. When he tilted his head, I noticed a tattoo of a dragon curling around his left ear. "Yeah, girl, you and everyone else here. Get in line. He'll see you if he has enough time."

Rylan sized the guard up. Rylan had at least several inches on him, but the security guard weighed twice as much. Then again, Rylan had a bit more going for him than the average human. "How much longer is he here for?"

" 'Til six. Get in line before I throw you two out. He'll see you when he sees you."

"We don't exactly have time to wait," Rylan continued.

"Then get out. No one sees Red Comet without a wristband." The guard pointed to a red band on a nearby girl's arm. "And you only get one by waiting in line, so if you don't have the time, leave before I escort you out myself."

Rylan snorted, and I noticed his chest puff out a fraction. He wanted to go all alpha-male-superhero on this guy's ass, I could tell. Surely he would win, but he'd definitely expose himself in the process.

Pulling Rylan's arm, I said to the guard, "We need to talk to Red Comet. Right now." I noticed a microchip glowing blue under his skin. "It's life or death, and I know for a fact he'll be furious with you if you don't let me see him. All the other fans can wait. Just go ask him," I added when the guard opened his mouth to argue. "If he says no, he says no, right? No big deal, and then we'll leave."

The guard slunk away to Connor's table. He whispered something in my brother's ear, and Connor turned toward us. I couldn't see his eyes behind his mask, but I knew he wouldn't leave us hanging. Every girl in line followed his gaze. If looks could kill. These fangirls were ruthless.

Connor nodded, and the guard returned. He pointed to me. "He said he'll only see you. Your friend needs to stay here."

"Shocker," Rylan grumbled.

I shrugged apologetically. Connor stood from his meet-and-greet table, gave the teen girl standing before him a quick hug, and led me through a door into a storage room. Books overflowed from boxes onto the floor, and a pack of mechanical pencils was scattered along a tiny table next to a half-empty coffee cup.

As soon as the door closed, Connor pulled off his mask and went in for a hug. Damp pieces of hair clung to his sweaty forehead, but he grinned so wide his mouth almost looked too big for his face.

"Hey there, Abby! I didn't know you were stopping to visit, but I'm glad you did. I was suffocating out there! Weird place for a meet and greet, isn't it? I wanted to do it in a strip club, but I'm trying to appease my younger audience. And sorry about Mike, he thought you were some groupie trying to get to me. I told him off for it, he won't do it again. Don't know why I even need security anyway, you know? I can always just fly—"

"Connor!" I yelled. He threw a hand over my mouth to silence me in case someone was listening, but got distracted seconds later and began clicking the lead out of the pencils on the table. "Connor, can you focus, please?"

He dropped the pink pencil in his hand. "My bad. What's up?"

I chose to blame my pounding headache on the horde of hormonal girls outside. Rubbing my temples, I said, "Do you know where I can find Dad?"

Connor shrugged. "I don't know, work maybe?"

"Did he move offices again?"

"Umm . . . yeah. I wrote it down, but the paper's somewhere at home. Why?"

"Because . . ." I took a deep breath. "I think he did something really, really bad, and I need to fix it."

"What are you talking about?"

If Rylan was here, he wouldn't have wanted to tell Connor. And even if he did, Rylan certainly wouldn't have cried. I did both. And after, while I wiped my nose on the shoulder of Connor's super suit, I felt a little better. Until . . .

"I don't believe any of that," Connor said.

"What?"

"Dad wouldn't do that. He wouldn't just force people into feeling things so he can control them. He's trying to help people, not—not *hurt them*."

"Connor, please—"

"Did Iron Phantom tell you this? Are you seriously still in contact with him?"

"No. It wasn't him. It was my . . . friend."

"Is it the friend who came here with you? Abby," Connor yelled, "wake up! He doesn't know Dad. *We do*. Dad would never do anything to hurt anyone."

My chest tightened. I was angry and confused and didn't know what to believe anymore. It seemed like anything could be possible.

"Look, even if Dad isn't involved, *someone is*. Someone lied to us. The microchips don't detect emotions," I repeated Rylan's words. "They change emotions. And if you want to be a hero, then stop sitting around signing autographs when people could be in serious danger. Do something, Connor!"

Connor's fingers balled into fists. He clenched his jaw and closed his eyes. I could pinpoint the exact moment when he moved on from petty anger to something resembling acceptance. I hadn't mentioned our mom this time, but it didn't matter. When Connor's shoulders slouched and he slowly slipped his mask back on, I knew I hit the same nerve as before.

"At least take out your microchip," I begged. "Please just do that. You don't have anything to lose."

Connor pulled off the glove on his right hand and glanced at his wrist. "How?"

"Cut it out. That's what I did. And tell Hunter to do it too."

He pulled his glove back on. "I don't know, Abby. . . ."

"Please. It's not what you think it is."

"Fine. I'll see what I can do. I have to get back out there, and you need to get ready for your show. Dad and I are coming. We'll all talk about this after and figure everything out. You can even bring your . . . special friend." Connor gagged, and I swatted at his head. He ducked easily. "Break a leg tonight, Abby. You'll kick ass."

Connor reentered the bookstore to shrill screams and unnecessary sobbing. By the time I pulled it together and left the storage room, he had already resumed his seat and was taking a selfie with a middle-aged woman wearing only slightly more clothing than some of the teens.

Rylan rushed over immediately. "How'd it go?"

I scowled at my idiot brother. I was so sure he would help, so sure he would be on my side. "Horrible."

"Fan-freaking-tastic."

"Abby, are you ready?" Mrs. Miller approached me ten minutes to curtain. My face had been caked with foundation and eyeliner and lipstick, my eyebrows drawn darker by one of the makeup mothers backstage. I wore a flowy beige dress and a corset that made my boobs look awesome even though I could barely breathe, and my honey-blond hair hid under a long brunette wig. A ring of small flowers circled my head. I looked nothing like Abby and everything like Angeline. That should have excited me. My heart should have been thumping with anticipation, but all I felt was fear.

If fear had a color, it would be black. It would drip like tar and stick to your fingers no matter how many times you tried wiping it off. It would smell acidic, burnt plastic melting into the ground, into your soul. Fear sometimes sneaks up on you when your back is turned. Other times, it stands before you in plain sight. That's the worst kind. When it's so obvious it had been there all along, but you were just too blind to see. Fear is when you find out someone you loved and trusted wasn't who you thought they were. Fear is when you realize you've been lied to.

I nodded to my director, taking a few deep breaths. I tried to imagine the coil in my muscles as I danced, the tickle in my throat after hitting a high note. I imagined the warmth that spread through my chest when Rylan wrapped his arms around me. I felt a little better.

"Yeah. Yeah, I'm good," I said.

"Excellent! You are going to be fabulous! Break legs!" Mrs. Miller tightened a lime green cardigan around her shoulders as she waded through racks of costumes and cans of hair spray to search for Isaac.

I felt awkward leaning against the wall by myself as I counted down the minutes until curtain. The rest of the cast was busy taking pictures and chatting away. The only person I wanted to talk to before going onstage was Rylan, but he was busy fixing a wheel on the bottom of the papier-mâché crocodile. Interesting how I waited and agonized over my shot as a lead in a Morriston musical, and now that I had it, all I wanted was for it to end.

Rylan and I came *this close* to blowing off the show completely in the face of what we learned this afternoon. We might have actually done it too, if disappearing wouldn't have triggered my father's suspicions that we were onto him. So we were stuck waiting until after the final curtain call before we could do anything worthwhile. The musical didn't matter in the grand scheme of things. Not anymore.

Feeling a tap on my shoulder, I turned to find Sarah rocking on her heels, glancing nervously at the hallway leading to the stage. We hadn't talked much lately, between the E.D.D. injections and our late nights spent at rehearsal, but she was still my best friend. I leaned in to hug her, hoping that if I held on to someone safe and familiar, then maybe it would drain my fear away.

It didn't work very well, but you can't blame a girl for trying.

"Are you nervous?" Sarah asked me. "Because I'm nervous. Like, so-nervous-I'm-going-to-barf nervous." She pushed a piece of hair from her eyes, revealing the inside of her wrist where the light from her microchip flickered. I instinctively hid my own wrist in the folds of my dress.

"Don't picture the audience in their underwear," I advised. "It never works out quite the way you want it to."

"Noted." She straightened her blue dress and bubble-gum pink sweater, which clashed horribly with her red hair. Someone needed to be fired from costume duty.

"Places!" a girl on stage crew poked her head into the dressing room before quickly ducking out.

My heart skipped a beat, and Sarah's face filled with a frightened deer-in-the-headlights look.

"No underwear?" she asked.

I nodded. "No underwear."

She pulled me a second hug. "You'll be amazing, Abby."

"You too. Hey, Sarah!" I called as she walked away. She turned around with a smile plastered to her face, and I knew I couldn't keep lying to her. She deserved better. "Come find me and Rylan after the show. We really need to tell you something."

"You're not pregnant, are you?"

"What? No! Just come find us."

As I rushed to stage left for my first entrance, a warm hand gripped my wrist, pulling me to a halt. I almost didn't recognize Isaac with his slicked-back hair and pointed silver crown. He wasn't supposed to be on this side of the stage, something I knew he was well aware of.

Isaac's eyes flitted around the hallway. "We got this, right? If those damn supers can put on their tights and rescue people from fires and shit, then we can go out there and sing."

"Of course we can." I watched as Isaac dabbed at the sweat on his forehead. Was he, of all people, nervous? A microchip blinked under his skin, and I tried to ignore the plummeting feeling in my gut. "I think the supers have grown on you since you moved here."

"You might be right. I know he's a villain, but I'm somewhat of a closet Iron Phantom fanatic. I guess I'm a sucker for an underdog."

Me too, Isaac, I thought. *Me too.*

Isaac smirked. "And black is also my favorite color. Anyway . . ." He took a deep breath, washing away the nerves, then grinned at me. "Break a leg."

Orchestra music swelled just as I reached the wings. I scooted past a few chorus girls and a sophomore boy named Danny who was holding a microphone and reciting the prologue before the first song.

"On one desolate winter night, inside a majestic town not unlike our own . . ."

"Are Connor and my dad here?" I whispered to Rylan. He sat on a stool with a flashlight and a copy of the script, preparing to pull open the curtain.

". . . humanity was targeted from all sides by an unknown assailant . . ."

"Connor's been here awhile. He's saving your dad a seat. Last time I checked, he wasn't here yet."

I gulped. "Okay."

"*. . . And this savage enemy emerged not by land nor air nor sea. For it lurked inside the very walls of the kingdom it sought to destroy . . .*"

The wings filled with a blue glow from the microchips under my castmates' skin. Rylan and I tugged at our sleeves. "Everything's going to be fine, Abigail. I promise."

"*. . . draining life from all who dare approach it.*"

The show started off good, fine, as well as anyone could expect of a bunch of amateur high school students. We had an audience primarily made up of students, teachers, and parents who cheered loudly at the end of each song and laughed every time Prince Arthur said something suave. Rylan rewarded me with a huge smile and a thumbs-up after my big solo number, "Better Than This," where Angeline dreams of leaving her run-down servants' quarters for life in the countryside with a pasture full of flowers and a loving husband like Arthur.

The stage lights were so bright that I couldn't see past the first two rows to find Connor or my dad. Were they enjoying the show? Did Dad eventually come? I had no clue.

But other than that, *Hall of Horrors* was going smoothly.

Until . . . the kiss.

I'd kissed Isaac plenty of times this week, something Rylan reminded me of with frequent groans and eye rolls. The whole thing turned out much better than the first time—nothing like kissing Rylan, but at least Isaac quickly figured out licking me and yanking my butt looked (and felt) disgusting onstage.

The song leading up to the big kiss required Angeline and Arthur to profess their undying love for each other. Isaac's hands were slick with sweat while they held my own, and I knew I wasn't doing much better. The stage felt like a burning inferno, but we worked our way through, taking deep breaths in the right spots and belting out high notes in others.

"Living in shadows, I never felt free.

You became my sun, and I could finally breathe.

And as we stare into the stars,

Your head pressed against my heart . . ."

The entire cast joined us onstage, egging on Arthur and Angeline to confirm their everlasting love with a big, sloppy kiss. Sarah caught my eye and winked. As anxious as I had been before the show, I couldn't help but enjoy myself a little bit. This was exciting, an adrenaline rush. All eyes were on me, and I felt like I could do anything.

". . . I know now that we're together,

This love starts today and lasts forever.

Because nothing can be better . . ."

I moved closer to Isaac, our hands clasped tightly together and our chests nearly touching. Part of him looked terrified, but another part—a larger one—was enjoying this too.

"Nothing can be better . . .

Nothing can be better than the prince and . . ."

Isaac winked playfully, and for once, I didn't want to spit in his face.

". . . I!"

When we kissed, the audience held their breath. And so did I. I held my breath and looked up with wide eyes. Because just above us, one of the lights had come loose and was tumbling down, making a beeline for my face.

CHAPTER TWENTY-ONE

It happened in slow motion—or at least it felt that way. Funny how that works. Pleasurable moments fly by, the memories hazy after a few months, but the horrible ones drag on and on and on.

I froze, unmoving until a pair of hands shoved my shoulders. I fell with enough force to send my head snapping back and cracking against the stage. Stars popped before my eyes. The world turned black. I thought I passed out until I heard the screams. They came from every direction—in front of me, behind me, inside me. I tried to move. My head hurt so much. I felt someone next to me—Isaac probably, his fingers running through my hair. It felt nice. All I wanted to do was sleep.

"Abigail! Abby! Look at me, okay?"

Someone shook my shoulders, and my eyelids fluttered open. Every light in the auditorium was now lit, ruining the magic of the Hall of Horrors. Maybe Mrs. Miller was right: This show was horrible. Cursed.

Either the room had quieted down or I ruptured my eardrum when I hit the deck. Considering my head was hurting, not my ears, and I could easily hear my pained whimpers, I decided to go with the former. The audience sat silently in their seats, looking patiently at the stage. Except Connor. He bounded up the aisle, leapt through the air, and landed right next to me and . . . Rylan. Rylan was the one stroking my hair, his eyebrows pulled together, forming a crease.

"What's going on?" I moaned, looking at my feet. One of my sandals had fallen off, and my dress had suffered a long tear from ankle to knee. The shattered remains of the light were strewn along the floor. Isaac was gone. Go figure. It was too far-fetched to think he'd stick around and see if I was okay. He was probably on his phone again. Or eating.

"You're fine, everything's fine," Rylan said. "Sarah, come here!"

I propped up on my elbows, watching Sarah. She wasn't freaking out, which freaked me out. She stood with her hands clasped in front of her dress, a brilliant smile gracing her lips. Never mind that I probably had a concussion and almost got knocked out by a stage light. Sarah was calm, cool, and collected. Not normal.

Her hands shifted, and I noticed her microchip now blinked not blue . . . but red.

She said, "Do you need something, Rylan?" Sarah's voice sounded soothing, musical, and so unlike herself. Her eyes looked blank, staring but not really seeing.

"S-Sarah?" I looked from her wrist, to my castmates, to the audience. Red. Red. Red. If the microchips glowed blue when dormant, then they glowed red when they were . . .

"No!" I yelled, lunging for Sarah's skirt.

Rylan pushed me down on the stage again. "Sarah, make sure everyone gets home safely." He turned to the audience. "Go. Follow her right now."

They stood in such bone-chilling synchronicity that my mouth went dry. With one short command from Rylan, they filed out the door.

Connor gasped, his fingers digging into my skin. "What the hell . . ."

"Those chips are programmed to turn the entire city into submissive zombies. They aren't meant to help people like *you* save anyone," Rylan snapped. "Exhibit A." He gestured to the line of men and women slowly walking past. I watched in horror, listening to the soft footfalls of my classmates, teachers, and neighbors until they disappeared down the hall. "Didn't Abigail tell you?"

"Well, yeah—"

"So you weren't listening? Or don't you understand words? Because those are the only reasons I can think of for you to completely reject everything your sister told you!"

"I didn't completely reject her. I cut out my chip, didn't I?" He pushed up his jacket, flashing his scabbed wrist. "Listen, kid, you have no idea who you're messing with."

Rylan snorted. "Oh, *I* have no idea? You have no idea—"

"Rylan!" I tugged on his T-shirt and groaned. My head pounded so hard I thought something was growing out of my skull, and their arguing wasn't helping.

Connor's fingers probed through my hair. "She needs to go to a hospital."

"No, she doesn't."

"Are you shitting with me right now? Look at her!" I'd closed my eyes again, and I felt rather than saw Connor wave his hands around my face.

"Just move back for a second," Rylan said.

"No way!"

"*Move* away. I don't know if you noticed, but you're wasting time arguing with me."

With an agitated sigh, Connor scooted back, and Rylan's hands replaced my brother's. His fingers rubbed the growing bump on the back of my skull. "Hold still, Abigail."

"Rylan, don't." I knew how much my head hurt, and the last thing I wanted was for Rylan to take my pain into his body. If we were going to destroy the nanobots, he would need his strength.

But my plea was futile. As soon as Rylan touched me, I felt my skin grow warm. I relaxed as the tingle spread toward my forehead and the throbbing trickled away. When I opened my eyes, I noticed Rylan panting in pain.

Connor looked on in horror. "What are you doing?"

"Healing," Rylan grunted.

"Healing? Wait, you're . . ."

The last of my headache faded, and Rylan pulled me to my feet. Apart from us, the auditorium was now empty. Rylan swayed a bit and braced his hands on his knees.

"You have superpowers? *You?*" Connor asked. "Hang on, who even are you?"

Rylan straightened up and held out his hand. "Rylan Sloan."

"No, that's not what I meant. I mean . . . wait. You're the guy from the meet and greet today. And you have healing powers? Just like . . . no. No way. You're him? *Iron Phantom*. You're *him*!"

Rylan was still breathing heavily as he waited for the impact from my concussion to dissolve. "Yeah, uh, sometimes I am, yeah."

"Oh, okay, then." Connor crossed his arms, and I caught a hint of a smile cross his lips. Was he actually just going to let this go? Then his eyes grew dark. No. No, he wasn't. "I am going to *kill you*!"

Connor charged, and I jumped forward, blocking his path. Which was a horrible idea. Connor's chest hit me like a train, and I flew back into Rylan's arms. "Connor, stop! Rylan's not a villain; he's just trying to help!"

"No, Abby, he's not." Connor gripped my shoulders and tugged me toward him, but Rylan wouldn't let go. Connor pulled at my wrist but stopped when I backed up into Rylan's chest.

When we were kids, Connor always tried to tug me along. He would drag me outside to play superheroes or to our parents' room to rummage through their drawers, searching for "buried treasure." Whenever my brother reached for me, I always knew to follow. But not this time. Not when I knew he was wrong.

"So, what? You're choosing him over me?" Connor tilted his chin up and tried to look tough, but I knew, deep down, he was terrified he might be right.

"It's not about choosing, Connor," I said. "It's about doing what's right. Rylan never killed anyone; he's not the bad guy. But someone else is. If we can find the server sending the signal to the nanobots, then Rylan can destroy it and everyone will be normal again. We can save the city."

"Fine, then." Connor waved his hand toward the door. "If you want to pick him, if that's what you want to do, I don't see what's stopping you."

He was missing the bigger picture. Maybe I had it all wrong. Since Connor received his powers, I thought he was superhero first, brother second. But now, Red Comet didn't even think about coming to the rescue. As his lips curled at the sight of Rylan's arms around my waist, I realized Connor cared significantly more about saving me than saving Morriston.

Rylan released me and stepped forward, squaring off against my brother. "What's stopping us is that we don't know where to find the server. I have an idea—city hall. But no one knows where they moved their offices to . . . except maybe you." Rylan ran a hand through his hair, then hesitantly stretched out his hand. Connor hated Rylan, and Rylan wasn't particularly wild about Connor, but he wanted to make a truce. "As much as I hate to admit this, Connor," Rylan said, "we need you."

Rylan and I waited in the hallway for Connor to change into his super suit. I had traded my *Hall of Horrors* costume for my street clothes, and Rylan already wore his full Iron Phantom regalia. I was beyond thankful the school was empty. Seeing Morriston's most worshipped and most feared supers together in the same room would be difficult to explain.

I bounced on the balls of my feet and pulled at the sleeves of my sweatshirt. Connor could be worse than a teenage girl when it came to getting dressed, and I was afraid that if he didn't hurry up, we would be too late. He clearly wasn't taking mine and Rylan's fears seriously. Connor had seen the nanobots work for himself, but I didn't think he truly believed what was happening. In his mind, anything city hall did was good.

"Connor, get out here!" I yelled, pounding my fist on the bathroom door. My nerves were starting to make me nauseous again. "I feel like I'm going to throw up."

"What? Are you okay?" Rylan urgently pressed his wrist to my forehead. "Do you need to sit down?"

I kicked the door of the men's room with the tip of my boot, wincing and hopping on one foot when I crushed my toes. "No, Rylan. Since I met you, I always feel like I'm about to throw up. Connor, *come on*!"

Rylan leaned against the wall and smoothed out a wrinkle in his mask. The lights in the school were shut off apart from the dim red glow of the emergency exits. Rylan's dark suit rendered him practically invisible, and I jumped when his disembodied voice muttered in my ear, "I'm choosing to take that as a compliment."

"Take it however you want."

"I shall."

"Will you lovebirds shut up?" Connor emerged from the bathroom with his Red Comet tights intact and his phone pressed against his ear. "You disgust me. Dammit!" He scowled at his cell, and I thought I heard a piece of the plastic case crack beneath his fingers.

"What's wrong?"

"Well, first, I called Hunter. That's Fish Boy to you," Connor said to Rylan. "He's meeting us downtown. And second, I called Dad, and he's not answering his phone. I keep trying, but . . ."

My stomach plummeted. With the excitement of the show and the terror that ensued after the stage light crashed down, I forgot to ask Rylan if he ever saw my dad come in. I thought back to that moment, lying on the filthy stage with my head beating like a drum. I tried to picture the scene in my mind. The audience had been still. Connor jumped out of his seat and ran to help, and to his left—I remembered now. To his left had been an empty seat. Dad never showed up.

And now we didn't know where he was.

With one long sniffle, I managed to hold in my tears. This whole mystery with the nanobots was so unbelievably confusing and wrong, and crying wouldn't make it better. Straightening my shoulders, I forced my face into a blank, emotionless mask. Because that's what all the supers did in the midst of catastrophe. Even if a building was blowing up or someone was dying, they didn't show fear.

"Fine. So, what now?" I asked.

Both Connor and Rylan seemed taken aback by my abrupt change in attitude. Clearing his throat, Connor motioned for us to follow him outside. Icy tendrils of air crept up the back of my neck and stung my cheeks. I quickly pulled up the hood of my sweatshirt.

Rylan watched my every move. "She doesn't have a mask," he observed.

Connor didn't bother glancing over his shoulder as he led us into the trees behind the school. "She'll be fine. Worse comes to worst, I'll play it off like I just saved her from you."

I punched Connor in the back. He didn't even flinch. "*She* has a name," I said. "And *she* doesn't appreciate you talking about her like she isn't standing right here."

"Yeah, yeah." Connor turned to face us in the middle of a small clearing. His red boots crunched in a pile of dead leaves. "Look, here's what's going to happen. I'm taking Abby," Connor reached for my arm. "You teleport downtown or whatever it is you do. Meet us on the corner of Springfield and Sixth. You know where that is?"

Rylan nodded. "Sure, but I think I'll take Abigail with me, if you don't mind."

"Actually, I do mind." Connor pulled on my right wrist, and Rylan held on to my left. This felt like two little girls fighting over a rag doll, and we really didn't have time for it. Every second we wasted, all of Morriston was going further and further out of their minds. They would do anything they were told without a second thought. Didn't anyone else understand how dangerous that was?

Rylan gave my arm a tug, and I fell into his chest. "Look, I'm really not trying to be a jerk, but it's freezing out here. Do you think Abigail would rather fly a million miles an hour with you or teleport with me?"

"*Abigail* is turning into an icicle," I interjected. "Teleporting sounds lovely."

Connor harrumphed, knowing Rylan had him beat. Tonight in Morriston, for one night only: *Battle of the Testosterone: My Brother vs. My Boyfriend.*

"Okay, great, fantastic," Connor said, though I could distinctly feel him rolling his eyes behind his mask. Before I could call him out on it, he bent his knees and rocketed into the sky.

We watched the red blur that was my brother grow smaller and smaller until he disappeared completely. Rylan shrugged and held out his hand. "You ready?"

I gulped, suddenly nervous that, no matter how much I disliked Morriston High, something bad would happen tonight and I would never see it again. I lied when I said, "Yeah, I'm ready."

I held my breath, and we rode the Black Vortex of Terror into town. Connor was waiting for us when we arrived, leaning against a parking meter and trying to look debonair. The tights kind of took away from his desired level of sophistication, not to mention no one was even on the streets to see him. As usual, Morriston turned vacant after dark. The only way people would be outside tonight was if someone forced them. Which wasn't highly unlikely.

A gust of wind blew off the river, chilling me to the bone. Rylan and Connor were too busy glaring at each other to move, so I picked a random direction and started walking down the street. Someone had to take initiative.

Connor grabbed the back of my hood and pulled me to a stop. "Where are you going? That's the wrong way."

"Right, uh, yeah. Yeah, I totally knew that."

Connor snorted. "Right. City hall's new offices are this way." He pointed to the nearest intersection, and we followed behind him.

We crossed the street and passed a line of shady-looking shops, including but not limited to: a toy store, an abandoned café, and a filthy ice cream parlor next to one of the dirtiest, smelliest alleyways known to mankind. When Connor finally stopped, I craned my neck and looked at the building stretching toward the sky. As far as offices went, it was pretty unassuming. Made of gray brick, it housed a bank and a deli on the ground floor next to a revolving door. It wasn't a tiny building, but it certainly wasn't one of the tallest in the city.

Connor looked up and down Springfield Street with his hands on his hips. A lamppost flickered on the corner, then went out. "Where the hell is Hunter? He told me he took out his chip. There's no reason he shouldn't be here."

As if on cue, a rumble sounded from the next street over. The sound grew louder and louder, culminating in Fish Boy's motorcycle screeching around the corner, coming to a halt in front of us. Hunter tugged off a helmet, straightened his mask, and ruffled his hair with two webbed hands.

"Hey, friends. Ready to save the world?"

"We saved it already," Connor said dryly. "You were too slow."

"Yeah, right. This baby goes zero to sixty in three seconds." He patted his handlebars. "Speaking of which, should I feed the meter, or do you think I'll get a pass tonight because of this nanobot nonsense?"

"I think you'll be fine," Rylan said. He was watching Hunter like he couldn't be sure whether to take him seriously or not.

"Cool. Oh, hey! It's you!" Hunter looked Rylan's Iron Phantom suit up and down. "You don't look anywhere near as scrawny as you do on TV."

Rylan's green contacts caught the light as he stared at Hunter. "Um . . . thanks?"

"You're welcome."

"Can we go inside now?" Connor asked. He was chomping on something beneath his mask. Gum, probably.

"You're sure this is the right place?" Rylan asked. His voice sounded determined, but when I cast a sidelong glance, I noticed Rylan anxiously pulling at the back of his mask.

"This was the address written in my dad's office at our house. So I'm going to avouch that this is it."

"Avouch? You mean *vouch*?"

"Nope." Connor smirked, and the corners of his mouth formed

a crease in his mask. "Avouch. It was on my Word of the Day calendar. Look it up, wise guy."

No, he wasn't lying. Connor really did own a Word of the Day calendar and used the words he learned at extremely stressful and unhelpful moments. He also used insults from the 1890s and pretended like they were a big slap in the face.

Rylan was obviously sick of arguing with my brother because he didn't say anything further. Instead, he squared his shoulders and strode through the building's revolving door like he owned the place. Hunter followed, and Connor and I brought up the rear.

"So . . . who came up with the name Fish Boy?" I heard Rylan ask.

Hunter shrugged. "My grandma picked it out. Couldn't tell her no."

Unsurprisingly, the lights in the lobby were low. An overturned janitor's bucket and mop lay on the floor, soaking the gold tiles with sudsy water. Whoever had been using them clearly left in quite a hurry—or was forced into leaving.

A single guard sat behind a gleaming reception desk. He straightened when he saw us, and Connor gave him a little wave.

"Evening, sir. We're just heading upstairs. Don't mind—"

The guard stood, raising his gun. The red glow of his microchip flickered. He fired off two shots at our heads, forcing us to duck.

"Don't worry, guys. I got him." Connor stood, rearing back his fist as the guard ran around the desk. Just as he raised his weapon again, I stuck my foot out, sending him crashing to the lobby floor. Rylan kicked the man's gun away and punched him out before Connor had time to move.

"Too slow," I told my brother while Rylan chained the guard to the desk using the man's own handcuffs. Connor grumbled something incoherent. It looked like he was trying really hard not to flip us off.

With the guard incapacitated, we headed for the elevator. As we waited for the car to arrive, it finally hit me how serious this was. I thought I knew what we were getting into, but I was wrong. The force of what we could face in the city hall offices beat me down until my legs wobbled like jelly. Injury, destruction, something worse? Sure, Rylan, Connor, and Hunter had badass superpowers, but we were all so young. I looked at my feet. I felt tiny, like a child. I was nothing but a kid, and Rylan's, Hunter's, and Connor's tight costumes and silly superhero names suddenly made them look ridiculous instead of intimidating. How was this going to work? I was stupid to think we could do anything about the nanobots. Could the four of us really make a difference in the lives of thousands?

"What floor do you think?" Rylan asked when the doors opened in front of us.

Without thinking, I said, "Twenty-sixth. Top floor."

"How'd you know?"

The shiny brass walls of the elevator car displayed our reflections. They scrunched my features until I appeared short and squat and stretched the boys into string beans. Looking like clowns in a fun house didn't exactly help my diminishing confidence.

"We're talking about my father," I said. "He wouldn't want to sit in an office any lower than the highest floor."

"Okay, listen," Connor said. "When we get in there, just follow my lead."

Rylan grumbled, "Does your lead involve distraction by means of recitation of your fancy calendar?"

Connor paused, scratching his head. "Re-ci-ta-tion," he sounded out.

"Whoops, sorry. That must be tomorrow's word. Didn't mean to spoil it for you."

Hunter leaned toward me, whispering, "Thanks for inviting me. This is way better than reality TV."

By now I was pressing my temple against the wall to soothe my flourishing migraine. "Do you guys need to keep fighting?"

Apparently the answer was a resounding *yes* because Connor and Rylan were still going at it when the elevator dinged on level twenty-six. It was a wonder either of them managed to rescue anyone with their abundance of sensitivity issues.

Hunter and I watched as Connor pushed Rylan's mask over his eyes. Rylan retaliated with a swift kick to Connor's shin.

Grabbing them both by the shoulders, I nearly bashed their heads together. "Focus," I growled.

We crept down the hall into the labyrinth of cubicles. Each space appeared empty, and my nerves eased slightly. If no one was here, it would be easier to destroy the server. And if the server wasn't here, then we could go home, gain some intel about city hall, and form another plan—one less dangerous than creeping into a building practically blind.

I clearly wasn't cut out for the superhero life.

"Do you hear that?" Connor whispered.

We paused in the middle of the floor, outside a dark conference room. Someone was speaking, laughing deep in the office. Rylan crouched low and looked around the corner of the nearest cubicle. No one. Hunter inched forward across the floor, and Rylan followed. I linked one hand with Rylan's and the other with Connor's, and we formed a chain as we made our way through the building.

More laughing. A bit of singing. Then an advertisement for a tanning salon.

Someone had the radio on. Talk radio.

My father loved talk radio.

Hunter waved his hand and motioned to a glass wall in the corner of the office. The room was huge, lavish, filled with couches and leather chairs that undoubtedly belonged to my dad. Nothing less than the best for the mayor of Morriston.

A blaring radio sat on an immaculately clean wooden desk next to three computers and a tall, humming server bank. Green lights flashed across the server at random intervals. Bright orange cables were coiled in a heap on the floor. Part of me expected the computers to be bigger, more impressive and less like the average laptop. But that's what they were. And they were also so close I could almost feel myself picking them up and smashing them into the office's white walls.

"Is anyone in there?" I asked.

"Can't tell," Rylan whispered. "I could teleport in and see. . . ."

Connor shook his head and pulled us toward the door. "No. We all go in, or no one goes in at all."

The door didn't creak when we pushed it open. The radio was louder in here, and the tanning-bed commercial had turned into an ad for a grocery store chain. The high-backed office chair faced away from us, overseeing a panoramic view of Morriston through floor-to-ceiling windows. The chair shifted, and I heard Rylan's breath catch as the occupant's shoes brushed along the carpet. We weren't alone.

"Dad?" Connor called tentatively.

A light chuckle sounded from the opposite side of the desk. My dad didn't laugh much, but when he did, it was much deeper—nothing like this.

"Dad?" Connor called again. Ever so slowly the chair squeaked, turning around.

My feet froze to the floor.

Rylan should have teleported us back home. Though, judging by the pale and sweaty sheen his cheeks adopted, I doubted he could've run, let alone use the Black Vortex of Terror.

Connor's hand fell slack in mine. I felt a panic attack coming as our father's hand reached forward to shut off the radio. *In. Out. In. In . . .* I tried to remember how to breathe. Just then I realized how much I was counting on Rylan being wrong. It couldn't be him. He couldn't have destroyed the city he loved so dearly. I squeezed my eyes shut, hoping when I opened them that the world would vanish to dust. But my father was still there. He was still responsible.

Please, anyone but him.

When he caressed the computer controlling the nanobots, a dazed smile appeared on his face. Against my better judgment, I took a step forward, choking back the bile that threatened to rise in my throat. Maybe I had dared to hope too much.

My father was sitting right in front of me, perched in his office chair. But there was something else too.

A microchip blinking red in his wrist.

CHAPTER TWENTY-TWO

"I'm sorry." Dad's voice came out hoarse as he struggled to breathe, like the power of the nanobots was too much to bear. "He told me to call him if someone came." His hand shook as he reached for the phone on his desk.

"Call who?" Connor asked.

But Dad didn't seem to hear him, or if he did, he didn't care. "He said . . . he said to call. I need to call," he mumbled. The top buttons of his shirt had sloppily come undone, and his hair stuck up in tufts.

"The server," Hunter whispered, nudging me. "Get the server."

The server. That was why we came, but I could barely force myself to lift a finger, staring at my dad, as wilted and obedient as the men and women in the auditorium tonight. Rylan was the one who had his emotions in check, and so it was Rylan who teleported across the office, grabbing for the keyboard on the desk.

Dad's head snapped toward him. My father pulled a pistol from his lap, the bullets blasting holes in the wall when he pulled the trigger. We dropped to the ground. I expected to feel a shot, to see blood falling thick on the carpet, but neither came. After several more shots, the room quieted. When I looked up, Dad's arm was still outstretched, aimed at nothing. The gun fell to the floor, but he didn't even notice he'd dropped it.

"Dad!" Connor ripped off his mask, running to our father's side. "Dad, come on. Snap out of it. We're going to help you, okay? We're going to fix this. Dad?"

He didn't answer. He didn't even blink.

Rylan made a second attempt at destroying the server, but another shot—this time from the doorway—had us diving for the ground again.

"Just wonderful," came a bored voice. Wallace stood just inside the door, flanked by two burly men and an even burlier woman, all three with chips in their arms and murderous expressions on their lips. The barrel of his gun was pointed at Rylan's heart. "It's you again."

"Hey there." Rylan waved. "You're looking well. You have a little spring in your step. And a—a very large gun . . . in your hand."

Wallace fired another shot. Rylan teleported to avoid it, and the bullet hit the window instead, leaving a spiderweb of cracks in the glass.

"You also have a bit of color in your cheeks," Rylan added.

Hunter piped up, "I really think it's just his rising blood pressure."

"Enough." Wallace took a step into the office, slamming the door behind him with such force that it rattled on its hinges. After cocking an eyebrow at the four of us, Wallace turned to his men and said, "Detain them."

Wallace's beefy assistants advanced on us, cracking their knuckles. Connor and Rylan snapped into action, throwing kicks and punches with incredible precision. Wallace's two men—twins by the looks of their identical square jaws and stubby noses—quickly advanced on Rylan, moving in to hold him down. Rylan smirked and teleported behind them, kicking their backs and sending them tumbling headfirst into the side of the desk. Connor flew at them, attacking from behind, while Hunter was left to deal with the woman.

"Wait, guys! I don't hit ladies," Hunter said, backing against the wall as she advanced on him.

Hunter wouldn't hit a woman, but she would sure hit him. She shifted her weight, preparing to throw a right hook at Hunter's jaw. Just before she could make contact, I leapt through the air, landing on her back, sending us both crashing to the floor.

I hit my head against a table leg on the way down, and I lay there for a moment, dazed. She recovered quickly and turned on me, her large face contorted furiously, her eyes slate gray and deadly. She pulled her arm back for a second punch.

With a battle cry, Hunter rushed at her, smashing into her ribs like a battering ram and sending her flying.

The twins jumped up and reentered the fray. Connor was busy duking it out with Wallace, unaware of the two large men behind him. Rylan was in the middle of prying the woman's hands away from Hunter's throat. Stumbling to my feet, I rushed forward, trying to warn Connor. But before I could take two steps, I was hindered by a pair of enormous arms around my chest.

I kicked my foot backward, my heel striking the newest attacker's kneecap, but the guard's fingers shot upward and tightened around my neck. Squeezing, squeezing, squeezing. My head went foggy, and I felt myself slump against his chest.

Connor, Rylan, and Hunter realized at the same time that I was in trouble. As they made a move to help, Wallace, bruised and bleeding on the floor, managed to snap the end of a long steel cuff around Connor's shin. Wallace fastened the other shackle to a metal pole jutting down from the ceiling. The female guard hurried to do the same to Hunter.

Rylan paused when he heard the loud clang. If I could have breathed properly to warn him, I would have, but the guard only squeezed me tighter. Rylan didn't see it coming. The twins tackled him from behind, and Wallace snapped handcuffs around Rylan's wrists and ankles, chaining him to another pole on the opposite side of the room.

My father hadn't moved an inch since Wallace entered the room. He sat with his hands folded on his desk. His eyes darted around, catching mine for a moment. His mouth opened, but he didn't speak.

The guard let up the pressure on my neck just enough to keep me from passing out. I attempted a perfectly aimed kick at his crotch, but was too dizzy and weak from lack of oxygen to follow through.

Wallace pushed himself off the floor, grinning as he holstered his pistol.

"Leave us," he said to his assistants. The twins dashed from the office, the female guard not far behind. Only the guy holding me remained. "So let's see. We have two Hamiltons, a fish, and a phantom—"

"This sounds like the start of a really bad joke," I said.

Wallace let out a mirthless laugh. "You have no idea." He paced in front of us, only stopping to rip off Rylan's and Hunter's masks. When Rylan's face was revealed—a bruise blooming around his eye and blood dribbling from his lip—Wallace scoffed, obviously unimpressed that Morriston's resident supervillain was really a high school senior with only trace amounts of facial hair.

"*You're* Iron Phantom?" Wallace's lip curled. "How . . . disappointing."

"To be honest, I think it's rather impressive. But what do I know? I'm the one chained up."

"Speaking of that . . ." Hunter rattled the cuffs around his wrists. "How about getting us out of here, huh?"

"Umm. I actually can't do that. . . ."

"Come again?"

Rylan blushed. "The thing about teleporting is that I can't exactly do it when I'm attached to something really heavy." He glanced at the chains trailing toward the ceiling. "This building fits the bill."

Wallace snorted.

We were officially stuck.

"I was actually concerned that the chains wouldn't do the trick," Wallace said. "I can see now that I overestimated your abilities. You call yourselves heroes?" He crossed his arms as he turned to me, fixing me with an icy stare. "Or do you call yourselves villains? After the display at the warehouse, I'm a little unsure. That was you with Iron Phantom, wasn't it, Miss Hamilton?"

I refused to give him an answer either way. Instead I clenched my jaw until my teeth were ready to shatter, meeting his gaze head-on. Behind him, still trapped at the desk, Dad's mouth dropped open.

Wallace took slow, confident strides across the office, stopping only a foot in front of me. I thought about spitting in his face, but I decided to save that maneuver for later.

He took my wrist in his hand, his stubby fingers examining the spot where a microchip should have been blinking beneath my skin.

"How—? Did you all take them out?" he asked.

I kept my vow of silence. Beside me, Connor, Rylan, and Hunter did the same.

"Not up for chatting? Shame. I was only trying to prolong the inevitable for you."

"Wallace," Dad croaked, pleading. Without bothering to turn around, Wallace snapped his fingers in my father's direction.

"Quiet," he said, sounding almost bored. Dad's jaw clenched shut automatically. "So let's get to it, then, shall we?" Wallace headed for a short cabinet beside the desk, opening the doors to reveal three shelves full of liquor. After choosing one of the larger bottles, he began filling a square glass with an amber liquid.

Wallace gave us a mock salute with his glass, then took two long sips, nearly emptying it. "Anyone care for a drink before we start? Or are you a bit tied up at the moment?"

Connor groaned. "Villain jokes. I hate villain jokes."

Rylan stared at Wallace with such intensity that it looked like he was trying to set the man on fire. "You're not going to give us the stereotypical villainous spiel where you reveal your evil genius plan in excruciatingly gory detail, are you?" he asked. "Because I have to say, I haven't been sleeping well, and I don't think I could stay awake for that."

Wallace strode over to Rylan, backhanding him with four rings on his right hand. Rylan's head jerked to the side and he spit a glob of blood on the white carpet. The guard tensed behind me.

A steady stream of red dripped down Rylan's cheek. It made my heart hurt.

"You've been quite the source of commotion, Iron Phantom," said Wallace. "Whether you intended to or not. Did you know I hired one of my guards to masquerade as you?" He nodded to the big man standing behind me. "Just on occasion, only when I thought it was necessary. He robbed a jewelry store. I had him vandalize my car to draw away suspicion. . . ." Wallace chuckled.

"The rest, of course, I took care of," Wallace said. If only I had the ability to shoot lasers from my eyes. The subway flood, the theme park malfunction, the drive-by shooting, the bomb in the mall . . .

My dad looked like he was about to cry. I could feel the anger rolling off me; I could feel it spilling from my brother, Rylan, and Hunter too, bringing the office to a boil until we were all suffocating in rage. Rylan should have killed Wallace when we had the chance.

Hunter shifted in his spot, his chains clanging. "So this was all you? Mayor Hamilton had nothing to do with it?"

"Mayor Hamilton doesn't have it in him," Wallace snapped.

"And Iron Phantom? He didn't have anything to do with it either?"

Wallace eyes narrowed. "Are you slow, or just stupid?"

"Neither." Hunter grinned. "I'm just trying to get the full picture."

Rylan caught my eye, and we looked at Hunter strangely. I couldn't figure out what he was doing, but if he had some grand plan up his sleeve, then now would be a good time to start using it.

Connor spit at Wallace, a large glob of saliva landing on his shiny loafers. "Why would you do this? Why would you hurt people?"

"Because it was a means to a much better end." He slammed his glass down on the desk, waving a hand in my father's direction. "The great Mayor Hamilton thinks he can detect when someone is about to commit a crime? Give me a break. This city is so tainted with criminal filth that it wouldn't make a difference. You've normalized murder. This city is *toxic*. Your father hasn't been able to do anything about it, and neither have you, Connor. You're too soft. You're both too weak—"

Another glob of Connor's spit landed on Wallace's shoes. "So you think you're the only one who can save Morriston, is that right?"

"I'm the only one who has the gall to do what needs to be done."

"Do you even understand how hypocritical you sound?" Rylan shouted. "You destroyed the entire city! You're no better than any other criminal."

Rylan took another slap to the face. "Have you ever felt the pain of loss, Iron Phantom?"

"More than you know," Rylan replied through clenched teeth.

"Then you should understand. All of you should understand. Everyone in Morriston has known someone who has been killed. Well, not anymore. I ordered those nanobots months ago, but I knew no one in their right mind would agree to Mayor Hamilton's *emotion detection devices*," he said with a sneer, "unless the city was in mortal peril. And that's where you came in." Wallace eyed Rylan's super suit, giving him a demented smile. "When you set the fire in city hall, it gave me an idea. If the citizens had a new threat to fear, not just an ordinary criminal, but one with powers, someone who could be anywhere at any time, who could kill them in an instant, then they would flock to receive a microchip. They wouldn't have another option. And they would never suspect the nanobots I'd hidden inside.

"Now that the nanobots have been activated, Morriston will finally be compliant. No more fighting. No more killing. They'll listen to anything I tell them. *Your father* will listen to anything I tell him." He looked longingly at the chip in my dad's wrist. "No one else will die."

Rylan's jaw unclenched and fell slack. His eyes were no longer full of loathing but filled with pity. I just felt numb. A human icicle.

"Someone was killed, weren't they?" I asked, trying my best to sound sensitive lest he snap. "Someone you cared about. Who was it?"

Wallace turned to me with leering, bloodshot eyes. "My younger brother, David. He was robbed at gunpoint last year." Wallace's voice trembled. "No one saved him. Not your father. Not your brother. They were too busy protecting everyone else."

Connor swallowed hard. "Wallace, I'm . . . I'm sorry. I didn't know."

"Of course you didn't know!" Wallace roared. He pounded his

fist on the desk, and the computers shook. *Hit the server next,* I thought. *Smash it to pieces and this can finally be over.*

"There's always someone else to save," said Wallace. "Someone more important, maybe someone closer in reach. But what about the rest? What about the ones who fall through the cracks?"

Shame filled Connor's blue eyes. He knew how much it hurt to fail. "Manipulating people using those nanobots isn't going to help. It will only do the opposite. This won't bring your brother back, and I know how much it hurts, but I'm sorry," Connor whispered. "He's gone."

With a swipe of his hand, Wallace smashed the lamp on my dad's desk to the floor. He picked up a photo, sending it crashing into the wall. The glass shattered. A corner of the picture poked out from the frame, and I recognized my mother's wedding dress.

He rifled through the drawers, tossing aside papers and folders with little care. When he found what he was looking for, he paused, grinned, and slowly stood.

I leaned forward to get a closer look at the object clenched in his fist, but the guard quickly pulled me back, knocking my head against his chin.

"I've heard enough," Wallace said. There was a flash of silver as he thrust whatever he was holding into my father's hands. "Inject them."

"No!" I kicked at the guard, trying to escape, but his fingers bruised my skin. I twisted in his grip, screamed and punched, stilling only when Wallace held a short knife to my throat.

"Red Comet can go first," he said, nodding to my dad.

Another round of screams burst from my throat. Dad jerked to his feet, out of his own control. Sweat soaked his forehead. The eyes that looked down at Connor were not my father's eyes. They were dull and unfeeling, the eyes of a man long since beaten into submission.

"It's not me," Dad said, his movements robotic as he knelt at Connor's side. "I swear it's not me."

Connor nodded. He struggled against the chains as he sat on the floor, but they were unbreakable. He hadn't been shorter than Dad since before the giant growth spurt that accompanied his superpowers. But now he looked like a little kid again. Powerless. Connor's eyes were red, but he pursed his lips, refusing to shed tears.

I looked from Connor to Rylan to Hunter. Each struggled to break free, but each failed.

"Go ahead," Connor finally said. "You know you have to do it."

Dad reached for Connor's arm.

"Wait."

Wallace held up a hand, and the world seemed to stop spinning. For a second, I dared to hope he changed his mind. But then he said, "He took it out once before. Put it somewhere he won't be able to get at it. The neck, I think."

This time, I didn't hear myself scream, but I felt the burn in my throat. I didn't decide to kick Wallace in the stomach, but when he smashed my face into the wall, I knew I must have tried. I didn't want to see the flash of a syringe as it plunged into my brother's neck, but it consumed my vision. Connor cried out, trying to scoot away, but he had nowhere to go. He whimpered when our father depressed the plunger.

"Connor!"

Connor jerked on the floor, his chains clanging. Too soon, he stilled, his heavy breathing straining the seams of his suit.

"Connor! Connor, look at me!"

His head snapped up, and his bright blue eyes locked with mine. "Yes, Abby?"

My heart nearly stopped when I heard his voice. It was slow and soft instead of boisterous. And his eyes . . . they lacked any type of emotion. Connor was staring right at me, but I wasn't sure he recognized me. Not like he normally did. Not in the brotherly way where he made me laugh until I cried or teased me until I stormed from the room in anger. Connor wasn't Connor anymore.

"Connor, please!" Tears trickled down my face and fell on the guard's forearms. "Come back, Connor! You can do it. You have to come back to me."

Connor's eyes flitted around the room as he shifted in his seat. I hadn't given him a command, not by normal standards, but he was trying so hard to obey. Except he didn't know how. I could read the anxiety in his eyes, and that small display of emotion gave me hope. *Come back from what?* he was thinking. *I don't know what to do.*

"Don't look at her," Wallace commanded. "She's not your sister anymore."

Connor's gaze quickly dropped to his boots. "Yes, sir." He pulled his legs to his chest and rocked back and forth, muttering, "Yes, sir. Not my sister. No sister. Yes, sir."

"That's sick," Hunter said to Wallace. "You need serious help."

Wallace retreated to the desk, motioning for my father to follow him on the way over. Dad shakily got to his feet, his fists balled up as he stared down at Connor.

I noticed three more syringes next to the computer, and my blood ran cold.

"Iron Phantom next." Wallace smirked as he handed the syringes off to my dad. The guard's fingers scraped against my neck as he struggled to hold me still.

I watched my father approach Rylan. He tried in vain to teleport, rivers of sweat pouring down his face as he stared at Wallace over my father's shoulder, hatred spiraling from his body like smoke.

"Stop!" Rylan yelled as my father lifted the syringe. "Don't come any closer."

Dad froze.

"Don't listen to him, Benjamin." Wallace actually had the nerve to yawn as he leaned against the desk, like dealing with us was nothing but an inconvenience. "Get on with it."

Until recently, I never considered myself particularly brave or strong or anything that would help convince me I could act in the face of evil. I wasn't famous. I wasn't my brother. But when I caught Rylan's horrified glance out of the corner of my eye, I knew I could stop this. Hunter was immobile, Connor was still quivering on the carpet, whispering to himself. It had to be me.

The guard didn't see it coming. Throwing my head back, I smashed my skull into the bridge of his nose. I didn't dare pause when I felt the warm spurt of blood hit my neck. Kicking him in the crotch, I dove for the last two syringes on the desktop.

They were heavy in my hands, filled with a creamy white gel and a small silver chip. My father was inches away from Rylan, the tip of the needle nearly pricking the vein pulsing in Rylan's neck, when he noticed me gripping the syringes with white knuckles.

"Drop it, Dad. Please."

His hand shook, and slowly his fingers uncurled—one by one . . .

"I don't think that's a smart idea." Wallace's hot breath crested my ear, and I tensed up, my skin crawling. His tie brushed against my shoulder when he closed in on me, and the cold barrel of his gun sent ice down my spine as he pressed it against my temple.

I bit my lip, fighting the terror that clawed inside of me. How many times had I been in this position before? In my nightmares, in the warehouse. Each time I gave in. Each time I let the fear eat away until nothing was left.

"Drop the syringes," Wallace said. "I don't want to kill you."

I almost laughed. Wasn't that what he was doing anyway? Killing us, just in a different way.

Rylan's eyes went wide as I leaned into the gun, letting it dig into my skin. Confusion rolled off Wallace in waves. He expected me to beg, he expected me to cry. He expected me to be afraid. But I wasn't afraid. Not for myself, not anymore.

What Wallace never expected was for my foot to wrap around his leg, catching him behind the ankles. With one hard pull, he stumbled to the ground. His gun went off, a bullet lodging in the ceiling, but I kicked it away from him before he could use it again. The pistol skittered across the carpet, landing under the liquor cabinet against the wall.

Wallace looked up at me from the floor, curled into the fetal position as he rubbed his back where it hit the ground. I raised the syringe in my right fist, but then I hesitated.

Wallace noticed. His eyes darted over to my father, still standing in front of Rylan, the syringe of nanobots dangling from his fingertips. He opened his mouth, another command forming on his lips. Even though I had him practically cornered, he thought I was too slow. He thought he won.

He thought wrong.

I lurched forward. It took Wallace a few seconds to notice there was a needle in his neck, and by then it was too late. I depressed the syringe.

Wallace pushed himself to his knees, rubbing at his skin as if doing so would erase the nanobots working their way to his brain. My eyes welled up with tears, but I felt too exhausted to wipe them from my cheeks. I made the same choice that he would have made. Worse yet, I didn't even feel bad about it.

Not all villains needed superpowers.

Rylan sneered at Wallace, Morriston's greatest criminal who didn't look so great anymore. Now he just looked lost.

"Go to hell," Rylan said.

I watched with pity as Wallace tried to figure out how to go about obeying that command. Eventually, I placed my hands on his shoulders and whispered, "Just go to sleep, Wallace. Just go to sleep."

And he did.

The guard snatched up the gun and ran from the room as soon as he saw what I did to Wallace. What *I* did. I did the same thing to him that he did to thousands of people all over the city. In the end, I was no better than a criminal.

"You didn't have a choice," Rylan reassured me. "You had to put an end to it somehow."

I wiped my nose on my sleeve while I dug through the drawers of my father's desk, looking for a key that might unlock the chains binding Connor, Rylan, and Hunter. My brother was now snoozing on the floor, a long string of drool dripping from his lips. When I told Wallace to go to sleep, Connor and my dad unceremoniously decided to submit as well.

I found a ring with several brass keys at the bottom of a heap of heavy binders. Quickly, I got to work testing them out, first on Connor's handcuffs, then Rylan's and Hunter's, until I found the correct ones. After freeing his wrists and ankles, Rylan ran for the server, examining it and the wires trailing into the three computers on the desk. He tapped on the keyboard, flipping through screen after screen of blinking lights and complicated codes. His brow wrinkled.

"I'm afraid of messing up the program and hurting someone." Rylan glanced at Connor when he let out a particularly hefty snore. "And even if I manage to fix this, I don't want Wallace waking up."

"Me neither. Do you think anyone is going to believe Wallace was behind this? People might blame it all on you. We don't have any proof."

Hunter came up beside us, smirking. "Oh, ye of little faith. Abby, I've told you before that I'm a whiz with a video camera." He pointed to a small black disc clipped onto his suit near his collarbone.

"You filmed it?" Rylan crouched down to look into the tiny lens. He rolled his lips between his teeth to hold back a laugh. "All of it?"

"Every word. I can edit out our identities, but I got Wallace's entire confession." Hunter shrugged. "I know I don't have much in the way of powers, but this is enough to put him away for a long time. Possibly forever."

Forever. The word rang out like a bell, and I launched myself at Hunter, hugging him fiercely. "Thank you, thank you, *thank you.*"

"Don't mention it. Fish Boy to the rescue, you know?" When I finally let go of him, his cheeks were pink. He snatched his mask off the ground and quickly pulled it on. "Anyway, we should get out of here. See if we can patch up your dad and Connor at a hospital or something—"

"Connor can't go to a hospital."

Hunter slung my brother's sleeping form over his shoulders like he weighed no more than a sack of feathers. "It's cool, I know a lady." Turning to Rylan, he said, "Think you can teleport us there?"

Rylan rubbed at his cheek, smearing the blood from Wallace's slaps. He slipped his mask back on. "I can try. But I think I need some fresh air first."

"No worries. I'll grab Abby's dad. You take the scumbag—sorry, Wallace—and we'll take the elevator down."

CHAPTER TWENTY-THREE

Hospitals were a place of limbo. Neither here nor there. A revolving door of nurses and doctors and nurses again. A never-ending stream of waiting . . . followed by more waiting. Waiting for a diagnosis. Waiting for surgery. Waiting for Connor to wake up.

I'd experienced my fair share of emergency rooms, but Morriston's Valley Hospital was a major departure from the trend. Rain soaked the streets when we arrived behind the building, in front of a service entrance, several dumpsters, and a garage likely belonging to the morgue. Rylan and I huddled underneath an awning, balancing my father and Wallace between us while Hunter tipped his head skyward, drenching his scales and plastering his hair to his forehead. Once he was satisfied he was wet enough, he approached the service door, knocking four times, then six times, then two times. The nurse who finally answered dropped her jaw and adjusted her crooked glasses while she took stock of us. Three supers (one bloody, one soaking wet, one unconscious), the mayor of Morriston (also unconscious), Wallace (who really cared about him?), and me (there wasn't much to say about me, but I had an inkling my face was as pale as a ghost).

"Ummm . . ."

Hunter shifted Connor over his shoulder so his butt directly faced the nurse, making her flush bright red and become even more alarmed—if that was possible. "Is Jackie working tonight?" he asked.

The nurse nodded, eyes wide.

"Can you bring her to us? If you can't tell, we've got a bit of an issue on our hands."

Because the girl's microchip was activated, she didn't hesitate to listen to Hunter and scurry away.

As it turned out, Hunter's friend Jackie was a fifty-eight-year-old ex-superhero who used to go by the alias of Tornado. Tornado was never on active duty during my lifetime, but Connor read a lot about her while cultivating his powers. She possessed super strength and super speed, but retired once she tore her ACL after a fight with some gang members in the early '90s.

Fast-forward over twenty years and Jackie Bolman was now Valley Hospital's top surgeon. Like us, she hadn't trusted city hall's intentions were noble when it came to the microchips. The long slice in her forearm was proof of that. After ushering us inside, Jackie personally locked Wallace in a private room, then rushed my dad and Connor into surgery.

And so I played the waiting game.

Rylan changed out of his super suit so no one was frightened by Iron Phantom's appearance, and then he and Hunter took turns playing checkers with me in the lobby. The halls of the hospital were deserted; most nurses and doctors had been ordered to return home, and those who hadn't stayed far out of our way.

The only contact we had with the outside world was when two little girls whose mother was in labor asked Hunter for his autograph. He happily signed *Fish Boy* on a hospital band, then let them touch his flippers.

"I told you, Abby," he said when they ran away squealing, "ladies love the flippers."

I hadn't prayed in a long time, since before my mom died. But as I watched the girls disappear around the corner, I prayed that Dr. Bolman could find a way to fix Connor and my dad. And if she could fix them, she could fix the rest of the city. No one deserved to be manipulated and forced into action. Especially those precious little girls.

The waiting room was deathly quiet, but my thoughts had never screamed so loud.

I was curled up on a hard plastic chair in the early hours of the morning, my head in Rylan's lap, when Jackie appeared in the waiting room. I bolted up in my seat, elbowing Rylan and Hunter to wake them. They jolted, and Hunter slipped from his chair onto the floor.

Jackie's face was tough to read. Was the corner of her mouth quirked up because she was successful or because she was preparing to break some earth-shattering news? She adjusted her low ponytail as she reached for an empty chair, sinking into it as she studied the clipboard in her hands.

"So here's what we're dealing with," she said. "Your father's chip was easy enough to remove. He's still unconscious, but he should wake within an hour or two. Your brother's, on the other hand, was a bit tougher."

I swallowed hard.

"I performed a modified anterior cervical discectomy on Connor's neck. Usually, a cervical disc is removed to alleviate pain and numbness, but I did the procedure purely with the intention of reaching the microchip Wallace injected. I made an incision here"—Jackie drew her finger over the front of her neck—"and luckily, the chip was still in place and I was able to get to it. I don't know if all the chips work this way, but there were still a few nanobots left inside acting as a control station, if you will, sending signals to the others that had moved into Connor's brain. I didn't feel comfortable performing any extensive neurosurgery, so I destroyed the microchip and the nanobots left inside and waited to see how Connor would act when he came out of anesthesia."

Rylan started rubbing the back of his head when Jackie mentioned neurosurgery. "And . . . ?" he prompted.

"It seems to have worked. Connor remembers how it felt being under the influence of the nanotechnology, and he doesn't feel the same sense of forced obedience he did before. He's essentially back to normal. I'm hoping to bring in other surgeons from out of state to help me return everyone who received an injection back to their usual selves." Jackie spoke quickly and looked like she was making extra effort to avoid eye contact with me.

Rylan caught on to the tension flickering in her eyes. "Wait, you said he's *essentially* back to normal. I'm sensing a giant 'but' here."

When Jackie loudly exhaled and hung her head, I knew something did not go according to plan. She had to cut into Connor's neck. Was his voice gone? A few days ago, I would have admitted that Connor losing his voice would be God's greatest gift to humankind, but now the thought of him unable to tell me jokes and useless facts from his Word of the Day calendar made me sick.

"The nanotechnology doesn't have an effect on him any longer, but while it was functioning, it did manage to severely addle part of his brain." I held my breath and felt the gut-wrenching punch even before Jackie dropped the bomb. "As far as we can tell, Connor is unable to access the part of his brain that controls his abilities. Simply put, he doesn't have superpowers anymore."

The first time Connor Hamilton suited up as Red Comet, I thought the whole thing was a little weird. Not that superheroes were weird—they had been around all my life—but that my brother actually *was* one. Connor's first costume was a compilation of items he picked up from the local thrift store—red tennis shoes, a red-and-gold figure-skating unitard, and some red spandex he cut to fit snugly over his head. His tights clung a bit too tight around his pelvic region and butt, giving him a kind of permanent wedgie, which I made fun of until Red Comet grew famous enough to have a designer make a super suit on his behalf. The inability to see his face behind his mask freaked me out too. Connor had a tendency to show his emotions through his eyes, and it took months for me to figure out what he was thinking whenever I couldn't see them.

Connor's first mission involved saving a five-year-old from falling into the tiger exhibit at the zoo. The kid was pretty short, so his aunt picked him up and sat him on the ledge overlooking the tigers so he could see. There was no barricade separating the observation platform from the animals, which was pretty dumb in my opinion, but I guess no one expected the kid to take a tumble and become cat chow.

The little boy was about one second away from being eaten when Connor swooped down, caught him just as he was about to land in the tigers' jaws, and returned him safely to his family. And thus began Red Comet's rise to fame.

Connor was on an adrenaline high for at least a week. Dad was sure Connor would blow his secret to his friends at school, but he surprisingly took his new position in Morriston society very seriously. Connor practiced his powers constantly, often dragging me out of bed in the middle of the night to throw acorns into the woods for him to catch and hone his super vision. I always complained about my brother's new life, but he never did. Not when he had to leave his friends, or miss a meal, or abandon a date. Popping out of nowhere to rescue a kid or a grandmother was Connor's new hobby, a cool skill that his friends didn't have. Being a superhero was fun for him, nothing more. But eventually, being Red Comet consumed Connor's entire life.

I wasn't very concerned about Connor losing his powers, but I was concerned about how he would handle it. I didn't know if he could function without them. Having superpowers gave Connor a major confidence boost. I was worried that without them he wouldn't be able to find confidence in other ways.

The only light in Connor's hospital room came from a small window on the far wall. Connor lay curled up on the bed, his back to the door with only a thin blanket covering his legs. The line of his IV was draped over his shoulder, attached to a vein in his hand. The beep of his heart monitor echoed in the stillness of the room. Connor's shoulder twitched when my shoes squeaked on the tile floor, but he didn't speak.

"Connor?" I hesitantly pulled a chair to the side of his bed. He didn't acknowledge me. He was much too quiet to be sleeping; Connor snored like a freight train.

I tapped his shoulder. He shrugged my hand off and buried his face in his pillow.

"Connor, just talk to me. Talking's what you do best."

"Just go away, Abby," he croaked. I knew immediately that he had been crying.

"Can I get you anything? Water? A pudding cup?"

Connor's shoulders tensed and he said a bit louder, "Just go away."

"No." I scooted my chair around to the other side of the bed so I could see him. He quickly rolled over so his back was to me. When I rounded the bed a second time, he didn't bother moving. Connor's nose was red and puffy, and his eyelashes shined with tears he was too tired to wipe away.

Seeing him this way brought me back to the hours we spent in the waiting room the day our mom died. My heart felt broken. But I guess you had to have a heart for it to feel broken, right? I wasn't sure what I had after injecting Wallace tonight.

"I know you need to talk to someone," I said. "I'm as good as anyone." When Connor didn't speak, I continued, "And I know I can't relate to what you're going through, but I do know what it's like to lose someone. I'm guessing this doesn't suck any less."

Connor toyed with the bandage over his throat where Dr. Bolman made the incision. I hoped he wasn't in too much pain to carry on a conversation. After much deliberation, he said, "If you're going to stay, you need to come closer."

"Why?" I got off the chair anyway and knelt next to his bed, my forearms on the mattress.

"Because I feel like I'm blind now. I can't see anything more than a foot in front of me."

"So your super sight's really gone?" I had hoped that maybe only his ability to fly would disappear. Anything to keep him feeling like himself.

"Yeah," Connor said, "along with everything else."

Here it was. It didn't take long. The beginning of Connor's deep, dark depression.

"I feel empty. Millions of people on this earth don't have superpowers. But no matter how hard I try to reason with myself that if they can do it, I can do it, I can't help thinking that my entire life is just going to spiral downhill from here."

"Connor, you're *nineteen*. Your life's just getting started."

"You don't understand," he snapped. "Our mother is dead, our father is lying in a hospital bed unconscious, and I just lost the only thing that remotely made me feel like I was somebody. Now I'm nothing. I have *nothing*."

"You have me." My voice was so low I wasn't sure he heard it until I caught his eyes soften. "And I wish you wouldn't talk about yourself like that. You're funny and kind and all the girls think you're really cute. You're going to be fine, Connor. You don't need screaming fans to convince you you're special because *I'm* telling you you're special. And if you can't see that, then I'm sorry because you're really missing out."

We sat in silence while Connor twisted his hospital band around and around his wrist. He'd found a red pen and scratched out his last name so it only read *Connor*. Because that's who he was now. Not Connor Hamilton. Not Red Comet. Just Connor.

Finally, the corner of his mouth quirked up. "Thank you. I really needed that."

"Anytime."

Without warning, Connor squeezed his eyes shut and let out a loud moan. I jumped up, thinking the worst—that the surgery went wrong and there were still nanobots working in his brain. I was on the verge of running to find Jackie until Connor grabbed my wrist and said, "I just realized, now that I can't fly and the transmission in my truck is probably two miles away from blowing up, you're going to have to teach me how to do *normal-people things*." He shuddered. "Like ride the bus."

The tension drained from my body, and I collapsed into the chair. "Oh, the horror! Now you'll finally know what it's like to sit on people's germs and crumbly food. Now that I think of it, there was a dirty diaper left on one of the seats last week."

Connor's voice squeaked. "A what?"

"Relax, I'm only kidding." I shot him a wink. "There were *two* dirty diapers."

Connor threw back his head. "Ugh! Being normal sucks!"

"You'll manage. I won't leave you to fend for yourself, you know." I poked him between the eyes. "First, because you'd never survive. And second, because I'm not that mean. I'm not going to just abandon you, Connor. We're in this together."

Connor held out his pinkie. When we were kids and Connor liked to snoop through our parents' closet in his spare time, he'd always pinkie-promise that we'd never get caught. I was a giant worrywart, but whenever Connor held out his little finger, I knew he'd protect me from trouble. The whole thing seemed silly once I grew up, but back then, Connor used the coveted pinkie promise as a way to show he would always be there for me. And now it was my turn to be there for him.

"Promise?" Connor asked.

I linked my finger with his. "Promise."

Thanksgiving came and went. Stores filled with Christmas shoppers and the smell of peppermint coffee. Radio stations played holiday songs around the clock. For a visitor to Morriston, everything appeared relatively normal on the outside.

But on the inside, life was far from normal. The day after Connor lost his powers, Jackie Bolman called in surgeons nationwide to assist in removing the microchips. The procedures were relatively simple. All the injections had been in the arm, not the neck, so destroying the nanotechnology was quick and painless. In about a week, Morriston citizens were back to their usual nonsubmissive, rule-breaking selves.

As for Wallace, the video evidence Hunter filmed was far too incriminating for him to walk away unscathed. He was shipped off to a penitentiary on the other side of the country, cussing and screaming the whole way there—or so we heard. Good riddance.

And then there was my father. It took him almost a day to wake up after his microchip was removed, and another day before he would even speak. First he had been overwhelmed by the guilt of losing my mother, and now, just when he was trying so hard to heal, the guilt of hurting Connor and standing idly by as Morriston was torn to pieces came crashing down as well. Liquor bottles covered our kitchen counter, cigarette butts littered the bathroom floor, and the amount of nightmares he'd developed had eclipsed mine. It quickly became apparent that the whole ordeal had been too much for him. He resigned as mayor, packed his belongings, and checked into an inpatient rehab facility in the middle of the state.

Happy holidays.

Connor visited him a few times. I went once, but I kept finding excuses to prolong my return. Seeing my father so broken was a wound on my heart that was still far too fresh to reopen.

With Dad gone, Connor had appointed himself my new guardian. Too bad it definitely wasn't me who needed guarding. Dad had granted Connor temporary permission to use his shiny new car, as well as access to his bank account. The first thing Connor purchased with his newfound wealth was two dozen doughnuts and a subscription to *Playboy* magazine. Superhero or not, Connor would always be Connor.

Sarah now spent almost every day over my house. Rylan and I finally told her about his superpowers, and Connor broke the news about his lack of superpowers. She'd teared up, but her sadness was quickly remedied thanks to Hunter. Red Comet may have been gone, but Sarah had found a new fan fiction project in the form of Fish Boy. I guess the ladies really do love the flippers.

The five of us were like a weird little family now. We had game nights on Thursdays and potluck dinners on Sundays. Iron Phantom's name had been cleared, and Rylan was quickly climbing the ladder as the city's most loved super, thanks in part to Isaac, who had joined up with Morriston's paparazzi and started hounding Iron Phantom for photographs to publish online (he was almost as bad as Sarah). Occasionally Rylan and Hunter would leave us to save the world, something Connor would respond to with a roll of his eyes and a vicious scowl. But he was coping, slowly adjusting to his powerless new life as a civilian. Or he was trying to anyway.

"Ladies and gentlemen, I have an announcement!" Connor bounded down the steps and landed on the living room couch between me and Rylan. We were in the middle of a Christmas movie marathon, and Connor's sudden violent invasion sent our bowl of popcorn crashing to the floor.

"You're finally going to cut your hair?" I asked. Connor's hair had recently grown so long that he had a constant crick in his neck from flipping it out of his eyes.

My brother ran a hand over his scalp. "Well, yeah. But that's not what I'm talking about." He took a deep breath, stood, and extended his arms out to either side. "After careful deliberation—"

"Was that today's word of the day?" Rylan interrupted.

Connor's lip curled. "Maybe. Shut up. It's my turn to talk." He cleared his throat and continued, "Anyway, after careful deliberation, I have decided that I'm going to quit taking online classes and go to real-people college."

Snickering, I skeptically asked, "Real-people college?"

"Yep. Like with actual humans. Girls."

"Girls?"

"Girls," Connor confirmed with a wiggle of his eyebrows. "Lots of pretty girls. I'm majoring in communications . . . because I don't really know what else to do, so . . ."

Rylan asked, "What does someone with a communications degree actually do?"

"Beats the hell outta me." Connor shrugged and picked up a fistful of popcorn scattered at his feet. I wasn't surprised when he shoved it all in his mouth. "Communicate with people I guess. Communicate with girls," he mumbled through the kernels.

I tried to picture my brother on a legitimate college campus, studying in the library with an overpriced cup of coffee on the desk beside him. The vision was difficult to imagine, though Connor did wear glasses now that his super vision reverted to a more human state. Large hipster ones with black frames. He couldn't see a thing without them, but they made him look somewhat studious, which might fool people for a little while until they got to know the real Connor Hamilton.

Nevertheless, Connor was willing to try almost anything once, and college didn't seem like a terrible idea. He'd certainly had worse.

"Communications sounds good for you, Connor," I said. "It's about selling stories to the public, and if anyone can do that, it's you. You've had more experience than almost anyone."

"Why, thank you, Abby. I always knew wearing those tights would pay off someday. Speaking of tights . . ." Connor's eyes homed in on Rylan's arm resting along my shoulders, the fingers of his left hand entangled with mine. "Don't you have to go save the city, lover boy?"

Rylan relaxed into the couch, a yawn escaping his lips. "The city doesn't need saving right now."

"Fine," said Connor. "But just an FYI, Mrs. Richardson over on Union Avenue loses her cat at least once a week. Good luck taking care of that one now that I'm gone."

"Duly noted."

Connor smirked as he left the room, but I caught a hint of his real smile. It made his eyes soften just a tad.

"He's trying," I said. Maybe one day Connor and Rylan would be real friends—not frenemies. Connor could use another friend.

"Yeah, he is. You're pretty good with him, you know. He really loves you."

"Well, he's not difficult to manage. You just feed him a lot. Make sure he gets plenty of exercise." I twisted my fingers in my lap. Talking about the l-word in Rylan's presence tended to make my stomach run off and join the circus.

I thought about telling him so, about finally confessing and letting my heart spill out of my chest, but the quirk in his lips and the warmth in his eyes made me think he already knew.

Hopping off the couch, Rylan offered me his hand. "Let's go on an adventure."

"Rylan, I think we've been on enough adventures the past few months to last a lifetime."

He chuckled, agreeing. "Okay, how about a tame adventure? Somewhere not snowing, perhaps?"

The snow was piling up outside on the deck, and the temperature was well below freezing. Warmth would be rather nice. "Where?"

"It's a surprise. Do you trust me?"

I looked from Rylan's wiggling fingers to his wide toothy grin. And then I knew. No matter what happened, no matter who tried to hurt us, Rylan would always be there. He saw me in a way I hadn't realized I wanted to be seen until I met him. Not a hero, not someone with powers, but just a girl. Just Abigail.

Morriston was a city of heroes and villains—those with masks and those without. But in a place where the impossible could become a reality, I knew only one thing for sure.

There was Rylan and there was me. And that was more than enough.

I took his hand.

And we were gone.

ACKNOWLEDGMENTS

This feels a lot like an Oscar speech. With that said, please don't play me off the stage.

First and foremost, thank you to you, the reader. You picked up this book, and that means more than you will ever know. You rock!

To the incredible team at Swoon Reads: Since I was three years old I have wanted to share stories with the world. You made that three-year-old's dream come true. I cannot express how grateful I am for all you have done on behalf of this book. Jean and Lauren: Thank you for believing in me. It is an honor to write for you.

To my fantastic editor, Emily Settle: Where would I be without you? You are a genius and an absolute delight. Thank you for picking up this story and helping me shape it into what it is today. If anyone is a superhero, it's you. But don't worry—your secret is safe with me.

To the lovely, talented, insightful people I have met on Swoon Reads: Thank you for always brightening my day with your feedback, ratings, and comments. I quite literally could not have done this without you.

My friends at Wattpad: You believed in this book long before anyone else. Your constant kindness kept me going when I couldn't figure out what to write next, and your support of my characters surpassed anything I could have imagined. Thank you.

To the plethora of chocolate chip cookies I ate while writing to keep my juices flowing: Thanks a million.

Katie, Sierra, and my "twin brother" Sara: Thank you for indulging in my eccentricities throughout our many years of friendship. I would not be the person I am today without you.

Saint Francis de Sales: You, sir, are the real MVP. I hope you aren't sick of me yet.

Cooper: You are a dog and thus unable to read this, but thank you for being my number one cuddle buddy. You slept on my lap a lot while this book was being written, which made typing difficult, but you always kept my legs warm.

And finally . . . to my parents: This starts and ends with you. I love you more than you know.